THE STRIKE ZONE

THE NEW YORK LIONS: BOOK FOUR

LULU MOORE

Cover Design by Emily Wittig

Interior Design by Cleo Moran/Devoted Pages

Illustrated Shirt Design: Lyla June Co.

Editing by Perfectly Write Editing

For Erin and Amanda,
because this book probably wouldn't exist without you.

If you get three strikes, even the best lawyer in the world can't get you off

BILL VEECK

1

Scout

"Man, I wish my ass looked like that."

I winced as my head thudded on the underside of the table, but it clearly hadn't been loud enough to cause concern, given the current conversation was still in full flow.

"Squats, bro. You gotta stick to squats."

"I squat. I squat, dude. My ass still doesn't look like that."

"Don't be too hard on yourself, these guys work out for a living. What's your gym regimen?"

Cyrus clapped a hand onto Joey's shoulder, only for him to drop his head with a shameful shake.

"Clearly not good enough to make it look like I'm smuggling a pair of honeydews in my pants."

There was a moment of silence as the guys continued their observations—let's say—of the guys at practice, until a slow rhythmic beat kicked in. Alice tapped a stirrer against her coffee cup, enough to serve as a warning she wanted this meeting underway.

Or she wanted the guys to stop talking. Or that she wanted to go back to bed. Probably the latter.

Whatever it was, I could tell she was about to crack.

I gave up trying to get the screen to work, carefully avoided banging my head again, crawled back from the tangle of wires under the table, and slid onto my seat. Taking one look at the presentation I'd written, which was now kind of pointless, seeing as I couldn't present it, I closed my laptop.

Guess I'd be winging it. At least I'd brought a couple of printouts.

I didn't bother to look at Alice, I could already feel her eyes lasering into me, urging me to kill the chatter.

"Guys, can you stop talking about your butts for one second? I need your full attention. I promise you'll have time to discuss them after I've briefed you."

Joey and Cyrus—the two interns who'd been assigned to the social media team for the next three months—and for some reason I'd been put in charge of—managed to tear themselves away from whatever was happening down on the field. Reluctantly, I might add. Joey gave a longing double take out the windows before he sat down.

Cyrus moved to a chair that still allowed him enough of a glance at the field that I knew he wouldn't be paying full attention to anything I said anyway.

It was like they'd forgotten they'd still be required to work during their internship, that this much-coveted assignment did not mean they'd be doing nothing but hanging around with the players and gawping. Not that they would be hanging with the players, but I was beginning to wonder if they'd picked the social team because it had the most exposure to the Lions roster on a daily basis.

"Sorry, Scout," they muttered in sync.

"Interns," grouched Alice, under her breath.

With the tip of my finger, I eased her coffee cup closer to her and mouthed, Drink the caffeine, while declining to remind her she didn't need to be here at all, seeing as she was part of the sales team, and this meeting was to discuss social media plans.

But Alice Tan kind of did what she wanted.

I still hadn't figured out if the reason she was working in baseball was because her workdays didn't typically start until mid-morning, therefore she could legitimately exist as a night owl and party after each game, or because she genuinely enjoyed baseball.

She liked the guys, I knew that much.

"Okay." I clasped my hands together once I was confident

I had the most attention from the interns as I was going to get, attempting to sound as commanding and "in charge" as I could. "Tomorrow is the first game of the season. We have a big year of work ahead of us. In the company meeting on Monday, we were told our team's key objective is to grow the social channels. Under the entire communications umbrella, we've already succeeded in shedding the reputation as being the 'loser club of the MLB' and, according to the latest set of data, we're now seen as fun and energizing. The demographic of attendees has become younger, and we're bringing in new fans to the games."

Taking a breath, I waited to see if either of the guys wanted to say anything, but unsurprisingly the room stayed silent.

"Great," I continued. "We're very hands on in this team, we have a weekly schedule dedicated to responding to comments, and we will continue that. Because we've grown so much, we have decided to split the work up for the year. Our focus will be TikTok—"

"Awesome—"

"It is, and the persona we put out is that we take the games seriously, but we don't take ourselves seriously."

"Yeah, we don't want people to start thinking we have a stick up our butt like the Yankees," mumbled Alice.

Joey snorted a laugh.

"Exactly." I turned to her. "That everything?"

She gave one long nod of her head. "Yup. And don't forget that we also need to keep up team morale while we're creating content. The guys aren't going to want to respond to you the second they walk into the club if they had a crappy game the night before, or they're in a losing streak. When morale is up, we win more games."

"And let's not forget Shepherd wants the Commissioner's Trophy this year."

The pair of us stared across the table, doing our best to hold the eager gazes of the two boys. Maybe eager was overreaching. Interested? Perhaps not even that. Distracted? Definitely.

It was a miracle I still had a shred of their attention. Cyrus was once more looking out of the huge plate glass windows, where far below a few of this season's roster were practicing ahead of the Opening Day game tomorrow.

We should have held this meeting yesterday when the stadium was quieter, and there were fewer players around to get sidetracked by. Or earlier this morning before anybody arrived.

"Cyrus…"

His head snapped back to me.

"I get it, I really do. Including and especially the ass admiration. But I need your focus for now, then you can go down there and get to work. Give me twenty minutes, deal?"

"Sure. Sorry, Scout."

"Thanks." Over the table I slid the printouts illustrating a couple of graphs from the wider data that had been presented to us earlier in the week. "If you look at this, you can see what worked last year and what we need to change. A key point from the fans was player interaction, they love it when we make the players seem more human and accessible. The best performing posts last year were game day fit, anything involving cute stuff, like puppies and players, or posts that bring out personal details—favorite cereals, soda, what's in their refrigerator—things like that."

The pair of them flicked through the pages, nodding as their eyes scanned across the figures. I couldn't tell if they found it interesting or they were nodding because that's what they thought they should be doing. Cyrus picked up his pen and began doodling on his notepad.

"As members of the social team, your opinions are valid. Everyone chips in with ideas. We bounce off each other, we learn, we improve. If you have ideas, then you share them. No idea is a bad idea."

The pair of them sat there in silence. I was half expecting a dust ball to blow past any minute. I caught the end of Alice rolling her eyes.

"Guys? How about now? What's trending, what's new? Any ideas—"

Joey's hand shot into the air before sheepishly lowering it. "Um, well, you know the mom trend that's always popular. The one where they empty their bag and go through it…that could work."

"How'd you mean?"

"When the guys come in the building, we grab them before they get to the locker rooms. Ask them to show us what's in their bag."

"Oh yeah, good. I like that." I nodded in a way I hoped was encouraging. "We can build on that too. A day in the life—"

"A week in the life of the Lions."

"Hey, don't the Lions always have a bat dog for special games? We could do more there if the fans like dogs—"

"Ha-ha, like who can get around the bases faster," Joey interrupted.

"A New York Lion or a New York Labrador?"

"You mean Barclay?" I asked, quickly jumping in.

"Yeah, whatever he's called." Cyrus continued, "NHL teams always do a doggy day with the local shelters—calendars, or photoshoots, that sort of thing. Bring your dog to work."

"I like it." Alice sat up straighter and took a long sip of her coffee. It might have been the light, but I was sure Cyrus's cheeks flushed a little at her compliment. "We can work more ad sales in for pet brands. Have pet-focused days. The Dodgers hold a dog day, we should do the same."

"Good, what else?" I asked, spinning around at the knock on the door to find Tom, one of the guys on the comms team, poking his head through the gap.

"Scout, we have this room booked."

"No, we're booked until—" My eyes flicked to the clock across the stadium, and I realized that we'd spent so long messing around with projectors and staring at butts, that I'd lost track of the time.

Crap.

Tom walked in and dropped his stuff on the table, not even bothering to wait for the four of us to stand up. What's more, he was followed by approximately fifteen members of the comms team, so it became a bustle trying to get out while everyone else was swarming in.

"Jeez, give us a second to get out of your way, why don't you?" grumbled Alice as she finally pushed through the crowd. "There must be a dozen meeting rooms on this floor, how are they all booked?"

Instead of answering, I grabbed the boys before they attempted to take off and pulled them away from the thoroughfare of the corridor to finish the meeting.

"There were some good ideas in there, guys. Well done. Your first assignment is to create a social media posting schedule of ideas for the next two weeks, and we'll see what we can take from it. Can you send to me by the end of the day?"

"Sure thing. Um, Scout, will we get to watch the game tomorrow?"

I nodded. "Yes. I need you helping the rest of the social team capturing the warm-ups. Also we have a bunch of the Lions shirts to give away, so for the game you'll be out on the boardwalk, handing shirts out to anyone who catches a home run ball."

"Awesome!" muttered Cyrus, hitting his fist against Joey's, who looked equally as delighted at their roles for the Lions Opening Day game, before taking off down the corridor.

"Come and find me if you need anything or have questions," I called after them, and turned to Alice. "Could they have left any quicker?"

"Yeah, probably. Bet they've gone to find the boys on the field, pump them for information on their workouts," she replied, rolling her shoulders back and letting out a wide yawn. "They have a point, you know."

"About what?"

"Those butts are noteworthy."

"Only when I don't have to concentrate on other things. Come on, let's drop our stuff and run out for a coffee before we get back to work. Or in your case, start working." I nudged her shoulder with a laugh.

"Hey, it's called efficiency, and delegation. Two things I happen to excel at."

In the short time we'd been in the meeting, the hustle and bustle of the New York Lions communication department—located on the fifth floor of the stadium—had kicked into full throttle.

I'd only been with the Lions for little over a year, but we'd already doubled in size, thanks to the combination of a healthy operating budget and the challenge of turning around the reputation of a club, which, as I told the guys earlier, had been less than stellar. Recruitment for the best and brightest in the industry had gone into overdrive, and there were now more than a hundred people on this floor alone.

It hadn't always been like that.

The New York Lions had historically been seen as the worst team in baseball. For decades it was found at the bottom of both the National League East and the National League, as well as bottom of the entire points table.

All this changed, however, when Penn Shepherd bought the club a few years ago and injected both some much-needed cash and an infectious love for America's favorite game, which seemed to have been forgotten.

Overnight, the club transformed from a graveyard where players were unofficially retired before retirement, to being seen as a serious contender in the postseason. Not only did the starting rosters get overhauled, but so did the stadium, the club grounds, and the front offices. It was no secret that Penn Shepherd wanted the Commissioner's Trophy, and he was fully prepared to pour as much money into the club as needed in order to make that happen.

And happen soon.

In case we forgot our goal, the Lions' mantra was painted across the back wall of the comms department in giant font above the intertwined letters of the Lions logo.

king of the jungle, king of the field.

we're not here to play ball. we're here to win.

Last season saw us win our division and lose in the NLCS.

Each season since Penn Shepherd took ownership, we'd progress a little further.

This year the guys were expected to make it to the World Series. And while the starting nine might be there to hit the balls and sprint around the bases, the responsibility of winning that trophy fell on every single one of our shoulders.

Whether that was the crew who kept the locker rooms clean and tidy, along with the shelves and fridges stocked full of the players' favorite drinks and snacks; the groundskeepers who kept the grass cut at the perfect length for optimal ball rolling—between one and two-and-a-half inches tall—or my social media team, keeping the fans entertained in between games, and the players relevant.

We were all integral.

We were one team.

Alice took my laptop and jogged over to the far-left corner where ad sales sat, dropping it with hers on one of the empty desks.

The marketing team was on the other side of sales, and social—where I worked—was sandwiched between them. With only eight of us, we were the smallest team on this floor, but arguably the busiest. The biggest team—public relations—sat down the right wall.

Finance, legal, HR were all on the floor above, while more customer-facing roles like ticket operations were the floor below. Anything directly relating to the stadium, or games and players, such as security or travel were all on the lower ground floors, nearer to the training facilities.

While the players might have a rest during the offseason, the front office spent the down months planning strategy for the following year, so it wasn't a novelty that everyone was busy—it was always busy. But since Monday, there'd been a buzz in the air not present since last season—reminiscent of that first day of term mentality I used to get before each new school year.

Spring Training was over, and Opening Day was right around the corner.

The elevator doors pinged open right as Alice reached me and we made our way down to the huge atrium of the New York Lions headquarters.

The vast gold and black logo taking up most of the marble floor glinted in the sunlight as we walked over it, and past the empty plinth Penn Shepherd had installed, ready for the Commissioner's Trophy to be placed on top. I wasn't a superstitious person, but I still hadn't decided whether keeping a pedestal for every single person to walk past each morning was tempting fate, or simply an example of the sheer amount of faith and hope he had in his players.

The gates were already heaving with tourists and Lions fans all lining up to enter the grounds. Over the past few weeks, each day had gotten busier and busier. Most of those waiting looked like they were heading for the store to buy their favorite player's jersey or new season merch, though a large, excited group in the middle were clearly there for the first stadium tour of the day to begin.

Passing under the huge stone Lion arch, the two of us made our way along the boardwalk and past the giant Lions flags gently waving in the breeze.

In less than twenty-four hours, the Hudson on our right would be heaving with guys in canoes and dinghies waiting to catch any home run ball soaring over the stadium walls. Cyrus and Joey would be positioned on dry land ready to capture all the action and upload it to the social channels.

I briefly wondered if this year I'd convince my boss to get us a Lions dinghy to take out on the water and join them.

Next to me, Alice inhaled slowly and deeply. "Ahh, do you smell that?"

I sniffed the air but came up empty. I smelled nothing except the usual salty, dirty kind of way it was normally. "Nope. What?"

She threw me a wry smile. "The start of baseball season, baby."

"Oh yeah?" I chuckled. "What does that smell like?"

"Sweat. Popcorn. Baseball pants." She smirked, nudging an elbow into my side and nodding to the stadium wall on the left.

In the past few weeks, the groundskeepers had removed last year's ginormous posters plastered against the paneling on the sides and replaced them with fresh ones. Each poster featured a player from the current season's lineup.

Since Penn Shepherd's ownership, it had become a popular marketing move to announce the start of the new season. With giant flags flying around the city with the players' faces on them, and a takeover of the screens in Times Square, the New York Lions were virtually impossible to escape.

The message was clear—the Lions had been forgotten for far too long, it was time to remind the people of New York City there were three baseball teams in contention.

A couple of the posters already had fans posing by them, having their photos taken, and it wouldn't be long before they were covered in graffiti, messages from fans, and scrawled love notes to their favorite players. It was encouraged by the club, and made for great content, especially from the more enthusiastic fans.

Everyone had their favorite players—Ace Watson, the Lions pitcher, was usually fighting for top spot on the sexiest man of the year list, along with Jupiter Reeves, the Lions' third baseman and resident bad boy. Alice was a big fan of Jupiter Reeves, along with most of New York's female population. Something to do with a body covered in tattoos, thick-set muscles, and constant scowl.

If I was choosing, I'd pick Parker King any day of the week.

Owner of the best butt at the Lions, according to an unofficial poll of everyone on the fifth floor, possibly even the entire MLB—otherwise known as the Lions starting catcher.

From the many yet all too brief encounters I'd had with him last year filming content, he was a good guy. Always smiling, and very easy on the eyes with a flop of light brown hair that always looked like he'd just run his fingers through it. He also didn't seem to take himself too seriously, something I'd quickly learned was rare among elite sportsmen.

I didn't know a ton about him, beyond what I heard around the club, which was mostly from the girls, but he was usually found cracking a joke or two with Ace.

Alice nodded ahead to where a larger-than-usual group was gathered in front of one. "Who are they crowding around?"

"Ten bucks it's Reeves," I replied right as a gap opened up in front of the poster. It wasn't Reeves. "Huh, I stand corrected."

Yeah, I would definitely pick Parker King.

His face was usually hidden behind the catcher's cage mask, but here on the board, his smile beamed out, green eyes glinting mischievously under his Lions baseball cap.

Parker King, along with Ace Watson, Lux Weston, and Tanner Simpson, made up a small group of players known as the Lions' fab four and were widely regarded as the future of the club. The four of them trained together, hung out together, and when they weren't on the road hopping from hotel to hotel, lived together.

"He was so into you last year."

"No, he wasn't," I shot back. "It was a rumor. The gossip around the club last year was out of control. If he'd been into me, he'd have asked me out. And he didn't."

It was a conclusion I'd come to recently, during a period where I'd briefly questioned my life choices. I'd found myself fantasizing about different paths, one of which was spent wondering if the whispered rumors were true, that Parker King had liked me, and where I'd be now if he had asked me out last season.

It might have saved me some time dating douchebags, or maybe he'd also have turned out to be a douchebag himself.

But you live and learn.

And what I learned about dating my most recent ex was that I had terrible taste in guys, and/or I needed to do better at picking them. Probably both.

Alice shrugged. "I dunno. Those rumors are still going strong."

I turned to her, my brow furrowed, though more from annoyance that my ex-boyfriend popped up uninvited once more in my thoughts. "According to whom? How do you know all this? The season hasn't even begun, how is it you're already at the center of the gossip?"

"Hey, gossip doesn't discriminate between seasons."

"Alice—"

"I listen—"

"Ali—"

"Pablo told me," she replied with a grin. "I always bring him a coffee in the morning, and we spend a little time catching up before I head up to start work. He doesn't take time off during the breaks, he sees everything that happens here and keeps me updated on the news."

Pablo Garcia was the security guard who manned the reception desk. He'd been with the New York Lions longer than I'd been born, as he liked to remind me, and nothing got past him. He knew everything and everyone.

"That's how I knew about Lux Weston dating Radley Andrews before the papers got it. He brought her to the gym."

"And he told you that Parker King is into me?"

She nodded solemnly. "Yup. According to Pablo, Parker King's had the hots for you for a while now, but then you started dating Shit Head and he thought he'd blown it. He's been waiting for you to be single again so he can swoop in."

"Oh come on." I scoffed so hard it burned my throat, and I coughed out the rest of my sentence. "There's no way that's true."

Alice jerked a shoulder up. "Hey, I'm just telling you what I heard. You wanna know what else? Which we could possibly call bigger news, it's gonna cause some problems at least."

"Sure—"

"You know how Ace Watson screwed up last Opening Day?"

"Yeah." I shuddered, because how could we forget.

It was unlikely we ever would. A day to go down in history.

It had been a blood bath. Ace absolutely crumbled on the mound in Philly, and in front of President Andrews, who'd made the first pitch, then stayed to watch her precious Philadelphia team annihilate us. I could still feel the humiliation and tension that clogged the air when the guys returned to the hotel after the game.

It was the worst start to a season the Lions had ever had, and for weeks everyone was on edge.

Ace had been immediately replaced by Riley Rivers as starting pitcher, and rumors quickly spread he had the yips.

It didn't last. Miraculously, Ace turned it around to make last season his best season ever and ended it by winning the CY Young Award.

Probably the first pitcher to ever win after tanking an Opening Day.

"I heard it was because of a girl."

I tore my eyes away from Parker's face and the daydream I was about to slip into, and glanced at Alice. "Is it just everyone's sex life that you and Pablo gossip about?"

"Unless there's something more interesting and worth discussing," she replied with a pursed lip, "but I'm not there yet. Anyway, Ace tanked because of a girl, and after what happened between Boomer Jones and Leanne in accounting—"

"Wait, what? What happened?"

She looked at me like there was a possibility I'd grown two heads, then tutted loudly. "Oh right, I forgot that was the week you finally ditched Shit Head, and you went through your single-girl-surviving-on-ice-cream-chopping-your-hair-off phase, then disappeared to Spring Training." Alice turned to look over her shoulder, before tilting her head closer to mine and lowering her voice. "Okay, according to Pablo, Boomer and Leanne hooked up a couple of times right at the end of last season. I think it started the night the guys celebrated getting into the postseason. Anyway, I guess they didn't clarify their relationship status or whatever, so when he was photographed after New Year's with that model, Leanne made her displeasure known and she emailed HR about it."

"Okay…"

"All the players have been asked to sign a workplace dating clause. The email went out this morning."

My eyes bugged. "Whoa."

"I know."

Opening my phone, I scanned through my emails. "I don't see it. When did it go?"

"It's just the players. I guess they don't care if front office staff date. But if we want to date a player, we have to declare it. HR is covering their ass, I guess. And Penn Shepherd doesn't want another Opening Day disaster like last year, or any distractions. Apparently his view is that the dating clause will discourage players enough, they won't even bother trying."

"Boys will just have to keep their dicks to themselves." I laughed, shaking my head.

"Only on club grounds." She snorted, before nudging me gently. "How long are we betting it takes Parker King to sign one and date you?"

Out of nowhere, somewhere in the depths of my core, there was the tiniest flicker of interest as I once again very briefly wondered what it would be like to date Parker King. And just as quickly reminded myself it was a terrible idea.

"He can take as long as he wants. Not interested."

"Yeah, yeah," Alice replied with a pursed lip and a thickly raised eyebrow.

"I'm not. This year is about making better relationship choices. Dating a professional athlete does not qualify for that. Or anyone working with professional athletes," I replied, slashing my hands crossed through the air. "No one in sports. Period. I want to be single for a while. Plus, HR is right, dating at work is a terrible idea."

"Okay. Chill." Alice chuckled. "I take it Shit Head is still messaging you? You should block him."

I was about to reply that I intended to block him, I just kept forgetting, when a couple of girls stopped next to us.

"Hey, are you two just going to stand there and stare? Or can you move to the side so we can get a picture?" One of them huffed.

"Actually, we're not staring, we're making better relationship choices. Isn't that right, Scout?" Alice smirked as she tugged my sleeve. "Come on, let's get our coffee."

My gaze flicked back for one last look at Parker and his grin, before turning to the girls. "You're welcome to him."

2

Parker

"Fucking Reeves—"

"Did you see her? She looked right at me. She looked right at me and waved—"

"I'm not getting goddamn friend-zoned. It's official, Scout's single—"

"Millie definitely waved. I'm telling you, I'm finally in. I'm getting closer—"

"I'm asking her on a date. The next time I see her, I'm asking—"

"I said I'd catch her a ball, and I did. Who needs more than that?"

“Did you see where she was sitting? I couldn’t find her. She’ll have seen my homer, right? D’you think she saw it?”

“I’ll get that ball back, then I can give it to her as a gift. I’ll write something cute on it. Girls love that shit—”

“I haven’t hit like that since the middle of last season, and I go and get a home run on my first pitch during Opening Day. It’s a sign, I know it—”

“I’ll ask her on a date—”

I stopped dead.

Tanner stopped next to me.

The pair of us were standing in the middle of the corridor heading to the locker rooms, which wasn’t the best place to stop after a game, seeing as it became an interstate of players, staff, coaches, and sports journalists all rushing around, dodging each other to avoid a collision.

I pulled him to the side before we got taken out by someone not looking where they were going.

It wouldn’t be the first time it had happened.

“What?”

“What?”

“What are you talking about?” we asked in sync, both looking more confused than we probably should.

I held my hand up before he started talking again. “What were you talking about just then? Who are you asking out?”

“Millie. Who are you talking about?”

"Scout." I sighed.

Scout was all I ever seemed to talk about right now.

Think about.

Dream about.

I was almost at the point where I was boring myself, let alone everyone else.

Nah, who was I kidding? I'd never get bored of talking about Scout Davison.

Tanner held his mouth in a straight line and gave one single understanding nod. "Okay, bud. You go first."

Dropping a hand on his shoulder, I squeezed in gratitude.

He knew the seriousness of this situation, because he was living it, too, and pining over Millie Robinson, who wanted nothing to do with him. But at least he didn't have to see her every day.

Now the season had started, I'd be seeing Scout *every damn day,* and I had no plans to go through the same torture of last year, when I took too long to ask her out.

I was not about to sit on my ass again while another dude swooped in and snatched her up.

I was the only one who'd be doing any swooping.

Me, Parker King, catcher for the New York Lions.

Swooper.

"Thanks, man."

My cheeks puffed, letting out the deep breath I'd taken,

and my mind homed in on Scout again. I don't know what it was about this girl that caused me to forget how to act like a normal human being.

It was miles away from the professional baseball player who could get any woman he wanted. The one who'd never in his *entire* life had a problem asking a girl out.

But Scout made me forget myself.

"Okay." I repeated, "I don't want to get friend-zoned or whatever the fuck Reeves called it."

Fucking Reeves.

The spiral I'd stopped myself from spinning into pregame, was threatening to take hold again.

This was all Jupiter Reeves's fault.

I'd been quietly having a conversation with my boys about how to ask out Scout now she was single, when Jupiter Reeves interrupted with his sole contribution by telling me not to get friend-zoned.

That was it. Don't get friend-zoned.

I was about to ask him what he meant when Coach called a meeting, and I hadn't seen Jupiter since, unless you counted the dugout. And even I wasn't stupid enough to talk to Jupiter Reeves about a girl during Opening Day game.

That was the sort of shit Ace pulled.

"You think I should go and find Reeves and ask him what he meant?"

Find Reeves, or find Scout. It was debatable which was

more nerve wracking.

I waited for Tanner to answer. Instead, he pulled his cell out and began scrolling.

I was still waiting thirty seconds later. Did he not realize I wasn't asking a rhetorical question and did *actually* require a response?

"Duuude?" I tried again, making no attempt to keep the whine from my tone. "What should I do?"

I was about to slap the cell from his hands when he finally looked up, and a wide smile split his face.

"What?"

"I don't think you're in the friend zone yet. You're definitely still in the strike zone." He snickered, thrusting his cell in my direction. "She saw your home run."

The screen was open on the New York Lions TikTok channel—which Scout was in charge of. I found myself staring at a looped close-up video of me smashing the ball through the air, far into left field and the stands, jogging past the bases and off the field.

The last five seconds was in slow motion, my mouth curved up on the right and looking every ounce as smug as I felt when I saluted the fans before ducking back into the dugout.

The smugness returned tenfold as I read the text over the top.

KING OF THE FIELD ❤

"Check out the one underneath."

I scrolled down to find a video of Ace and me warming up.

My smile grew.

It wasn't us just throwing and catching or going over strategy. No sir. Those groin stretches the PTs had us doing on the daily were paying off in more ways than one, and I didn't mind in the slightest that a close-up of my ass was there for the world to see.

Not if Scout had videoed it.

The social media team usually had cameras set up along the field to capture each game, and they always stayed close by. But today I hadn't been aware of seeing any of them. Or rather, I hadn't spotted Scout.

Normally I knew when she was near, as though I had a sixth sense for anything concerning Scout Davison, but today I'd been too focused on making sure Ace had a better Opening Day than last year.

And I had. We'd annihilated the Braves.

But if these two videos were anything to go by, Scout's attention had been on more than the game. Especially as—from scrolling through the rest of today's posts—no one else had two made of them.

I glanced back up at Tanner, my chest puffing. "Do you think she's into me? That's what this means, right?"

Whatever Tanner was about to say died on his lips and

his eyes widened at something over my shoulder. There was absolutely no way he could have been any more obvious when I turned around to see what he was looking at and found Scout walking toward us, a laptop clasped to her chest as she typed away on her phone.

Fuck. She looked so pretty.

I hadn't seen her properly since last season. I wasn't counting the ice-skating fiasco from Christmas when she'd been with Rangers Douche, and I also wasn't counting the week she flew down to Spring Training, when I mostly ran in the opposite direction whenever she was near, just in case she was *still* with Rangers Douche.

But I wasn't running now.

Even from thirty yards out, the swell of her tits bouncing in the white tank top she was wearing woke my dick up. The Lions shirt thrown over the top did nothing to help, either, because all I could think about was her wearing *my* Lions shirt.

She'd cut her hair since last month. Instead of the long blonde waves I always dreamed about wrapping around my fist, blunt ends stopped just above her collarbone and brushed along the sliver of golden skin peeking out between the material. No matter, I'd make it work. And I don't know how, but it made her cheeks seem even rounder and her lips more kissable than ever.

And they'd always looked really fucking kissable.

"Hey, Scout," crowed Tanner in a way that made my jaw

clench, especially when his hand shot in the air with an overexaggerated, mom-style wave. I'd have kicked him if it wouldn't have been obvious.

Her head shot up, her face immediately flushing pink as her gaze darted between us. "Oh hey, guys."

Her eyes stilled on me. I'd never seen a shade of blue like it, as though an artist had mixed the color of my favorite pair of Levi's with the glow in the sky right before nighttime arrived, especially when they twinkled.

"Hey, Parker."

I held my breath as she passed us, just in case she decided to stop and talk, but instead she walked on by without another glance, without me waiting to say hey back to her.

Shit.

Once more, Scout Davison made me forget myself.

I'd never felt more like I was back in high school than when Scout was around. Except in high school, I never became tongue-tied. I'd owned the hallways.

My shoulders were on the verge of slumping when Tanner nudged me.

"She's into you," he said as we watched her walk off toward the elevator banks.

"You think?"

"No doubt. Of course she is. You know my motto—you're Parker Fucking King. Get it over with before the team meeting. Ask her out."

I rubbed my hands together. Okay. Yeah. I was Parker Fucking King. I could do this.

I'd already waited too long to talk to her, and over my dead body was Jupiter Reeves going to be proved right. I would *not* be friend-zoned.

If I ran, I could hit the elevator button for her before she reached it.

"We're talking about Millie when we get home," I called behind me before I took off down the hallway.

Here goes nothing.

"Scout," I called as loudly as I could, but not so loud that it made every single other person in the corridor turn around. I should have picked a better time. "Scout, wait up."

She stopped and turned, blonde hair flicking in her face.

Pushing it out of her eyes, she glanced up from her phone, wearing a confused expression. "Hey, Parker, what's up?"

I slowed. What is up? I hadn't thought this far ahead. Not enough to come up with a valid answer to one simple question without me looking like a total dick, at least.

Instead, I came to a stop in front of her, curling my hand around the peak of my cap before shoving both hands deep into my pockets.

"Um, hey."

"Hey," she replied. Her head tilted as she waited for me to fill the silence and explain why I'd just run down the corridor after her. "Well done on your home run, by the way."

"Thanks." I grinned, only my grin didn't drop. It froze while I was still trying to remember my words.

"Are you okay?"

"Yeah, yes. Just wanted to say hey. And—you know—great work on the TikTok today." *The* TikTok. Fuck my life. "I mean TikTok. Just TikTok. Not *the*, obviously—"

Parker, *shut up.*

Scout's brows dropped a fraction and her left eye twitched as she kind of narrowed it at me. Yeah, I definitely forgot to take my cool pills this morning.

If I could read her mind, it would be saying something like *What the fuck is happening right now?*

"Thanks." She laughed. "I can't take the credit today. We have a couple of interns on the social team for the next few months. They were capturing all the content and—"

"Wait, that wasn't you? You didn't take the videos of me… um…I mean us. Of the game? The warm-ups?"

She shook her head slowly. "No, Cyrus and Joey were catching all the pregame content, then went out to the boardwalk."

Cyrus and Joey.

I hoped it wasn't obvious my entire chest shriveled like a popped balloon. I glanced down at the floor, half expecting to see a piece of wrinkled rubber lying there. Everything Tanner said about Scout having the hots for me was all based on videos two dudes had made.

Two interns staring at my ass.

And I wasn't sure how I felt about it.

Maybe I had really blown it by taking too long to ask her on a date last year.

"Oh."

"Is everything okay?"

"Yeah, it's good. I just wondered is all. Thank them for including my home run."

"Sure. I will. No problem."

I rocked back on my heel. "So—"

"So—"

Think, Parker. *Think.*

"Let me know if you need any more content. Always happy to help out you guys on social," I added weakly, trying to avoid eye contact with a couple of the guys heading to the locker room.

I didn't need an audience for this, nor did I want to make it obvious something was happening that I'd then hear about later.

"Count on it. There's a lot planned," she replied with a broad smile that lifted my chest a little.

I was saved from another awkward silence by a movement to my left. On second thoughts I'd prefer the silence. Coach was jogging down the stairs next to the elevators, and the moment he spotted Scout and me, his step paused.

Please keep walking, please keep walking.

But luck was not on my side, and instead of walking by, he marched straight toward us.

Not only was I totally choking asking Scout on a date, now my dad may as well be peering over my shoulder.

"King. Don't forget to sign your form," he barked, before I could say a word.

A deep frown crossed my face, because first off, that made no sense and…nope, just the no sense thing.

"Eh, Coach? What form?"

His eyes flicked to Scout and back to me, along with a sly grin. A grin I didn't like the look of. Not one bit.

"The dating form." His finger pointed between Scout and me. "You two will need to sign it. If that's what's going on here."

The air caught in my lungs so quickly that no amount of cool I might have had saved me from choking on it. There was no rescue. Just straight, red-faced choking.

Scout's eyes were widening to the point they were in danger of falling out, and her cheeks weren't just pink, they were bright red.

"Damn, Coach. What?" I managed to splutter.

"Don't you read your emails?"

Not if I could help it. "Um, yeah. 'Course I do."

"Well then, you should know what I'm talking about."

I forced myself to look at Scout, in case *she* knew what he was talking about, except she was now looking anywhere else but me. The signs by the elevators were not *that* interesting.

Once again, I asked myself how was I this major league ball player with money, above average looks (according to several sexiest men polls), and an ass to die for, yet I couldn't ask out the one girl I'd been crushing on for over a year?

I waited for Coach to leave and continue his journey, perhaps to terrorize a few of the rookies or go and ruin someone else's life, though no evidence pointed to that happening. I stayed silent. In the end, Scout jerked her head behind her to the stairs, clearly providing a quicker escape option than the elevators, which had never been called.

"I need to…um…running late. See you around."

She took off before I could say another word.

I was yet to blink, even when I turned to Coach, who was *still* there looking like he hadn't just stirred a big pile of shit in my life. Come to think of it, I wasn't even entirely sure what he had done, but I knew I wasn't going to like it.

"Coach?"

"Check your emails, King. Then get your ass in the auditorium for a debrief," he replied, walking off before I could stop him.

I pulled my phone out and opened my inbox. Nothing was there that I could tell. Even among the fifty-one thousand unread ones.

Scroll.

Spam.

Scroll.

Casa Grayskull admin.

Scroll. Scroll.

Nothing except sports news. An email from my stylist for game day fits—save that baby for later. Scrolling. Scrolling. Scrolling.

Then I spotted it. Yesterday.

FROM: NEW YORK LIONS HR

SUBJECT: INTERCOMPANY RELATIONSHIP DISCLOSURES

To all players,

Following recent behaviors, the New York Lions senior management has decided that, with immediate effect, any player wishing to enter into a personal relationship of a sexual nature with another New York Lions employee is required to sign a confidential relationship disclosure.

Anyone caught failing to uphold this agreement will face disciplinary action. If you are already in a relationship with an employee, respond to this email.

Please note: signature from both parties is required.

Any questions should be directed to the New York Lions HR dept.

Sincerely,

HR

Fuck my life.

3

Parker

"Did you know about this?" I hissed to Ace as I slipped into the chair next to him.

He didn't answer. He was too focused on what was happening at the front of the auditorium, where Coach Chase was gathered with a couple of the other coaches, as well as Riley Rivers, one of the alternate pitchers.

At least his debrief hadn't started yet.

"What's going on?"

Ace shook his head. "Don't know, and I can't lip read from this angle."

"Cool, anyway, did you know about this?" I shoved my

phone in front of him.

He glanced down briefly, before looking back at me. "What?"

I swiped my screen open, again. "This. This email."

Taking my phone, he scanned the words. From the way his eyebrows shot up I could tell this was the first time he was seeing it too. I didn't appreciate the smirk growing on his face, however.

"Shit, bud." He shook his head. "That's rough. Is that because of Boomer?"

My mouth dropped. Fuck. It hadn't even occurred to me that there was a definitive cause behind this beyond HR being a giant fucking pain in my ass.

Boomer Jones, goddammit.

"Do you know if anyone else has seen it?"

Ace shrugged, his attention back on whatever conversation Coach was having. "Dunno. No one reads their emails, do they? Probably why they sent it."

I jerked to the right as Tanner dropped onto the bench next to me. Next to me was incorrect, *landed on* me was more accurate.

"Tan, Jesus. I'm literally sitting right here."

"I know, sorry, got too excited." He turned to me, his eyes wide in excitement. "Well?"

"Well what?" I grumped.

“Er…Scout. When’s the first date?”

“Never.” I groaned through the solid clench of my jaw and opened my phone again, handing it to Tanner. “Did you know about this?”

As Ace’s had done, Tanner’s brows shot up as he read over the email. “Whoa. This is fucked up.”

“Yeah.” I glanced down, scanning the words for the dozenth time searching for a loophole, for anything which meant I could ask Scout on a date without having to sign a declaration about it first.

But nothing. Nada. Zip.

Next to me, Tanner was shaking his head, reading the email on his phone.

“What’re you going to do?”

“I dunno.”

“You still like her though, right?”

“Yes, Tan, I still like her. My feelings haven’t changed in the last twenty minutes since I read this.”

“So what’re you going to do then?”

“I haven’t got that far yet.”

He was just about to jump in with another response, but instead, Coach’s voice boomed from the front. He was so loud, that sitting in the back row of the auditorium wasn’t just about not appearing like a brown nose. It was to save on hearing loss. Besides, we’d already done our time on the front row. That was rookie territory, and this season’s influx were all primed and ready.

"All present and correct?" he asked, not waiting for a response. "Good. Everyone, sit your asses down, and listen up."

It took longer than it should have for silence to descend, the energy in the room was buzzing hard off our win. The main doors to the auditorium clanged back and forth as the last few guys rushed in to take a seat, sprinting up the steps in case they were late, only to slow down when they realized there were still half a dozen others behind them.

Tanner's hand shot in the air as Lux walked in, taking the steps two at a time to where we'd saved him a seat. He looked like he'd come straight from the field, but the game ended an hour ago.

"Where've you been?"

"With Radley." He grinned.

I held in the eye roll. Of course he had.

I liked Radley, I liked her a lot. She was a sweet girl, and she was fun to have around the apartment. It also made me happy that my boy Lux was happy. On the flip side—without sounding melodramatic—it only served to remind me how completely alone I was.

I mean, not *alone* alone.

But I'd spent the whole of this year so far, and a good portion of last year, counting down the days until I could ask Scout on a date. Getting to this point had not been the easy path it should have been, and now this fucking form was making it even harder.

It was all my fault.

I should have asked her out the first time I'd laid eyes on her.

I still remember the day. I was walking back in from practice and the social team had set up a table by the doors with a sign next to it that read: apples or oranges?

On the table had been two huge crates of both, Scout had been standing in between them, long blonde hair tied up in a thick ponytail of waves, swaying down her back.

It had been her eyes I'd noticed first; big and blue, like staring into an ocean, but with a warmth you don't always get with blue eyes. Mesmerizing. Her smile came next, beaming from ear to ear with just that hint of challenge because she knew exactly what she was about to ask—juggle the fruit, and let us film it.

She was smart, too, lining up Ace first, who was easily the most competitive of us.

Like giving candy to a baby.

Ace being Ace picked up three oranges, tossed them in the air, and we all watched as they fell to the ground when he missed them. Scout's laugh peeled out—genuine and infectious—as Ace sprinted after one of the oranges that had rolled down the pathway.

"You next," she'd said eventually, with a twinkle in her eye and even more of a challenge to her tone.

Could I do better, or worse?

I had never, in any moment before or since, been grateful to my mom for forcing me to take part in Westlake Elementary's second grade talent contest. The one where I'd practiced nonstop for a week trying to juggle the baseballs that I always left lying around the house.

I picked up three apples and tossed them in the air. On the second rotation, I picked up a fourth, then fifth, at which point Ace snatched one away to eat, and I nearly dropped the rest.

"Show-off." She laughed.

That was the day my crush on Scout Davison grew roots.

I meant to ask her out. I *did.*

I wanted to. But every time I planned it, something got in the way. Ace's Opening Day, or one of her colleagues, or our insane work schedule, or the absolute douche-nozzle she started dating at the end of last summer.

I lost my chance. It was possible I sulked (not that I would ever admit it) for weeks. Okay, *months.*

Right before Spring Training there'd been rumors of her and the douche breaking up; I waited with bated breath for confirmation. Then, this morning, like a ray of sunshine on a rainy, miserable day, I heard the news.

Scout was single once again.

My plan not to waste any time in asking her out, lasted

until approximately thirty minutes after today's game ended and Coach alerted me to my emails.

My jaw clenched again.

"Okay, settle down," Coach started, then stopped.

The door banged back and Jupiter Reeves walked in and whispered something to Coach, who nodded and made his way to the back like he had all the time in the world. Jupiter Reeves did things on his own schedule.

"Gentlemen." He nodded to us, taking a seat next to Lux.

"Okay, can we begin now? No one needs a bathroom break? Snacks? Drinks," asked Coach, moving to the whiteboard behind him.

"I'll take some Twizzlers, Coach," called someone nearer the front, which caused another wave of chatter.

Coach responded in his usual manner—to stare until we were silent—though the corners of his mouth were twitching in amusement. "Okay, first off. You did good today. A game in the bag, we are one for one."

The energy in the room exploded. Whoops, cheers, hollers all echoed off the walls.

"Home runs, stand up. Weston...King...Jones... Velasquez..." Each time he called a name he tossed a piece of candy our way. I caught a packet of Skittles and ripped it open. "Where's Watson?"

Ace stood up slowly. I could tell he wasn't sure whether he was about to get called out for last year's Opening Day performance, even though he'd more than made up for that. A Snickers was launched through the air.

"You pitched good. Let's keep it up."

"Yes, Coach,"he mumbled through a giant bite of chocolate and peanuts. "Man, I'm hungry."

"Okay," Coach held his palms up, calling for silence once more, "now let's get down to business and what we can improve on for tomorrow."

For the next twenty minutes, he proceeded to rip apart everything we'd done. How we'd let the Braves score, how we'd not been paying enough attention to where the ball was. Twice it had been missed in the outfield and dropped, allowing the Braves to make too many runs off the bases.

Ace, who'd he called out earlier for doing a good job, was now being ripped apart for showing off with too many fastballs. I shrunk down in my seat hoping that I wouldn't also get picked on for calling them, because he was only doing what I'd suggested. More than once we'd gone against the coach's guidance, even though they'd resulted in a strike.

Next up on the chopping board was Boomer Jones, first base, who'd fumbled a catch.

I let out a sigh of relief.

"Is he talking about the game we just played? This sounds like a blood bath. Was he this pessimistic last season every time we won?" whispered Tanner.

I shook my head. "Nah, this is because of Shepherd. He

wants the trophy."

"He needs to start by getting rid of that goddamn plinth in the lobby. Gives me the heebie-jeebies every time we pass it," added Tanner ominously, letting out a dramatic shudder.

"Tell me about it."

"Okay, housekeeping time." Coach slapped his clipboard loudly. "It's the start of the season and I'm only going to remind you once. This is not a frat house. The locker rooms are not there for you to dump all the crap your wives and girlfriends won't let you take home. The laundry is not for your personal use…" He pulled his glasses off and peered over everyone until his eyes landed on Ace. "Watson, we're clear on this, right? Get yourself a housekeeper."

A chuckle went through the auditorium.

For reasons I still hadn't figured out, Ace had a habit of bringing in his laundry. I think it was because he used to have a crush on a girl who worked in the maintenance team, but he categorically denied it. Though seeing as it stopped once he got together with Payton, evidence pointed to the contrary.

"Last item on the agenda. For those of you who don't read your emails, which I assume is most of you, you have all received a note from HR." Immediately half of the guys pulled their phones from their pockets. "You will see that from today intercompany relationships need to be declared to human resources."

I could see the back of Boomer Jones's head.

He was a good guy, he was fun to have a drink or two

with. He'd been over to our apartment for a few games on PlayStation. I normally liked him. Not today though. Not *today*. Whoever was sitting next to him shoved him playfully in the shoulder.

Yeah. This was because of him.

"Let me make one thing very clear," Coach shouted over the volume of everyone snickering and jeering at Boomer. "I absolutely do not want to hear about this. I do not care who you date. Just keep it out of the locker room. King, that means you too."

I groaned. I knew it was too much to hope I'd get away without being singled out in the meeting. "What does that mean?" I grumbled.

I thought it was under my breath, or maybe Coach was better at lip reading than Ace was, because he shouted, "You know exactly what it means. And I don't want it in my locker room." He stood there, his eyes locked on me, until everyone else got bored, and decided it was time the meeting finished.

A couple of the guys stood up, and the chatter immediately kicked in as everyone else took their lead.

I leaned over Ace's shoulder so the three of them could hear me as we made our way out of the auditorium. "Was he talking about Scout?"

Tanner nodded. "I'd say so."

"Seriously, how does everyone know about Scout?" I hadn't made it *that* obvious, surely.

"Dude, you cried in the locker room when you found out she had a boyfriend."

"No, I did not."

I didn't. I absolutely didn't. I'd *almost* cried, because we'd lost by a run. And it had been so close. And I hadn't cried. Just gotten a bit sniffly. But it was because of the run, nothing else.

So what if I'd seen Scout with that dickhead on the way back to the locker rooms.

Ace nudged me before I fell down my rabbit hole.

"So, you gonna sign this form thing?"

I shrugged. "I dunno, I just found out about it. Not exactly the best way to start dating. 'Hey, babe, can I get your signature before I take you out.' Maybe this whole thing is stupid."

"You think?"

"Nah. Uh-uh. No. No way," a deep voice growled from behind us. "Not happening."

Tanner and I spun around.

"You okay there, Reeves?"

"I will be if you stop going on about Scout Davison," he snapped. "But we all know that's not going to happen, don't we? I mean, I shouldn't even know her fucking name. But I do. You know why?"

From the way he was glaring, it seemed like he wanted to answer his own question, so I stayed silent.

"Because you don't stop going on about her. Therefore,

you're going to see this thing through. And ask her on a date. And sign that goddamn form. Understand."

I waited to see if he was going to add any more, or if I was still expected to keep my mouth shut. Eventually, I moved his finger out of my face.

"Yeah, I don't think you can dictate—"

"I can if it means we all get to have a season without you sulking like a little girl."

My teeth gritted. "I did *not* sulk."

"You sulked."

I schooled my mouth into a hard line before I pouted and took another step forward out of this room and away from Jupiter Reeves. "What would you know anyway? You don't have to sign one of those stupid forms."

Come to think of it, *was* he signing a form?

Jupiter was in a relationship with Marnie Matthews, the Lions' head of baseball science.

"I am actually. The email said *all players*."

"You were already in a relationship." I huffed, the tip of my sneaker squeaking on the floor where I was scuffing it. "Doesn't count. Everyone already knows."

"Everyone already knows with you too," he shot back.

"Not the same thing, and I don't remember asking for your opinion," I snapped. "I'd prefer a little privacy when I ask her out, which isn't going to happen now I have to involve HR. Is it?"

I didn't even want to think about what would happen when everyone in the club knew I'd asked Scout on a date. Lux was getting enough shit because he was dating the president's daughter, but at least Radley was only here on game days and she came with armed guards who always added an air of intimidation.

Scout worked here, the guys would see her every day, they'd see *us* every day, and I didn't want to put that on her.

These guys were my buddies, and we all joked around. I just didn't want them to joke around with Scout.

"Did you even read the email, King?"

"Yes. A hundred times."

"Then you'll have seen it said *confidential.* No one needs to know you've signed it. No one needs to know you asked her out. The only reason everyone is well aware you've got the hots for her is because, as I already said, you spent last season sulking."

"Stop fucking saying that." I looked to Tanner. "I didn't sulk. Did I?"

Tanner looked at his feet.

"Tan? Tanner?"

"Um..." His mouth curled in a grimace, and his shoulders lifted in a halfhearted shrug. "Kinda, but it's okay—"

I scowled at him. Not like he hadn't been sulking enough the past few months.

"Parker. It's not a big deal, and I assure you no one cares, especially me. Just please, for the love of god, ask her out so I never have to hear about it *ever again*," Jupiter added, before giving me one last shake of the head and pushing through the four of us, jogging down the remaining steps, muttering under his breath about getting his locker moved.

"He's right, you know."

"About what?" I scowled at Tanner.

"About it being secret. No one needs to know."

I let out an exasperated sigh. It did make it somewhat easier if no one knew. "You think?"

"Yeah. I do. You're Parker Fucking King. She'd be lucky to date you. You've never had a problem with girls before, no need to start now." He grabbed his stomach as it rumbled. "Man, I'm starved. Let's get some wings on the way home."

"Sure, whatever you want," I muttered, not that I was paying attention to anything he said because I was too deep in thought.

I needed to summon the old Parker.

The one who got any girl he wanted. The one who could ask out the girl of his dreams and not tell a single person.

Parker fucking King.

4

Scout

"Hey, Scout, do you have five?" a voice behind me called, just as I hit the button for the elevator.

I spun around to find Ava Martinez, my most senior boss, and VP of marketing, next to Lowe Slater, *her* boss, and the Lions president of global media communications, standing in Ava's office doorway.

"Big guns," Alice hissed as she passed by me on the way back from the bathroom, letting out a low whistle at the same time. "You're in trouble."

"Shut up," I hissed back, though the way my heart automatically raced had me wondering the same thing while

I attempted to hurry over to them but in a way that made me seem totally casual and unpanicked.

I wracked my brains as quickly as I could to figure out what I could have done that would warrant a meeting with two of the most senior women in the company.

Was I about to get fired? I don't think I'd done anything fireable. And no one knew about the ton of Post-its I stole last month for my roommate to use on a bachelorette she was planning. Maybe this was about Cyrus and Joey gawping over players' butts.

Given the slightly bemused expression on both their faces, I wasn't sure I nailed the innocent look quite as well as I hoped.

All in all, being called into her office was way out of the realm of my usual day to day.

Ava's tight curls bounced as she turned back into her office and perched on the edge of her desk, while Lowe took a seat on the couch. I was still glued to the spot in the entrance, wondering what was going on.

I'd never been in a meeting with Lowe Slater before. Not one on one. In fact, she was so many rungs above me on the corporate ladder I'm not sure I'd ever properly spoken to her. It didn't help that she was married to Penn Shepherd and therefore intimidated 95 percent of everyone who worked in this building.

I knew Ava slightly better, very, *very* slightly. She was my boss's boss, which meant I usually only saw her once a month at the wider team meetings.

It was all the more confusing that they both looked entirely warm and welcoming.

"Come in, Scout. Take a seat." Ava gestured toward the couch next to Lowe and the spare chair. I sensibly opted for the chair and promptly rammed my hands between my legs to stop them shaking. "We won't keep you too long."

"Where were you off to?" asked Lowe, brushing her hands over her jeans and almost blinding me with the giant rock on her finger as it caught the light.

"Downstairs. To the entrance. We're setting up for some social content with the guys for when they come in today. We're asking them who was the last person they called on their cell. We usually get some fun answers," I blurted. "Especially as no one ever calls anymore."

"Cute, I look forward to seeing it."

I stared at Lowe, trying to come up with a response, better than *thank you*, but I couldn't. Instead, I smiled.

I mean, obviously she must look at the social channels for the Lions, because she oversaw everything, but the idea that she saw them—that she saw *my work*—was kind of a reality check. Because she was married to the guy who paid my salary, and if she didn't like it then maybe he wouldn't like it and…

"How did the intern briefing go this week?" asked Ava, pulling me from my spiral.

I nodded with a smile, trying to disguise the surprise she'd even known it was happening.

"Not bad, thank you. They had some good ideas. I think they'll be an asset to the team this quarter." Assuming they can stop talking about butts. "They seem very keen to get to work each day."

In fairness to Cyrus and Joey, they had produced some good work. Better than I expected them to. They'd totally nailed the task I'd set them to come up with content ideas for the next few weeks.

Two days ago, we'd filmed in the locker rooms as part of a before and after to assess the damage done during a game.

We'd gotten down there early before the day started and before anyone arrived. The place was spotless. Everything from towels to water bottles and snacks were all lined up, neat and tidy as usual.

That wasn't the case when we returned after the game when everyone had left. A disaster zone would be in better shape.

Wet towels were everywhere.

Who had left all the empty cans of Diet Coke piled into a pyramid on the floor?

Who'd left their shirt and shorts on the floor *next* to the laundry chute?

Who'd left their shower shoes *in* the shower?

The video was posted yesterday, and even for the start of

the season, there'd been incredible engagement. We'd had nearly three million views in twenty-four hours, and over five thousand comments. (It was widely agreed the shower shoes belonged to Ace Watson.)

"Happy to hear it. I look forward to seeing the results," Ava replied with a smile, her eyes quickly flicking to Lowe before focusing back on me. "Keep up the good work, Scout. You have great ideas, and your work during preseason was excellent."

"Thank you."

"Anyway, I"—she gestured over to Lowe—"we, wanted to discuss a new opportunity with you. We're creating an overarching Lions social brand, which includes the Jungle Kings—the Triple-A team out in White Plains. Penn Shepherd wants consistency, and we believe it's key for audience reach and strengthening our fan base. One of the roles will be a social manager who can create a strategy for each of our channels and lead a small team, reporting to Tim Chang, the VP of comms over in White Plains. We've been impressed by your work over the last year with the Lions and think it would be a great step up for you. I'll get HR to send the job description over, and the post will be announced externally next month. But we'd like you to apply."

My brows shot up, my already clammy palms became even sweatier. I didn't know what this meeting was about, or how it would go, but it hadn't been *this.* A new job.

"Oh wow, that's—thank you. Thank you for thinking of

me. I'm honored."

"You know the brand, you work hard, your ideas are inventive and creative. We'd be silly not to include you," Ava replied as she stood, indicating the end of the meeting. She meant it when she said she wouldn't keep me long.

Please don't ask me any questions, please don't ask me any questions.

My brain was whirring too fast to come up with answers, I only just remembered how to stand up, put one foot in front of the other, and make my way to the door.

Lowe followed close behind. "This is a great opportunity for you, Scout. I hope you don't need to think too hard about applying."

"No, no, ma'am," I stuttered, certain it was the first time I'd ever heard her say my name, and before ten minutes ago I hadn't even realized she knew who I was. "Thank you, again."

I barely took a step out of the office when Alice rushed over. If the meeting room wasn't made of glass, there's no way she wouldn't have been pressing her ear to the door. As it was, I found myself yanked back over to the elevator banks and out of sight.

"What was that about?" she asked, rapidly pressing the button for it to arrive. "You looked so nervous. Why was Lowe Slater in there?"

"Did I?"

"Yeah, you were doing that thing you do where you rub

your hands together. I thought you were getting fired. Tell me you didn't get fired. Do we have to pack up boxes?"

"I didn't get fired." I crossed my arms over my chest, ramming my palms into my armpits, which were still kind of nervously sweaty.

"Then why'd you look so nervous?"

"I've never been called in like that before," I replied, stepping into the elevator as the doors opened, and hitting the button for the ground floor. "But they're creating a new overarching Lions brand to include the Jungle Kings. They want me to apply for a role in it. Social manager for all the channels."

"No way!" Alice's eyes widened. "That's awesome, babe. Do you want to apply?"

I shrugged. "I guess. I literally found out about it two minutes ago. Once I get the job description, I'll check it out. I'd get more responsibility. It could be great."

"You should totally apply," she replied as we reached the ground floor. "When you get the paperwork, we'll go through it. Hey, do we have plans for after the game tomorrow?"

"Don't think so. You wanna go out?"

"Yeah, not a late one though. I'm still hungover from last week."

I was about to reply that it was unsurprising given what she'd drunk last week, when I realized I stepped out alone. "What are you doing?"

"Going back to my desk. I only rode down with you to find out what the meeting was about."

For the first time since I got called into Ava's office, I laughed. "Of course you did."

"Keep up the good work, hot stuff," she yelled through the narrowly closing gap. "See you at lunch."

I bit down on my grin, thankful—for once—there was no one around to hear her, and made my way out of the building to where the guys were setting up, waving to Pablo as I passed the desk.

A sharp breeze hit me as I walked outside, and I cursed myself for leaving my sweater on my chair upstairs. It looked way warmer from the windows.

"Hey, guys, what's going on? Are we all set up?" I asked, wrapping my arms around myself. Jeez. How was it *this* cold in April? Last week the weather guys had sworn summer was coming early.

Cyrus glanced over from where he was positioning a small video camera and microphone on a tripod, in front of which, Joey was hopping about.

"What about now? This good?" He took four paces back. "Or here?"

"Yeah, stop, stay there." Cyrus nodded, secured the tripod in place, and pointed behind him. "As long as everyone walks in via that door, we'll catch it all."

"Where's the sign for everyone to read?" I asked.

Joey turned around and picked up a large piece of card stock I hadn't noticed, along with a stand. "Right here."

"Cool. Have you seen anyone arrive yet?"

He shook his head. "No, no one's been through. And I checked with Pablo, it's all still quiet."

Flipping my phone over, I checked the time. "The early birds should start arriving soon. There are usually two or three who come for the gym or a steam, plus everyone who has PT scheduled. Then the rest seem to arrive all in one go."

As I was talking, a blacked-out Range Rover drove past us, heading around to the players' parking lot.

"Head's up, Joey. Jupiter Reeves is always one of the first to arrive."

"What?" His eyes shot to mine. "That was Reeves? That's Reeves's car?"

I nodded, and watched the boys try to contain their excitement. Joey especially was a big fan, he'd made it quite clear on his internship application that the New York Lions was his club. He came from a family of Lions diehards, and Jupiter Reeves had quickly become his number one favorite player.

While I didn't have a relationship with baseball or New York from my family, I understood the love and affiliation you had for a team. My dad was in the armed forces, and I'd been born in the hospital on the Ramstein Air Base in Germany. Originally from Texas, we supported the Longhorns, because that's where my dad had been at school, and college football was the focus for us.

As I said in my interview, *I enjoy sports, but I'm better at my job. Not being a fan of the Lions means I'll be more objective and focused, and I'm not going to be fangirling over the players.*

This was clearly not the case for Joey, who was now smoothing down his T-shirt and checking his reflection in the glass doors as Jupiter Reeves headed our way, holding the hand of his fiancée, Marnie Matthews, who also worked here.

"Dude, chill," muttered Cyrus, who didn't seem any more chill than Joey, given how red his face had turned.

"Good morning, Mr. Reeves," they greeted in sync. I could almost see their heart eyes.

Jupiter grunted his response with a single head nod, attempting to power past them, but Marnie pulled him back.

"Jupiter—"

"What?" he barked.

She pointed to the board, now set up on an easel. "You need to answer the question."

"Otherwise we can't grant you entry," Cyrus joked, only for his smile to die on his lips as Jupiter scowled.

"What question?"

"This one," replied Joey, moving away from the board he was standing in front of.

Jupiter squinted at the question. "Who was the last person I called on my cell?" He glanced at Marnie and shrugged. "I dunno. You, probably."

Marnie rolled her eyes. "Jupe, you literally just hung up on Drew."

"Oh yes. Yeahhh. So, I did." A very rarely seen, broad smile spread across Jupiter's face—making it clear why underwear ads of him along Sunset Boulevard had caused fender benders and traffic jams—and he looked directly into the camera. "The last person I spoke to was my brother-in-law, Drew Crawley, to remind him he still owes me a thousand bucks, because I won our fantasy football league this year." Jupiter peered around the camera to Joey. "You're putting this on TikTok or whatever, right?"

Joey nodded.

"Great." Jupiter grinned at the camera again. "And now everyone else knows, too, and you should all feel free to message him on his social channels as a reminder. Tag him in the post at Drew Crawley."

I bit down on my smile as Marnie hid a similar expression. Drew Crawley was a legendary New York hockey player and married to Jupiter's sister. It wasn't the first time Jupiter had used the social channels to give Drew shit, it wouldn't be the last. And it always got picked up by the sports press, so I didn't care.

"Have an awesome day, guys." Jupiter walked off, slinging his arm around Marnie and muttering, "That was fun."

"That was amazing," Cyrus cried as soon as Jupiter was out of earshot.

"It was. Well done. That's the kind of stuff we need, content that keeps rolling and more people visiting the channels."

The pair of them nodded eagerly.

"Who'd you think will be next?"

"Could be anyone," I replied, frantically rubbing my arms again to ward off the cold, and taking one step closer to the shelter of the building. "Okay, guys, you seem set up, I'm heading inside to work. Come and find me when you're done, then we'll edit the footage and get it scheduled to post."

"It's Parker King."

I spun back around. "What?"

"Parker King, Lux Weston, Ace Watson, and Tanner Simpson," Joey replied, his gaze locked on something over my shoulder.

I almost didn't want to look, but the temptation was too much. I turned 90 degrees, and sure enough, the four of them were walking toward us.

Out of nowhere, my core clenched.

I hadn't seen Parker up close for a couple of days, not since he ran after me in the corridors on Opening Day. When we stood staring at each other, neither of us able to form a full sentence. I'd been all but glued to the spot, gazing into his bright green eyes, before Coach Chase interrupted about HR's dating form.

I'd run back upstairs so fast it had taken me a minute to catch my breath.

Watching him now, running his fingers through still-damp hair, I was almost tempted to sprint up to HR and get the form myself.

Better relationship choices, Scout.

Walking next to the other three only emphasized the size of him. The *width* of him.

While shorter than the rest of the guys, he was still well over six feet. Where the others strode toward us with long legs, Parker looked powerful. Thick thighs from hours spent squatting behind the plate, strong enough to hold him in position for every game.

His tee had ridden up a couple of inches, showing off a stretch of tanned skin at the base of a hefty set of abs. I was so focused on it, that I didn't notice Parker had paused his step, and when I finally looked up, I found him staring at me.

The clenching doubled down.

My gaze hastily shifted, only to see a wide grin spread across Ace's face. It was the grin Jupiter had worn—dripping in trouble and mischief. Tanner nudged Parker in the ribs, wearing a similar grin. Only Lux remained expressionless, though as they got closer, I could see a faint smile twitching on his lip.

"Hi, Scout," Tanner and Ace chorused.

"Hey." I waved back, no doubt looking as awkward as I felt, my eyes darting everywhere but at Parker.

"Now, what have we got here?" Lux asked, staring at the board. "Who did I last speak to? Um, my girlfriend."

"What about you, Parker?" crowed Ace, in a way that told me he already knew the answer.

"My mom." Parker rolled his eyes and scowled at Ace. "You can shut your mouth, not like you don't call your mom every morning too."

"Not denying that, bro." He rubbed his hand over Parker's hair, only for it to be smacked away. "There's nothing wrong with being a mama's boy. Right, Scout?"

I shook my head, trying to figure out what was going on, because beats me. "No, I think it's cute."

Whatever I'd said resulted in the identical smiles of Ace, Lux, and Tanner to grow. Parker, however, pulled at his neckline, which was distinctly pinker than it had been a minute ago. Was he *blushing*?

"Scout thinks you're cute." Ace laughed, nudging Parker hard with his shoulder. "Was there anything you wanted to say in return?"

"Yeah, I'm sorry I didn't drive in alone this morning." He rolled his eyes and shoved Ace so hard he almost fell over, though that was more from Ace laughing.

Another gust of wind blew past us, reminding me that I'd been heading inside to the warmth. As I turned to leave, I allowed myself a glance at Parker through the reflection in the glass doors.

What I didn't expect was to find his gaze meeting mine once more, which is where it stayed until I forced myself to look away. And suddenly I wasn't so cold anymore.

Quite the opposite.

5

Scout

Ten minutes later I was sitting in the cafeteria, holding a piping hot mug of coffee as I attempted to focus and remember what I was supposed to be doing. The reason I couldn't was standing in the entrance answering questions about who he called last.

It was very annoying.

Since the other day, Parker had been taking up way more headspace than usual. I couldn't get away from him. It didn't help that nearly all the content I edited featured him and his stupid handsome face, or insanely hot muscles.

Like the video I was supposed to be editing right now—

Parker paused on my screen while I tried to decide whether I should cut him from the reel.

Was it too much to feature him two days in a row? Probably.

If only I could stop looking at him.

His face was hidden behind the catcher's cage.

His narrowed eyes were so dark in the shadows the bright emerald green was on the verge of turning black, menacing, almost. The antiglare swipes underneath were only adding to the effect. His smile was gone, along with the warmth. His constant approachable, easygoing demeanor had vanished.

Right now, this Parker I was staring at, showed a whole different Parker, a *dangerous* Parker.

An undeniably sexy Parker, in that sexy-that-absolutely-*shouldn't*-be-sexy way.

Better relationship choices, Scout. Better relationship choices.

I was so engrossed with thoughts about what this side of Parker would be like I didn't notice the protein shake being placed on the table until it was too late.

I immediately slammed my laptop shut.

"Anything interesting on there?" Parker asked, in a way that made it very clear he'd seen his face filling my entire screen, as well as me gawping at it.

I shook my head, forcing away the heat flooding my cheeks. "Nope. Just work."

Work…*that's* why I was sitting here. Work.

"Okay." He chuckled, pulling out the chair opposite me. "Can I sit?"

"Um…yeah…sure," I replied, taking a swig of my rapidly cooling coffee if only for something to do.

I watched as he settled into his seat. The distraction had moved from my screen to IRL.

"What's up, Parker?"

"Sorry about the guys back there, they're idiots most of the time."

"Oh, no worries."

I thought he was about to add to his sentence, but instead, he took a deep breath and leaned back, only to sit forward again.

His elbows were placed purposefully on the table, followed by his fingers lacing together. I found myself pinned with those eyes I'd just been looking at. They weren't quite as dark and dangerous without the mask, but they weren't as bright green as usual.

If I could use one word to describe the expression he was currently wearing, it would be *determined.*

"Do you want to go for a drink with me sometime?"

I blinked, my brain slowly trying to catch up. "What?"

"A drink. Tonight? After the game. Or anytime. Soon. This week. Tomorrow."

"With me?"

"Yes." He nodded. "You."

I swallowed hard, a poor attempt to moisten my dry mouth, wishing I hadn't finished my coffee already.

Parker sat back again, and this time he stayed there, arms crossed and eyebrow raised as he watched me with amusement spread over his face.

"You okay there, Scout?"

I closed my mouth and nodded. I didn't dare speak.

What was happening? *How* was this happening? *Now*?

Goddamn.

"Well, while you're thinking about your answer, I want you to know that I like you. I've liked you for a long time. I should have told you last year, except I blew it and then you started dating." His jaw clenched briefly. "But rumor has it you're single again, and I'm not about to waste this season doing nothing about it. So, what do you say? Wanna go for a drink with me?"

Did I want to go for a drink with Parker King?

Man, why couldn't he have asked me like eight months ago? Before Shit Head.

Or even a few days ago, before I'd decided I was going to make better relationship choices, and dating athletes was a bad idea.

And concentrate on work.

Crap, yes, *work.* Work including the new role I'd been asked to apply for.

"Um, wow...um."

Jeez, wanna say *um* one more time, Scout?

Parker picked up his shake and waited. It was unnerving.

"I..." My shoulders dropped with a resigned sigh. "Parker, I'm flattered, I really am. I—"

Narrowed green eyes pinned mine. "Tell me you're not getting back together with Rangers' Douche. Please, *please* tell me you're not."

"Who?"

"The guy you were dating. Rangers Douche." He frowned. "Didn't he work for the Rangers?"

"How did you—" I started, then remembered I was friends with the second biggest gossip at the Lions, who in turn was friends with the biggest. Did everyone here know that I'd been cheated on? God, how humiliating. "Never mind, I guess Pablo told you."

His head tilted as he peered at me, and he nodded slowly. "Sure. Let's go with Pablo. Well?"

"Well, what?"

"Are you dating Rangers Douche again?"

"No. I'm not."

Parker's shoulders dropped, the tension in his jaw immediately relaxed and a smile lifted his mouth. "Good, I'm happy to hear it. But if you got hurt in the process, I'm also sorry."

"Thank you."

"Now"—he brought the shake to his lips, and paused—"can I take you for a drink?"

My brain said screw everything. I was on the verge of saying yes. I *wanted* to say yes. It was right there on the tip of my tongue. *Y E S*.

Three letters, one tiny word. But instead I said,

"It's just not a good time."

"Okay—"

"My boss asked me to apply for a new job, and I really should concentrate on that," I blurted, making his eyes bug.

"You're not leaving?"

"No." I reached out to touch his arm but pulled it back before I did. What did I do that for? Weird. That was weird.

I had no business touching him. Even though I kind of wanted to. Kind of wanted to give his biceps a little squeeze, maybe see if those abs of his—still on show through his shirt—were hard or soft. Probably both.

He puffed out a deep breath. "Thank god, although if you were leaving, it would have solved a minor hurdle I have."

"What d'you mean?"

"Some dumb form we have to sign." He shrugged.

"Oh yeah, the one Coach mentioned."

"Right." He huffed a laugh. "Yeah. I forgot for a second you were there. Probably should apologize for that too." This time when he stared at me, a flush crept over my cheeks. "So, what's your new job? You won't be doing social anymore?"

"I will, but they want to expand the Lions brand and give me more responsibility."

"Wow," he said, his eyes momentarily following one of the PTs who walked in and over to the coffee machines, before coming back to me. "That sounds cool. Congratulations."

"Thanks."

"I love your work on the socials. I love the Tiktok. *TikTok.* Fuck. The TikToks you make. They're funny."

"Thank you." I smiled. "I literally just found out about it, so I don't have the details. It might not be what I want, but I should probably concentrate on that for the moment. Plus..." I glanced down to where my fingers were running along the edges of the laptop. Why was I suddenly so nervous? "I'm kinda staying single for the moment."

My eyes flicked up to see his mouth roll together and all I could focus on were his lips. Big, full lips. Soft looking lips. I wondered what they'd be like to kiss.

Argh. Scout. Con-cen-trate.

Relationship choices. *Work.*

"Sensible."

"Yup," I replied much too loudly and definitely like I was trying to convince myself. I was. I needed convincing. "But maybe we could be friends?"

Parker leaned forward again. The tip of his tongue peeked

out and slowly licked along his top lip, and his eyes never left mine.

Either the air thinned or the AC shut off, and out of nowhere my heart thudded erratically the same way it did when I was looking at his picture, only this time I could feel it through my entire body.

This was the dangerous Parker. The sexy-but-shouldn't-be-sexy Parker.

Man, was he ever sexy.

"Of course," he spoke finally, before standing up and downing the remainder of his shake. "I'd be lucky to be your friend. And Scout?"

"Y-yes?" I managed to splutter as he loomed above me. Big, strong, muscular.

"When you're ready to be more than friends, say the word. I'll sign that damn form any day of the week."

He walked off without looking back. If he had, he'd have seen confusion all over my face and my hands rammed between my crossed legs to quench the shivers that had shot down my spine.

Dammit.

Developing a crush on Parker King did not fall under the heading of better relationship choices.

I just needed to figure out how to stop it, and soon.

6

Parker

"Hey, has anyone taken my lucky socks?—and my deodorant?—Anyone?—Guys?"

I opened the fridge and grabbed a protein shake, wondering if Tanner would wear himself out with all the yelling before someone told him his lucky socks were in the laundry room where our housekeeper had left them.

Where she *always* left them, in the little cubby with his name on it.

Snatching up an apple while I chugged the shake, I watched Tanner sprint across the living room and disappear down the hallway only to return thirty seconds later, skidding to a halt in front of me, socks held high in his fist.

"I found my lucky socks."

"Were they in the place they always are?"

"Yes. Coincidently, they were," he replied, hopping about as he pulled them on one at a time. "Now I just need to find my deodorant."

"Dude, just get some from the club."

"Nah, I like mine. I like the way I smell with it." He lifted his arm, sniffing deeply against his armpit. "What's more, I think Millie likes it too."

I crunched on my apple. I hadn't realized Millie had ever gotten close enough to smell him or his deodorant. I was about to ask if that was the case when Ace appeared from his bedroom, and Tanner's attention was immediately taken.

"What about you? Have you seen my deodorant?" Tanner pounced, before Ace had barely taken a step.

"Yes. It's in my bathroom where you left it this morning."

"Next to your shower shoes?" I smirked.

"Shut up. I don't have fucking shower shoes," he snapped as Tanner once again sprinted across the living room. "That guy is going to forget his head one day."

"Yup."

"Are you ready to go?" Ace dropped his bag on the floor

next to mine. "Six days, baby."

"Excited?"

"Bet your ass I am." He picked up the remains of my protein shake and finished it. "Aren't you?"

"Yeah, totally. We're going to win this year, I can feel it."

Ace put down the bottle and held my gaze. "Me too. Me too."

I had the impression he was about to add something more, when Lux appeared with his phone wedged into the crook of his neck. His bag was dumped next to Ace's before he opened the fridge.

"…Yeah, Goldilocks. Call me later…yeah, love you, babe… work hard…you bet…speak to you later."

"Is Radley coming to the game tonight?" I asked as he placed his phone down on the counter, connecting it to charge while simultaneously removing one of the three apples Ace had picked up.

"Dude, stop ruining the fruit. If you want to get better at juggling, use a ball." He rolled his eyes when Ace huffed, and turned back to me. "No, she has a test tomorrow. She's studying."

"Radley's studying?" asked Tanner, returning with a can of deodorant in his hand, which he proceeded to spray over himself like it was air freshener.

Given he was the nearest to Tanner, Ace took the brunt of

the spray and simultaneously began choking while wafting his hand through the air.

"Dude, what the fuck?" choked Ace, frantically wiping his tongue with the hem of his shirt. "Couldn't you have done that in the bathroom where you found it?"

"Sorry," replied Tanner, though his focus was on Lux. "Dude, what's Radley's test?'

"Um, women poets."

"Women poets and what?" pressed Tanner.

Lux shrugged. "Nothing. That's it. They have five questions and three hours to answer."

"Snooze." Ace held his hand to me for a high five, which I hit hard in agreement. "Sounds boring as fuck."

"Does Millie have the same one?"

I glanced back to Ace at the sound of a loud thud, to find him face down on the countertop and banging his forehead as it became clear why Tanner was asking so many questions about Radley's class. Not because he had any interest in women poets, or whatever, but because the only thing he legitimately cared about outside of baseball was Millie Robinson, Radley's BFF.

Lux nodded with an eye roll. "Probably, they're in the same classes."

Tanner snatched up his phone from the counter.

"What are you doing?"

"Texting Millie good luck."

"She's gonna block you one day," Ace muttered with a shake of his head as he poured a massive bowl of Froot Loops.

"Nope." Tanner shook his head. "I make sure I keep it on the right side."

"What does that mean?" I scoffed, flicking on the coffee machine.

Tanner slid onto the stool next to Ace, his thumbs never slowing on the taps across the screen. When he was done, he placed the phone down with a broad smile. "I text her good morning, and good night. Plus, an occasional GIF during the day."

The three of us stared at him. Lux's eyebrows disappeared under his ball cap.

It was a combination of being not at all surprised at this behavior, while also being *very* surprised he hadn't given up on Millie yet. Tanner wasn't known for his staying power, but we were going on seven months despite Millie not showing the slightest bit of interest.

More than that, she'd not given him one sliver of hope that he was getting somewhere, like some girls did.

Some girls liked the attention even when they professed otherwise. Not *Millie.*

I got the impression Millie could quite happily live her

life and not think about Tanner Simpson once. Maybe that was why Tanner was so determined to get her to notice him. It was still a mystery how he'd managed to get her number in the first place.

I glanced over to Lux. "Did you know about this?"

He shook his head. "Nope. Radley's not mentioned it."

"Tan, how often does she reply?"

"Dunno." He shrugged, and his mouth curled down. "Not a lot. But she hearted a GIF I sent of a puppy sneezing the other day. She'd never done that before, so between the heart and the wave she gave me on Opening Day, I think I'm getting somewhere."

Ace grabbed Tanner's cheeks and squeezed. "Good for you, bud. There's no way she can hold out against this face for much longer."

"Right?! Thank you."

"Always here for you, man." He patted him hard on the back and turned to me. "But right now I want to know more about Parker."

I picked up my coffee and sipped. "What about me?"

"It's the first away series. Scout will be there. She'll be traveling with us. What's the plan?"

"Whaddya mean?"

"Well…" Ace glanced from me to Lux and then to Tanner,

before back to me. "You asked her out and she said no. And now you're gonna be 'friends.'"

I ignored the way he air-quoted *friends*. "So?"

"You seem pretty chipper for a guy who got rejected."

"I didn't get rejected."

"I think that's what 'no' means."

"By that logic, Millie rejected Tanner, he's still chipper," I shot back, turning to Tanner. "Sorry, bud."

But Tanner shrugged it off. "I am chipper. Because I know Millie will come to her senses soon."

Ace rolled his eyes and focused back on me. "But seriously, why?"

"Because..." I replied, pushing my fingers through my hair, and scratched hard on my scalp. "She likes me."

"And this is based on her looking at a picture of you on her laptop."

"Not looking. *Staring*."

"Which you don't do with a guy you want to be friends with?"

"*Just* friends," I corrected. "Exactly."

I closed my eyes, bringing back the memory I had of her sitting at the table in the cafeteria.

I hadn't even realized she'd be in there, but I'd spotted her the second I'd walked in. It hadn't been hard. The place was virtually empty during mid-morning, and she'd been sitting at a table right in the middle, her back to the door while she worked away.

Except from the angle she was at, I could see her screen clear as day. I could see exactly what she was working on.

Me. My face. Wide on the screen. Whatever she was working on had something to do with me. Not unusual, yet as I stood there and watched I realized she wasn't doing anything *but* staring at my face.

I waited for a good two minutes to see if she'd move on to another picture.

She didn't.

Even if she had been "doing her job" no one stares at a photo of someone for over two minutes if they don't also have other things on their mind. In a rare turn of events, Tanner was correct, Scout liked me. What sealed the deal was how badly she flustered when she spotted me, and her entire face turned a very sexy shade of pink.

A shade I wanted to see again, and more of.

Without sounding conceited, I know when a girl likes me, and Scout Davison fell right into that category.

"What's the plan then?'

"The plan is…we're going to be friends. Best friends. I'm going to be the best friend she ever had."

"Can I be there when you tell Reeves to suck it and stick

his friend zone up his ass?"

I laughed. "If it'll make you happy."

"You should give Scout your sweatshirt."

Once again, the three of us turned and stared at Tanner, waiting to see if he was going to add any more explanation. "Girls like any shit that smells of guys. Give her your sweatshirt."

"What? Like walk up and hand it to her?" I scoffed.

"No, just when she's cold, give her yours. Then she'll always have it and always be thinking of you. Smell is a strong association tool, I saw it on the Nature Channel."

"Since when do you watch the Nature Channel?"

"Sometimes I can't sleep." He shrugged his response. "I'm going to do it with Millie. It's part of Operation Strike Zone."

My mouth held in a line, Ace stared, confused. In the end Lux was the one who spoke, with a barely contained smirk.

"Tan? What is Operation Strike Zone?"

"It's my plan for Parker and me to get our girls."

"The name is TBC," I shot out.

"I like it, it has a certain ring to it," Ace said, picking up his bowl of Froot Loops and draining the milk. "And I can't wait to hear how exactly this is going to work."

Not that I had one, but I didn't get to answer before Tanner slung his arm around me,

"I can help you with this, I've thought about it a lot. You have to be everywhere Scout is. Not in a creepy way, obvs, but just be there. If she needs something, you're there. If she's carrying heavy bags and needs help, you're there. She wants a volunteer for social, put your hand up, buddy. Until one day you're not there, and she notices."

Ace snorted. "Yeah, and she'll be all, '*Huh, where's Parker, I miss him and his big strong arms and cute little butt.*'"

"She doesn't sound like that." I threw him a scowl and turned to Tanner. "Is that what you're doing with Millie?"

He shook his head. "Nah, I'm still working on her texting me back. But as soon as she does, then I'll be helping her."

"At least you have her number. I don't have Scout's, so maybe we're even," I replied and looked to Lux, who was generally considered the most sensible one of the four of us. "What do you think?"

"It could work." He nodded, though it was a little too uncommitted for my taste.

"Scout likes me, I know it. I just need to be patient until she's ready to date again, and make sure no other guy gets in first this time."

Ace grabbed his phone and hit Speed Dial. "Hold up, let's get a girl's opinion."

"Babe, I'm about to head into a meeting," answered Payton, before the first ring sounded out.

"We'll be quick, Parker needs your help," Ace said, pushing the phone toward me with an overly enthusiastic nod. "Pleeeease."

"Man, I knew I shouldn't have answered," she muttered, before barking out, "Parker…you're on a clock. Shoot fast."

"Oh. Hey, Payton…um…basically…" I began, trying to figure out exactly where to start. "It's about Scout…"

It didn't take long for me to explain the entire situation, mostly because she already knew I'd crushed on Scout for ages, which meant I could gloss over the finer details. But also because I talked so quickly it wouldn't take up any of her time, plus it didn't sound quite as lame when I strung every word together without taking a breath.

"Well, babe? What do you think?" Ace prompted after a couple of seconds of silence.

"Let me get this straight, you're asking me if it's a good idea to try and be a friend to a girl you have the hots for, in the hope that one day she'll want to date you because you think she likes you."

I didn't correct her and say I *knew* Scout liked me, because the four of us were all mentally checking she'd summed it up accurately. From her tone it sounded like she thought we were all idiots.

"Um, yeah…I guess. You think it's okay?"

"I think it's good you're all pretty." She sucked in a deep

breath, or maybe it was an exasperated sigh. "You know, guys, this is a learning opportunity for you. It's how regular people get together and build relationships. Not everyone can walk up to someone in a bar, snap their fingers, and expect to get what they want."

"Wasn't that what I did to get you?" Ace snorted.

"Do you really want to go there right now, Lucky Aces?" Payton shot back.

"No, ma'am."

I held my hand in front of Ace before he could say any more, because I still wasn't clear on what she was telling me. "Payton, are you saying it's a good idea?"

"Yes, it's a good idea, Parker. Be Scout's friend. I know you really like her, but don't expect it to happen overnight. Remember, it might not happen at all."

"It'll happen," muttered Tanner.

I breathed a sigh of relief. "Cool, yeah, thanks. Will do."

"Anytime. Okay, Gotta go. Bye."

"LOVE YOU," Ace yelled into the phone, but she'd already cut the call. He clapped his hands together. "Great, we're all set. The plan for Operation Strike Zone is in place. Parker is going to friend his way into a relationship with Scout, and Tanner will work on Millie."

"Sounds good to me," echoed Lux and Tanner in unison, before Lux added, "And now we need to leave or we're going to be late. We're not getting fined for tardiness this early in the season."

"Parker, you coming?"

I pushed away any thoughts I had about whether my plan to date Scout had just been hijacked by my roommates, because that would only mean one thing.

It would go drastically wrong.

7

Parker

"Ouch," I grumbled, rubbing my ribs where Tanner had just rammed his elbow. "What was that for?"

Tanner flung open the back door before Lux had a chance to cut the engine, and jumped out while almost pulling me with him. Dragging more like. By the time I'd managed to stand up, Ace had got out, too, both of us wondering why Tanner was hopping about excitedly.

"What are you doing?"

Tanner nodded over to the Lions Stadium entrance. "Isn't that Scout?"

Ace and I followed where his finger pointed, but all we

could see was a person carrying way more than any person should reasonably carry in one go.

Several bags were slung over each shoulder, while their arms were full from the boxes they were holding, piled on top of which were books. Even when I squinted it wasn't entirely clear who was under the bags and the boxes.

It could be anyone.

Until a flash of blonde caught in the sunlight, and a burst of nerves shot through me.

"Yes, it is." Ace spun around, took one look at me, and removed his ball cap, shoving it onto my head. "Wait."

"What are you doing?" I asked, pushing it up so I could see.

"You had bed hair. You don't want her thinking you're hooking up with other chicks, even if you are just friends," he replied, taking a step back to assess me. "Okay, you're good to go."

"Go where?"

"Go and help Scout with all that shit she's carrying."

"You think?"

"Yes," they replied in unison.

"Okay." I turned to Lux as he closed the trunk, sensibly staying out of this ridiculous situation, even if I did need him for one final seal of approval. "Yeah?"

"Yes, go, before someone else helps."

"Oh fuck that."

I shoved my bag at Ace and Parker and sprinted across the parking lot. Scout was carrying so much and moving so slowly that it didn't take any time to catch up with her.

"Hey, let me help you with that," I said, grabbing the boxes and the books, yanking them way too enthusiastically from her grip. In hindsight, I should have given her a little warning, seeing as she nearly toppled from the change in balance. "Whoops, sorry."

"What the..." Her blue eyes flared as they landed on me, and it took her a second to figure out what had just happened. "Parker...what are you doing?"

"Helping?" I grinned.

"Oh, okay, thanks."

"Sure thing," I replied, holding the book with my chin before it fell off. "Why are you carrying so much?"

Though maybe the question should have been *how* are you carrying so much? She could barely see over the boxes.

She shifted one of the bags back onto her shoulder. "I had to pick up some things on the way in this morning, and when my Uber dropped me, I realized I had way more stuff than I thought. It's video equipment, so I can't leave it outside."

"Seems I arrived just in time," I replied, also relieving her of one of the bags. Jeez, this was heavy. Scout was way stronger than she looked. "Where are we taking this stuff?"

"Oh, I can manage, you don't need to help me. I only have

to make it to the lobby, then I can get a couple of the guys to come down and help carry it."

"Hey, we're friends, remember. That's what friends are for, right?" I winked.

She glanced around me, based on her expression, I'd hasten to guess she had no idea what was happening right now. That made two of us. But I was too committed to back out now, so therefore I'd be taking these boxes wherever she wanted.

In the reflection of the glass doors, I caught Tanner, Ace, and Lux with identical grins plastered on their faces, as well as Tanner giving me a double thumbs-up.

"Um...sure, I guess. Thanks. I need to go to the fifth floor."

"Cool, not sure I've ever been up there. Lead the way."

I followed her through the giant revolving doors, and across the vast Lions logo on the floor to the security gates by the reception desk. Which is when I realized my first mistake. Or maybe it was my second, possibly *third* if you included allowing the guys to convince me running after Scout was a good idea.

Scout and I might only be friends, but I'd forgotten about Pablo on the security desk.

Pablo Garcia was a Lions lifer. He'd been with the club since he was a boy, and there was no one more loyal, which he felt gave him the right to act as an unofficial coach for each and every position on the field. And he had *strong* opinions.

Most of us had learned the hard way that it was much

better to listen to Pablo than ignore him.

Pablo also knew everything that went on in this stadium. And I mean *everything,* including how I felt about Scout.

"Well, look at you two. You sure look busy." His tone was light, but that meant nothing, especially as his beady eyes were trained pointedly on me. He was the biggest shit-stirrer in this building, including Ace. "Good boy, Parker, what a coincidence you were available to help."

My eyes narrowed while I attempted to somehow send him a telepathic message to please keep his mouth shut. Just this one time.

"Hey, Pabs." Scout smiled sweetly. Because that's probably all she knew him as, this sweet old grandpa figure. "How's it going."

"Good. Always good for me, especially on game days," he replied. "How about you two? Parker, you doing okay there?"

"I'm great," I replied, letting Scout go ahead of me through the barriers. I followed her as quickly as possible and tried to ignore Pablo's stare.

Unfortunately I wasn't paying attention to where I was going, and collided with one of the grounds staff watering the huge trees in the atrium. Pablo shook his head and turned away.

"Sorry, man."

"Parker?"

"Yeah, coming," I called and raced after Scout.

I caught up with her right before she reached the elevators and hit the button.

For the first time today, I had time to properly look at her, soak in those big blue eyes of hers sparkling like sapphires. Faint laughter lines fanned around the corners, and I realized I hadn't ever properly heard her laugh. I'd heard her giggle, I'd seen her smile, but I'd never been present for one of those big, deep laughs drawn from the depths of your belly. The type that made those creases, anyway.

What did Scout find funny? What made her laugh? Whatever it was, I bet she looked stunning. I bet her cheeks turned rosy pink when she did. She was so goddamn pretty.

I wanted to make her laugh, and then it occurred to me that even if I never got any further than this moment, being her friend and getting to know her—like normal people did, or however Payton put it—would still be totally worth it.

"Is there something on my face?" she asked after a second, scrubbing her spare hand over it before running her fingers through her hair.

"No, you're all good." I shook my head with a laugh and changed the subject before she could ask what I was staring at. "So, are you coming on the road with us?"

"I am." She nodded, a grin widening on her face. "Not gonna miss the first game of the season at Wrigley Field."

I matched her grin with one of my own. "It'll be a fun one."

"You want to tell me what you've got planned for the rookies?"

Slowly, I shook my head and did my best to ignore the way her eyelashes were batting as her eyes turned pleading. "No can do, I'm afraid."

Every year, the first away game in Chicago was a big one, and not because we had a game to play.

It was the setting for the rookies' rite of passage, a tradition that had them on an excursion to the nearest coffee shop in Wrigley Field with an order for everyone on the entire Lions roster, coaches, and additional staff. I don't know how or why it started, but it was something all the teams did—it was fun, team bonding, and always raised a smile, especially as we added an extra element—our rookies had to wear dress-up.

And what they wore was always kept a closely guarded secret until the last minute.

When I'd been a rookie the theme had been *Wizard of Oz*, I had the honor of dressing as Dorothy.

Today, the nine rookies coming on the road with us would be in yellow Minion costumes, all wearing their own shirts and numbers while they walked—or waddled, given the size of the costumes—through Wrigleyville.

"Are you sure?"

"I am. You'll find out soon enough."

"No fair." She chuckled as the bell rang and the elevator doors opened.

Stepping aside to let her in first, I noticed Scout glance down at her phone and frown deeply. Three small lines stretched across her brow and her eyes narrowed in annoyance.

"Everything okay?"

"Yeah. Just…oh, it doesn't matter." She nodded, and before she could stop it, her mouth opened in a wide yawn.

As her arm shot up to cover her mouth, her phone flew out of her hand. I bent to pick it up and pass back to her, trying my hardest not to look at the stacked-up messages on her phone screen from someone called Shit Head.

Rangers Douche.

"Do I need to fetch you a coffee once I'm done with these boxes?" I asked, doing my best to push through the irrational jealousy that had my teeth grinding.

Scout shook her head and laughed, her blonde hair coming untucked from behind her ear, and I found myself fighting not to place it back.

"Sorry…" She yawned again. "I usually pick one up from around the corner on my way in. But…" She glanced down at the boxes with a sheepish smile.

"What's your order?"

Her teeth caught the edge of her lip. "Oh…um, you know…"

I was waiting for her to add to that sentence, but she was now staring down at her feet, and we rode a whole floor without her looking back up.

"Scout?"

Her eyes shot to mine. "Oh…yeah, it's just…um…just

coffee."

If the tops of her cheeks weren't flushed, and she wasn't trying her best not to look at me, I'd have left it, but something was going on.

"Coffee and what else?" I pointed right at her. "I call bullshit."

Her eyes flicked to the monitor see how many floors we had left to travel, only to wince when there were still three left, and I couldn't hold in the laugh.

"Scout?"

Eventually she sighed in defeat. "In my defense, it's something I discovered during school and it got me through exams, breakups, finals. You name it. Now I like to start my day with one. It's a little ritual."

"What's the drink, Scout?"

"Don't judge..." She stared at me, and if my hands weren't full, I'd have held them up.

"Hey, I won't."

"Okay...it's a double espresso split in two—one to start and one to finish, caramel drizzled around the insides of the cup, half one percent, half almond milk, two shots of hazelnut, a packet of Splenda and a spoon size whip on top, with chocolate powder to finish."

My brain was still trying to keep up with what she'd said, and my mouth must have dropped open because I heard her grumble, "Hey, you promised you wouldn't judge."

I shut my mouth, then opened it again. "I'm not, I'm just…I mean…oh man, I dunno if I can do this."

"Do what?"

Pushing my cap up, I eased my fingers along my brow and let out a massive sigh. "This friends thing."

"What—"

"Yeah, I might need to rethink it." I shook my head with a grimace. "I can't be seen with someone who drinks that. I have a reputation."

Scout's mouth dropped open, and she shoved me hard on the shoulder. At least, I guessed she thought it was hard. I didn't move.

"Parker!"

"I'm kidding." I laughed, even harder when her outrage deepened. "What I meant to say was…how interesting and how ever did you discover it?"

She shrugged. "Well, maybe not so much as discover, more like invent."

"Wow." I blinked. "I'm impressed. Very inventive. And did I mention brave? How do you not get laughed out of coffee shops with that? It genuinely sounds like the most disgusting drink I've ever heard."

Her mouth dropped again, this time her cheeks turned fully pink. I kind of liked teasing her like this, especially when it meant her teeth sank into her plump, rosy bottom lip, like they were doing right now.

My gaze was still focused on her mouth when the elevator pinged and the doors opened.

"Welcome to where the magic happens," Scout announced, stepping out.

I followed her and stopped.

I'd never been up here. I'd been to the floor where legal sat, which was mostly made of glass meeting rooms, but this was all open. Everyone together. Noisy chatter, clacking on keyboards, shouting.

There had to be over a hundred people, and I could swear I'd not seen any of them before in my life.

"Is this just the social media team?"

"No, this is the whole communications and marketing departments." She nodded over to the corner, where a life-sized cardboard cutout of Jupiter Reeves stood, holding onto a Gatorade. Someone had drawn a curly mustache and glasses on it. "My desk is this way, where the social team sits."

Not one person looked up at us as I followed her in silence, walking past several banks of desks and over toward a wall of glass overlooking the entire stadium and field.

"Hey, cool view!" I marched over to the window. "You can see everything from up here. The batting cages, the bullpen…"

"Yeah, we can watch the game and work," she replied as she stopped at the desks next to where I was standing and dropped her things onto it. "This is me. Thanks for the help."

"You're welcome," I replied, my eyes still fixed on the view, where I'd be heading shortly. Usually at practice we were too busy focusing to think about anyone watching from the front office. There were always people wandering around—grounds staff, PTs, not to mention the occasional VIP who got backstage access with one of the execs. We learned to block it out.

It never occurred to me that Scout could be one of those people.

I kind of liked the idea that she was. Liked it a lot.

I placed down everything I'd carried for her as two chairs on the other side of her desk immediately swizzled around to reveal the guys who'd been on the entrance door yesterday.

Their mouths dropped open.

I nodded over to them. "Hey, guys."

"Hey, Parker," they echoed each other, staring at me in a way I always found unnerving, no matter how much I experienced it. "Good luck today."

"Thanks." I smiled and turned back to Scout. "I should go."

"Yeah, of course, thanks again." She shuffled a little, glancing down at her feet, at the pale blue Chucks she was wearing, then at her backpack and her laptop. "Good luck today."

She was looking at anything but me. I should have found it weird, except from the way she was worrying at her lip, it was clear her nonchalance was all an act in front of her audience of two interns, plus anyone else watching.

"Anytime." I took a step back with a quiet chuckle, wondering how far I would get before she gave in. "See you on the plane, Davison."

Scout's head shot up, her blue eyes flaring wide, eyelashes batting against her high cheekbones before she turned away with a flick of blonde hair. It wasn't quick enough for me to miss the smile growing on her face, however.

Yeah, this girl definitely liked me.

Operation Strike Zone was underway, or would be as soon as I came up with a better name.

8

Scout

Alice: Have you seen him yet?

Scout: Seen who?

Alice: Your new boyfriend?

Scout: What are you talking about?

Alice: *eye roll emoji* Parker King, who else would I be talking about?

Scout: I don't know what you're talking about half the time

Scout: But no

Scout: And he's not my anything

Alice: He wants to be

Scout: We're just friends

Alice: He asked you on a date

Scout: And I said no. Hence, we're friends. And you swore you wouldn't repeat it

Alice: I'm keeping my promise, but that doesn't stop me from saying you're only friends until the day he's in your panties *smirk emoji*

Alice: How soon will that be?

Scout: Why do I hang out with you again?

Alice: Because your life would be dull AF without me

Alice: How's Chicago anyway?

Scout: Dull without you

Alice: See, told ya. Bring me back some deep dish, will you?

Scout: I'll see what I can do. Gotta go

Alice: Same, probs should do some work and get selling

I shut my phone off, slipped it in my pocket, and glanced up.

Joey and Cyrus, along with a few of the other guys, were standing around in the loading bay of Wrigley Field, waiting for our rookies to arrive. A couple of them were tossing a baseball to each other; Jess, one of the comms girls, was on her phone, and the rest were leaning, bored, against the wall.

While it was—unfairly, I might add—assumed the social team did nothing more than stand around and capture whatever they happened upon, we did *actually* work our butts off. We ran to a tight schedule, especially on away stretches when we were under more of a time crunch.

Not to mention when things went wrong, we couldn't wing it as easily as we might be able to back at Lions Stadium.

Because something always went wrong, which likely accounted for the reason why we still hadn't started yet.

We were definitely too busy to have—one, two, three… seven of us—waiting like this. Usually there were three guys here max, all working on rotation because we always needed someone back at base in New York. But the first away game against the Cubs was always a popular one to travel to.

I checked my watch again, then the schedule on the clipboard. We were going on thirty minutes delayed. Any longer and it would get pulled because the rookies would be needed at practice, or whatever they did before a game.

"Does anyone know what the holdup is?"

The response I got was either a shrug or a head shake.

"I walked past the locker room an hour ago and could hear a lot of swearing, mostly," added Cyrus, without looking up from the mini handheld video camera we were using.

"Did any of you see the dress-up?"

Joey shook his head. "No, but they're big. I saw the carriers for them."

"Okay. We'll keep waiting, I guess," I replied as my phone buzzed again.

Shit Head: Scout, please answer.

Shit Head: I miss yo u. I want to explain.

Shit Head: Are you really going to keep punishing me for one stupid mistake.

Shit Head: It wouldn't have happened if you'd come with me like I'd asked.

With a scoff and a heavy eye roll, the phone was shoved back in my pocket. Unzipping my backpack, I rummaged around for the packet of Twizzlers I knew was in there somewhere and grabbed a couple of strands.

Urgh, boys were so annoying.

I didn't even know why he was still messaging me.

We'd broken up over three months ago, just after New Year. I'd seen him once to return his things and get mine back, and since then he'd barely stopped texting me. Possibly more than when we were officially dating last year.

Douche.

I bit down on the strawberry licorice, before stuffing the entire strand in my mouth and starting on the next.

As I stood there, trying my best to chew without my teeth being stuck together, the annoyance, the pain, all the infuriation I'd worked hard to rid myself of came surging back up. It sat on my chest and squeezed hard.

"Ugh," I grunted, pulling my phone back out.

Scout: Stop texting me. You explained yourself just fine the first time. I didn't come away for New Year and you found a girl who would. Congratulations. We're

> done, Mark. Get it through your dense skull.

With a deep breath, I hit the Block button on his contact—something I should have done a long time ago. This time my phone was chucked into my backpack, zipped away, and slung over my shoulder, but not before I grabbed another couple of Twizzlers.

I'd met Mark—or *Shit Head*—on a night out last summer.

The Lions had beaten the Yankees during the Saturday afternoon and a bunch of us had headed for drinks after, riding that winning high. We'd been at the outdoor pop-up market in DUMBO, and he'd been standing next to me at the bar when it was my turn to pay. He'd leaned over me to grab a napkin before picking up the beer bottles in front of him.

He was cute, with deep dimples that were present whether he was smiling or not. In hindsight, those dimples were the whole problem. They gave the illusion he was a decent guy, because no one with dimples like that could ever be a dick, right?

Fucking dimples.

For the next two hours we'd caught each other's eye from across the seating area, lit by twinkle lights. As the sun lowered onto the horizon, we snatched glances, traded soft smiles, locked gazes. When the guys and I called it a night to head home, we stood up. Mark decided this was his last chance, and before I knew what was happening, he'd rushed over to get my number.

In front of *all my friends.*

He messaged the next day.

Our first date I discovered that he worked for the New York Rangers. But the Mets was his favorite New York team, followed by the Giants. He was *not* a Lions fan, he told me.

So what? No big deal, it's just where I work, I had thought. New York has three baseball teams, it stands to reason not everyone is going to be a fan. And sure, it was kind of funny that he didn't ever seem to have any interest in my job, or whether I'd had a good day as it revolved around a team he'd hated since he was a kid.

Because it was my first year with the club, I was still learning about all the players and their history, so I didn't always notice the small gripes he made about them.

Or how his mood always seemed to be so much better when the Lions lost, even more so than when the Mets won.

One time, I got him tickets to the Lions and Mets. The Lions won and I didn't hear from him for nearly forty-eight hours.

He ignored me for *two whole days.*

Once the baseball season finished, we had time to hang out more because I wasn't traveling with the club. We went for dinners, we spent Sundays walking through the city or spending time with our friends. He took me to see Rangers vs. Bruins and afterward we headed up to Vermont for a couple of days. It was cute.

Except, looking back on our time together, I realized it wasn't all that cute because every five minutes he had to reply to one of a thousand group messages from his friends. Annoying is a better word.

Then New Year came around.

The week before Christmas, he'd been invited to one of his friend's ski cabins for the weekend, and I was invited too. Sounds awesome, right? Getting out of the city, breathing in that mountain air.

Any other time I would have jumped at the chance, but Alice had invited us to her New Year's dress-up bar crawl that she'd meticulously planned, and it's all we'd been talking about for two months.

We'd given our word, that's how we'd be spending New Year's. We could go skiing another time.

On Christmas Eve, Mark announced he'd changed his mind. He was going skiing. What's more, he didn't seem that bothered about me joining him either. That alone would have been the final nail in our coffin if a couple of weeks later one of his friends hadn't uploaded pictures onto Facebook of their weekend without properly vetting them.

Mark might have returned to New York after the holidays pleading apologetically with claims of missing me, but that wasn't entirely true.

Instead, he'd found someone to help him get through the difficulty of being without me. I found out later that she was his ex-girlfriend—the one he used to complain about all the time.

As is always the case in situations such as these, she did me a favor. My eyes had finally opened wide to what a dick he was, and no doubt still is. We broke up. I cried for a couple of days, ate some ice cream, and cut my hair.

And felt a whole lot better for it.

I've mostly got over my annoyance, until I'm reminded of it when my phone buzzes. I'm pissed I could have enjoyed the offseason doing what I wanted to do, instead of spending it with a douche. But now I had the time to make up for it, plus a new job opportunity to work on.

I'm free to figure out what I want from my life and can make the most of being single.

"Hey, Scout—"

My head shot up to the sound of Joey's voice and I swallowed the giant lump of red licorice I'd been attempting to chew my way through.

"Two minutes."

"Thanks," I mumbled, trying my best to remove the candy wedged in my back teeth.

My fingers were still working against my molars, when a loud laugh echoed out as the doors to the changing rooms clattered back against the walls.

"Awesome. So awesome. Cy, make sure you're getting this," cried Joey.

"We're going viral with this, for real."

"Dude, watch where you're going!" yelled someone, jumping out of the way as a giant, bright yellow Minion almost knocked them flying, followed by another one.

"What the—" Was all I could manage, simultaneously amused and horrified as I watched nine Minions—all easily eight feet high—make their way into the corridors where we were waiting for them.

They were so wide that only two could fit down at a time, and given whoever was inside each Minions costume couldn't really see where they were going, they all ended up colliding into each other—between bursts of loud laughter and a lot of swearing—before bouncing back to the walls, like we were playing bumper cars. A couple of them had already ripped the shirts they were wearing—custom, Minion-sized Lions shirts, all bearing their name and number.

"You're on my foot—"

"It's like a furnace in here—"

"I can't see—"

Now I knew why we were running late.

After one of the Minions was knocked so hard he fell over, and it took five minutes to get him back upright, it quickly became clear this was going to take way longer than I was expecting it to. There was also the issue of their legs—easily half the length of mine, and I didn't have long legs.

We were supposed to be going to the coffee shop across

the other side of Wrigleyville, but there was no way we'd have time.

At this rate we'd miss the start of the game.

I leaned into one of the guys. "Hey, is there anywhere nearer we can visit?"

Joey pulled up the local map to search. "Yeah, there's one in the other direction, it's a five-minute walk instead of fifteen."

"Let's go there. No one's going to miss us."

"Got that right. Or we could get an Uber."

"How are they going to fit? We'd need one each."

"Yeah," he replied, looking back at the guys. "Maybe not then."

I stepped back, the small space we'd been waiting in was now overcrowded with Minions, a couple of the coaching staff, and definitely more of the comms and social guys than were here earlier. I was half expecting to see the guys from the starting roster join us, but I guess they were all in practice.

Spotting a small box over on the side, I grabbed it and stepped up. Didn't help—I was still towered over by giant yellow cartoon characters, who couldn't see me anyway, given the size of their heads.

"Okay, are we all together?" I yelled, and several of them jerked to where they thought the voice was coming from, only 50 percent got it right. I waited as a low chorus of *yesses* mumbled through them. "Who has the coffee order?"

A yellow hand—belonging to Luke Coggings, according

to the name on his shirt—shot as far into the air as it was able.

"Cool. We're running a little behind, and we're short on time to get you back here, so we're going somewhere closer than planned. I'll lead the way, so follow me. Anyone not in dress-up, grab a Minion's hand and be their guide," I added, jumping off the box and waving them forward.

They were going to need all the help they could get.

Have you ever tried walking down a busy road with nine giant Minions?

How about giant Minions in baseball uniforms walking around a rival territory on game day?

I thought it was going to take forever to walk five hundred yards to the coffee shop. It took way longer.

Every single person stopped us.

Cubs fans took selfies before loudly pronouncing the Lions were going to lose this series.

Several of the guys were jostled enough that I wish we'd brought security.

Luckily no one else fell over, but only through sheer luck. Traffic stopped to let us cross the road, people got out of their car and videoed us, and by the time we reached the coffee shop there were almost two hundred tags on social.

I stepped inside with a huge grin on my face.

Last year the guys had been dressed as Where's Waldo, which isn't as immediately obvious, and we had some traction, but it clashed with Ace's poor throwing streak, and many of the comments on social were from fans who felt we should be paying more attention to the game.

This year was a different story.

I stepped to the side, holding one of the doors open, while Jess held the other. One by one, the Minions stepped inside, guided by their helper. Luckily the doors were bigger than the costumes, and no one lost their head.

Amazingly the place was relatively empty, and the Minion with the list was guided over to stand in line behind the only other person waiting.

"Hey, Cyrus, make sure you capture them ordering, and who each order belongs to."

"Sure thing, boss," he replied, hurrying over to the counter and peering down at the crumpled-up form, clenched tight in the little hand.

It took ten minutes of ordering, plus another ten for the drinks to be made and stacked up before the Minions were ready to get back to the stadium. It was a good thing so many of the staff had come with us, because there was no way we'd be able to carry back all the coffee *and* guide a Minion at the same time.

"Hey, guys," I called to Cyrus and Joey from where I'd been editing the footage from this morning's *game day fit* content. "Let's hang back and edit what we've got, then we can get it uploaded before the game."

"Sure." Joey slid into the booth next to me and removed

the ID card from the video camera, turning to Cyrus. "Hey, Cy, pass your footage over."

"Man, I can't believe Parker King drinks that," he announced, pulling out the chair opposite Joey and me, and placed the camera down.

I glanced up from my screen, trying not to focus on the jolt zipping through me at the mention of Parker's name. Or simply the thought of Parker.

"Drinks what?"

"The coffee he ordered is a tragedy. I figured he'd be black with half-and-half at the most, not a heart attack waiting to happen."

"It can't be that bad," I replied, but as mine could be considered a little skewed, my opinion on others' wasn't always valid. However, Parker had been very clear on his thoughts about my coffee order yesterday.

"Here. Read it and tell me you don't think that's sick. And not in the good way. I mean, who drinks that?" He scrolled back through the video and paused the screen before passing it to me.

I looked down at the list. Out of nowhere my belly flip-flopped, giving way to a warmth that had my chest pounding. Parker King wasn't a coffee-ordering freak like me.

This wasn't his coffee order. It was mine with his name next to it.

He'd ordered *my* coffee.

Joey was peering over my shoulder and making gagging noises. "Urgh, that sounds disgusting. How can he drink that and be in peak physical fitness?"

"Yeah, if it hadn't been a ball player dressed as a Minion asking, there's no way she would have made it. Coggings had to hand the form over to her because she didn't understand it. Neither did he." Cyrus snorted.

But I wasn't listening.

Parker had not only remembered my drink, he'd ordered it. And this did not bode well for my plans to make smart relationship choices.

Not bode well, at all.

9

Parker

"Didn't expect to see you so early," I called over to Ace as his G-Wagon pulled up next to mine and he hopped out.

"Yeah, but my girlfriend works a real job, and I didn't want to stay in bed by myself. Plus, I was hungry," he replied, rubbing his stomach as he stretched out of a wide yawn. "I love Payton, but her cooking sucks. The only time her apartment has any food in it is when I bring it over, and seeing as we've been away for a week, the fridge was bare."

"Yeah, why d'you think I came in early?"

He slammed the door to the trunk shut, threw his arm

around my shoulder, and we made our way toward the front door to Lions Stadium.

I pulled my ball cap down and glanced around; a dull pang of disappointment flickered in my belly as it didn't appear there was any social media content planned for today. It was a long shot. It had been so late when we'd finally landed last night, and I guess Scout had to sleep sometime.

Based on how empty the players' parking lot was this morning, everyone else had had the same idea.

The only staff I spotted were the groundskeepers preparing the eleven-acre Lions site—tidying the flower beds and clipping the Lions-shaped bushes before the gates opened to fans later this afternoon.

"Because we're synced as fuck and you love me?"

"Yeah, that's why. And also Radley stayed over, so Lux wasn't up to make breakfast as usual. I couldn't wait. I'm starved."

"Did I miss anything last night?"

"Whaddya mean?

"When you got home."

"It was one a.m. You missed me crashing if that's what you're talking about."

He dropped his head on my shoulder. "Did you miss your nighttime snuggle with me?"

"I did actually."

"Good. Which brings me to my next topic. When are you

going to replace me?"

I stopped walking, shifting my bag back up onto my shoulder, and looked at him. "What? Seriously, what are you talking about?"

"Scout."

"Oh." I rolled my eyes and pushed through the revolving doors into the entrance lobby. "What about her?"

"What's the next move in Operation Strike Zone."

I winced and stopped walking again, this time directly over the lion's mouth on the logo in the floor, which I should take as a warning. "Dude, don't say it out loud. It's lame as fuck."

"No, it's not. It's awesome."

"You think?"

"Yup. So, what are you going to do? That was a cool move with the coffee." He snorted out.

I shoved him hard in the shoulder. "Oh, fuck off."

"What? You didn't know."

I groaned. On our first day in Chicago when one of the travel staff had come around for our coffee order, I didn't think twice before I gave them Scout's nausea-inducing morning special. If you're wondering how I remembered something so complicated, I'd ask you how could I forget?

The thing was burned in my memory.

Anyway, I thought it was funny.

I knew she'd be down with the rookies making her TikToks

and taking them out to get the coffee order. And I thought it was cute that one of them would ask for hers. I figured she'd see it and think, *Wow, Parker's so amazing, he remembered my particularly disgusting order, he must really like me. Maybe I should rethink my decision to not date him.*

That didn't happen.

Instead, the coffee order was posted as part of the reel on the Lions TikTok.

I was outed as having the most repulsive coffee order anyone has ever seen.

The post went viral.

In three days, it clocked up seven million views. I was publicly mocked by the Jimmys Fallon *and* Kimmel, by sports journalists who questioned my diet, regimen, and dedication to the club, and by the guys in the locker room who said that coffee order had clearly gone straight to my butt.

An amazing butt I'd hard earned through thousands—no, *millions*—of squats.

I hadn't spoken to Scout, but every time I'd seen her, whether it had been by the field or on the plane, or walking through the lobby of the hotel we'd stayed in, she'd smiled at me. A sly smile, with a crooked curve of her lip. A smile I chose to interpret as her telling me how funny and cute I was, but she was funnier.

A smile which held a little secret only the two of us knew.

A coffee order–shaped secret.

I hadn't seen her at all yesterday, or the day before that. Now I come to think about it, I hadn't seen her properly since our flight from Chicago to Milwaukee when I'd walked down the plane to find my coach, and she'd been a couple of seats farther along.

"Something else will be news next week," Ace added, pulling on my bag and dragging me over to the reception desk. "Come on."

"Good morning, gentlemen," greeted Pablo from behind the desk, his balding head looking shinier than usual.

"Morning, Pabs, how're you doin'?" saluted Ace.

"Never better. I'm living the dream, especially this week. Well played, boys, well played. You got some good hits in, Parker."

"Thanks, Pabs. Thanks for holding down the fort while we were gone," I added, swiping my access card against the reader.

"It's what I do best. How're you feeling about the games this week?"

"Goddamn awesome," Ace replied, flexing his bicep. "We got this."

Over the next few days, we were playing the Yankees. It would be the first time we'd play them this season, and given last season we lost 90 percent of the games every time we met, the air should have been thick with anticipation.

Instead, we were buzzing off the best start we'd ever had.

We were eleven games without a loss.

On the flip side, we were going to lose at some point.

Statistically there's no way we were going for much longer without a few foul balls and thrown away runs, but it would be better all-around if we didn't lose to the Yankees. We were playing the Nationals after that; we could lose to them instead.

"So, what's the news here?" Ace leaned across the reception desk, propping his chin on his fist. "What happened while we were gone?"

Pablo's beady eyes narrowed a fraction as they flicked between us. "Not a whole lot happens when you boys are traveling. But I did find out something interesting. Wanna hear it?"

"Um...yeah, obviously."

"The other day, my granddaughter was showing me this video. I'm not so much into the apps or whatever the kids use, but my granddaughter likes them and sometimes she shows me things she thinks I'd find funny. I'd told her you were out playing the Cubs and that it was time for the rookies' initiation, so I guess she was looking out for it."

I'd never been totally convinced I had a sixth sense, but right now my belly was fluttering in a warning, making it very hard to ignore. This conversation was going in a way I already knew I wasn't going to like.

"I'll tell ya, I don't know whose idea it was, but those Minions were funny, especially when they were ordering coffee. But you know what I found the most amusing?"

"What?" Ace said, his chin resting in both his palms while he listened to the most fascinating story he'd ever heard.

I could tell him the ending to save time. I knew exactly where this story was going.

"Parker's coffee order. It's an unusual one, I've only ever known one person to have that coffee order before." His head turned slowly, and he pinned me with a stare.

"Pabs, it's not like that." I groaned before this story went on any longer. "We're just friends."

"Parker, I know how you feel about her."

"Yeah, you and everyone else in this building," I grumbled. "I like her, it's not a crime."

"Scout's a good, hardworking girl, who got treated badly by her last guy she was dating."

My jaw clenched at the mention of Rangers Douche. "Pablo, I haven't done anything. I asked her out and she said no. We're friends."

But Pablo continued like he hadn't heard a word I'd said. "Don't be doing anything stupid."

Each word was punctuated with a wag of his finger.

"I'm *not*. Jeez."

My tone had Ace interrupting before I got even more annoyed with this conversation. "Pabs, Parker's done nothing wrong. He's just got a new friend, is all."

Pablo was still holding me with his glare. It was intimidating at best, terrifying at worst. I'd heard rumors he'd made grown men cry with it; while he always came across like your favorite grandpa, in my opinion he was way closer to Tony Soprano.

His thick, bushy black eyebrows shot up. "I know what you boys got up to last year with your sex magazines."

Ace scoffed. "They weren't sex magazines. It was *Cosmo*."

"Same difference. Scout's worked so hard since she got here, she's building a career. Don't mess it up for her."

I frowned deeply. "Pablo, are you warning me off her? Because you don't have that right."

"No. I'm not. But I'm saying don't fuck up her career because you can't keep your dick in your pants." This time his finger jabbed straight toward my groin.

"Hey, Pabs, what the fuck? You know how long I've liked her. I want to date her." I huffed, stepping back from the desk, trying to guide Ace with me so we weren't stuck here any longer. "She said no."

"Hmm."

We stepped back far enough that I could legitimately walk off. "See you around, Pablo. I was in a good mood when I drove here." I added with a grumble to Ace.

"Ahh, it's not that bad. He's messing with you," he replied, turning toward the corridor leading to the locker rooms, right before a broad grin spread across his face.

"What?"

"Don't turn around."

Obviously, I turned around.

Scout was running down the staircase by the elevators.

"Dude, what did I just say?" Ace nudged an elbow into my rib.

Instead of freezing on the spot, I jogged over to her quick enough to catch one of those little smiles cross her face as she spotted me.

"Hey, Davison, you know how much shit I've gotten since you posted that goddamn coffee order?" I stopped at the bottom of the stairs. "Even *Late Night* has been talking about it. You know how hard I've worked to cultivate my reputation as being cool?"

She shrugged with an innocence no one was buying. Or at least I wasn't. "I couldn't leave it out. It was part of the video we shot."

My eyes narrowed. "I think you could have left it out."

"Yeah? What you gonna do about it?" she challenged. "You mock my coffee order, you need to handle the consequences. Why do you think I don't share it with anyone?"

"You shared it with me."

"Huh." Her blue eyes held mine and she sucked in her cheek. "I guess I did."

I kept my smile to myself, stepped in a little closer, and lowered my voice. "Are you sure you don't want to change your mind?"

"About what?"

"Dating me."

The hesitation right before she answered was all I needed to bring my good mood back in full force, and it wasn't just good. It was excellent.

Her bottom lip curled into her mouth, eyes scoured my face before they rolled to the sky. "See you later, Parker."

I watched her walk off down the corridor.

That smile I'd kept to myself was now beaming out for anyone who wanted to see.

10

Scout

"What're looking at?"

I spun in my chair, coming face to face with a pair of high-tops crossed at the ankle on my desk. Ankles and high-tops belonging to Alice. I pushed them off.

"Nothing."

"Oh yeah?" She leaned around me and peered out of the window by my desk. "You sure do have a good view of nothing. In fact, d'you wanna swap desks? Yours is obviously sooo boring here. Mine's far too distracting."

I peered over to hers, easily the messiest in the office. Piles of magazines, stacks of paper she'd printed out and not dumped in the recycling, empty cans of Diet Coke—you name it, it was on her desk. The cleaning staff had long given up trying to tidy around it.

"I'm not sitting over there."

She turned to me with a grin. "I was kidding. There's no way I could sit next to a window like this. It's not even a window. It's a wall of glass. No, it's like one of those walkway things at the Empire State or whatever where you're standing directly above a mile high drop. You know if the window breaks there's nothing stopping you from falling out."

She shuddered dramatically.

"Let's hope that doesn't happen then," I replied. "Are you going to tell me why you're interrupting me? What do you want?"

She shrugged. "Nothing. Just noticed you'd been staring out the window for twenty minutes instead of working. Obviously, I wanted to know why, and now I do."

"No, you don't," I answered way too quickly.

"You're not staring out the window because Parker King is down there at practice waggling his cute little butt?"

"He's not waggling." My eyes darted around to all the occupied desks in earshot, though thankfully that wasn't many, given it was nearly lunchtime and people were already starting to head out into the sunshine. But there were still ears around to pay attention to what Alice had to say. "And will you keep your voice down?"

Her focus went back to the field. "I'd say that was waggling."

"Alice…"

"What? If you're not staring out the window at Parker King and his cute butt, wondering what it would be like to date him, then what does it matter who hears?"

"I don't know why I tell you anything." I huffed and focused back on my laptop.

"Hey, when a hot major league ball player asks you out, not once, but twice, it's only normal to wonder what dating him would be like."

"I wasn't wondering."

She spun around and pinned me with her big brown eyes. Alice was kind of intimidating when she wanted to be, especially when she didn't blink.

"I wasn't, I was thinking about the new job."

It was half true.

I hadn't yet had the job description, so I'd been wondering when it would arrive. That's what I'd been thinking about. She didn't need to know I was also thinking about Parker because, yeah, I'd been watching him practice.

And I hadn't been thinking about dating him. I'd done that already.

I'd been thinking about the way my belly did that little flip whenever he smiled at me.

Or how big his smile grew when I caught him looking at

me—which was way more than I should have.

Or maybe Parker was catching *me* looking at *him*. Because however you viewed it, the pair of us spent a lot of time staring at each other.

"You could do it for me, you know."

"Do what?"

"Find out what that cute little butt is like." She laughed.

I pushed her chair to the side, making room for me to roll in next to her, and resumed my staring at what I'd been staring at for far too long before Alice rudely interrupted me.

Not much had changed.

Grounds staff were prepping the stadium for the game later—picking up any trash left from last night's game, followed with hosing down the stands and bleacher seats. On the field, the lawnmowers trimming the grass had left behind thick green stripes. More staff were cleaning the bases, tidying the wide fan of terracotta that ran around the diamond, and brightening up the Lions logo in the center.

But it was in the corner, behind the Lions' dugout, where my attention had been, and was once more.

Parker was in the batting cages, running drills with the coaches and a couple of the relief catchers.

While I couldn't tell who was pitching to him from this distance, I knew without doubt that the guy crouching behind the plate was Parker, even with his ball cap and cage mask. It was the width of his shoulders, the thickness of his thighs, the way he was rocking ever so slightly on the balls of his feet from side to side. Something I'd noticed he did every time he got into position.

I guess it could be interpreted as waggling.

I leaned into Alice so only she could hear. "I agree it's a cute butt."

"Hmm," was her only reply, before she side-eyed me. "Have you heard any more from Shit Head?"

"Not since I blocked him."

She reached behind and picked up a pot of lip balm from my desk, twisting the top off to sniff before putting it back down. Her eyes barely left the batting cages however. "Sure you don't want to get back on the horse?"

"I'm sure," I replied firmly, though even as I said it I wasn't quite sure I meant it.

"Because that horse sure is sexy," Alice continued, like she hadn't heard a word I'd said. "With his cute little waggling butt. And the coffee thing…come on, that was adorable."

"He made fun of my order."

"It *is* disgusting, Scout. He'd have lost points if he *hadn't* made fun of it." She scoffed.

"That's why I don't tell anyone about it."

"You told Parker."

"Yeah, I know."

She didn't respond, and two minutes passed before she

said anything else, which had to be some kind of record. Her forehead rested against the glass as we stared down at the field. It was kind of hypnotizing, and not at all surprising how little work I'd gotten done today.

Perhaps I should move my desk away from the windows.

The pair of us were so engrossed in staring out at the green expanse, that neither of us was particularly focused on any one thing. Alice noticed it first, and by the time I caught what she was saying, it was too late.

I couldn't hide. I couldn't duck behind my chair. I couldn't do *anything* except watch Parker King turn and stare directly at the window, *my* window, and wave.

Not a small wave either. Parker's big arm shot right in the air, moving side to side like a windshield wiper. It was obvious enough that one of the guys he was with turned around.

"OMG," said Alice.

"No. Nothing happened. That didn't happen."

"Um, we both know he just waved at you."

"No," I hissed again, turning to make sure no one else was looking out of their window. Thankfully, just me who was obviously not doing any work. "There's no way he can see it's me from this distance. And he doesn't even know where my desk is. Or the window."

"You can see him," she countered, "and I was here when he came up, remember? He's obviously worked out which your window is."

"No way, he didn't. Who does that?"

"Parker King," she replied as she stood up.

I thought she was finally returning to her desk, but I should have known better.

Instead, she waved back, if you could class what she was doing as waving. Jumping up and down while her arms flailed about. If he wasn't two hundred yards away, he'd probably be able to hear her banging on the glass too.

I pushed as hard as I could against the window, zooming away in my chair, and shrunk down so no one could see me. Though thankfully I don't think anyone paid the slightest attention, they were all far too used to Alice's behavior to care what was causing it today.

She finally turned away. "Phew, well, I've done what I came to do, and watching those guys is really making me crave hot dogs. Let's go and get one for lunch."

"Sure." I snatched up my purse, anything to get out of here and away from the window.

"Hey, Scout?" she said, pressing the elevator button. "If you don't want Parker, can I have him?"

I bit down on my cheek, though I didn't need to think about the answer. "No."

"Yeah, that's what I figured."

11

Parker

"King, a word."

Slamming my locker door shut, I turned to find Coach standing in the archway, only for him to walk off. I guess it was my cue to follow.

A loud chorus of *ooohs* from the guys trailed me as I jogged after him, though not before I flipped everyone the bird.

He was waiting for me by the couches, arms crossed and perched on the back of the longest one, which separated out this area of the locker room. We called it a locker room, though it was kind of misleading for the facilities we had here, given the overall space—at five thousand square feet—was bigger than most houses.

Shepherd had the place specially designed to provide anything we needed when we needed it and separated out into zones, including downtime before a game—board games, cards, Xbox, or PlayStation—there were even bunk beds for anyone who wanted a quick nap. At the opposite end of the couch we were currently standing by, two of the rookies were fighting it out on *Call of Duty*.

I stopped in front of him. "Yeah, Coach."

"What's the latest on this form you're signing?" he barked out.

Coach Chase had come from the Yankees, where he'd been bench coach.

A phenomenal player in his day, spending the majority of his career as shortstop for the Mariners before moving to the Braves, where he'd won two championship rings. After a couple more years bouncing around teams, he retired and moved into managing.

In the nearly fifteen years since, he'd become well respected for handling both the players' needs and the clubs' in equal balance. He could relate to what we were going through because he'd lived it. He was fair, rounded, and well liked.

Over that time, however, he'd certainly perfected that stern *don't mess with me* scowl, just like the one he had trained on me right now as he peered over his bifocals, expecting me to know what he was talking about.

I didn't.

"What?"

"Have you signed it?"

I tugged at the collar of my tee, which suddenly felt way too tight. "You mean the dating thing?"

"What else would I be talking about?"

I shrugged. "Beats me, Coach."

"Well?"

My brows knotted tightly in annoyance. "I'm not dating anyone."

Coach stayed silent, though the way his eyes bored into me spoke volumes. He didn't believe me. Which pissed me off.

"No. I've not signed it, because I don't need to…I thought you only had to sign it if you started dating someone who worked here. I'm not, so I haven't. I asked her on a date, she said no. End of story." I stared at Coach, Coach stared back. "Wait…I have to sign it just because I like her? That is fucked up."

"Nothing fucked up about this season, King. Shepherd is not fucking around. HR is not fucking around. I need you on this team, otherwise we have Barry to work with," He snapped, mentioning one of the Lions' backup catchers.

I closed my eyes and took three deep breaths. God, this was humiliating.

"I don't see what difference it makes who I'm dating. Or not dating," I added quickly. Not that he believed me.

"We don't want distractions this season."

My hand flicked between the two of us. "Isn't this a distraction? Pulling me up for something I've not done."

"Do I look stupid to you?"

"Eh?"

"You think I don't know what's going on right under my nose? You don't think I don't notice you trying to get that girl's attention? You don't think that's a distraction?" Biting down on my cheek was all I could do to stop the grimace, especially when Coach was still staring at me. "I'm telling you that it is. While you're here in this stadium, your focus should be one hundred percent on the task at hand. You're a catcher, Parker. You have to see the whole field and be able to read the play five steps ahead. And you can't do that if you're distracted by getting this girl's attention."

"I'm not distracted." I gritted as my cheeks puffed out the breath I'd been holding. "What do you want me to do? I can't make her date me."

"I've told you, I don't care. Just keep it out of the locker room." He pushed off the couch back, making it clear this confusing-as-fuck—and totally pointless, if you asked me—conversation was over. "Now get your ass to the cages before you're late."

As he walked off, my eyes flicked to the clock on the wall. I had thirty minutes before practice started. I was already changed, and it took me approximately five minutes to walk from here to the cages, walk *slowly.*

Maybe Coach was losing it. That would explain his weird behavior. And this weird conversation.

And why he made no sense at all.

Given his parting shot was about not caring what I did, I assumed that meant he didn't care about what I didn't do either. Therefore I wasn't signing that stupid form for no reason.

I was still chewing on it when Ace appeared. "Hey, what was that about?"

I shook my head. "I dunno. Coach is…he's being so weird about this form thing. I don't get it. Why does he care about me being friends with Scout?"

Ace shrugged. "Maybe it's about what happens when you become more than friends."

"But there's no guarantee that's ever going to happen," I snapped.

As I said it, my chest squeezed tight enough that it was all I could do to rub away the sensation I hadn't felt in a while; the sadness dragging through me as it dawned on me that there was a strong possibility Scout and I would never be more than friends.

No matter how much I joked around with her, or helped her carry shit, ordered her coffee…anything to get her to notice me, maybe the timing was all wrong.

She had her new job to concentrate on. Not that any of it mattered to Coach.

I shook it off as quickly as it arrived. *Focus, Parker. Get your head in the game.*

"Hey, you wanna come up to HR with me?"

"Nope."

"Okay, put it this way. You're coming up to HR with me."

"I can't." Ace's head flopped back with a loud groan. "I have to go see the doc. I have the VO2 max test."

My own groan echoed his. I wasn't sure who wanted to do their thing less. Him or me. The VO2 max test was gross, and something every player in the roster had on their schedule once a week. But I'd take it over a trip to the sixth floor.

"I'll swap with you." I laughed.

"Seriously, dude, why are you going up to HR?"

"Because Coach will ask. He wants me to sign the form."

"But you're not dating," he added unhelpfully.

"I know we're not. But if Coach asks whether I went up, I can say yes."

"Hmm." He scratched his head, followed by ten seconds of silence as we walked down the corridor. "You know, this could be a positive. That everyone has faith you'll seal the deal."

"I guess."

"Well"—Ace slapped me on the back as we stopped by

the stairs leading down to where Ace was headed—"good luck. I'll be done in an hour if I haven't died."

"You'll be fine," I assured him, though I was also aware death was a distinct possibility. Even occasionally preferable.

Five minutes later I stepped out on the floor where HR sat and stared at the welcome board that split up the floor, detailing where each department was located. It definitely wasn't as welcoming as Scout's floor, and there were no cardboard cutouts of Jupiter either.

I'd only ever been up here a couple of times. HR was on the same floor as legal. While I'd never had any need to visit the legal department, the first season Shepherd took ownership, Ace used to drag me up to complain on a near daily basis about how PlayStation hadn't got his likeness right for *The Show*. It was therefore up to legal to do something about it.

It hadn't been long before he'd been banned from visiting them.

Come to think of it, I wasn't sure if that ban still stood, or if it was on a season-by-season basis.

What was I even doing up here? This was so dumb.

Scout wasn't distracting me, my stats already this season could attest to that. My on-base plus slugging was .568 so far. I'd had six home runs in seventeen games. I'd been catching well and hitting well. I'd been training my ass off.

In fact, I'd never felt better.

Nothing to do with Scout.

I peered around, everyone looked way too serious. What exactly was I supposed to say? Hey, I like a girl that works here, d'you want my signature?

Yeah, no.

I was still staring at the board, trying to figure out what to do, when the elevator doors pinged behind me.

"Parker?"

I spun around and came face to face with the reason I was standing here in the first place. Or chest to face, given that's about where she reached.

Was this a coincidence?

"Oh, hey."

"Hey." Her smile lit up her face. "What are you doing up here?"

"No—oh, um, nothing. Ace needed me to come up for something," I spat out the first thing that came to mind. "He's not allowed up here. It's a whole story."

Scout gave me a look that said exactly what I was feeling right now. Dumbass.

"What are you doing here?"

"This stopped working, I need to get a new one." She waved her access card at me. "Are you on your way back down, or just got here?"

I thumbed behind me. "Heading down."

"I'll be two minutes if you want to wait for me?" She shrugged.

"Yeah. You bet," I replied, then wished I hadn't been so enthusiastic. But fuck it. "I mean, sure. Go and I'll wait here."

I stayed where I was as she rushed off.

Visiting HR hadn't been quite as dumb as I'd originally thought.

12

Scout

You know you can build a house out of Twizzlers?

They're kind of like Lincoln Logs, except red. And instead of being made of plastic logs it's made of candy.

If you lick the ends, you can get them to stick to each other, which makes it easier to create stability in the structure. It's a great way to pass the time when you're supposed to be concentrating on anything else.

Plus, at the end you can eat it.

It's something I learned while reading through the very extensive job description I'd finally been sent: develop strategy, create content, analyze data, manage channels. All the usual roles. It was what I did now.

Except, right now, I only had one brand to oversee. This would add another two: the Jungle Kings, and this new brand—the New York Lions corporate brand, which currently didn't exist.

I would need to build it.

I'd started working on my Twizzlers house while staring at my screen because it stopped me from flicking between the job description, the New York Lions corporate website, and the Jungle Kings website, and any other website I could read to pass the time.

This would be a bigger role than I'd originally thought. Much bigger.

Full days. Longer hours. More traveling. I'd need to go out to White Plains, for sure.

I wasn't even entirely sure where White Plains was.

Could I do the job? Maybe.

Did I want the job? I hadn't decided.

Was I excited about a new opportunity?

It wasn't the word I would use. Or perhaps I would, but I'd also add nervous, anxious, and apprehensive. Even though I was sure they all meant the same thing.

I'd only been at the Lions for a year. I'd come from a small social brand agency where I'd started as an intern straight out of school. Moving from an office of six people to one where it seemed to double in size every week was daunting.

It took me a month to learn everyone's names, and a year on, I still saw a new person every day.

It was only now, with one season under my belt, that I felt fully comfortable in my role. I'd worked my butt off. I'd learned from mistakes I'd made and gotten better at my job as a result. All I'd felt coming into my second year was excitement. Excitement about building the team and watching it grow.

Now I'd have to start over, find my feet again, figure out how to do a job with three times the amount of work. Plus I'd never built a social presence from scratch before. The comfort zone I built wasn't quite so comfortable anymore.

It wasn't like anyone was forcing me to take the job

Or that I'd even get offered it if I did apply.

Yet a small, *tiny* part deep inside me was whispering that I'd be letting someone down if I didn't, and I wouldn't be given another opportunity like this again.

I should be *grateful.*

"You're missing a piece of the roof," Parker announced, pulling out the chair and sitting down opposite me.

Leaning forward, I peered over the top of the house and spotted the gap he mentioned, snapped off another strand of red licorice, and stuck it down. "Thanks."

"Is this what counts as work in the social team?" he asked, folding his arms behind his head as he leaned back.

His biceps flexed so impressively I almost forgot what I was doing. I didn't even think he was doing it on purpose, that's just how they were.

Giant biceps from years of baseball. I wasn't sure if his black Lions tee made them look bigger because it was slightly on the snug side, or if the tee was snug because they were so big. Because *he* was big.

Athletic. Honed. Taut.

Take a picture, Scout. It'll last longer.

I managed to tear my focus away from his body to his face and watched as the corner of his mouth lifted higher on the left, almost disappearing into the stubble on his cheek.

A crooked smirk, shooting straight at me, that said he knew exactly what I was thinking, or not thinking, because that smirk vanquished all the questions whirling around in my brain and the anxiety in my belly, and replaced it with a heat I'd not felt in a while.

"Yeah. You get to catch a ball for a living, I do this." I laughed back eventually.

"Fair argument."

"Shouldn't you be at practice?"

"I'm on my way, happened to be walking past and spotted you," he looked around the empty dining hall, "and I'm never going to pass up an opportunity to say hello to my *friend*."

There was that word again. Or rather, the way he said it.

Like there was so much more to it.

Like it was the beginning of something, a path I hadn't yet walked down.

"Do they frown on candy houses upstairs?"

"It's quiet down here." I shrugged. "I needed to think."

"With Twizzlers?"

"I like Twizzlers."

"I see that, and playing with them requires a lot of brain strength," he teased, leaning forward. The front legs of his chair thudded on the ground.

"It does, actually. You should try it sometime."

"I might," he replied, propping his arms on the table. It brought him closer to me, close enough that I couldn't quite meet his eyes. But I could feel them on me, studying almost. "Scout, you okay?"

I nodded. "Yeah."

"You sure?"

"Yes, I'm fine," I answered, but then my gaze flicked up to his deep green eyes, and a sigh escaped me before I could stop it. "Remember I told you about this job they've asked me to go for?"

"The one stopping you from dating me?" His lips rolled tight as he tried to hold his grin. "Sure, how could I forget?"

He was playing with me, but it I didn't stop my shoulder dropping. "Oh—never mind."

"Davison, I'm teasing." He reached over and nudged my clenched fists. "Come on, tell me. I promise I'm a good listener."

"I got the job description yesterday, and I've been reading up on it. It's way bigger than I thought it was, more hours. More work. It's doing things I've not done before."

His head tilted left. I could see from the look on his face that he was having a hard time figuring out why I didn't sound more excited, because it really was an awesome opportunity. "Is that not a good thing?"

I shrugged. "Yeah, I guess."

Parker picked up a piece of Twizzler and stuck it into the roof, like a little chimney. "You don't sound so sure."

"It's a big step up. I've only been here a year."

"But can you do it?"

I nodded. "Yeah, I think so."

He was silent for a minute, sticking down another piece of Twizzler, this time into a little path in front of the house. "Scout, if they didn't think you could do it, they wouldn't have asked you. I've been with the Lions since before Shepherd took over, and I speak from experience about what it was like before, and the difference it is now. I can tell you that Shepherd only hires the best. He has no weak links here."

I glanced up as a couple of the team PTs wandered over to the coffee machines. I half expected them to tell Parker to get to practice, but neither of them seemed to notice he was in here.

"Shepherd didn't hire me."

"But he hired whoever hired you. Therefore, he hired you,"

Parker shot back. "Scout, what's got you worried about this? You're awesome on social. We have so many more followers since you took over. Plus, you're funny. You kill it with replies to our haters."

My brows knitted together.

It was true, I did like to reply to the Lions haters, and a couple of times they'd been pulled out by bigger social channels like MLB.com or ESPN, but I was part of a team, and they could have come from anyone.

"Um, Parker? How do you know someone else didn't write them?"

He shifted forward slightly, *just* slightly, but it was enough to make my heart rattle against my rib cage, especially when he pinned me with those bright green eyes of his. "Because I like you, and that qualifies me to know which ones are yours and which ones aren't yours. I know."

"Oh."

"So I'm saying with my qualifications—"

"Of liking me?"

"Yes. In my qualifications of liking you, I can wholeheartedly say that you will be awesome for this job. And you know what else?"

"What?"

"You're a Lion. We were born out of adversity. We rise to a challenge, and we usually come out on top. If we don't, then at least we tried. If you don't want to apply for the job, then don't apply for it. But don't not apply because you're worried you won't be able to do it." He sat back again, his eyes darting to the doors before back on me. "I have no doubt that you can."

My cheeks burned at his compliment. "Thanks, Parker. I appreciate the support."

"Hey," he shrugged, "what are friends for?"

Smiling, I picked up one of the packets of Twizzlers and thrust it at him. "Want one?"

"Thought you were never going to offer." He grinned, easing one out and biting down on it with straight white teeth, shining through his perfect smile as he stared at me.

It should have had my nerves in a tizzy with how intense it was, but perhaps my nerves at figuring out this job description had all been used up because I did nothing but smile and stare right back as the pair of us chewed down on our Twizzlers.

"Can I ask you something?"

"Sure?" he replied.

"Why didn't you ask me out last year?"

A laugh bubbled up from his chest. "Because I'm an idiot."

"Seriously—"

"Yeah, seriously because I'm an idiot." He grinned again, though taking in my raised eyebrow, he leaned forward. "I guess the long version is that last season was hard. Ace started so badly, and we're a team. The two of us play so closely together, and he was hurting. It was hard when he got benched. I wanted to give him all my support. If I'd asked you out, then I would have wanted to spend all my time with you, when Ace needed me and the boys. Then when he started pitching again, and I went to ask you out, you were dating Rangers Douche."

I blinked a couple of times. "Oh."

"So, I waited." He stayed there, once more holding my gaze, until he pushed out of his chair. "I need to head to practice before my coach sends out a search party."

"Okay."

"I'm okay with waiting for you, Davison. I've already gotten good at it. Once you have the job, and you're ready to date me. I'll be here." He winked.

My mouth dropped.

By the time he'd disappeared out of sight, I still hadn't closed it.

It took a lot to shock me into silence, but Parker King seemed to have been managing to do it for the best part of a month.

And when the afternoon rolled around, a box arrived on my desk filled with Twizzlers and a note signed, *For your next construction project,* I realized how truly screwed I was.

13

Parker

"Doc…you're…killing…me…"

"One more minute," Dr. Marnie Matthews replied, not showing any signs of giving a shit that I was about to die.

"I'm…gonna…be—"

"Parker, if you stop talking it'll be easier. Not to mention I can't hear you through the mask anyway."

I grunted at her loudly instead. I guess she understood I was on the verge of collapse as she hit the Decline button and slowed the treadmill down to a stop.

"Okay, hop off."

I'd never jumped to the sides quicker. Ripping off the mask, I attempted to suck down as much oxygen as I could.

My lungs burned. My thighs burned. My calves burned.

Even my ass was burning.

"Stand up straight, you'll get more air in," she ordered.

Snatching the towel, she was holding out to me, I did as I was told, doing my best to mop up the sweat pouring down my body, even with the AC on full, but I'd been running flat out on a 4 percent incline while my oxygen levels were monitored, and now I was the equivalent of a human furnace.

"I'm not built for sprints, doc…I'm a catcher…I'm built for squatting…" I puffed out, rubbing the towel over my face right as she rolled her eyes.

"Yes, Parker, I know. You tell me every week."

"And every week you still make me come in here and do them. Even though I hate sprinting."

Hated it. Always hated it. Hated it at school. Hated it now. *Hated.*

Marnie was still talking like she hadn't noticed or didn't care I could barely stand. "…and your results are good—oxygen extraction figures are higher than they were at the start of the season. You're getting fitter, Parker."

Huh. That was interesting. "Yeah? How fit? I'm already fit."

"*Fitter*," she repeated, peeling the disposable heart monitor from my chest and plugging it into her laptop.

Immediately her screen filled with colored graphs and

wavy lines containing the data she and her team monitored closely.

I stepped down off the treadmill and grabbed a bottle of Gatorade from the fridge and another sweat towel from the shelf, and sat down while she worked her magic.

Doctor Marnie Matthews, the Lions' president of baseball science and data, had been brought to the Lions by Penn Shepherd when he'd taken ownership of the team.

An astrodynamicist—or superbrain, as most of the guys called her—by profession, she'd come from NASA, where she'd spent the previous decade launching rockets into space. Because, *If she could launch a rocket, she could make a baseball fly more efficiently*, according to Shepherd.

She'd been tasked with helping the team win.

No small feat, but she'd succeeded and almost single-handedly turned the club's losing streak around overnight. The data she collected on how each of us individually played our game had been the biggest contribution to the Lions winning, beyond the players themselves.

Through a series of tiny changes she'd implemented—from the way we traveled, ate, and slept, to how our bats were stored and the dugout was kept—we'd become a slick, *almost* unbeatable team.

She'd introduced Penn Shepherd to a new type of material embedded with tiny sensors that could monitor everything from heart rate to hydration and muscle fatigue to oxygen levels during a game, and account for them in real time.

Therefore, she could make any necessary adjustments in real time.

If our sweat levels were up when we played during the high summer months and we were close to dehydration, then we'd be sucking down hydration packs during the batting. Last season we had 47 percent fewer injuries than the season before, which had 70 percent less than the season before that.

Her team of data scientists focused on each player as individuals, and when we came together, we were fitter and stronger because of it. I wasn't entirely sure I understood everything she did, but we were winning, therefore I didn't care a whole lot.

She could do what she wanted.

On the flip side, she was engaged to Jupiter Reeves, so she had her faults.

I watched as she flicked through the different charts she'd brought up.

"Hey, doc, how are my results compared to, say, Ace's?"

"Ace is a pitcher. He doesn't have the same cardio abilities you do. He doesn't bat, he doesn't run bases," she replied, not looking up from the screen.

"Okay, what about Weston?"

"He's center field. If you want a fair comparison you need to go with Robson Barry."

I rolled my eyes.

I liked Robson. He usually started a couple of times a week

when Riley Rivers was pitching instead of Ace, but I didn't want to be compared to another catcher.

It was too easy.

I wanted to know the goddamn hill sprints I'd busted my guts for were at the same level as the fielders.

"What about Reeves, doc. Am I fitter than Reeves? He's heading toward old man territory now, right?" I chuckled, wiping another cascade of sweat from my face. "Must be nearly forty."

"He's thirty-four and does he know you call him an old man?"

I shook my head. "Of course not, I don't have a death wish."

She chuckled in response, her head flicking up to one of the guys on her team as he walked into the lab. "Marnie, Scout Davison is here for you with a couple of guys. Can I let them in?"

Even through the haze of sweat and lack of oxygen, my ears immediately pricked.

Scout was *here.*

If my heart wasn't still pounding from the treadmill, it would be pounding from that news. I hadn't seen her for a couple of days, except from far across the field during the home games we'd played.

I'd been toying with the idea of going up to the fifth floor to see her but hadn't decided if that was too much, especially because I couldn't come up with a decent excuse as to why I'd be up there.

Which reminded me, I needed to get her number somehow.

But this…this was perfect.

Nothing forced about her doing her job while I was doing mine.

I jumped up from the seat and stood in front of the mirror. I might have been on the verge of collapsing only minutes ago, but I also looked *good.*

My muscles were popping, my skin was still wet with sweat and these shorts made my ass look super peachy. It was all on display for Scout to get her fill. I eased the waistband down an inch so it sat on the divots girls went wild for.

I couldn't have planned it any better.

"Scout? What for?" Marnie's eyes flicked over to me and frowned, then back at the guy by the door.

"Something for the website. She said you'd okayed it last week."

"Dammit." Her eyes widened and she slapped a hand to her head, turning back to her screen. "I forgot. Crap. Can you ask them to come back in thirty, can they wait until then? Parker's done—"

"No!" I shouted as I was forced out of another one of my fantasies where Scout fell in love with me. And if the expression on Marnie's face was anything to go by, too loudly. My head snapped to her colleague. "Tell them they can come now, I'll do it. Whatever you need me to do, I'll do it." I turned back to Marnie. "If that's okay, doc?"

"No, Parker. Boomer can do it, he'll be rested. We're doing the VO2 max test."

I was too busy buzzing with the renewed energy of Scout being outside to panic about what I was volunteering for. "Please, doc. Just go with it. I'll do it, get me on the treadmill again."

Her entire face screwed in confusion. "Why?"

"Just 'cause," I pleaded, throwing in my best puppy dog eyes. The ones I knew the girls liked. "Please, doc?"

She shrugged and puffed out an exasperated sigh and nodded to the guy. "Okay, tell them they can come in." As soon as he left, she turned to me with narrowed eyes. "What's going on?"

"Nothing." I tried to keep my tone as casual as possible. "Just want to help out, is all."

Suddenly her brows shot up. I could almost see the lightbulb hanging above her head, shining bright.

"Oh, wait. Is this the girl you like?"

"What?

"The girl you like? Scout's the one you like?"

"Jupiter's got a big mouth," I grumbled.

"He likes to tell me about his day." She smiled, a smile so sugary sweet it made my guts churn. Gross. "Sometimes you come up in conversation."

"What else has he said?"

"Not much, that you like a girl and won't stop talking about her."

"I don't talk about her all the time." I huffed.

"And I'm right, it's Scout? She's cute."

"I *know*."

"Wow, you must really like her if you want to go through a VO2 again."

"We're just friends."

She popped a hip and crossed her arms over her chest. "You're offering to put yourself through something you just told me under no certain terms that you absolutely hated. I think you're more than friends, Parker."

"We're not," I grumbled, again.

"Uh-huh." One of her eyebrows shot up, and I could tell she was trying to keep her amusement to a minimum. "Shall I fetch you a T-shirt then? Wouldn't want her to get the wrong impression with you exercising in only a tiny pair of shorts."

"C'mon, doc…gimme a break," I pleaded again, really stretching out the vowels until a loud knock sounded at the door.

Marnie's eyes flicked back to mine with a wink, before she greeted Scout with a big smile.

"Scout, hey. Come in. Come in."

"Hey, Doctor Matthews, thanks so much for doing this, we

thought it would be fun content..." Scout stopped walking as her eyes fell onto me. "Oh! Parker!...I, uh, um...didn't know you'd be here."

If I had any doubts about this stupid plan of mine to get Scout's attention, they vanished into the air.

Her mouth dropped into a perfect oval, her full lips pursed. Lips I wanted to see wrapped around my dick.

I'd thought about it before, more times than I should admit, but now with her in front of me while I was only a pair of shorts away from being naked in front of her, it seemed almost real. Especially with her eyes wide in shock, and the longer she stood there staring at my damp chest, the pinker her cheeks grew.

Oh yeah, I could definitely see my dick in her mouth.

Fuck, she'd look incredible.

"Scout, I'm finishing up with Parker if that's good. I have a couple more tests to run with him, and you can film those if that works for your content."

In the future if anyone asks me what the hardest part of this session was, I'd answer trying to keep a straight face when a broad grin was threatening to break at the struggle Scout had to tear her eyes away from where they were currently trained on my abs.

Yeah, I should win an award.

"Oh, sure. That works, thanks..." Scout turned to me. "I mean, if that's good for you, Parker. We're doing a piece for the website. It's a week behind the scenes at the club."

I was about to respond when Marnie jumped in, "Parker's fine. Let's get started, shall we?"

The two guys, who seemed to follow Scout everywhere, were closely behind, each with a tripod under their arm.

"Scout, you good if we set up here?" the skinny one asked. "Doctor Matthews, anything we need to avoid?"

"Yes. My screens. You can film Parker on the treadmill, and that's all."

"No problem," he replied and placed it directly behind me.

Fine by me, my ass would look great on camera. It was almost unnecessary for Marnie to whisper, "I'll make you look good, don't worry."

I already did look good. Even if I did have to wear an ugly as hell mask.

"Can you explain what we're doing here today?" asked Scout, pointing the microphone at Marnie, though she wasn't paying attention, seeing as her eyes darted to me every couple of seconds.

"Yes, we're measuring the VO2 max levels in Parker, which is to say we're looking to see how his body uses oxygen. The higher the level, the better his cardiovascular function, which is needed for sprinting around the bases."

"Sounds good," Scout replied, her eyes darting my way again. I wasn't even sure she'd looked me in the eye yet, she'd just been staring at my chest the whole time. Chest, abs, arms, ass.

"Parker, hop up on the treadmill."

I did as I was told.

The whole process was the same as it had been thirty minutes ago when I'd walked in fresh, Marnie fixing the monitor around my chest so she could track my heart, while I eased on the mask. I could hear the guys behind me, setting up their equipment.

"We do this in stages, we keep increasing the speed until Parker is working at his max effort." Marnie reached over and checked the straps holding the mask in place. "You ready? We'll begin at a quick jog."

I nodded.

"Scout, are you ready?"

"Yes, ma'am," she replied, from somewhere out of my eyeline. "We're good."

Marnie set the speed and incline on the treadmill.

Regret set in almost immediately.

I didn't know what Marnie meant when she said she'd make me look good, but I definitely wouldn't look good if I collapsed dead, which is exactly where I was headed if she increased this speed by even a little bit more. And that would be a shame because I kind of wanted to see this thing with Scout through, especially as it felt like I'd been getting somewhere over the last week.

Since we'd shared Twizzlers.

I had barely settled into my stride when Marnie turned up the speed again. My mask hid the scowl I shot her. There's no way I was going this fast during my actual VO2 max test. I don't think I'd ever gone this fast. The incline hadn't been this steep either.

Definitely not.

My legs were pumping so quickly to stop me from falling off the end, they were about to dislodge from my body.

I was concentrating so hard I barely heard Scout talking.

"Why do you keep increasing the speed?" she asked.

"Because we have to build to stop his lungs plateauing. We can't measure his capabilities until he's at max effort."

"And does everyone run at the same speed?"

Marnie shook her head. "No, it depends on their personal capabilities and how well their body works to convert oxygen. Parker is above average, so we always start him much harder. Due to his dense quad and glutes, he can handle a lot. Parker holds a lot of power in his thighs."

I made a mental note to tell Marnie I loved her, especially when I caught Scout's eyes dropping to my ass again. The euphoria only lasted a couple of seconds, however, before it gave way to panic that my lungs might explode.

My legs were definitely going to fall off.

Or I was going to fall off.

The power of the treadmill belt would splatter me against the wall, like a cartoon.

This is how Road Runner must feel.

If I didn't die, I'd need to be stretchered out of here. I'd have to spend the afternoon in rehab just to regain the use of my legs.

Marnie dialed up the speed again. The only thing stopping me from collapsing was the fact I could see Scout from the corner of my eye, standing at the side of the treadmill.

Scout was watching me.

Why was I putting myself through this again? To impress her?

What a chump.

I didn't know how loudly I groaned, but it was loud enough that Marnie called time on this stupid plan of mine.

"Okay, we're done. I think we've pushed Parker as far as he can go." Marnie hit the Slow button on the treadmill, and it was all I could do to grab the bars on either side of the belt. I didn't even have the strength to jump to the sides.

"Wow, Parker, I'm impressed," Scout said as I ripped off the oxygen mask and jogged to a stop. "That was really something to watch."

"Thanks," I puffed out, wiping myself down for the second time with a sweat towel.

If I hadn't been concentrating on not throwing up, I'd have seen Scout track the movement, eyes wide.

"Thanks, Doctor Matthews, I think we got what we need."

"Are you sure?" Marnie replied in a tone full of amusement

as her eyes flicked to me. "We still have a couple of tests to run."

There was no need to translate the grunt I let out.

"I'm sure." Scout laughed, while the guys packed up. "Thanks for letting us interrupt, we have a few more things to add, but the video will be up some time next week."

"We all look forward to seeing it." Marnie grinned at her.

"Bye, doc. See you around, Parker."

The second Scout left the room, I grabbed the trash can and hurled my guts up, before collapsing onto the floor.

Through the black spots blurring my vision and the ringing in my ears, I could just make out Marnie standing over me. "Are you okay?"

Even if I could speak, I didn't have an answer.

"I have to say, Parker, that was truly impressive, and I can tell you now Robson Barry couldn't have done that twice. Maybe not even Jupiter."

I perked up a fraction. Not even the great Jupiter Reeves, though it was debatable he'd do something this stupid to begin with.

If I wasn't careful, this friendship thing with Scout was going to kill me in more ways than one.

14

Scout

There was no mistaking the familiar shape in the distance, outlined against the bright May sun shining down from the clear blue sky.

Broad shoulders tapering down to a narrow waist and the best butt in baseball. Unofficially. Even if that butt of his hadn't been haunting my dreams for the past few nights, I'd have recognized it.

It was pure coincidence he was out here, arriving at the same time he always did when we had a home game.

It wasn't that I'd chosen this exact moment to run and grab a coffee from the shop and arrive back through the gates at the exact same time Parker pulled up, hopped out of his car, and made his way across the parking lot to the stadium entrance.

No, sir.

Pure coincidence. Just like it was a coincidence I happened to have an extra coffee in my hand, made exactly how I knew Parker took it.

I'd like to think this was a well-thought-through plan, but it wasn't.

Obviously. I wasn't even entirely sure what I was doing, except to say I'd already attempted it twice, but both times he'd arrived with his roommates—one or all of them—and this wasn't something I wanted witnesses for.

Not that I knew what this *something* was.

He was twenty yards out when I finally decided to open my mouth. "Hey, Parker, wait up."

I'd barely finished shouting his name before he spun around, and even from this distance I could see his eyes light as he lifted his sunglasses up, followed by a smile that split his face. Perhaps this wasn't such a stupid idea.

Thick stubble coated his cheeks, though it did nothing to disguise the sharpness of his cheekbones or the ruler-straight line of his jaw. He seemed to get more handsome every time I saw him.

The stadium was always quieter when the boys were gone, but this past week had felt like a ghost town. I wouldn't fly out with them every time they left, just like I didn't attend every away series last year, but I don't recall noticing the team's absence quite so much.

Though I was beginning to realize it was simply the absence of the one striding toward me.

On the flip side, I'd been very productive and had actually gotten ahead with work. I'd edited the *week in a life* feature for the website, and the guys who'd flown out on the trip had sent all their content back to me, which I'd compiled into enough TikToks to last until next week.

Without Parker around to distract me, or watch from the window by my desk, I'd also started the presentation I needed to give for my job interview.

"Heeyy." He grinned, stopping just short of where his sneakers would hit the tips of my Chucks.

Close enough that he needed to peer down at me with an expression that was ego boosting to say the very least.

I had an overwhelming urge to hug him, but instead, curled my fingers tighter around the coffee cup.

"Are you my welcoming party?"

"Maybe." I laughed. "I got you a coffee."

I may as well have been handing over the Commissioner's Trophy for how his eyes flared wide. "You got me a coffee?"

I nodded, willing my cheeks to stay their normal peachy shade. "Yeah. You got me one. Thought I'd return the favor. That's what friends do, right?"

Even as I said it, and even as I watched him nod, it felt weird to hear. I might not be ready to admit it, but I wasn't sure we were in friends territory anymore. I wasn't sure where we were. Some kind of weird no-man's-land before we reached the space that *more than friends* belonged to.

His eyes flicked between the two cups I was holding. "Which one's which?"

"You wanna guess?"

"Nope. No, I do not." He laughed, taking the boring black coffee I held out and sniffing it. "This smells safe. Thank you."

"Sure you don't want to try mine?"

"Bleugh. No thanks," he said, sticking his tongue out, and lifted the cup to his lips, then paused. "Actually, yeah, I kind of do."

"Of course you do." I passed mine over and watched as he eased the lid off to peer inside like he was expecting something to pop out. By the time he'd sniffed this one, too, before gingerly taking a sip, I was ready to hand him an award for the overacting.

"Huh." Was all he said as he placed the lid back on it.

"Huh? Does that mean you like it?"

He shook his head. "No. Definitely not. But I don't hate it. It's not as bad as I thought it would be. We can still be friends," he added solemnly, making me laugh.

"Oh, thank god for that. Aren't I a lucky girl?"

"I'm the lucky one."

He might have mumbled it, but it was loud enough to hear an underlying seriousness, which heightened when he held my gaze. It set off a succession of little somersaults in my belly until I had to look away.

"So," he nudged me gently, "how's your week been? Have you missed me? It's hard to check in when I don't have your number. You best be coming to the game today."

"Is this you asking for my number?"

He shook his head. "No, simply stating a fact."

"My week's been good, I've managed to get some work done without you distracting me all the time."

"I distract *you*?"

"Maybe."

His hands clasped to his chest. "Why, Scout. I think that's the greatest compliment you've ever given me."

"Shut up."

"I will not." He laughed, nudging me with his shoulder again, and we walked toward the entrance. "How's that website film coming along? Are you going to make me famous?"

"Aren't you famous enough already?"

He shook his head. "Nah, I'm only baseball famous. Not star quality famous. I'm expecting your film to do that for me."

"It's a film now, is it."

"Yep, so when's it premiering?"

"This week."

"I'll let the mail room know to expect extra fan mail then."

"Oh, you and your ego." I laughed, patting him on the shoulder.

"Hey, there's nothing wrong with my ego."

I stopped and allowed my gaze to drop, before it slowly inched upward. I did my best to make it look all show, but I could happily admit to myself I was enjoying every second. It was almost as good as last week when he'd been nearly naked, dripping in sweat as his muscles worked to exhaustion.

"I dunno, looks too big to fit through the doors."

"Nope. Watch." He marched forward and pushed through the wide revolving doors into the lobby, only to come right back out again as they spun around. "See."

"They must have been widened or something."

"Uh-uh," he said, and before I knew it, he'd grabbed my hand and pulled me into the next go-around. I barely had time to shriek, it was a wonder neither of our coffees spilled as I found myself hard against his even harder chest. And there was no escape. "See, I told you."

The revolving doors might have been big enough to fit us both in, but barely. The five seconds of time it took for us to pass through into the lobby could have been days as his green eyes bored into mine.

All we'd done was taken a couple of steps, but the flip-flopping in my belly was akin to riding the big drop at Six Flags, and just like I always did on roller coasters, I held my breath.

"Shall we go again?" His lips brushed the shell of my ear and I lost all train of thought; my brain ceased to function. I was all set for another go-around, when loud shouting yanked us out of whatever moment we were having.

A couple of security guards were standing with their back to us next to the security desk. Pablo was behind it with his arms crossed, and wearing an expression so murderous that I almost ran back outside, and it wasn't even aimed at me.

Whoever was currently shouting was far braver than I was.

Parker leaned into me and let out a low whistle. "Someone's got balls. No one messes with Pablo and comes out unscathed."

I was about to agree with him, but it was only when I heard Alice's voice among the din that I really paid attention. As I hurried forward, Pablo turned. "Here she is. Now you can see her, then you can fuck off." He thumbed out.

I frowned, there's no way Pablo would be telling Alice to fuck off. But then the security wall parted and in the middle was one person I'd hoped never to see again, at least for a very long while.

"Mark?"

I barely noticed Parker tense next to me, because Mark pushed through the two security guys and rushed toward me, only for Parker to step in front and block his way.

"What the fuck do you think you're doing?" Mark snarled.

"I'd ask the same question. But first I want to know who the fuck you are."

"I've come to see Scout," Mark replied, attempting to sidestep around Parker, only for Parker to move too.

In the split second Parker turned to me and back to Mark, he'd realized exactly who this guy was demanding to see me.

"Did you make an appointment?"

"I don't need to make a fucking appointment." Mark tried again, only now Alice had arrived and flanked his other side. "Jesus. Scout, c'mon, talk to me. Call the dogs off."

Parker looked over his shoulder, where I was standing, 50 percent shock, 50 percent annoyance. Though the shock was waning into anger.

I'd had a couple of weeks of peace from Mark; I'd almost forgotten about him. I'd been having fun with Parker, enjoying my days without being bothered every hour by a whiney message. It hadn't in a million years occurred to me that blocking him would result in this.

Him, here at my work. With Parker, Alice, Pablo, and two security guards staring.

At least it was early enough that the players hadn't arrived. And we didn't have filming scheduled for this morning.

Parker turned back to him. "Doesn't look like she wants to talk to you, buddy."

"That's what I've been telling him," bit out Alice.

Mark's jaw clenched, and his fists balled. "Move out of

my way."

Before Parker refused, or before Mark attempted to punch him and got punched back, I stepped to the side, summoning as much of Pablo's murderous expression as I could. "What are you doing here?"

Mark's eyes sliced to Parker and back to me. "I want to talk."

"I don't know what gave you the impression I wanted to talk to *you*, or that it was okay for you to show up here *at my work*," I seethed, "but I don't."

"You haven't replied to my messages."

"Because I blocked you."

I couldn't decide what was more strange: that he was surprised that I'd blocked him, or that he hadn't realized I'd done it in the first place. But he stood there for a good ten seconds before he said anything, until he did.

"I'm sorry."

I wish he'd stayed silent. "Cool. Can you leave now?"

His eyes dropped, into what I guess he thought was a pleading expression. "No. I want to explain."

"You already did. Why can't you get it through your thick skull? We are over."

Mark stepped closer, or as close as he could get with Parker still half blocking me while Alice looked on venomously, and lowered his voice so at the very least Pablo and the two security guys couldn't hear him. "I want to make it up to you."

If I wasn't still holding onto my coffee, I'd have

crossed my arms, instead I moved back.

"And you thought coming to my place of work was the best way to do that? This is so embarrassing." I glared at him. "You need to leave."

"Sco—"

"You heard the lady," Parker snapped, twisting Mark to face the doors and shoving him forward. "Out."

"Get your hands off me."

"Then do as you're told and get out," Parker repeated calmly, not in the least bit fazed Mark's knuckles had turned white from the tension he was holding, and nodded to the security guys rushing over. "Or these two will lift you up and carry you to the gates. I wouldn't test it either. I've seen them take on an entire busload of Jupiter Reeves fans single-handed without breaking a sweat."

Mark yanked his arm out of Parker's grip, glancing around with obvious disgust. "Don't know why I bothered coming to this shit hole. You can repaint all you want, still be the worst club in the league."

"Dude, seriously, is that all you have to say? You insult like a twelve-year-old. No wonder you couldn't handle Scout." Parker laughed. "How you managed to get her in the first place is beyond me."

Mark stopped struggling and stood there. His eyes narrowed even further on Parker. He either didn't know or didn't care that he was standing in front of one of the greatest catchers in the MLB.

No, *he knew.*

"Get her…what?" He snarled, before his face took on an entirely different expression, wild eyes darting between me and Parker. "Wait…have you got the hots for her? Is that what this is about?"

Parker turned to me and winked; my chest squeezed until I almost couldn't breathe. Blood whooshed so loudly in my ears that I never caught his reply, or even if he did reply, because Mark decided he'd finally had enough. It was unfortunate, however, that as he stormed through the doors, Ace Watson and Tanner Simpson arrived for the day.

"Whoa, bud, where are you off to in such a hurry?" asked Ace as Mark barged past him.

Tanner's eyes followed as Mark finally made it outside, the security guards in close pursuit escorting him until he was fully off Lions premises. "Why do I recognize that guy?"

The second he was out of sight I finally managed to pull much-needed air into my lungs. Blood was still pounding through my veins, and it took all my energy to fight the urge to cry, especially when Alice pulled me into a hug.

"Are you okay?"

I eased myself from her grip and took a massive glug of my coffee. I hadn't had anywhere near enough to cope with this so early in the morning. "What was he doing here?"

She shrugged. "To see you. He'd only been here a couple of minutes before you arrived. Pablo called up, but you weren't there."

Another couple of the guys walked in, and I stepped away from the doors, turning my back before anyone could spot me. "This is so embarrassing."

Alice didn't get the opportunity to answer because Parker appeared, having stayed by the entrance to watch security escort Mark away.

"Are you okay?" he asked, his head dipping down to my height so all I could see was his bright green eyes and the concern that filled them.

It was making it even harder to hold back my tears, and I gave a loud sniff.

"Yeah. I'm fine. I'm sorry—"

"You have nothing to apologize for," Parker snapped. "That guy's a dick."

"Got that right," mumbled Alice.

"I wasn't apologizing for him. I was just…" I stopped talking, I actually didn't know what I was apologizing for. "God, this is so embarrassing."

"It's not," said Alice.

"It is, and it's unprofessional. Everyone will know about it," I wailed. "I'm supposed to be applying for this new job. They're not going to give it to me when shit like this happens."

"Sco—"

"No one's going to find out about this," interrupted Parker. "I give you my word. Beyond me, you and…" his eyes flicked to Alice, "your friend here. The only ones who saw were Pablo and security. Plus, Ace and Tanner, and they won't say anything."

"Pablo is the biggest gossip. This club runs on gossip."

"I promise he won't say anything," Parker insisted, and given the firmness of his tone, I was inclined to agree with him. It didn't make me feel any better however.

"It's still embarrassing."

"Scout, you're holding the world's most disgusting coffee, and you're proud of it. That's what you should be embarrassed about." He grinned.

I managed to return a weak smile, but that's all it was. The excitement I'd buzzed on this morning, and—fine, being honest—about seeing Parker had drained away, leaving nothing but an aftermath of annoyance and frustration.

He must have sensed it, because the next thing my shoulders were held in his grip.

"Scout, the Lions is not the place to be embarrassed. You don't think every single one of the guys who works here has done something they'd rather forget. I mean, look at Ace."

He nodded over to where Ace and Tanner were laughing with Pablo.

"He choked last year in front of the president, and seventy thousand people, and he still summoned the strength to pull his pants on every morning. A few years ago, on my very first day here as a rookie, my mom sent me the biggest bunch of balloons, like the biggest you'd ever seen, and the idiot who delivered them didn't tie the weight properly, and they got loose."

Parker pointed upward, and the three of us tipped our heads back until we could see the top of the stadium seven floors up.

"Yeah, we couldn't get them down, but every time one of those fuckers finally popped or died and floated to the ground, Pablo announced it on the loudspeaker to come and collect it. It went on for two whole fucking months."

My eyes had widened so much, it was almost impossible not to smile.

"That's better." Parker said softly, "I like it when you smile."

"Thank you."

"You're welcome. Now drink your disgusting coffee and get back to work," he replied, his tone full of jest.

I was so busy staring at Parker that I'd almost forgotten Alice was standing next to the two of us, until she coughed pointedly. The pair of us managed to break out of the staring competition we were having and turned to find her watching us. I was about to ask her why she was looking at us so strangely when she spoke.

"I like you, Parker King. Keep up the good work."

Parker scoffed a laugh. "Thanks. I appreciate that. Now I need to go and rescue my coffee from Ace before he drinks it."

"See you later." I chuckled, though he only managed a couple of steps before I had the urge to call him back. "Hey, Parker?" Moving away from Alice for a shred of privacy, I asked, "Did you tell Mark you had the hots for me?"

He shook his head. "No."

I wasn't expecting the disappointment at his words to hit me quite so hard. Hard enough that I had to swallow down the tears that threatened to make another appearance.

"Oh. Cool."

"I don't have the hots for you, Davison. The hots are for sixteen-year-olds, jerking off to posters of models on their bedroom walls." He continued, "I *like* you. A lot. I have done for a long time. I want to date you, and you better believe I'll treat you a damn site better than that fucking douche. I told you I'm okay with waiting, and when you're ready, I'll show you exactly how fucking awesome you are and exactly how you should be treated. And I will wake up every morning knowing how fucking lucky I am to have you."

My mouth must have dropped open because he tucked his finger under my chin and gently closed it.

"See you around, Davison. Thanks for my coffee."

15

Parker

"STRIKE."

My ear rang from the volume of the umpire yelling. I swear he was getting louder with every call he made.

Or he was trying to be heard over the din of Lions fans cheering at the call, especially the ones behind the strike zone.

It was like they'd collectively decided to play umpire, several thousand of them sitting there, eyes trained on the ball flying straight into my glove and shouting the strike before he could.

Change over.

I stood, stretching out my thighs and glutes, while Ace

jogged over from the mound and we walked to the dugout together.

I tapped my fist to his. "Nice work."

"We're on fire today."

We were heading into bottom of the third against the Marlins, at Lions Stadium, and up by two runs to nothing.

Even though there was still over half the game left to play, there was an extra special buzz in the air that felt a lot like winning. It was all to do with us playing at home.

At Lions Stadium.

I'd been in every major league stadium in North America several times over, but I'd never felt anything like the electricity that ran through the fans when we stepped onto Lions field.

It made winning that extra bit sweeter, and I knew that's where we were headed today. I could feel it deep in my bones.

Ace and I were syncing beautifully, more of the Marlins than not had been sent off without making first base. Today, the field was nothing more than a paint-by-numbers exercise, the Marlins' defense was predictable to the point of boring. It was like they hadn't even tried to make this difficult for us.

Yeah, we were definitely heading for a win.

Ducking my head, I stepped down into the dugout and took a seat next to the pitcher's chair—Ace's chair—as the rest of the guys made their way off the field.

Our current team had been playing together for a few seasons now, give or take a couple of transfers and the new rookies, but we'd spent hundreds of hours in the dugout that I could close my eyes and tell you exactly what was about to happen.

Saint Velasquez, our Puerto Rican right field, would be first in line for snacks, ripping open a packet of the sunflower seeds he loved so much while yelling out calls for the guy up at bat, no matter how many times Coach told him to stop.

Jupiter Reeves would grab a bottle of the blue Gatorade, take one sip, snatch up his bat and helmet, then make his way to the bullpen because he was always first at bat.

The rest of the guys would file in; some would find their coaches, some would grab snacks and drinks, and some would sit in silence for a minute, thinking about the next inning.

"Heads up," yelled Tanner, and I turned just in time to find a protein bar hurtling toward me, snatching it right before it hit me in the face.

I should have kept my cage on.

"A little more notice next time." I frowned at him as he dropped onto the bench next to me.

"Sorry." He took a swig of the apple juice he was holding and passed it to me, leaning around to peer at Ace. "Hey, Lucky Aces, your pitching is on fire today."

Ace finished the bottle of water he was guzzling down like he'd been in the desert for a month, and tossed it into the trash. Given he wouldn't be at bat, he didn't need to worry about water sloshing around his belly as he ran bases. Not like the rest of us.

A wide grin split his face as he looked back at Tanner. "It fucking is. Isn't it?"

"Is Payton here?"

"Yeah, she's up with the girls." He thumbed in the general direction of the stands behind us, though really, he was aiming for the owners' box.

Payton Lopez, Ace's girlfriend, happened to be best friends with Penn Shepherd's wife, and therefore whenever Payton came to games, she mostly watched up there.

She said it was because she didn't like being surrounded by hundreds of girls all wearing Ace Watson shirts and screaming about how hot he was. But she'd also admitted it was because she didn't like standing in line for drinks.

"Where's Weston?" Tanner asked.

I nodded to the end of the dugout where Lux was talking to his coach, head bent down in concentration at whatever he was being told. Tanner didn't seem to care, however, and if the umpire hadn't burst my ear drum with his call, Tanner's voice nearly did.

"Weston!"

"Tan, what the fuck?" I grunted, attempting to stop the ringing in my ear as Lux, along with everyone else in the dugout, including all the coaches, turned their attention to Tanner waving emphatically.

Tanner was just about to start shouting again when Lux made his way over, likely at the urging of Coach to get Tanner to stop making so much noise.

"You best not be calling because you wanted snacks," snapped Lux as he got closer and positioned himself against the boards.

"I wasn't, though it wouldn't have hurt you to pick up some protein bars on your way over here."

Lux rolled his eyes. "What is it then?"

"I was just wondering where Radley's sitting."

Ace barked out a laugh. "Seriously. Tan, come on."

"What?" he replied, his tone verging on huffy. "You know where Payton is. Parker knows where Scout is. I just want to know where Millie is. They weren't here for warm-ups."

Lux dropped his head with a shake, though it was only to hide a grin.

"I don't, actually," I offered up.

Tanner turned to me. "What?"

"I don't know where Scout is. I haven't seen her since this morning after Rangers douche stormed away."

Tanner's eyes bulged in response. "Shit. That's who that guy was? I should have knocked him out when he barged me. What was he doing here?"

I shrugged. "To talk to Scout, I guess. Not that he got a chance."

What an absolute tool that guy had been. Still was. Always would be, most likely. I'd been thinking about it all day and couldn't figure out how Scout—sweet, lovely Scout—had wasted so long with him. Or what she'd seen in him in the first place.

He wasn't even good looking. Close up, I could only describe his face as punchable.

Ace pulled a protein bar from his pocket and unwrapped it. "Yeah, I'd say you were rocking that protective vibe this morning. Did Scout finally see you as boyfriend material and agree to a date?"

I shook my head. "Not yet."

He reached over and patted my knee. "She will, don't worry. Did you get her number yet?"

"Nope."

"Well, that needs to be the next plan in Operation Strike Zone."

"Only if we stop calling it that."

Tanner turned to me. "What's wrong with Operation Strike Zone?"

"What's right with it? It sounds so dumb."

"It's cool. Like we're in the CIA or something."

"But we're not in the CIA. We play baseball."

Tanner shrugged like he didn't see the difference and stood up. "Well, I think it's cool. And you know my motto..."

He reached over my head to the shelves of helmets and grabbed his. Without saying another word, he turned around, jogged to the end of the dugout, removed his bat from the bin, and vaulted the boards on the way to the bullpen.

Lux had long since lost interest in the conversation and was now looking out to the field where the Marlins were getting into position on the field. I turned to Ace, wearing an expression of amusement identical to his.

"What is his motto?"

"Beats me," he replied, nodding to the field. "Reeves is up."

Nudging Lux with the tip of my shoe and gesturing him to move out of the way from the boards he was still leaning over—the guy made a better door than a window—I watched the field. The Marlins were all in place, preparing themselves for the force of Jupiter's hit. He hadn't made a home run yet, but the last two innings he'd got around to third base before the ball stopped him.

Jupiter up at bat was always a sight to see. I remembered being a kid and obsessively watching Dodgers games just to catch a glimpse of the great Jupiter Reeves.

Watching him was like watching art come to life.

The calculated positioning of his body, the roll of his neck, the subtle way he shifted his weight from right to left. It was the same every single time, and no matter how much people tried to copy it, they never came away with the same result.

"Fuuuck," hissed Ace while Lux let out a low whistle, though it was virtually impossible to hear over the roar of the crowd. "That's gotta be three hundred and fifty feet."

And just like that we were up another run.

As he took off, Jupiter tossed his bat high into the air, and it landed back on the ground with a thud. It had been known to snap in half before, but from what I could see this time it stayed intact.

His run around the bases was slow and deliberate as he soaked in the deafening cheers from fans. And not just Lions fans, everyone. Jupiter Reeves might be a Lion, but there wasn't a single person watching who couldn't appreciate what they'd just witnessed, because he'd long ago cemented himself as one of the greatest players of all time.

"Hello, ladies," he said, stepping into the dugout wearing a massive grin, and marched down to the end of the row, high-fiving everyone he passed.

He might be the GOAT, but he was also a massive dick when he wanted to be.

"Fucking Reeves," muttered Ace, because that's all there was to say, and just like we all did, he flip-flopped between hero-worshipping the guy and wanting to punch him.

"Tan's at bat," announced Lux, sitting in the spot Tanner had vacated.

"SMASH IT, SIMPSON," yelled Ace.

The three of us sat in silence as Tanner readied himself for the ball. Even though he acted a clown 99 percent of the time, the second Tanner stepped onto the field, his entire demeanor changed to one of serious concentration. You could see it from the way he spun his bat in the palm of his hand

and got into position; there was an intensity in his expression you never saw him wearing at any other time.

"That'll get him to second," said Lux as Tanner grounded the ball to the outfield, the Marlins shortstop narrowly missing it rolling past his leg.

"He might get to third if he sprints," I replied, eyes narrowed on Tanner powering onto second base, where he stopped.

"Next time." Ace chuckled.

It was as Boomer Jones stepped up to the plate that I felt the presence of someone sliding along the benches next to me.

"How's it going with the social chick?" asked Jupiter, taking a long swig of the Gatorade he'd picked up when we first came off the field.

I side-eyed him. "Fine."

"Got her number yet?"

I shook my head, answering the question for the second time in ten minutes. "Nope."

"Hmm—" He reached into his pocket and pulled out a folded, crumpled piece of paper, which he held between his fingers. "It's your lucky day then, isn't it?"

"What's that?" I asked, one eye still on Boomer, who'd managed to get to first base, while Tanner moved to third.

"A cell number," he replied, snatching his hand away when I tried to take it.

Dick.

"Reeves, I'm not in the mood, and I don't want a random cell number."

"It's not random. It's Scout's."

Turning my entire body toward him, I tried to pin him with one of the menacing scowls he used on us most of the time. But it wasn't anywhere near as effective. Maybe you needed to be nearing forty in order to accomplish that, or however old he was. Retirement was calling, that was for sure.

"You're telling me on that piece of paper in your hand is Scout Davison's cell phone number?"

"Yup."

I took a deep breath, willing my racing heart to calm so I could at the very least give the impression of being cool. "What's the catch?"

"No catch."

"Then why?"

"Because you're a good catcher, you're good for this club, and you're going to go far in baseball."

My brows dropped so quickly a bolt of pain shot me right between the eyes. I rubbed against my forehead. "Seriously, what are you doing, Reeves?"

"Marnie told me about the VO2 max test and how you nearly killed yourself to impress this girl. We kind of need you on the team, so I'm helping you out."

"By giving me her number?"

"Exactly." He held the paper out to me again, this time allowing me to take it.

I still wasn't 100 percent certain that I'd open it to find a cell number, but sure enough scrawled inside were ten digits, with Scout's name above them. And this crumpled-up piece of paper became the most precious thing I owned.

"Thanks, man, I really appreciate it," I said as he stood up to leave. "I apologize for calling you a massive dick."

"You didn't call me a massive dick."

My gaze flicked to his, though it didn't quite meet his eye, instead offering a wry smile. "Oh, didn't I?"

He walked off with a head shake, mumbling something I didn't catch.

I glanced back down at the number—Scout's number—before folding it up and slipping it carefully into my pocket for safekeeping.

For the rest of the game, we were untouchable. I was untouchable. Ace and I took the Marlins out fastball after fastball. I hit two home runs. The final score was Lions: 8, Marlins: 2.

Once the final play was done, I sprinted off the field before anyone could catch me, heading straight to the locker room. Ignoring coach, ignoring reporters waiting for a quote, ignoring everything. They could all wait until I'd completed this one task.

Yanking my locker open so hard I nearly pulled it from its

hinges, I grabbed my phone.

Parker: Hey, Davison, how about we try for coffee again in the morning? No douches invited. Same time, same place?

16

Scout

Parker: Get ready for the hella sexy game day fit I'm rocking.

Scout: I'll be the judge of that.

Parker: I'm counting on it…

I bit down the smile and focused back on the task at hand. Namely repeating myself to Joey and Cyrus about what we were doing right now, but given it was eleven p.m. and probably way past their bedtime, it wasn't sinking in quite as quickly as I hoped.

"The guys come out of those doors." I pointed to the entranceway leading into the loading bay under Lions Stadium, where three large buses were waiting to take the guys off to the airport. Tonight they were flying out of New York and down to Dallas for an away series against the Texas Rangers. "They have to come down the ramp, then they walk around the front of the bus."

"Where'd you want the cameras set up?"

"One straight on, and one at forty-five degrees coming down the ramp." I turned to Cyrus who was still looking kind of confused. I was putting it down to the fact it was way past his bedtime. "Fans like the action shots. Plus, some of the guys jog down the ramp, and the girls go wild for those, especially when we put it in slo-mo."

"How 'bout we each man one. Set them up on a tripod?"

I nodded to Cyrus, holding in a yawn of my own. "Yeah, and I'll stay up at the front to make sure the guys come down with a little separation between them."

"Why are we doing this again? When they're all going to be wearing the same thing," asked Joey for the dozenth time.

"Because it's funny. It's a 'who wore it best,'" I explained, *again.* It was definitely more than a dozen.

"Oh."

"Guys, you can sleep on the plane, so let's keep it together for a little longer. Then you get on the bus with the comms team, and I'll edit this in the morning."

"Okay, sure." Joey nodded, turning to Cyrus. "C'mon, let's get these done. I'll go by the ramp."

The whole time we'd been talking, the doors had slammed back and forth, as everyone readied themselves for the trip. It might be eleven p.m. but it was possibly the busiest time of the day so far.

A little under an hour ago the boys finished playing their home series against the White Sox, which hadn't gone as well as everyone wished it had.

The Lions narrowly lost the final game, and everyone was a little bit quieter because of it, and likely a whole lot pissed. But leaving for another series meant there was no time to dwell on it. At least until they got on the plane and Coach laid into them.

While the boys had come straight off the field and headed to the showers, everyone else jumped into gear. Front office staff, assistant coaches, and PTs were running around making sure everything and everyone was where they were supposed to be.

The travel staff, who had meticulously planned arrangements down to the second, had already left for the plane waiting at Teterboro, overseeing the transportation of equipment, staff and players' luggage, and transport manifest.

That was to say, nothing of the advance teams who prepped the hotels the boys would be staying in, including the swapping out of custom mattresses for each of the starting nine to be set up in the hotels for when the guys arrived. Penn Shepherd went to every length and more to make sure his team was well rested before each game, and if that meant they slept on what was as close to their own bed as possible, instead of lumpy hotel bedding, then he would happily foot the bill.

It was all part of his strategy for the Lions to be crowned World Series champions as soon as possible.

"Scout?"

My head flicked back to the doors to find Dave, one of the locker room attendants, standing there.

"You wanted a five-minute warning. This is it."

"Cool, thanks." I waved back at him, then turned to the guys. "Okay, I'm going up there. You all good?"

"We got this," Joey replied, lining up the camera so it was in the exact spot he wanted it, and opened his mouth with another wide yawn.

A couple of the rookies walked out just as I got to the doors, giving me a nod of acknowledgment. Thankfully we hadn't planned anything more elaborate after the loss, because it was always so much harder to get any content. At least tonight all they needed to do was walk onto the buses, which was what they'd be doing anyway.

I smiled back, the mood too somber to attempt any form of conversation. Plus, there was only one guy I really wanted to talk to. I kind of wish he'd hurry up, too, or at least not arrive at the same time as any of the coaches, including Coach Chase. I wasn't certain, but I swear the last few times I'd seen him he'd scowled at me.

Boomer Jones, Stone Fields, Saint Velasquez all passed by, unsmiling, followed by a couple of the base coaches.

"Hey, Scout. Fancy seeing you here. How're you doing?"

I was glad to be leaning against the wall for how suddenly my core clenched at the sound of Parker's deep voice, only for it to double down as the heady, earthy scent of him floated under my nostrils.

"Hey, Parker. I'm good, how are you?" I grinned, while doing my best to ignore the fluttering in my belly.

No, not belly. Lower. Right between my thighs.

"Great now I've laid eyes on you. Did you watch the game?"

"Of course. Sorry you guys lost tonight."

He jerked a shoulder up. "Yeah, sucks because we played well. But what I really want to know is why my home run isn't on social yet."

"You know," I started, crossing my arms over my chest and adding a little foot tap. I had the feeling Parker kind of liked it when I sassed him, and after tonight, I wanted to make him smile. "Other people get home runs as well. It's not all about you."

"Yeah, but when you feature mine, it means I know you've seen it. Makes me feel important."

"Hmm. I'll see what I can do."

"Hey, that's all I'm asking." He rubbed his hands together. "So what have you got us doing tonight?"

"Told you, just game day fit."

He frowned, glancing to a couple of the rookies walking past. "You know we're all wearing the same thing, right?"

"Yeah, it's a 'who wore it best.'"

"Oh really?" He grinned wide. "Then pray tell, how good am I wearing it? C'mon, be honest. I'm the best, right?"

Holding my mouth in a straight line, I leaned back slightly. My eyes dropped and coasted slowly up from his sneakers.

Game day fits were some of our most popular posts.

Last year there'd been roughly a hundred, and we'd done a dozen or so already this year. They always attracted a slew of comments from Lions fans, as well as a barrage from Lions haters, but that's what made it fun.

Some guys, like Lux Weston, clearly spent a lot of time deciding what to wear for each game. They hired stylists, they had their outfits selected weeks ahead of time, they liaised with designers. Others, like Jupiter Reeves, wore the first thing they found in the closet and gave zero fucks what anyone thought, but still looked better than everyone else.

Parker was usually someone who fluctuated on the scale between Lux's enthusiasm and Jupiter's apathy, but he always looked good. Always.

Didn't matter if he was arriving for practice, heading to the gym, or on the field, Parker King was a certified snack, and any of the girls on the fifth floor would agree in a heartbeat.

But this week we'd decided to do something different, inspired by a copy of *Us Weekly* I'd spotted open on a feature with a bunch of celebrities all wearing the same thing. I knew the guys would be flying out late after tonight's game, and they always wore the Lions sweats to fly.

All of them dressed the same.

Not that I could recall every game day fit of Parker's because he mostly liked to wear a suit—a really well-fitted suit—but right now, standing in front of me in the black sweatpants and soft black hoodie, his hair still damp from the shower, cheeks a little pink under the thick stubble, I knew for a fact I'd never seen him looking quite as good as this.

Not even fresh in the mornings.

How was it fair that at nearly midnight, after playing baseball for the last few hours, he looked like this?

"I like it," I replied finally, trying to force myself to swallow before my mouth completely dried up. "Maybe you'll win the award."

Even under the harsh strip lights of the loading bay, his eyes brightened. "There's an award?"

"Yeah."

Parker leaned in slightly, his lips curling with a slow smile, and I was once more intoxicated with the scent of him. "I'm okay with that, if you're picking the winner."

I'd almost gotten used to the way my heart kicked up whenever he was near me, or the way my mouth dried a little as I stared at his lips and I tried not to think of what they would feel like to kiss, like I was doing right now. But it was hard.

Sometimes, when we weren't surrounded by a hundred people all hurrying around us, I drifted off into a fantasy of what else Parker could do with his mouth.

What his tongue was capable of, what *he* was capable of.

My dreams were still being haunted by visions of his rock-hard body, powering on the treadmill as he dripped in sweat, until I bolted awake drenched through with a weird electricity buzzing across the surface of my skin.

It was a wonder I was getting any sleep at all.

The good-night messages didn't help, either, though I had a feeling he knew exactly what he was doing. Sending me a message every night ensured he was the last person I thought of before I closed my eyes.

He might be the reason I'd been getting no sleep this week, but he was also the reason I'd ended each day with a smile on my face, the reason I jumped out of bed to meet him for our morning coffee, and the reason I carefully selected each item of clothing I wore.

It was nearly the middle of May, the regular season was barely six weeks old, yet all plans I'd had to concentrate on my career and stay single were hanging on by a thread. I couldn't even tell you how he'd done it, but Parker King had successfully become the best part of my day.

The downside of all this time I'd been spending with Parker was that I'd become so engrossed with him, I forgot where I was.

"Get a room," jeered someone passing, who sounded a lot like Ace, especially when Parker jerked forward from a slap on the shoulder, though it was hard to tell when I only caught the back of the perpetrator's head, hoodie pulled up and looking exactly like everyone else.

My cheeks burned red, something Parker noticed. He immediately stepped back.

"I'll leave you to work." Hitching his bag up, he held my gaze for a second. "See you on the plane."

I shook my head, and my eyes fell away. I couldn't look at him. "I'm not coming."

"What?" he barked out, frowning deeply at me. "Seriously? You didn't come last time."

"I have a lot of work to do, the job application needs to be submitted next week and I haven't started it yet."

"Oh." He tried to hide his disappointment, but his face dropped before he could stop it. I fared no better. Worse, even. Because from the way my belly was swirling, there was no denying it anymore. I liked Parker King. Like, a lot. "In that case, staying behind is a good idea. You're going to nail that job, Davison. I can feel it."

"You'll be back before you know it," I replied quietly.

"I guess I'll have to miss you instead." He leaned in. "And you know what they say?"

I shook my head, my breath catching in my throat. "No, what?"

"Absence makes the heart grow fonder." He winked.

It wasn't until he boarded the bus that I could finally breathe again.

17

Parker

Parker: Texas coffee sucks

Scout: I'm from Texas

Parker: That explains it then

Scout: Have you ever been to White Plains?

Parker: For the Jungle Kings?

Scout: Yeah, what's it like?

Parker: They're a lot of fun. Tanner played there before he moved up to the big leagues. Why?

Scout: Working on my presentation, just trying to come up with some ideas

Parker: My brain is for hire if you want to borrow it

Scout: Thanks

Parker: And any other part of my body you might need too

Scout: *eye roll emoji*

Parker: How's New York? Miss me yet?

Scout: Quiet. And no.

Parker: Never counted you as a big fat liar, Davison

Scout: Awesome home run

Parker: Just giving you the content everyone wants. My lack of presence on TikTok recently has been noticed

Scout: Oh really?

Parker: Yup

Scout: How about I set up something real special, just for you

Parker: I'm listening

Scout: *eye roll emoji*

Scout: I'm sorry about tonight, there's no way that ball was caught before you reached base

Parker: Yeah, Coach complained but it won't be overturned. Only positive is we're heading home. Are you ready for our big reunion?

Scout: Our what?

Parker: Our reunion. Tomorrow. Our spot, same time as usual

Scout: I'll be there

Parker: Can't wait

Scout: Me too

"Where are you?"

"Waiting for you," I replied, scanning through the dozens of people wandering along the boardwalk running around Lions Stadium.

I just couldn't see the one person I wanted to.

"At the coffee shop?" Scout asked.

I knew she was close because I could hear the music playing inside the shop, both through the phone and because I was standing outside.

"Obviously."

"I don't see you."

I spun around, searching again until I finally spotted her walking next to a behemoth of a man wearing a Velasquez jersey.

Her eyes darted left and right, with two identical creases forming between her brows while she tried to find me. Before I could stop it, my face split with the biggest grin as my chest thudded erratically, as though it had been months and not the six days that had passed since I'd left her standing in the loading bay.

But the difference between this away series and every other one where she'd been left behind was that I returned home to New York knowing—okay, 95 percent certain, because she never actually admitted it—that Scout had missed me. And it was all down to Jupiter Reeves.

I'd never been much of a texter, definitely never spent hours sending messages back and forth until my thumbs got sore, but in the last week nearly every spare minute I had was spent messaging Scout.

Countless times over the last week I'd taken back every bad word I'd ever said about Jupiter, and I did it again.

I'm sure I'd pay for it at some point, and when that time came, I'd happily hand over my Amex.

I'd never thought of my cell phone being a beautiful thing before, and yet it had become my most prized possession. Since last Tuesday I'd flown across two time zones, a dozen states and played six games while learning as much as I could about this girl currently searching the early game day crowds for me. *Me.*

This girl I'd crushed on for nearly a year was here meeting *me.*

This girl whose favorite color was green. This girl whose roommate traveled so much Scout almost qualified for living alone.

The one who used the same dryer sheets her mom did because they reminded her of home, and I held back from telling her that the fresh, cottony scent permeating the air whenever she was within a couple of feet would always and forever make me think of her.

Scout's favorite holiday was July 4, her birthday was in October, and the last vacation she took had been to Mexico with Alice, her friend at work—the girl I'd met the day Rangers Douche turned up.

I'd learned her dad was pretty high up in the Army, and while her family home was now in Virginia, she'd grown up in Germany where her brother was still out there serving in the Air Force. But her heart belonged to Texas, because that's where both her parents were from. Even though the coffee sucked.

My cheeks were beginning to ache from how much I was enjoying watching her try to find me. I'd stay here all day, but the pull of being face to face was too strong.

I stepped forward a little. "I'm behind the middle pillar down the side."

"What are you doing standing there?" she asked, her eyes scouring the space until they locked on mine.

"Because I didn't want anyone else to spot me after I ordered your revolting coffee, it's too embarrassing."

Her perfectly arched brows shot up. "I thought you said Lions pride themselves on being embarrassed."

"We have to draw a line someplace, this is my line." I grinned as she stopped in front of me, arms crossed over her chest.

My grin widened as her foot tapped a little annoyed beat. Man, *this girl.* If my hands weren't full, I'd wrap my arms around her, pick her up, and swing her around. Instead, I stood there, taking a second to soak her in while her brows knitted even further, her lips pursed a little tighter.

I'd never been so desperate to kiss someone in my entire life.

I'd even settle for brushing against one of her perfectly rounded cheeks. But while I was certain she'd missed me, I was also certain we weren't at the greetings-kiss stage, and I knew without doubt that the first time I kissed her wasn't going to be surrounded by a bunch of Lions fans, plus all the people who'd escaped their offices for a morning coffee.

But she sure was cute when she was annoyed. If possible, it made her eyes seem even bluer, matching the color of this morning's cloudless sky.

"Hi."

I clicked my headphones off, ending our call. "Hey there."

Her gaze flicked to my hands, and back, frown still very much present. "What's that?"

I held one of the coffees out to her. "Your coffee."

"What's it in?"

I glanced down at the cup, mashing my lips together as hard as possible to stop the grin becoming crazed.

"A travel cup I thought you might like. A gift." I pushed it out to her again. "And I put your coffee in it."

She peered around my hands at the reusable coffee cup I'd picked up on the way here.

If I hadn't gotten it for free, it would have been the best fifteen dollars I'd ever spent. In my rush to see Scout, I'd arrived early, happened to spot the Lions store staff prepping for the day's opening, and my eyes landed on this beauty in the window.

I hadn't even known they'd existed. But now I did, I'd be buying them as gifts for all my coffee-loving friends.

"It's your jersey…"

"Yes." I grinned, turning the cup around. "And my number. We can work up to the stage where you're wearing my actual jersey to games, but this is good enough for now."

She took it from me, our fingertips brushing enough that we both felt the shock between us. Not shock. *Spark.*

Yeah, we had a fucking spark all right.

"You know," she started, before clearing her throat, "some would interpret this as saying you think my coffee is so good it deserves its own special cup."

"Uh-uh. Nope." I shook my head. "That's not what this was. I told you, this is purely about you forming a relationship with my shirt. It's a gateway to wearing it."

"Hmm." Her shoulders lifted in some kind of half-assed shrug. "Well, I see it differently. I think you love my delicious coffee." She giggled through a sip. "Mmm, delicious."

"I don't. This"—I tapped on the cup—"is a favor. I'm

raising your cool points because it tells everyone you're clearly a Parker King fan, while also making drinking the coffee less embarrassing for you."

"I'm not embarrassed."

I leaned in closer. "You should be."

Her eyes never left mine as she took a long, slow sip.

I was almost disappointed that a tiny foam mustache wasn't left behind on her top lip, because it meant I couldn't wipe it off. But I'd settle for the coffee-drinking standoff we were having, waiting to see who'd crack first, though I knew it wouldn't be me.

I'd stay here all day if it meant I got to stare at her; count the smattering of tiny freckles across her forehead, which had developed in the week I'd been gone, or study the way the blue of her iris darkened the closer it got to the edge.

I'd stare at her all day and never get bored.

Unfortunately all good things must come to an end. Our end was brought on by someone shoving a phone in my face.

"Excuse me, are you Parker King? Can I get a photo?"

I turned to my left, to find a shortish girl wearing a pair of cutoffs, and a shirt with my name on it. Exactly like the cup.

Glancing over to Scout, I couldn't tell if she'd noticed the number, but the two frown lines had made a reappearance, and for some reason, seeing them again almost made me as happy as I'd felt when I'd spotted her walking over to me.

"I like your shirt." I grinned to the girl, wider when it was clear Scout was doing her very best to look unbothered by our interruption, but I'd spent enough time with her to know when she was annoyed.

The tiny vein in her temple protruded that little bit further and her lips rolled in on themselves right before she sucked in her cheek.

Oh man, was she annoyed.

Any second and she'd start studying her fingernails.

"Thanks," the girl replied, peering up at me through thick, clumpy black lashes, "you're my favorite. All our favorites." She pointed over to a group of girls standing by the hoardings. "But I got to come and ask for a photo. And maybe a signature." The eyelashes batted hard as the girl pulled a Sharpie from her pocket.

"Of course. Hey, Davison, you see this shirt, with my number. Cool, huh. Matches your cup."

"I see it."

The curtness of her reply only had my grin widening while I scrawled my name across this girl's back.

"You wanna get in this picture with that matching cup of yours?"

Scout shook her head. "No, I think you can handle this on your own."

"Okay." I shrugged, taking the girl's phone, ready to snap some selfies.

Given how disinterested Scout seemed to be, it was

unsurprising this girl had incorrectly figured there was nothing going on between us, and wrapped her arms around my waist.

It didn't occur to her that Scout would care she was pawing her boyfriend. Or that I *was* her boyfriend.

An exasperated huff had my eyes flicking back to Scout, and the vein was now really popping. I could be mistaken, but I know I wasn't.

Scout Davison was *jealous.*

My heart made a little happy skip.

Halle-fuckin-lujah.

"Okay, that's enough," I announced after ten seconds of this girl's fingers digging into my side.

"Good luck tonight," she replied, staring up at me.

"Thank you. Hope you're coming with that shirt on."

"Yeah, of course." Her teeth sunk into her lip as she answered. "Actually, there's a bunch of us going to Rocket Bar after the game if you want to come and join us."

"Thanks for the invite, but I don't party during the season."

"Well, if you change your mind, we won't tell anyone." She winked with a giggle, taking a step backward, followed by another. She held on as long as possible before turning around and heading back to her friends.

Scout was finishing off her coffee as my attention focused once more on her, not that it ever really left. "Sorry about that."

"Hey, who am I to stop the fans of Parker King when he's out and about in public drinking his morning coffee." She smiled, and 90 percent of her annoyance vanished. "He's a fan favorite."

Dipping my shoulder, I nudged it gently into hers. "As long as I'm your favorite, I don't care."

She peered up at me, teeth caught in her bottom lip, like she was on the verge of saying something. I waited for it to come, but after a second, she turned away. "I need to get back. Are you coming?"

"Sure thing, Davison. Lead the way," I replied, falling into step next to her. It could be wishful thinking, but it sure felt like there'd been a shift between us. I'd put it down to our constant texting, which meant we weren't starting from scratch again, like every other time I'd returned. But right now, I wanted to ask what she was thinking about silently walking at my side, but I went with the answer I wanted more urgently. "So, did you miss me?"

She shrugged, bringing the cup to her lips again, even though it was empty. "Maybe."

"Then *maybe* come with us next trip."

"*Maybe* I will."

"Great, I'll make sure I have a shirt with my name on it delivered to your desk."

The eye roll she gave me warmed my heart for the rest of the day, and I almost credited it for the two home runs I hit in the postgame press conference later that evening.

18

Scout

"What's that."

My eyes flicked to the coffee cup Parker had given me and back to the screen where I was trying to concentrate. "A coffee cup."

"Where did it come from?"

"It was a present."

"From whom?"

I sighed deeply, enough to let Alice know I wasn't in the mood for her games this morning, at least until this new job presentation had been sent off. Why they wanted it before the interview was above my pay grade.

"Can you let me finish this and then I'll answer all your questions." I glanced back at the screen. "Do you think I should add a final slide? Like, 'the end'?"

"No." She pushed off my desk and turned to the window where a bunch of the rookies were in the bullpen. I knew it was the rookies, because Parker had been there earlier and was now in the gym.

And how did I know that? Because he told me. Every time he was at practice he'd message me to say he was outside my window, like we were teenagers in an '80s rom-com. But did I look? Of course I did.

He was taking up so much of my days that I honestly couldn't remember what it had been like last season when I wasn't so aware of every movement he made. Or every place he was. Even if he didn't tell me, I'd look out for him.

"Hey, Scout?"

I held a finger in the air. "One minute."

"Scout…Scout?"

"Jeez. Give me a minute," I snapped, cursing myself for not charging my headphones so I could legitimately ignore everything around me.

Sticking my fingers in my ears, I read over the final page one last time and pressed Save. It was good enough, and I'd only drive myself crazy if I kept reading. Before I could make any more changes, I dropped it into an email for HR and pressed Send, praying it was enough before my formal interview next week.

I glanced up to where the voice had come from. "Yeah?"

Joey tapped on his screen. "Can you sign this off before we post it, please?"

Cursing again, this time for not moving my travel bags, which I'd dropped by my feet the second I'd arrived, I stepped over them and walked around his side of the desk.

Peering over his shoulder, he pressed Play on the content they'd filmed earlier this week.

I hadn't seen it in full, I hadn't been there when the guys shot it. It was the segment they'd thought up before the season started—the mom style *what's in your bag*.

We'd been waiting until the team was fresh off a series win, and as luck would have it, the away trip to Dallas, followed by Cincinnati, achieved just that, so the second morning back we set it up outside and let them know.

It was the first segment the guys had managed totally by themselves.

While they'd been on the trips without me, there'd always been someone else to oversee or step in and answer any questions. But the team was now familiar with their faces, and rapport was building. They could do it alone.

"How long is this?"

"Ninety seconds."

First up was Saint Velasquez, the giant right field, sauntering up as only he did, wearing a pair of exceptionally bright flowery board shorts, flip-flops, and a white tee. Give him a surfboard and you'd never know he was one of the best fielders in the league. I liked him a lot, he was always happy and smiley, and when I'd manned the content shoots all last year, he'd helped with every single one.

More unusual than it sounds, because some of the guys just wanted to get into the stadium and walked straight past with only a nod hello.

I watched as he stopped at the table, opened his bag, and pulled out a massive bunch of bananas, a bag of sunflower seeds, a protein shake, and a toiletry bag filled with more products than I'd seen in Sephora.

"Wow." I chuckled.

Boomer Jones followed with nothing more interesting than a towel and a PlayStation remote.

Jupiter Reeves walked straight past without anything in his hands; Sawyer James, our second base, carried a bag of protein powder and a sweater he'd picked up from the dry cleaner on his way in.

The rookies produced better results; on being asked the question, one of them turned bright red and opened his bag to reveal a pair of girl's underwear, which resulted in a lot of jeering from the two guys he'd arrived with.

The moment Parker appeared on the screen, my stomach flipped, and I forced my entire body to still just in case it did something stupid like leap into the air with a loud cheer. Ace was next to him, both of them stopping at the table and dropping their bags onto it with a thud.

Joey turned around and glanced at me. "This is a great one."

In sync, the pair of them opened up their bags, and the camera zoomed in. If I didn't know they worked at Lions Stadium, or played for the club, I could believe they'd committed a store robbery. Ace lifted his out first.

"Did you guys know that the Lions store now has to-go cups for each player? They just came in this week." He beamed into the camera, holding up one of the cups. If he decided to leave baseball he could easily slide into a career on QVC.

I didn't need to see inside Parker's bag to know he was about to show everyone his to-go cup. The exact same one currently sitting on my desk.

"Are there any left in the store?" Cyrus laughed from behind the camera.

"Sure are, but get there early. And I have a dozen to give away on my Instagram, plus enough for all my favorite people to have one. All coffee deserves to have a good cup, even disgusting coffee."

"Oh, Jesus," I mumbled, my eyes rolling to the skies.

"What?" asked Joey.

"Nothing."

After Parker and Ace, came a couple of the coaches and PTs who had nothing interesting, followed by Riley Rivers, Robson Barry, and Lux Weston, none of whom had bags but emptied their pockets to reveal car keys, a phone, an assortment of gum, and headphones.

Last up was Tanner Simpson, who sprinted through the entrance without so much as an acknowledgment.

"Good work, it's a bit long though, so trim it to sixty seconds. Keep Tanner Simpson but cut the first two rookies and Sawyer James. You need to cut those panties."

I should have predicted the objection.

"No way. People will love them."

"We can't have panties on the Lions channel."

Joey thought for a second, and spun around to face me. "What if I block them out with an emoji, or something. Everyone sees his reaction and how embarrassed he is, plus the guys laughing. It'll make for good comments."

"Sure, okay. But can you cut Parker King out and just leave Ace Watson?"

"You wanna cut Parker King?"

"Yes. We feature him too much, we don't need that bit about his giveaway. What?" I asked as Joey continued staring at me.

"Nothing." He shrugged, his eyes snapping back to the screen. "They're funny together, people like it."

Annoyance bubbled under my skin. It didn't help that Joey was right, people did like Parker and Ace, they always had ever since they started playing together. The two of them were a double act that had captured the hearts of all Lions fans.

"Okay, but lose the bit about the giveaway. We don't need it."

"Don't need what?" asked Alice, who'd clearly grown impatient with staring out the window.

"Parker King and his coffee cup."

I almost knew it was going to happen before it did, all in slow motion as Alice lifted the cup from my desk.

"Like this one, you mean."

"Hey, yeah! That's so cool. I want one." Joey grinned as I snarled at Alice as best I could without making it too obvious she'd earned herself a space at the top of my shit list.

But she had, though given the smirk she was now sporting, I'd say she didn't care.

"Okay, you're good with the edits?" I asked Joey, who nodded. "Great, it can be scheduled once you're done. Thanks."

Heading back to my chair, I stepped over my travel bag and sat down.

"Where did this come from again?" Alice asked, pointing to the cup.

"I told you."

"You didn't actually." She leaned back in the chair next to mine, propping her feet on the desk as she always did.

And just like I always did, I knocked them off.

I pinned her with my sternest glare, though it was just as ineffective as my snarl. "You know where it came from."

"I want to hear you say it."

"Say what?"

She leaned in, her voice dropping to a whisper. "That you've got a crush."

I rolled my eyes again.

"Say it."

I tried to buy some time before I responded, giving her a shrug instead. But she sat there and stared until I swore if I glanced down there'd be a giant hole in my chest where her eyes had bored through me.

It was pointless denying it. I couldn't any longer. Not after two weeks of messaging or the morning coffees, or the cup Alice was turning around in her hands, or the Twizzlers, or the rescuing me from Mark, or his all-around sweetness.

It was all pointless.

"Fine," I whispered back, so quietly I was almost mouthing the words. "I have a crush on Parker King."

I expected her to jump up with a loud whoop, but instead, she leaned in further.

"And you're more than friends?"

"No. We're friends."

"Who…"

I waited to see if she'd finish the rest of her sentence. "Who what?"

Her head quirked. "Nothing else has happened?"

I shook my head. "Like what?"

"All this time you've been spending together and you

haven't been making out in the janitor's closet or screwing in the locker room after dark?"

"No…Alice, jeez," I hissed, "where are you getting all this from?"

She let out a disappointed huff. "My active imagination, I just figured something was going on and you'd tell me when the time was right, especially after that thing with the shithead. But it's been a couple weeks, and I was getting impatient."

"Please take my sex life out of your imagination. Nothing's happening."

"No." She shook her head. "Not nothing. You guys are flirting."

I gave one long, deep nod, because she'd got me there. Parker and I definitely flirted. We flirted in person. Over messages. Every time I closed my eyes and saw him, we were flirting. And what's more, I liked it. I liked his stupid jokes, I liked that he tried to make me laugh with them, and I liked his teasing.

As stupid as it sounded, it made me feel…good. Special. That I was important to him.

"Yeah, we flirt."

"Well, you know what happens next."

I shook my head, confused. "No, what?"

I wasn't sure if she paused for dramatic effect or if she was really considering her answer, but then she threw her head back with a loud cackle.

"You become friends who fuck."

My own head snapped around, checking to see that absolutely no one in the vicinity or neighboring desks heard her. "Alice! Don't say '*fuck*' so loudly. And that absolutely isn't what happens next. Jeez."

"Mark my words," she said, jabbing the air with her finger, "it's going to happen. So you better be ready."

"Ugh, shut up."

Pushing out of the chair, she rubbed her hands together in glee. "Ooh, I can't wait for you to tell me how right I am."

"I'm not going to," I snapped back.

"We'll see. Hey, you wanna go out after the game tonight?"

I shook my head, purposely focusing on my screen, or anything other than Alice. "I can't, I'm heading to L.A."

She dropped down in her chair again, gripping onto the armrests of mine and spinning me until I faced her.

"I didn't know you were scheduled for this away stretch. Haven't you been on three of the four last away series?"

"No, I haven't been away for the last two. I went to the plane for game day fit. But I wasn't on the plane, which you know. And for this one, Dave took vacation, so I volunteered."

"How convenient." She smirked. "Looks like I'm going to be correct much quicker than I thought."

I rolled the chair out of her grip and pursed my lips.

"You've not been on any away trips, so you don't know but there's actually very little free time."

"I don't think that'll stop lover boy."

I opened my mouth to respond, only to close it again. I had no response.

It wasn't because I thought something was going to happen with Parker, I didn't. Not yet. But it would be a lie if I said I hadn't volunteered because it meant I could spend a little more time with him, do a little more flirting.

Even though we'd both be super busy working, I kind of wanted to stay in the same state and time zone as him for a while longer.

"I'll take that silence as confirmation." She chuckled. "Come on, let's go and get lunch, I'm hungry."

"I need to pee first." I jumped up, suddenly desperate.

I rushed into the first stall open. I hadn't noticed the other stalls, or whether anyone was standing at the sinks, but by the time I'd finished peeing, there was a conversation happening. Once the faucets and hand dryers stopped running, I realized the conversation was about me. Not just me, me and Parker.

"Do you think they're hooking up?"

"Who?"

"Parker King and Scout Davison. I saw them again yesterday, they're always together."

If there's a less dignified place to freeze, sitting on the toilet with your butt hanging out, I'd like to hear it, because that's exactly what I did. I barely took a breath as these two girls discussed my dating life like it was daily news. I didn't even dare shift to peer through the gap so I could see who it was, because I didn't recognize their voices.

I should've known something like this would happen, it had only been a matter of time.

I hadn't noticed it at first, but the more Parker and I were together, the faster we became friends. Little things I'd previously brushed off—the odd look here, the whispered conversation there—were becoming more obvious, and more frequent.

This place ran on gossip, the more scandalous, the better. And clearly, the more *elaborate,* the better, because Parker and I were *not* always together, I knew that. We met for morning coffee then went our separate ways until the following day when we'd meet again. And that was it.

Not to mention, our morning coffees were a new development.

"I dunno, I heard he asked her on a date and she said no."

"There's no way that's true. Who'd say no to Parker King, that boy is H-O-T."

"True. Do you think she signed that form? Maybe it's legit."

"God, she's so lucky. First Leanne, now Scout. Who else is single on the team this year?"

"Stone Fields, Tanner Simpson…"

"Nope, playboy. Not interested."

"They're all playboys."

"Hmm. What about Sawyer James? He's hot."

"Hate to break it to you, ladies, but Sawyer James has a girlfriend," shouted Alice right before she flushed the toilet.

The next thing I heard was a muffled giggle, followed by a shuffle of heels on the tiled floor and the sound of the door opening and closing.

"You can come out now," called Alice, turning on the faucet. "Rookie mistake not checking the stalls for feet. Ten bucks it was the interns in PR."

I pulled up my jeans, flushed, and opened the door to find her standing there, leaning against the sink with her arms crossed and a grin spreading from ear to ear.

I held my hand up before she started talking. "Don't."

"Hey, you know you've made it here if people are gossiping about you. And you wanna know what I think…"

I raised an eyebrow, holding my hand under the soap dispenser. "I'm not sure why you're pretending I have a choice."

"Exactly. I think if people are gossiping, you may as well enjoy it by making it true."

I couldn't decide if it was better or worse that she had a point.

19

Parker

"Oh man, I am beat," announced Tanner, dropping his bag on the floor as the elevator doors closed behind us.

Lux hit the button for our floor. "Didn't you sleep on the plane? You were snoring like you did."

"I don't snore."

"Dude, you snore." Ace scoffed. "Snoring like a little baby."

"No, I don't."

"You're gonna need to get it under control if you want to hook up with Millie. She won't put up with sleeping next to a jackhammer."

Tanner lifted his head from where it was resting on the elevator wall and frowned at Ace. "I don't want to hook up with her. I want to be her boyfriend."

"Saying it as it is. I like it, Tan."

Tanner yawned wide and shrugged. "No point pussying around it. I do. You should take my advice."

The best I could do was nod in agreement.

I didn't bother to point out he hadn't given any advice because I was currently lacking the energy and mental capacity to add to this conversation.

It was somewhere around three a.m. Eastern, but we were on the West Coast where we'd be enjoying the California sunshine for the next few days, before flying home via Chicago. I normally didn't mind the travel, I could sleep anywhere, but this journey was particularly brutal. At least we could sleep until lunchtime tomorrow before we had to be over at Dodger Stadium.

The only plus side of it was the efficiency of the Lions travel department, which meant we were off our plane and onto the buses waiting for us within five minutes of touchdown, forty-five minutes after that and we arrived at our hotel for the next three nights.

Or would have been if we hadn't got stuck in traffic.

"Was Scout on the plane?"

I opened one eye and nodded at Ace. "Yeah, she was up at the front."

He waggled his brows in response, which I ignored, and went back to leaning against the wall with my eyes closed.

She'd been one of the last to get on the plane, and so I hadn't had a chance to talk to her. Once we'd been wheels up, the air stewards came around with our usual postgame snacks, then it was lights out for everyone to get as much rest as we could. She'd gone onto a different bus, and I hadn't seen her since.

Man, this elevator was taking forever.

"What room are you?"

"Sixty-two fifty."

"I'm sixty-two forty-five. I asked to have joining rooms again so we can set the PlayStation up."

"Not tonight, we're going to bed."

"In the morning."

"Those numbers don't sound like you're joining," muttered Lux, who also seemed to be giving in to the tiredness.

"If they're not, I'm having another word with the travel team." Tanner huffed.

I was saved from having to answer by the bell dinging to announce our floor. "Fucking finally."

Checking the signs outside the elevator for which direction we needed to head, I took off to the left without bothering to look back.

"Night, dudes. See you *mañana*."

I could hear Tanner mumbling about joining rooms as he turned right and walked away.

It was impossible to stifle my yawn as I passed each door, checking the numbers until I found mine. I was so focused on getting in and collapsing on my bed, that I didn't immediately notice a small, person-sized lump slumped on the floor at the end of the corridor. But as I got closer, it became very clear that there was indeed a person sitting on the floor, knees pulled into her chest.

One more step and I realized that this person was *my* person.

Tiredness whooshed so quickly from my body that I almost saw it flying back the way I'd come, while a million questions whirled around in my brain—mostly, was I really this lucky that Scout was waiting for me? Because if so, screw sleep.

Although it looked like she *was* asleep.

"Scout?"

Blue eyes flew open to meet mine, and she let out a yawn wide enough I had to stifle my own. "Parker?"

I stopped in front of her, holding my hand out for her to stand up. "What are you doing here?"

"I'm waiting for housekeeping. What are you doing here?"

Glancing at the door she'd been sitting against, I spotted the numbers 6248. "This is your room?"

She nodded. "Yeah."

I spun to the door behind us. Sixty-two forty-nine.

Holy shit.

This was *way* better than being next to Tanner. If he'd been in this room, I'd currently be having a conversation about what time we'd kick up the PlayStation. Or at the very least, ignoring him while he talked about PlayStation.

The Lions travel gods must have been shining on me.

I glanced once more at my key card just to double-check I wasn't imagining things. Nope. I was correct. For the next three nights, Scout and I had adjoining rooms.

"I'm next door to you." I grinned. "But what are you doing out here? Doesn't your key work?"

She nodded, her shoulder dropping with a loud sigh. Not exactly the response I was expecting after delivering the best news ever. "Yeah, it works."

"Then why are you sitting outside?"

"There's a bird in there."

"A what?"

"A bird. Or was, I dunno now."

"There's a bird in your room?"

She nodded and rubbed her eyes. "Yup."

My focus flicked to the door and back to her. "I know it's three a.m., but could you rewind a little?"

"When I got to my room, someone…housekeeping…I dunno, had left the balcony door open. And there was a bird sitting on the bed. A massive bird."

"A bird?" I repeated.

"Yes, a seagull or something. Anyway, it's massive and crapped everywhere. I walked in, it started flapping, I screamed and ran out. And now I'm here."

My body might have woken the second I'd spotted Scout sitting on the floor, but my brain was still struggling to catch up.

"Did you say housekeeping was coming?"

She nodded. "Yeah, but that was…" She glanced at her phone. "Twenty minutes ago."

"Did you go back in?"

"No way. I called them from my cell, and I called the travel team, but no one's answered. I guess everyone is asleep."

Taking a deep breath, I held my hand out before I could decide whether what I was about to do was really fucking dumb, or the best idea I'd ever had.

"This is my key, I'm next door. Go and take your stuff in there and give me your key."

"Parker…" She frowned. "We're not swapping rooms."

I shook my head. "No, but we need to get rid of the bird before we make any decisions, and housekeeping hasn't arrived yet. Give me your key," I repeated.

Placing it in my hand, she swapped them out, though the expression on her face never changed. It still told me she thought I was nuts.

A possibility.

"I'll be a couple of minutes," I told her. "Go on, go next door. If you're going to sit down, at least make it a couch. Leave the latch on for me to get in."

"Okay." She picked up her bag, hoisted it over her shoulder, and trundled a couple of yards down to my room, giving me one final look before entering.

I swiped the key over her lock and carefully pushed open the door. The light was still on from when she'd entered earlier, the drapes at the end of her room flapped from the swirl of air, and there on the bed, where she said it had been, was a very large seagull. Though from a distance it could be mistaken for a small dog.

This is not how I thought my night would go.

The bird stared at me, with its big beak and beady eyes.

From the looks of the half-eaten bowl of fruit on the table, it had clearly been making itself at home, and from all the crap on the floor and desk, he'd been here a while. Though I couldn't understand why he hadn't left already, even if the room was cozier than a Los Angeles rooftop somewhere.

As my eyes scanned around, I spotted the problem. The drapes had blown into the room and were blocking the gap the bird had come in from. All I needed to do was open the door wider and move the drapes.

"Easy, fella, I'm going to help you out..." I inched along the far wall, avoiding the crap on the floor. "Because, you might not know it, but you're helping me out."

He watched as I eased open the window, and pulled the drapes back far enough that I could wedge them behind the chair in the corner to stop them falling back in place.

"There you go." I gestured to him, the first time in my life I'd ever had a conversation with a bird. The bird didn't move. "Okay, suit yourself. But you can't stay here forever, and I'm going to bed."

Passing by the connecting door, I flicked the lock to open, saluted the bird good night, and let myself out the way I came.

I found Scout on the couch, kind of slumped against the cushion, doing her best to stay awake. The noise from me dropping my bag on the floor had her sitting upright.

"Was it still there?"

I nodded with a grin. "Yep. He said thanks for the bed."

"Ugh. I am so tired." She groaned. "Housekeeping didn't arrive?"

I shook my head. "Did you try them again?"

"Yeah, but no one answered."

"I'll call them. But…" I paused, momentarily questioning my sanity. "You can sleep here tonight."

Scout stared at me, I could see every single thought running through her brain, which was *almost* exactly the same thoughts I was having. Except she probably wasn't worrying about how she'd keep her hands to herself while she slept next to me.

Because that's all I could think about. Maybe I could

fashion a straitjacket out of my sweater.

But whatever decision she was battling, tiredness won. "Are you sure? I'll sleep right here. I won't be any bother." She patted a spot on the couch next to her.

I shook my head. "Uh-uh. No. You'll take the bed, my momma would never allow me to sleep on the bed while a girl took the couch. Do you want to go and get ready or whatever you need to do? I'm going to run back down to the front desk."

"Parker, you have a game tomorrow. You need rest," she argued.

"I'm good. I'll be back in fifteen," I blurted, running back out so quickly I forgot to grab the key. But there was no way I was sticking around while she got changed into pajamas or whatever.

And that's when it occurred to me. What did Scout wear to bed? What if it was panties and a tank, or worse…nothing?

Oh fuuuck.

Maybe I should go and sleep with Tanner. His snoring had to be a thousand times better than the torture of sleeping next to Scout in panties.

And then I remembered that *I* usually slept naked and I couldn't exactly do that now. Nor could I even remember if I'd packed anything appropriate for sleeping.

What the fuck had I set myself up for?

I panicked about it all the way down to the lobby. All

through the conversation with the front desk about what a shit show Scout's room had been while they apologized profusely and promised to fix it immediately. Then I panicked all the way back up to the room, where I trudged slowly out of the elevator and down the corridor, trying to prolong the freedom I had before my suffering began for real.

Sleeping next to Scout. Something I'd dreamed about for nearly a year, but not like this. Not with the torture of not being able to touch her.

My bedtime routine included a jerk-off in the shower, but I wouldn't even be able to do that. Not with Scout less than ten feet away.

Stopping outside the room, I gave it another minute to both summon the courage to knock and give her longer to get dressed, or undressed. Whatever.

Fuck my life.

I rapped hard on the door. Scout opened it so quickly I had a feeling she'd been waiting for me.

Immediately I was assaulted with the scent of lavender and fresh cotton, warm and heady, with a hint of toothpaste lingering in the air. It should have been enough to make me fall asleep there and then, except it had the opposite effect.

My body pinged awake as I stepped inside and took her in. Her hair was tied up with one of those bow things girls wore, her face so clean and shiny it almost sparkled. She wasn't in bra and panties, it was worse. I don't know how or why, but it was much, *much* worse.

A full pajama set covered in baseballs.

Baseballs, baseball gloves, baseball bats.

A wet dream come to life.

A freight train couldn't have stopped my mouth falling open.

"I know, it's dumb," she tugged on the hem of her shirt, completely misreading my expression, "but they're my lucky pajamas. I bring them on every away series I come to, and so far they have an eighty-seven percent success rate."

"Are you telling me that eighty-seven percent of the time you've worn those, we've won?"

She nodded. "Yeah, on away series."

"Well...they're definitely not dumb. And maybe you should travel with us more often. In fact, you tell Penn Shepherd that and he'll have us all wearing them." Scout meant to laugh, I'm sure of it, but instead she snorted loudly. Her hands flew up to her mouth as my eyes widened. "Maybe I should go and sleep with Tanner, he might snore, but he definitely doesn't snort."

This time her face fell into her hands. "Oh no, I'm so sorry. I'm really putting you out."

"Davison, enough. You aren't at all. It's only one night, it's no big deal."

She turned around to face the bed, though it was more like the elephant in the room, then back to me. "I don't want you on the couch, it's not fair."

"I'm fine on the co—"

She held her hand up. "Let me finish. I was thinking the bed is so big, that we could just build a line of pillows down the middle then it's like we're in separate beds. My brother and I used to do that when we were kids."

I pointed to the bed. "You want me to sleep in there? With you?"

She must have sensed the nervousness in my voice, or seen it all over my face, because her tone became way more assertive than it had been two minutes ago.

"Yes. We're both adults, right? Nothing's going to happen. And it would make me feel a whole lot less guilty."

"Okay…sure, we can try your pillow line." My eyes flicked to the bathroom, thank fuck it was a proper bathroom with a closing door and not one of those all-access area type ones without walls. "You get it ready, and I'm going to hit the shower, and I'll see you back here in five…no, ten."

I'd probably only need thirty seconds for what I had planned.

"Sure." She smiled, her fresh pink cheeks reflecting the downlights. "I can do that."

I snatched up my overnight bag and marched into the bathroom.

"Which side do you sleep?" she called out as I locked the door, staring at myself in the mirror, still trying to find any clue as to what I thought I was doing but it was nowhere to be found.

"Doesn't matter. Whichever side you don't want."

I didn't bother to add it was unlikely I'd be getting any sleep at all.

Turning the shower on full blast, I stripped off. The baseball gods must have taken pity on me because as I waited for it to reach that scalding temperature I really loved before bed, I rummaged through my travel bag and found some workout shorts and a T-shirt I didn't remember packing.

The second I stepped under the water my dick hardened, a Pavlovian response to a nighttime routine. I reasoned for both our sakes it was better to follow through with jerking off than risk Scout being nudged awake in the night if I rolled too close.

Pillow fort be damned.

As predicted, it took me less than a minute—thanks to the very real fantasy in my bed and one flimsy hotel wall between us—before the force of my orgasm punched me so hard that I needed to prop myself up. Almost immediately, tiredness took over.

I'd been awake for eighteen hours, played an intense game of baseball, flown across three time zones, and tried to extract a Labrador-sized bird from Scout's bed.

I was done.

Scout was scrolling on her phone over the far side of the bed beyond a wall of pillows so high I could barely see her in the dim light. She'd even taken the cushions from the couch.

"Are you okay over there?" I chuckled, setting my phone to charge on my side of the bed.

"Yes, I'm good. Any water left?"

"I left you enough," I replied, sliding between the sheets, and switched off the light only to immediately flick it back on again. "Sorry."

"It's okay, you can turn it off."

There's something about having a conversation in the dark, whispered, reverential almost. Even the most trivial topics become memorable—I knew I'd never forget this, anyway.

"What time do you have to be at practice tomorrow?"

"We report at one p.m. I'll sleep late, what about you?"

"I'm meeting the team at ten thirty."

"Do you need the alarm set?"

"No, I'll wake up. I'll move back next door so I don't wake you, the cleaning crew came in. The bird is gone."

"That's good." I chuckled, staring up at the ceiling as my eyes adjusted to the darkness until a soft glow shrouded the room.

"Is this the mattress you have at home?" The gruff, sleep-coated tone of Scout's voice was not going to help me fall asleep.

"Yeah, awesome, isn't it."

"So comfy, I feel like I'm on a cloud."

"Same."

"Parker?"

"Yeah?"

"Thank you for sharing your bed with me."

"Anytime."

"Good night, Parker."

"Night, Davison."

There was silence.

I held my breath, waiting for the moment when she finally succumbed to tiredness and her breathing leveled. Thirty seconds passed…sixty…and then the pillow between our heads moved, and I found myself staring at Scout's sleep-filled face barely six inches away.

Her warm breath ghosted over my skin. Her eyes barely opened as she leaned in and brushed her lips against my cheek. They burned as a brand would, intensely hot and shocking me awake.

Call it tiredness. Call it whatever you want. But a man can only take so much of having the girl he's wanted for a year lying in bed next to him.

Twelve months of pent-up frustration, of longing, of lusting after this girl in my bed, and I couldn't hold it anymore. The feel of her lips on my skin was a step too far.

My fingers speared through her hair, pushing into her pale gold strands, barely held together with the tie until they loosened in my hands, and I pulled her to me.

My mouth surrounded hers, spearmint and peppermint

clashing as my tongue slid inside, warm and wet.

A soft moan rumbled up her throat and down mine as she relaxed into me. Warm fingers tickled my beard, my grip tightened on the back of her head, trying and failing to get closer, deeper. I needed more, but the mountain of pillows between us thwarted me, though without their protection, I knew I'd already be nestling myself between her thighs.

That one truth had me pulling away, because when the time came, it wouldn't be an exhausted and rushed ten minutes. No, I planned to worship her for hours.

Her eyes were still closed when I pressed my lips to hers one last time and rested back on my pillow, falling into the deepest sleep I had for months.

When I woke up, she may have been gone, but I was still wearing the smile I'd had when I closed my eyes.

20

Scout

How long can you stare at someone sleeping before it's considered creepy?

My eyes flicked to the clock. I'd been sitting here for fifteen minutes, give or take an hour. That was probably entering into creep territory, right?

I'd never stared at someone sleeping before, so I wasn't sure on the etiquette. Come to think of it, there probably wasn't any etiquette.

Yep, this was weird.

The problem was I couldn't tear my eyes away from the

lump in the bed, also known as Parker King, currently so fast asleep the fire alarm could go off and he probably wouldn't stir. On the other hand, I hadn't had many opportunities to really *look* at him, so I was taking it.

A lone shard of morning light sliced through the blinds and landed on the pillow in front of his face. The glow highlighted his perfect bone structure and razor-sharp jaw that even sleep couldn't soften, along with a set of lashes I'd kill for.

Thick, light brown scruff coated his cheeks, the same as it always did, only right now a little shorter. I'd noticed over the past month or so that Parker's beard varied in length; he'd let it grow, then take a pair of clippers to it and start again, the only constant was how soft it looked. I'd always wondered if it would *feel* soft, and last night I got my answer.

Yes, ma'am.

There was yet a day to pass where Parker didn't get more good looking. I'd even been wondering recently whether a situation existed that would result in him looking normal, like us everyday folk. I wanted to see him wake up with a massive pimple, or hair sticking out at all angles. I'd even settle for a couple of face creases from how hard he'd been pressed into the pillow. Bit of sleep drool…but no.

Even now, one massive arm tucked under his pillow with the other curled into his side and a huge thigh wrapped around the sheets while his lips softly popped with each exhale, he could have fallen from the sky and hit every branch of the handsome tree to soften his landing.

Man, *those lips.*

I stifled a yawn; it had been a long night. I'd almost been counting down the hours until the sun made an appearance on the horizon so I could get out of bed and check I hadn't been dreaming.

I hadn't. And it almost made it worse.

That kiss really happened. I was living in a reality where Parker King and I kissed. Kissed while lying in bed together.

So you can see why I spent the next hour pondering on the most intense thirty seconds of my life before I needed to sit down.

I'd thought about it. A lot. More than a lot.

Never had I ever been kissed like that.

I couldn't even tell you how it happened.

Not only had it been dark, we'd been lying in bed on either side of a pillow wall after the longest day in history, which included a standoff with a bird, and dressed in the world's un-sexiest pajamas—or I had been. Either way, nothing super conducive to setting up *the best kiss in history.*

Thank god I'd been lying down because I wouldn't have been standing by the time he pulled away.

I smiled into the growing light as a memory popped into my head.

My nana once said Grandpa had knocked her socks off. I'd been young, and working off logic. It made no sense, even when she tried to explain it to me. But somewhere around two a.m. this morning, I finally got it. Everything clicked into place.

If I'd worn socks to bed, Parker would have knocked them off, like he'd been doing since the start of the season.

It wasn't just that he was hot. It wasn't that he was a professional athlete. It was almost *despite* those things.

Parker King made me laugh. He was kind and thoughtful. He helped his friends.

And he kept his promises.

It had been a couple of weeks since Mark had shown up, yet I'd not heard it mentioned by anyone, just like Parker had said—not even Pablo—which had to be some kind of record.

So yeah, I kissed Parker King. Or Parker King kissed me. And I'd been sitting here trying to figure out what to do about it, we were going on an hour and twenty minutes. It would have been longer if Parker hadn't stirred and rolled over, prompting me to grab my bag and sprint out as fast as I could through the connecting doors into my formally bird shit–covered room, before I got caught for creeping.

Still catching my breath, I flicked on the coffee machine. Today would need to be powered by caffeine.

The weather on the West Coast was already 10 degrees warmer than the East, and I'd planned my outfits accordingly.

Usually when I worked I stuck to jeans and a tee with a Lions shirt thrown over the top, but when I'd been hurriedly packing things into my travel bag the night before we left, I'd found a dress at the back of my closet I'd never worn.

Pulling it out, I laid it on the bed. Short but not too short, with puff sleeves and a pie collar, totally plain and appropriately Lions black, but also super cute. It would do perfectly for today, paired with my usual Chucks.

Taking one sip of coffee and burning my tongue in the process, I hotfooted it into the shower. I stood there, letting the water blast away whatever was going on in my belly. Nerves churned as my thoughts picked up from where I'd left them, along with a whole barrage of new questions firing into my brain from all angles.

Too fast for me to make any sense of them, that's for sure.

Parker and I had kissed. One *hot* kiss.

Now what?

He was going to sleep until lunchtime. It was quite likely I wouldn't see him again until tonight. He had practice, I had work to do. We'd have to talk about it at some point, wouldn't we? Would we?

Yes. We would.

Should I bring it up? Do I wait for him to bring it up?

Does it change anything? Do I want it to change anything?

I shrugged to myself and squeezed out a dollop of shampoo.

Parker wants to date you, do you want to date Parker? I dunno. It didn't exactly fit into any plans I made to focus on myself.

What will you do about work? Ugh, *work*. A ten-minute shower was not long enough to figure out that conundrum.

Do you want to kiss him again?

The answer to that question was the only answer I'd had all morning. *Um...Yes. Most definitely.*

Then what are you going to do about it?

Hmm.

By the time I'd rinsed the shampoo and followed up with everything else that one did in a shower, I was still no closer to an answer. Nor had I figured one out after downing another cup of coffee, drying my hair, carefully applying makeup so I didn't look as tired as I felt, and getting dressed.

It was not to be found.

Replacing my search for an answer with a search for my cell charger was easier, but no less anxiety inducing when I remembered exactly where I'd left it.

Plugged in next to Sleeping Beauty.

Crap.

I had to meet my team in twenty minutes, which could easily be spent wearing out the carpet with the amount of pacing I'd already completed trying to decide whether to get it or borrow one before concluding I was being entirely ridiculous.

Thankfully, in my hurry to rush out I hadn't closed the connecting doors properly, which meant, in theory, I could sneak in while he was still sleeping and grab it.

Carefully inching my fingers around the door, I eased it open enough to peer around.

Parker wasn't still sleeping.

The lump in the bed was missing, but the sound of his shower running came in loud and clear. This was perfect. Parker was preoccupied in what was technically another room, I could definitely grab my charger and leave without him noticing. I wouldn't even need to run.

Easy.

I was halfway across the room when it dawned on me the noise of the water was way too loud, and all the confidence I'd had in my plan drained away.

Parker hadn't closed the bathroom door, like he had last night. Nope. It was wide open. And from where I was now frozen in place—miles away from my plugged-in charger—Parker King was standing, his back turned and water cascading over his gloriously, *totally naked* body.

I'd already stared at Parker way more than anyone should stare at a person, but it didn't seem like I had any plans to stop now. I don't think I even blinked.

His head bent as he faced the wall, torrents of water traversing down thick, sculpted muscles either side of his spine until it hit the wedge of his ass. Immediately I was taken back to the day in Marnie Matthew's office where he pushed himself to exhaustion, and I'd spent the rest of the afternoon wondering if his ass was as impressive as his shorts made it look.

Yes, it was. Resoundingly, yes.

Oh boy, what an ass.

I was so focused on his ass that I didn't immediately realize that Parker wasn't *just* showering. The rhythmic movement of his arm couldn't be mistaken for anything else. Nor could the hand flat on the shower wall, so tense that his fingers were almost digging into the tiles.

Every cell in my body stood to attention. My breath shallowed. I had a sudden need to crank the AC.

I shouldn't be watching this.

I should leave.

I shouldn't know the two divots at the base of his spine deepened as his ass clenched tight. *Tighter.*

I shouldn't be imagining what he looked like when he came. Whether his lips softened and his mouth dropped. If his eyes stayed opened or closed. What color they turned.

I shouldn't wonder if this was when dangerous Parker made an appearance, the one I saw every time he stepped behind the plate. Focused and ready.

I *really* shouldn't be watching this.

Never in my wildest dreams did I think that seeing a guy jerk off could be this hot.

Okay, maybe somewhere in my wildest dreams if I ever had a dream featuring Parker jerking off, it would be hot.

But not *this hot.*

Parker's fist pumped harder, faster.

My teeth sank so deep into my lip I almost drew blood. My chest heaved. Goose bumps erupted on every spare inch of my skin.

I really needed AC.

"Ahhh…fuuck…Scout…"

It wasn't loud, but it may as well have deafened me.

He jerked forward a split second before his cum hit the wall. My eyes stayed glued to that spot while my ears still rang with the sound of him calling my name. Even as Parker stroked himself down and rinsed the wall clean, I never looked away.

I was so dazed, I didn't notice him turn around until it was too late.

The bright green had given way to something darker as they found mine and held my gaze.

Only then did I manage to blink.

Any normal person would have been embarrassed…maybe shocked, at the bare minimum, that something so private had been witnessed. But the expression playing out on his perfect features was nothing short of conceit.

I'd just watched him jerk off, and he was now staring at me with undiluted smugness. I could almost see his brain ticking over, calculating his next move.

My legs were too heavy, every cell in my body was too busy throbbing for me to run back out as I had this morning.

I'd need to sprint. But there I stood as Parker cut the shower, reached for a towel, and slowly wrapped it around himself.

Never had a thick white terry towel looked as obscene as this one did, resting on those equally obscene divots stretched above his hips. Abs. More abs than I'd seen in my life, except you know, the last time I'd seen them.

But that time hadn't felt like we were trying to make a porno.

Right now, it was debatable.

"Good morning." He stopped in the doorway and his gaze dropped to my bare legs. It was debatable who felt more naked, me or him, as his eyes slowly tracked up again. "Nice dress."

I tried and failed to calm the thudding in my chest. "Th… thank you."

"You're welcome."

Grabbing another towel, he rubbed it over his head and down his torso. It was a poor attempt to dry his damp skin. We both knew he was putting on a show. A show for me.

I still hadn't moved. I still hadn't looked away.

I was staying right where I was, and he knew it.

I had zero clue for what was about to happen and the anticipation was enough to have my heart trying to break free of my rib cage.

"Enjoying yourself?"

"I…"

"Oh, come on now, Davison, don't go all shy on me." He stepped nearer, though from the way his narrowed eyes never left mine, stalked would be a better description, one steady foot in front of the other. "Did you enjoy yourself?"

My flushed cheeks answered for me.

One more step.

"If I'd known I had an audience, I'd have really dialed it up."

Parker was about ten feet away now, and for the first time my eyes dropped only to dart right back up to his grin, one that could have been taken from the devil himself.

His incredibly impressive dick I'd just watched him fist, and was suddenly desperate to experience for myself, was standing to attention under his towel.

A towel that now looked in danger of falling off.

"What do you expect?" He shrugged. "You come in here teasing me in that little dress and you want me to pretend you're not wearing it for me? Nah, I can't do that."

I opened my mouth to respond, only to close it again.

One more step.

"And you think I don't know you're soaking wet under there, aching for me to touch you. Wanting me to give you what I just took for myself?"

Again, I couldn't answer. My entire body was frozen. He was right about one thing. I *was* soaking wet. This wasn't the sweet Parker who'd kissed me last night, the one who'd made my knees weak.

But I had a feeling this Parker was going to make my knees weak in a whole different way.

One more step. "You want to know what I was thinking about as I fisted my cock?"

This time I forced myself to nod.

"You, Davison. Always you. On your knees, lips wrapped around my cock." He scratched the edges of his jaw. "Or sometimes I wonder what you'd be like ass up, my hands gripping into your cheeks as I slide into you. Or how you'd look riding me, tits bouncing in my face. Fucking amazing is my guess. Should I go on?"

My mouth dropped. My entire body hummed with static buzzing through the air, I didn't think I'd ever been so turned on in my life. It was a wonder I could still remember how to breathe. My stomach almost convulsed as Parker's pink tongue darted out and licked along his lower lip.

"On second thought, I have a question…"

"Yes?"

"Do you think about me?"

Slowly, I nodded. I didn't have the brain cells to deny it.

"How much?" he asked, his head tilting as he waited for an answer. "Scout, how much?"

"A lot. More than I should."

"What do you think about?"

My cheeks still hadn't cooled from five minutes ago, but they heated up all over again, and he noticed.

"Okay, let's try it like this…" One final step and Parker was so close that I had nowhere to go. The scent of him overpowered me until I was fighting for oxygen. The heat coming off his damp chest was enough for a tiny bead of sweat to materialize between my shoulder blades and roll down my spine.

There was *nowhere* to go. My knees hit the edge of the bed, and I fell back.

Immediately Parker dropped to his knees, placing himself right in my eyeline. Green eyes bored into mine, seeking permission for what he was about to do. Or waiting to see if I was going to stop him.

I wasn't.

My gaze followed the path of his fingertips inching up my thighs until they reached the hem of my dress and disappeared underneath. I couldn't see his fingers, only feel them. And with sight taken away, all my other senses heightened.

His fingers hooked around the elastic of my panties. "Have you ever thought about what it would feel like to be spread out in front of me?"

I managed a nod as he eased them down and slipped them over my ankles. My eyes were open enough to see his darken another degree. The dangerous Parker was well and truly in the room, and right now he was pushing up my dress until it sat around my hips, and there was nowhere to hide.

Never in all my life had I felt so exposed. Never had I been so turned on.

Combustion was imminent.

His fingertips dug into the flesh on my thighs.

"Fuck, Davison. You are better than every dream I've ever had about you," he breathed out, sending goose bumps over my skin as he leaned in.

His face was inches from the apex of my thighs. If I had any second thoughts about this, they vanished along with my self-consciousness when I took one look at the expression he was wearing.

"Have you thought about how my fingers will feel sliding inside your tight, wet pussy?"

I could only moan in response as his thumb pushed through my wetness and circled my clit, followed by one thick finger slowly easing inside me. And then those magic hands of his, the ones which had caught so many balls, cupped around me and ground down.

"Oh my *god.*"

The muscles along his shoulder popped with each flex of his wrist. He looked incredible, only surpassed by the reverence on his face aimed directly at me.

"You're squeezing me so tight, the thought of my dick sinking inside is making my head spin." The timbre of his voice had reached a pitch that vibrated across my bare skin, even more so when he narrowed the space between his mouth and the spot I directly wanted it to hit.

It was possible the moment he made contact I blacked out. Warm, wet laps of his tongue with the perfect amount of pressure shot sparks along my spine, twisting it like a corkscrew.

"Fuck, you taste incredible," was all he muttered before getting down to work.

There's no way I was holding out. The sensation of his soft stubble against my hypersensitive skin was the sexiest thing I'd ever experienced.

My bones were on the verge of snapping from the tension building inside me. As much as I wanted to watch the magic he was performing, I couldn't stay upright.

I wasn't sure if I fell back or if he hooked his arms under my knees and pulled me into him, but either way my head hit the soft comforter and my eyes rolled into their sockets.

His mouth surrounded me, devouring like I was a lifeline he needed. With each precision-targeted swipe of his tongue and curl of his fingers inside me, I hurtled toward the finish line.

It was only a matter of seconds before I exploded.

I'd been running on a heightened state of arousal since Parker had found me sitting outside my room in the early hours of the morning.

"Gahhd. Oh god, *Parker.*"

The rhythm he set matched each one of my violent

convulsions, until I was pushing him away. I couldn't take it any longer. I needed reprieve, and it took a second for me to realize he'd given it to me.

A cool breeze alerted me to the fact he was no longer within inches of me. Summoning the bare minimum strength I needed to push myself up on my elbows, I found him looking impossibly smug, staring straight at me.

"Are you okay?"

"I'm way better than okay. Hearing you come with my name…" He shook his head. "Fuck me, Davison. I've been waiting a year to do that. Waiting a year to taste you and watch you fall apart…it was more incredible than I could have imagined."

As he spoke, his hands rubbed along my thighs, up and down. I didn't have a clue what time it was, I barely even knew *where* I was. The only thing on my agenda was to experience *that* again.

I expected Parker to drop his towel, I was desperate for him to drop it. Only he dropped his hands and leaned back.

"Wh…what are you doing?"

"You're going to be late for work. There's no way I'm rushing this."

I had to force the lump in my throat away. "We're not rushing. I'm ready."

He shook his head. "No, Davison. When I said rushing, I meant I'm not rushing our first time. I plan to take all night long, I'm going to worship you, starting the second the game finishes tonight." His eyes glanced over to the clock and back to me. "Thirteen hours."

It was going to be a long day.

21

Parker

"Why are you being so twitchy?"

My eyes sliced left, I couldn't see him properly, but I knew Ace was staring down at me with a deep frown. A deep frown and his dick hanging out. "Dude, can you get dressed?"

"What's the rush? You know I like to air dry," he replied, though humored me by covering himself with a towel. "Have you been on the Red Bull again?"

"What?"

"You're super twitchy. The entire bench is shaking."

I eased my hands under my thighs to stop them tapping. "I'm not twitchy. I'm tired."

"You don't seem tired. You seem twitchy."

"I want the debrief to be over so we can all go to bed. Why's everyone taking so long? Where's Coach?"

He raised an eyebrow; I couldn't tell whether he bought my explanation.

To be honest, I didn't really care.

The only thing I did care about was getting the fuck out of the locker room and back to the hotel, but it didn't look like the meeting was going to start any time soon, given half the guys were still in the shower, and Coach was nowhere to be seen.

I thought if I ran off the field, showered, and dressed at lightning speed, it might encourage everyone else to move their asses, but evidence pointed to the contrary.

Ace stopped drying himself, or whatever he was doing, and frowned again. "We're not having a debrief."

"What?"

"We're not having a debrief. And Coach is talking to ESPN."

"We're not having a debrief?"

"What did I just say? Seriously, why are you being so weird?"

"We're not having a debrief?" I jumped up, making no effort to contain my outrage. "Then what the fuck are we hanging around for?"

Ace pulled on a pair of briefs—fucking slowly, I might

add, but at least we were heading in the direction of being fully dressed.

"Dude, no one's hanging around, we all came off the field and got showered just like we normally do. You're the only one who left dust behind. We're all getting ready at the same speed, and the bus is leaving in twenty."

I peered around the locker room. Perhaps Ace had a point, though I still didn't understand why everyone was behaving like they had all the fucking time in the world. It was past eleven p.m., why did no one want to go to bed? At this rate it would be after midnight before we got back to the hotel.

I let out a huff and sat down again.

"Come to think of it," he continued, "you were also twitchy in the dugout. Quiet too."

"I was watching the game."

"Nah, I think it was more than that. You didn't find my joke funny, and you always find my jokes funny."

I pulled my phone out, so tempted to message Scout and tell her I'd see her soon, but I didn't want to do it with Ace peering over my shoulder. I hadn't told him about this morning, I hadn't told anyone. I knew that the second I opened my mouth and spilled my secret I'd make it that little bit less special.

And I kind of wanted at least twenty-four hours of having Scout to myself before it became public knowledge.

Or at least before the boys knew.

I wouldn't be able to go longer than twenty-four hours before they guessed. My face would give it away, plus all the jumping for joy at finally sealing the deal with Scout that I'd be doing.

"Parker, did you hear what I said?"

"Um…" My eyes flicked up to his.

Nope. No chance I was even lasting twenty-four hours. I couldn't focus on anything. I could barely remember the game we just played beyond knowing we'd won and I'd racked up two RBIs. I definitely couldn't remember him telling any joke, and it was a toss-up on which would be received as worse news—that I didn't find his joke funny or I didn't listen in the first place.

I was saved from making any admissions by the arrival of Lux wearing one of his neon sweatpants and hoodies. I'd lost count of how many he had, but I knew I'd never seen this one before. *That* I'd remember. It was so fucking bright, if the power went out, we'd just use Lux to guide the way.

"Dude, that color is enough to make my eye tic. You need to warn people when you're going to wear it. Or provide sunglasses."

He chuckled but said nothing, opting to pull out his phone, no doubt to message Radley. Maybe I should message Scout.

Nope. Someone would see. Fuck, I wanted to get out of here.

"Where's Tan?" asked Lux.

"Dunno. Probably still showering."

"We're never leaving," I grumbled, my head falling back onto the locker with a thud.

"What's with you? We only got off the field fifteen minutes ago."

I checked my watch. Huh. Lux was right, it had only been fifteen minutes, even if it felt like an hour. It was official, Scout made me lose all concept of time. Lux and I were the only two ready to leave.

Maybe if I headed for the bus, everyone would grasp the sense of urgency and hurry the fuck up.

"What's up with you?"

"NOTHING! I just want to go to bed."

His expression was the same one Ace was wearing, and I ignored that one too.

"Okay…"

I stayed silent. My bad mood would only get questioned further, which would lead to a place I didn't want to go. And I wasn't in a bad mood per se. I mean, I was definitely impatient to the point of exploding, but that's all. Who could blame me? I had the most perfect girl in the world waiting for me back at the hotel. At least I hoped she'd be there; I hadn't spoken to her all day. I hadn't even seen her. Not since she'd left my room in a post-orgasmic daze.

I adjusted my shorts before I started getting hard at the memory.

Even in the depths of my fantasies I'd not conjured up the image of her watching me jerk off, but holy crap, the look on her face when I turned around and saw her…chest heaving, cheeks flushed, jaw slack. She was exquisite.

No one had ever looked at me the way she had been looking at me. I'd had to consciously stop myself from sprinting across the room and picking up from where I'd finished.

I was on the verge of drifting into a fantasy about Scout when Tanner returned from the shower, dripping wet.

"Who's coming to my room to unwind with some *Call of Duty*?" he asked, shaking himself everywhere.

"Tan, Jesus!" griped Lux, probably because his brand-new sneakers now had a water spot on them.

I was much less annoyed, because it appeared that during my time dreaming about what I was going to do to Scout later, everyone had gotten dressed. Or mostly dressed. My mouth was open, ready to tell Tanner to hurry up when Coach walked into the locker room, wearing a scowl.

"What are you all still doing here? The coaches are waiting, get a move on."

Fucking *finally*. Someone talking sense.

Two minutes after I arrived back at my room, cleaned

my teeth, and took a piss, I was standing in front of the connecting door.

I'd always figured the first time Scout and I had sex would be following a proper date, where I'd picked her up at her place, taken her to dinner in the best restaurant New York had to offer, and walked her home. A world away from right now, yet a connecting door during an away series did seem kind of appropriate, if unconventional.

The performance anxiety attempting to creep into my brain, however, was all new and it would absolutely not do.

I was not about to fuck it up.

This was my dream girl, the one I'd thought about virtually nonstop for the past twelve months. And assuming I didn't fuck this up, it meant that I'd get to take her on a proper date another time. I'd take her on all the dates.

I could only pray she hadn't fallen asleep, given how long I'd taken to get here.

It was hard to believe that less than twenty-four hours had passed since I'd found her sitting outside her room and rescued her from that seagull. If I ever met him again, I'd take him out for a fish dinner, or set him up with a hotel suite of his own—for that seagull had done more for my sex life in five minutes than I'd managed in a year.

Here goes nothing.

My knuckles had barely brushed the door before it was opened. Every single worry I'd had about her falling asleep vanished as I laid eyes on her.

It might have been midnight, and time for bed, but from her fresh face, and wide-awake expression, I'd hasten to bet she wasn't planning to sleep for hours. That and her pajama pants were missing, revealing the stretch of smooth, golden legs I'd had my face between at the start of the day.

And I planned to finish my day between them too.

A smirk curved her lip. "If it isn't tonight's MVP, powering his team to victory."

Reaching out, I tugged on one of the buttons of her shirt. "Hey, I think your lucky jammies can take the credit."

"I told you they worked."

"I never doubted you," I replied as Scout stepped back for me to follow. "It looks significantly different in here without bird shit everywhere. Smells better too." I leaned closer, slowly, my nose gently brushing along her jawline to breathe her in. From the angle her neck tilted, I could see the frantic hammering of her pulse. "On second thought, that's you."

"I smell good?"

"You smell edible."

"Yeah?"

Craning back, my gaze locked into hers and I nodded slowly, pausing only to soak her in. I knew for a fact she had no clue how momentous this moment was for me. A million thoughts spun in my head. I wasn't about to rush it, and I wasn't about to rush *her*.

"Parker, are you okay?"

"Yes, I'm perfect."

"Then why are you just standing there?"

"Because…"

"Because?"

"Because…" I reached for her hand, suddenly overcome with what we were about to do. I'd had sex a thousand times, but this wasn't *sex*.

This was *Scout*.

I didn't want to tell her I'd paused because she looked so perfect to me I almost couldn't cope. That now I knew what she looked like when she came, the scent of her arousal, the taste of her, I would never experience anything better. And it fucking terrified me.

"Because…this is going to change things between us. And I'm a thousand percent ready for that. But if you decide you don't want that at any point, starting right now, I will walk out the door and we can go back to being just friends."

I could do that. I *think* I could do that. If I moved to Canada, I could do that. No, Canada was too close. England. I'd move to England. Australia?

My thoughts swirled, air lodged in my throat while I waited for her to answer.

"Do you think we're *just* friends, Parker?"

I shook my head.

"Me either," she replied softly. "I've thought about you all day."

"You have?"

"Yes. I know things will change, and I'm okay with that."

"You sure?"

She stepped in closer, her hands running across my chest, I'd never noticed before how tiny they were. "Yes. I want to finish what we started this morning."

My dick twitched. He knew how she felt.

"Oh yeah?"

"Yeah." She peered up at me through fluttering lashes. "Plus, you scored today, it's only fair that I get to even the field and score too. Or maybe the MVP needs his prize."

My head fell back with a loud laugh, and just like that, all the tension broke. The air unclogged itself and made way for the insane electricity crackling between us.

"You are so cheesy."

"Yeah, but I think you like it."

"I more than like it."

Scout stepped out of my arms, her fingers slowly working the buttons on her shirt until she eased it over her shoulders, and it billowed to the floor. And she was left wearing only a pair of tiny, black lace panties. Totally different from the white cotton briefs she'd had on this morning.

"Show me how much."

Saliva pooled in my mouth. My dick was so hard it was almost painful.

Her nipples were the shade of pink her cheeks turned when she was nervous, pale rose and standing to attention—pointing right at me. In less than a second I'd scooped her ass into my hands, carried her over to the bed, and laid her down. As I did, the final golden strands of her hair fell out of the tie, and using the tip of my finger, I brushed it away from her face.

"There you are."

Even in the minute since we'd been standing near the doors, her pupils had dilated, turning the blue almost navy. Full peachy lips I planned to spend the rest of the night kissing, parted as she gazed up at me, and the goose bumps marking her chest had nothing to do with the AC.

"Hey."

I didn't know where to start.

Where to touch her first.

How to make her feel the very best I could.

The pressure of Scout watching me, waiting to see what I would do, was almost more intense than game day against the Yankees. More intense than I'd ever experienced.

Reaching behind, I eased my shirt off. Her gaze tracked the movement. The mattress dipped as I knelt between her legs, while she soaked me in. And I made my decision. Slowly, like unwrapping the present I'd saved for last, I hooked my fingers under the loosened elastic and tugged them down.

I hadn't seen her properly naked this morning, but now,

staring down at her, I was kind of thankful.

I'd been distracted enough all day as it was, if I'd known *this* would be waiting for me, I'd have never made it.

She was incredible.

Her skin, already beginning to tan from the early summer sun, looked like it was glowing gold in the dimmed uplights around the room. The shadows they cast made her legs look seven feet long, ending in the rounded curve of her hips, and sweeping into the dip of her waist.

If I'd been correct when I said she smelled edible, she looked it too—soft and delicious.

"Oh man, I was right. You are better than any dream I've ever had," I whispered, slowly crawling over her body until I hovered above her.

Before she could respond, my mouth dropped to hers. Her tongue darted out as mine licked along her fat bottom lip, before my hunger took over. This wasn't the kiss we'd shared last night, sleep filled and languid. This was the starter pistol, lust fueled and preparing us for what was to come. Tongues collided hot and heavy, she moaned so deeply it vibrated through her chest to mine, and she took exactly what she needed.

Until it wasn't enough.

Tilting her neck back, she arched into me as I licked a path along her jaw, nibbling her earlobe, slowly traveling down her throat to her shoulder, and lower. Her moans intensified as one pebbled nipple found itself surrounded by my lips.

"You like that?"

"Hmm."

My mouth slid across her belly, and my hand slipped between her thighs. She dripped into my palm. Somehow I could almost still taste her from this morning, sweet honey bursting on my tongue, and by the time I found myself back in the same spot I'd left thirteen hours earlier, my dick was harder than my bat.

This morning had been about me. I'd wanted to show her exactly what I was capable of beyond jerking off in the shower.

Right now, was all about her.

Pinning her thighs open, I took one long lap.

Up to this point in my life, 95 percent of the girls I'd had in my bed put on a show. Screaming, thrashing, panting. I enjoyed it, even when I'd known it was as natural as their tits, but Scout was quieter. Even this morning, her body did all the talking, flushed pink and bowing off the mattress with each flick I took of her clit.

Sliding a finger into her slick, hot pussy had her bunching the sheets. If I hadn't been so distracted with licking up every drop of her, it would have been the sexiest thing I'd ever seen.

Adding another finger, stretching out her tight, slick muscles, I built up the pace. The trembling in her thighs turned violent, I was in very real danger of having my head squeezed like a watermelon.

"Fuuck, harder. I need it harder," she breathed out, grinding her pussy into my face, desperate for more.

"Because you asked so nicely."

Sucking hard on her clit, I flicked the tip of my tongue over it one last time.

She exploded just as ferociously as she had this morning. Her entire body shattering from the force. Unlike this morning, I had no intention of sitting back and letting her go.

My pants were in a heap on the floor, and I'd sheathed up before she'd even come down to earth.

The sensation of sliding my dick through her soaking wet slit tightened my balls so severely I almost blacked out.

"Scout?" I murmured against her lips. "Look at me."

Her eyelids flickered open, revealing eyes so glazed with desire it punched me right in the chest.

"Are you ready?"

"Yes."

The first squeeze of her pussy and I knew I wouldn't last. Red hot pokers shot down my spine with each inch I gave her. If I didn't think it would finish this before we'd even started, I'd get it over with and drive myself into her until I wasn't sure where I ended and she began.

"Jesus, Scout…"

Her eyes flicked up to mine. "Parker, this is…you feel…" she stuttered, and I would have laughed if I wasn't exactly the same.

She'd robbed me of words. The ability to think. Everything.

This moment.

This exact moment, holding her gaze as I filled her to the hilt, was everything I didn't know I'd been waiting for. I stilled, staring down at her, so completely aware of every single sensation. The feel of her, the smell of her, the way her lip caught in her front tooth. Only the sudden clench of her pussy got me moving.

It was better than I'd ever dreamed.

Slowly rocking inside her, I built up the pace and she met every thrust of mine with one of hers, lifting her hips until I was grinding against her swollen clit with each drive forward. It didn't take long until perspiration slicked across her body, making it look like she was sparkling.

This morning I'd missed her orgasm, too busy stretching out her climax with my face between her thighs. But I wasn't about to miss this one. I wanted to know everything that happened when she exploded under me.

Right now her cheeks glowed pink, and her nose scrunched as she tried to hold on.

Gathering her hands in one of mine, I hooked a leg over my hip and kicked up the pace until Scout's thighs shook uncontrollably. Or maybe they were my thighs trying to cling onto a shred of control. Her pussy clamped down, squeezing the life from my dick, and it was all it took.

Control *lost*.

Every fantasy I'd had, every lonely moment wondering what it would be like to finally get Scout—*if* I ever got her—was silenced as we exploded together. My mouth fell on hers, molding together as I gave her every breath she ripped from my lungs until I finally collapsed.

I was running on five hours of sleep, a full game of baseball, and if you counted the time difference, it wasn't far off my usual morning wake-up. It was all power to Scout that I was still awake.

"Parker…wow…"

Easing off her, I fell down on the pillow and turned to her, lifting a strand of blonde hair soaking up the sweat on her forehead to tuck behind her ear. "Just think, Davison, if you'd said yes to me the first time I asked you out, we could have been doing that weeks ago."

"Well, I'll just have to live with the regret." She chuckled.

"It's okay, you can make it up to me."

She scooched closer, her lips pressing against mine. My eyes were so heavy as I wrapped my arm around her and pulled her into me.

For the second time in as many days, I fell asleep next to Scout Davison.

Only this time when I woke up, she was still there.

22

Scout

"I'll come up when you're finished, and we can go to HR…cool?…Scout?"

Turning away from the window, my eyes met Parker's, who was simultaneously trying to keep one eye on the road while also clearly waiting for me to respond to whatever he'd been saying. Only I hadn't been listening.

Mashing my mouth, I offered up some kind of apologetic shrug and leaned forward as quickly as I could to kiss him while we stopped at a red light. Just even the fact I could kiss him felt both so incredibly alien and comforting all at the same time.

"Sorry. Please could you repeat that?"

"Wow, already ignoring me." He chuckled, brushing my knuckles to his lips.

At least two dozen people crossed haphazardly in front of us, from the looks of it, all of them on their way to work. I wondered if any of them also had a job interview.

Gah, my job interview that should have been tomorrow, so I'd have one more day to prepare, but got brought forward instead. *That* was why I was all kinds of churned up this morning, and it wasn't even nine a.m.

Job interviews at nine a.m. should be illegal.

At the very least they were unconstitutional.

"No, I am. I just—"

"I'm teasing, it's a big morning for you. Are you feeling okay?"

I nodded. "Yeah, I think so."

"Sure?"

I glanced back to the window just as a cyclist sped past, cutting through the traffic and causing several cars to slam their brakes, and drivers to hit the horns.

"I'm a little nervous, I guess. It's a big role. I wish I'd had one more day to prepare."

"You don't need one more day, you'll crush it," Parker added without hesitation, and I couldn't help but smile at his enthusiasm, or his constant and unwavering belief in me.

Always wanting me to do my best.

It was why I was currently sitting in his very comfortable Mercedes SUV, instead of my usual smelly subway car on my way to work.

Parker had insisted he'd drive me. I'm sure it also had something to do with him sleeping over last night because my roommate was out of town, and neither of us was ready to burst the bubble we'd been living in during the away series.

Boy oh boy, what a bubble it had been. I'd left for California just regular ol' Scout Davison, but after spending six nights in Parker King's bed having the most fun she'd had in ages, someone else returned.

Someone different, newer, with a sparkle in her eye and a fresh bounce to her hair.

I'd been thinking about it this morning, standing under the shower, but then Parker had joined me and naturally after that my entire focus became him.

But the biggest difference wasn't quite so obvious to the naked eye.

In the space of a week my heart had softened. Become happier, almost. Skipping a joyful beat. I felt more confident while—ironically—at the exact same time much more anxious.

Truthfully though, I couldn't put it solely down to the last week. It was the whole season. Two months ago, I'd been adamant about starting the year fresh, enjoying my single life, and living it to the max.

Two months ago, Parker King and I had barely spoken.

Now I'd spent six mornings in a row waking up next to him.

Now I'd spent six nights with Parker twisting my body like a pretzel, drawing out orgasm after orgasm, until I'd been convinced I'd never walk again.

The man certainly knew his way around a body. After almost a week on the road, I wasn't certain he didn't know my body better than I did. He'd made it react in ways it hadn't before. Made it feel things it hadn't before.

Every expectation I'd ever had about Parker King had been blown out of the water.

Everything I already liked about him was only intensified by his insanely hot body and his ability to whisper sweet nothings, while somehow being so incredibly dirty as he described exactly what he wanted to do to me that it made my head spin.

I don't know how he'd managed his days playing ball after our nights in bed, but if he was anything like me, he'd have woken up invigorated with the energy of a two gallon bottle of Red Bull—without the dangers of a looming heart attack, obvs.

It was addictive.

I was living in a world where Parker and I were having sex, and the scariest thing about it being that I honestly wasn't sure if I wanted to ever go back to one where we weren't.

A week ago we'd been *just* friends, and now I had something much bigger to lose.

And that right there was the crux of why my anxiety kept trying to shoot through the retractable roof of the stadium.

It was unsettling to say the least. Unsettling and unfamiliar. I'd never had this gut-churning, heart-pounding, chest-on-the-verge-of-exploding sensation when I'd dated Mark, and I wasn't entirely sure what to do about it.

"Scout? Have you got your presentation?" Parker reached over and squeezed my knee, only the slight change in his tone told me he'd already asked that question.

"Sorry, I'm sorry. I'm listening, I promise." I smiled, vowing to myself not to drift off into another spiral of anxiety-inducing thoughts. "Um…no, HR will have set it up. I just have one printed with my notes on it."

"Sounds good. And speaking of HR…" Parker started, accelerating through a yellow light before it turned red. "I'll come and meet you after, so we can go there."

"Where?"

"HR"

"Why are we going to HR?"

"We have to sign that dating form thing."

Oh. Fuck. Fuuuck. The HR form. How, *how* did I forget that?

"Scout?"

"Yeah?

"The form?"

"Do we have to sign it?" I mumbled, chewing on an invisible hangnail. Unfortunately, it was loud enough that a tiny crease formed on Parker's brow.

"Um, yeah, kinda. Coach is already on my ass, and that was before…you know…this last week…and we got together."

"Together?"

"Yeah, you and me."

I took a deep breath and stopped short of pushing my hands through my hair to tug out the ends. Instead, I found my fingers threading into Parker's, still resting on my knee. We drove another couple of blocks in silence, enough to reach the first set of signs directing us to Lions Stadium.

Before I even realized the car was slowing down, Parker had already pulled into a parking bay, cut the engine, and was now facing me.

"C'mon, Davison, what's up? Talk to me. Are you having regrets? Do you want to go back to being just friends because…"

I shook my head, stopping any more words from coming out of his mouth. "No. No. I'm not…of course I'm not. I don't want to be just friends."

"Then what? I can see something is up." He tugged my lip free as I chewed on it, "Talk to me."

"It's nothing…it's just…" I dragged a hand down my face. "HR is managing this new job role."

"So?"

"If we sign the form then they'll know about us."

"Um, I think that's kind of the point of the form."

I sighed. "Yes, but what if us being together influences whether I'm given this role or not. I mean…I don't even know if I want it, but if I do want it, I don't want to be offered it on anything but my own merit."

Parker frowned so deeply it almost hurt *my* brain. "Why wouldn't you be?"

"Because what if they give me the job because of you. Or don't give it to me because of you."

A broad grin stretched across his face, the head tilt he added did nothing for my anxiety because it was clear he thought I was nuts. "You're giving me way too much power in this scenario."

"Parker, I'm serious." I almost snapped. "Getting a promotion while dating…you know…you. It doesn't look good. People are already talking about us. This will make it worse. I don't want it to look like I haven't earned the job on my own merit."

"Why do you care what people say?"

"Because…" I stopped, trying to find the words. "They're not talking about it in a good way."

"I'm not following."

"It's girls gossiping. And with this job interview…"

Parker pressed his finger to my lips, silencing me. "You're

asking me not to sign it?"

"I'm asking…" I cupped his cheek, I was doing such a shit job of explaining in a way that made sense to me, let alone him, no wonder he looked so confused. "The last week has been amazing, I really like you, which I realize is the entire point of the form, but I don't want them to know we're sleeping together." God, that sounded cringe. "Slept together…having sex."

"Dating, Davison. We're dating."

I blinked, trying to decide whether that made it better, only to shrug when I realized it didn't. "Same thing."

"It's not the same thing. Sleeping is casual. Dating is formal. It's official. I know we haven't technically been on a date yet, but we will."

"Okay, date." My shoulders dropped, but I couldn't help the little smile, because if I was to believe Parker—which I did—I was now officially *dating* Parker King. "I'll sign the form, of course I will, but please can we just wait until this interview process is over and they've picked someone? It'll make me feel better."

"I can't believe you want to keep me a secret," he replied, though thankfully his tone was all jest. "You know I should find that offensive, at the very least a huge knock to my confidence. Unless you're using my body for sex. Are you using my body for sex?"

My smile widened. "Maybe. Are you okay with that?"

"Sneaking around and having sex? Yeah, I could be, but

you'd need to make it worth my while."

"How?"

"Hmm." Parker stroked along the stubble coating his jaw. "I've always wanted to hook up at work, and there's a few places I want to try out."

"Like where?"

"Home plate, the locker room, the rowing machine in the gym…Think that would be super hot. Plus, the—"

A burst of laughter escaped, and I held my hand up to stop him continuing. "You had them all lined up and ready to go, there, didn't you, stud?"

"What can I say, I've been waiting for the right girl."

My heart kicked into double time. "Me?"

"Hell yeah. You know how I feel about you, Davison. I can put off Coach for a little longer." He pulled me into him and, so gently I thought my chest might cave in, dropped a kiss to my lips. "I'd do anything for you."

"I really do like you a lot, Parker King," I muttered, slipping my tongue along his.

"You'd better."

"But can you drop me outside the gates before we enter the stadium, I don't want anyone to see me getting out of your car?"

I didn't catch his gruff reply, but the poke in my ribs I also received had me laughing the rest of the ride.

23

Scout

"…and based on the data we have from the Lions social, we should see the new channels double in audience size every month for the first six months before growth steadies. Sales predicts that we can bring in revenues within the first month. In summary, we can soft launch the channel with the new brand before taking it public, and it will work to build presence much quicker."

Three sets of eyes stared at me. I stared back until it became clear they didn't realize I was done talking. I *knew* I should have added a final slide at the end.

Dammit.

"Any more questions?"

There was a pause as Lowe Slater, Ava Martinez, and Tim Chang shared a look I couldn't decipher, but it was enough to have me searching for the nearest trash can to puke in.

My guts had been churning all morning—actually, since last night—and had been gradually getting worse as my interview got closer.

I waited. Somebody. *Anybody* go first. Tim took the honors, thankfully before I hurled.

"Can you go further into how you're proposing to differentiate the channels from each other?"

I flicked back to the slide I'd shown them at the beginning of my presentation. "The Lions, the Jungle Kings, and New York Lions corporate have three very different personalities. The corporate channel will focus more on stats and data, charity projects, and news that encompasses the business as a whole. The other two largely stay the same, homing in on their individuality as teams in the MLB, and widening our audiences. We do want them to both be thought of as the Lions family, however. We want the players involved too—charity games against each other, that sort of thing."

I took Tim's nod as one of approval, though it was followed by another stretch of resounding silence that made me wonder if I'd answered the question totally wrong.

For the life of me I couldn't recall my interview for my current job being this nerve wracking. Or as long. And there hadn't been three people in it. It had been me and my current boss.

This time the silence was broken by Ava clapping her hands. "Well done, Scout. This was a really great presentation, exactly what we're looking for. Your ideas are fresh, I loved the one about the players taking over the account for the day. Let us regroup, and if we have any more questions, we'll follow up before the end of the week."

I returned her wide smile with one of my own. Mine wasn't quite as wide, and contained an element of unease, plus it was hard to ignore the ringing in my ears.

"Thank you, I'm happy to hear that."

Lowe stood, along with Ava. My time was up again; they had a very clear way of cutting things short, I'd give them that.

Guess that's why they were paid the big bucks.

"This is a big job, Scout," Lowe said. "We know we're asking a lot of you, but we think you're more than capable of delivering. And you can build your own team to support you."

I gathered up the notes I'd brought in and walked with them to the door.

"We still have a couple of other candidates to see for this role, and we'll be running a second round of interviews next week for those who go forward, but we'll be making a decision immediately after that. Needless to say, we're delighted you're already part of the Lions family. You're reliable, creative, and an asset to this company."

I held in the blush as best I could. A blush was probably unprofessional. "Thank you, I appreciate that."

"No, thank *you* for coming in early. Go and get a coffee, and I'll look forward to seeing what you have planned this week." Ava grinned.

I managed a small laugh now I wasn't quite so tense about messing up my interview. "It's going to be fun."

Lowe leaned against the door frame. "Do share."

"It was an idea the interns on our team came up with. Do you know the dog we use for Opening Day bat collection?" The two of them nodded. "He's coming in, and once I've found some willing participants, they'll race him around bases. The sales team is working with pet care brands for the week, and it's to announce the Lions for Dogs game."

Ava wagged a finger at me and laughed loudly. "See, this is why you're perfect for this job. Man, I'm looking forward to that game, I'm bringing Stanley, my doodle. It's going to be chaos."

I nodded, grinning wide. "It sure is."

Lions for Dogs—an idea that was added into the mix at the beginning of the season and immediately green lit—was taking place in a couple of months to highlight and support the role of service dogs, as well as raising money for several service dog charities. It was an idea entirely stolen from the Dodgers, but, as I understood it, once Penn Shepherd had caught wind, he immediately insisted it was made bigger and better.

The plans were still being finalized for the entire Lions eleven-acre site to be turned into a doggie paradise for the day—including grooming salons, play areas, and swimming pools. Each pup in attendance would receive a doggy bag containing a special dog-sized Lions jersey, lots of doggy treats, and heaps of Lions-branded dog necessities.

My personal favorite was the Lions poop bag dispensers coming out the dog's butt.

"My husband is too competitive for his own good." Lowe chuckled. "We'll let you get back to work, message us when you're filming the race this week. We'll come down and watch."

"I will do. Thank you again."

The moment I heard the meeting room door close behind me, I rushed down the corridor, ducked into the bathroom, and breathed the biggest sigh of relief.

It wasn't the best interview of my life, but it could have been worse. And now it was over, for the moment, until the next interview. If there *was* a next interview.

Standing in front of the mirror, I gave myself a thorough once-over. Not much had changed since the one I'd given myself right before the interview, save for a fresh glob of mascara under my bottom lash I hadn't noticed before.

My heart rate slowed, the tension across my brow lessened, my shoulders lowered.

I'd survived.

I turned on the faucet as my phone pinged.

Parker: Hey Davison, are you done?

Scout: Yes

Parker: Awesome. Meet me downstairs by the elevators in five minutes.

Scout: What for?

Parker: Surprise. I want to show you something.

Scout: On my way

Giving myself a couple more seconds to stare at my reflection, I finished washing my hands, wiped the glob of mascara from under my eye, and headed back out.

The way to the elevators took me past the comms team, the group who managed the chatter around the players.

They were the first port of call for any news coming out of the club, any inquiries from the press, along with the all-important reputation management. It was a big team, and I knew enough of them to say hello to, but there were still a couple that I never seemed to recognize, including the two currently staring at me.

Or they had been staring at me. Now they were looking at anything *but* me, and totally silent, having shut down their conversation the second I came around the corner.

If they'd stayed chatting, I wouldn't have given them another thought.

But they didn't.

I forced myself to look straight ahead and not roll my eyes like I wanted to.

Since the girls in the bathroom last week, Alice had tried to drill into me about gossip being a sign of positivity. It was a theory I was yet to subscribe to, but I guess until I signed Parker's form, it was something I had to get used to. Or maybe this is how it would be from now on.

It was like I was walking under a microscope with the magnifier increasing by the day.

By the time I reached the ground floor, I was still ruminating on being the subject of so much gossip and I forgot why I'd come down, until I heard a loud *pssst*. Spinning a full 360 degrees, I couldn't see where the noise came from until it happened again.

"Pssst." Parker's head popped from around the corner, followed by his finger crooking at me.

I walked over to where he was. "What are you doing?"

"Shhh." His head snapped left then right, and he grabbed my hand. "Come with me."

Pulling me down the corridor away from the elevators, barely stopping in front of a door I'd never noticed, I was yanked inside and shrouded in darkness before I knew what was happening. It smelled like cleaning supplies.

"Parker..."

"Hang on. There's a light," he said, followed by the sound of him slapping the wall before he found what he was looking for. Yep, I was standing in a cleaning closet. "Ah, there we go."

He looked so pleased with himself that all at once the annoyance from the two upstairs, along with the final shards of tension I'd been carrying throughout my interview, melted away when he took my face in his hands and his lips found mine. His tongue slipped along mine, leaving a hint of peppermint, like he'd just chomped down on a candy cane.

I didn't bother to hold in the moan as I relaxed into him.

This kiss was exactly the antidote I hadn't known I'd needed.

That was another thing about Parker. He was an incredible kisser. *Incredible.* I don't know why I was surprised the guy was so good, but he was. I could kiss him forever and never get bored.

"That's much better," he mumbled against my lips as he eased away, his green eyes sparkling with amusement and holding my gaze. "You know, I think you're even prettier since I last saw you."

I arched a brow at him. "You saw me two hours ago."

"I know, and you've gotten prettier…anyway, how was it?"

Blinking out of my lust-fueled haze, my forehead furrowed a little. "How was what?"

"The interview, Davison. The interview. Am I looking at the new social media manager for the Lions, or what?"

"Oh, well I don't know yet. They still have more people to see, but we find out in the next week."

He smacked his lips to mine once, twice, then a third time. "You'll get it."

Wrapping my arms around his waist, I took a deep breath, soaking in that distinctive Parker scent I'd become so familiar with; earthy, leathery, and rich, with a hint of sweetness breaking through, exactly like him.

"So, what's this surprise?"

Parker swept his hands through the air. "This."

I glanced around. Mops, bottles of Clorox, shelves of laundry detergent and fabric conditioner, floor cleaner…you name it, if you needed a domestic product, it would be in here.

"The supply closet?"

"Yup." He grinned. "It's our new at-work meeting spot."

"Our new meeting spot?" I replied, biting down my smile, because honestly…this guy.

"Yeah." He nodded. "Secret meeting spot."

Pushing my fingers through the silky curls at the base of his neck, I took his mouth with mine, kissing him with the full barrage of emotion coursing through me—lust pushing its way forward. It was debatable what was going to get me higher—the fumes from the cleaning products or Parker's mouth.

"You found this while I was having my interview?"

"I did. We'll stay a secret until we sign the form, but I'm still going to need a kiss to get me through the day, so this will have to do."

"It's only for a week or so," I muttered against his lips, while wondering if we could lock it from the inside and how long we could actually be in here before the fumes became dangerous.

"I know." One big hand cupped the back of my head, while the other slid down to my ass. "But I think I could get used to this. Making out in a supply closet is way hotter than I thought it would be."

"That's the fumes talking." I chuckled. "But seriously, thank you."

"Anything for you, Davison. Just name it."

His tongue slipped back into my mouth with a soft moan, right as the list of what I had to do this week flashed into my head. "Actually, there is one more thing…"

24

Parker

Why did I agree to this again?

Oh yeah, I was high off cleaning products and totally distracted by kissing Scout—something I was getting used to. Both the high and the kissing.

On the plus side, I'd successfully convinced Tanner to wear the Lions mascot costume instead of me. There's no way I was running around the bases wearing an extra fifty pounds. If I'd wanted to do that, I'd have joined the Army.

As I told Doctor Matthews on a weekly basis, I *hated* sprinting.

"It's so itchy," he griped, pulling down on the material

around his groin area as he waddled along. "If I get a rash from this thing, you're gonna owe me. I can't be dating Millie with a rash."

And that's how I convinced Tanner to swap places with me, because I agreed to help him with Millie. According to him, now I'd finally moved things along with Scout, it was "*his turn*."

I held in my grin and handed over the giant Lions head I'd been holding for him. "You're not dating her yet. Any rash will have gone by then."

"It best be." He nodded to the head. "And you can carry that until the last minute. Don't know why you're not wearing this too."

"Told you, Scout wanted the mascot running, along with a couple of the guys. Plus the dog."

"And we all agreed you look the cutest, which Millie will see when she watches it." Ace laughed loudly, slapping Tanner on the shoulder.

It was enough to have Tanner lose his balance and fall into me.

There's no way I wouldn't have been completely squashed if Lux hadn't rescued him in time by grabbing on the Lions shirt he was wearing. Maybe the costume was heavier than fifty pounds.

"Dude, watch what you're doing," I grumbled, straightening my tee.

"I have no control over what I'm doing," Tanner snapped back, his little lion paws shooting up in frustration.

"Not you, Ace." I nodded to where he was almost doubled over laughing. "It's not that funny."

"It really is." He swiped a hand across his eyes to dry them. "Explain what's happening again."

"Scout is shooting content for TikTok. We're running around the bases to see who's quicker—"

"Me, obviously," interrupted Ace.

"We all know it's not you, Watson. You don't run bases," shot out Lux, adding a punch to Ace's shoulder, though he managed to duck away before Lux's giant fist made contact.

"Can I finish?"

Lux swept his hand out. "Please do."

"We're running around the bases against the dog we have on Opening Day to collect the bats. It's for the dog charity game next month."

"We're racing a dog?"

I nodded as Ace rolled his eyes. "What did I *just* say?"

"How am I supposed to race a dog in this?" Tanner flapped his arms about again. "It's a thousand degrees, and I can only go one tiny step at a time. It's taken forever to walk from the locker rooms."

"We should have carried the costume out here so you could change in the dugout." Added Ace unhelpfully, though it was clear from the smirk he aimed at Tanner it was only to rile him up.

I couldn't tell if it was a purposeful retaliation from Tanner or simply because he now had zero spatial awareness, but when he bumped into Ace, the force was so great, Ace nearly fell over the boards.

"Now that *was* funny," he muttered, turning to me. "So where's the dog?"

"I dunno," I replied, glancing around at the field. Beyond a couple of the groundskeepers who were always here tending to the diamond on game days, I couldn't see a soul. It was eerily quiet. Out of habit, my eyes found the window by Scout's desk but she wasn't there, nor were any of her team. "They'll be here soon. I was told eleven, and it's just before."

"Can you text Scout and tell her to hurry up before I die of heat exhaustion? Or is that against the rules of keeping things a secret?"

This time, *I* rolled my eyes and ignored him.

"I *can* message her, but I'm not going to. She'll be here soon, she said eleven."

I think Tanner harrumphed in response, but it might have just been him groaning as he tried to duck down into the dugout. There was a reason the Lions mascot never came into the dugout and it had everything to do with the width of the entryway, that he didn't fit into.

After making several attempts, Tanner dropped down onto one of the steps before I could stop him because it was going to take all three of us to get him back to standing. The costume was so big that he barely had to look up to talk to me.

"There'd best not be anyone watching this. I don't want witnesses."

Lux stared at him, his brow dropping as the left side of his mouth quirked up. "Tan, it's going on TikTok."

"Yeah, but it'll have been edited by then. It won't be live."

"We're all running."

"You're not running dressed as a lion." Tanner doubled down on his scratching. "How does Billy wear this every day? My skin will be rubbed raw."

"You'll be fine, your clothes will protect you."

"What clothes?"

"What are you wearing underneath?"

"Nothing."

Lux inhaled sharply, which caused him to set off in a succession of choked coughing intermingled with hoarse laughter. "Please…no…are…you…com…mando…?"

"Yeah?"

"Dude! You have to wear something."

"No one told me." Tanner huffed, pulling at his groin again.

I didn't know whether to join Lux in his fit of laughter or feel sorry for Tanner. Instead, I ducked into the dugout, dialed the locker room from the phone on the wall, and asked the attendant to bring Tanner clean underwear and a tee.

It arrived five minutes later, which wasn't a minute too soon, given Tanner had already stripped off to change.

Ace and I were helping him step back into the costume when his eyes widened at something over my shoulder. "What's *he* doing here? Don't tell me he's watching this shit show?"

Lux let out a low whistle. "We'd best not fuck this up."

I spun around and lifted my sunglasses. Immediately my shoulders straightened, and my stomach dropped.

Even against the bright morning sun, walking toward us along the far edges of the field, was the clear and unmistakable outline of our boss, aka Penn Shepherd, accompanied by a couple of guys, and a black Labrador. I hadn't expected us to have an audience of this magnitude.

I hadn't expected us to have an audience at all.

I figured it would be the dog handler and the social team.

At thirty-four-ish, Penn Shepherd was the youngest owner in the MLB. Born into one of the wealthiest families in America, he was supposed to take over the family business a couple of years ago but instead bought or, depending on who you spoke to, *rescued* the Lions.

It was no secret that he lived and breathed baseball.

He never missed a game, and attended every single away series, nearly always traveling with us on the team plane. He was a good guy, unlike a lot of owners who were in it for the money and status, it was clear the New York Lions had quickly become his pride and joy.

His mission was to make the Lions a family club, and as such, he knew every single person by name—since he'd taken over, there hadn't been a birthday, anniversary, or kid's birth missed—from the cleaning crew up to Jupiter Reeves.

The flip side of this being he owned our jobs, and no matter how approachable he tried to make himself, it was hard to forget. Therefore, it was virtually impossible to relax in his presence, and this included running around the bases dressed as the mascot—in Tanner's case.

"Who are the other two?" I asked, my eyes trained on the way these guys were walking toward us like they owned the place.

In Penn Shepherd's case, it was true, but the two guys flanking him carried the same air of arrogance that anyone did when they knew they were top of their game, even in the jeans, tee, and sneakers they were all wearing.

I saw it every time I walked down the corridors to the locker rooms, or when I passed Jupiter Reeves—there was an imperceptible swagger quality, untouchable almost, but it set you apart.

There was no difference between businessmen, sportsmen, and whatever profession these guys were in—we all liked to win, and win big.

"The one with tattoos is Rafe Latham, the other is Murray Williams," Ace replied, leaning against the boards. "Rafe's a lawyer, Murray's in finance. I don't know Rafe well, but

Murray's married to Payton's bestie."

"He's a *lawyer*?"

I was expecting him to say the guy with the full sleeves of tattoos worked in security, or was, at a minimum, leader of a biker gang. He was the least lawyer-y looking lawyer I'd ever seen.

"Payton's bestie?" Lux's eyebrows shot up. "The one who's Radley's professor?"

"Yup."

I turned to him. "*That's* the guy you've hung out with?"

"Yup. He's cool." His shoulder jerked up. "But…you know…it's weird."

"Yeah." I nodded. "Like you're hanging out with your dad."

"Nah, I don't always feel like I have to be on my best behavior with my dad. I just don't want to be spending my free time with my boss."

Nudging into his side, I chuckled. "That's what happens when you date an older woman."

"Maybe, but the benefits outweigh who we hang with." He quirked an eyebrow, which needed no interpretation, and I dropped my head with a shake.

The three of them were twenty yards out when the Labrador spotted Ace and came bounding up to the boards, his tail wagging so hard and fast it was barely visible. You could only hear the *thud thud thud* every time it hit the post.

Ace knelt down to stroke him. "Hi, Barclay, buddy."

I turned around to Tanner, who was still on the step. "You want help getting up."

He shook his head. "Nope. I'm not moving until absolutely necessary."

"Good morning, gentlemen," Penn greeted as he reached the dugout, his hand outstretched to shake each of us in turn, pinning us with his steely blue eyes.

"Morning, sir." Lux nodded with one of those smiles where you're trying to be polite but not too cheery.

"So you're the poor, unwitting candidates who got roped into today's task."

"Yes, sir," replied Ace, while Tanner grunted quietly behind me.

"How'd that happen, I thought it would be the rookies today?" He laughed, peering around me to Tanner still on the step. "You okay down there, Simpson?"

"Yes, sir. Just conserving my energy for the big race." Tanner nodded, making Penn chuckle.

Ace being Ace, and the least unsubtle person ever, turned to me with the biggest shit-stirring grin he could muster, or that's how I was taking it.

"Parker, do you want to tell Mr. Shepherd how we got roped into this?"

It took all my energy not to grit my jaw and punch him in the nose. Instead, I plastered on my best fake smile and said, "Wrong time, wrong place. The social team caught us at a weak moment yesterday."

There. Not one part of my sentence was a lie.

I *had* been caught at a weak moment by the social team. It didn't stop the bead of sweat appearing on my brow, however. Penn simply nodded, his mouth held together.

Thankfully the awkwardness was saved by Barclay trotting into the dugout as he spotted a lone baseball on the floor. A second later it was dropped at Murray's feet, who immediately threw it across the grass for Barclay to sprint after.

"Murray, try not to carve up my field before the game today," Penn drawled.

"Hey, you want to tell my dog he can't play with a ball when he sees one? Be my guest."

Penn's response was to roll his eyes while the tattooed guy, whose name I already forgot and was yet to speak, turned to watch Barclay with a wry smile.

"What time does this thing start?"

"We were told eleven." My eyes drifted up to the large clock in the corner of the scoreboard. Man, there were still seven minutes to go.

Before I did something stupid like talk about Scout, I turned and sat down next to Tanner. "You okay, dude?"

"No, I'm fucking hot." He grumbled. "Please can you message Scout and tell her to hurry up. Pleeease."

"She'll be here soon." Just as I spoke the words, her two interns jogged along the wide path behind the boards edging the field, along with a couple of other guys holding tripods.

A minute later Scout made an appearance, striding out purposefully in a pair of jeans, an overly large white tee with the Lions logo on the front, and a laptop was clasped to her chest.

Barclay was still lying on the ground, a ball by his feet, Murray and the tattooed guy were laughing with Ace. Penn had stepped away to the boards by the side and was on the phone, but I noticed the second she spotted him, and a split second of panic washed over her face.

I guess having him here was a surprise for everyone, though it could have just been her reaction to being in Penn Shepherd's presence.

Biting down the smile I could feel forming, I resisted the urge to run to meet her and sent out a prayer she'd hear about this goddamn job before the week was up.

After a year of watching her from the sidelines, becoming virtually mute in her presence, and resigning myself to the fact I would never get a date with Scout, now that I had her, I didn't want to be keeping it a secret.

I mean, I wasn't about to be making out with her in front of our boss, but I'd at least like to smile at her without getting fired for it.

While I wasn't totally hating the sneaking around or the surprising amount of times we'd managed a brief hookup in our closet, it was becoming harder to avoid Coach and his beady eye, not to mention his questions.

Truthfully, I didn't think it would be quite this stressful, because ever since we'd gotten together, I'd been watching my behavior in a way I never had.

The ball of anxiety I'd been carrying around the last few days gurgled in agreement.

"Sorry we're late, we had a problem with one of the cameras," she announced, concentrating on the task in hand, while stopping as far away from me as she possibly could. "We'll set up quick and then we can get going."

After forming a small huddle with the guys and handing out instructions, they all took off and found their positions around the diamond, along with the angles they needed. Two tripods were set up—one near Tanner's position as shortstop and one by the mound. A third was holding a video camera.

"You think Shepherd knows about you two?" whispered Tanner, or he thought it was a whisper. *I* thought it was loud enough for the guy over in left outfield to hear, and therefore scowled at him.

"No. But you wanna say it any louder?"

In my opinion, Penn was far too busy to pay attention to any of the rumors circulating among his team.

Coach was a different issue, but thankfully we'd be safe from his watchful eyes this morning—his view on the content creation was that it took precious time away from practice, and he avoided it at all costs. He also wished the players would, but it wasn't a fight he was going to win against Penn Shepherd's brand-building juggernaut.

"What will you—" he started again, but I waved him off. My attention had been taken by something else.

"Shhh. I'm trying to listen."

Scout was standing with Murray, her fingers stroking Barclay's silky ears as they discussed what Barclay's role was for the day. It was all perfectly innocent, totally professional, and absolutely nothing untoward.

Except every time she smiled at Murray, my fist clenched so tight, it could crush a baseball.

When she laughed, I thought my chest was going to explode from the tension. And when Tattoos joined in, making her laugh even harder, I was ready to start a fight.

"Dude, chill." Tanner tugged on my shirt, breaking through the growing annoyance. "Sit back down, you're being so weird. Stop staring at Scout, she's just doing her job."

I glanced around, taking one look at Tanner's expression, and slumped back onto the step next to him. The anxiety ball that had exploded into jealousy raging through my blood simmered to a gentle wave, which I was now attempting to rub away.

It was official. I was losing it, something made even more pronounced when Scout turned away from them, her eyes locking onto mine long enough that when she smiled, I felt the full force of it hit me.

This time when Tanner spoke it was a barely audible whisper. "How much longer is this going to be secret?"

"Until the end of the week. They're doing second interviews now."

"Then you're signing the form?"

I nodded right as Scout called out, "We're almost ready. Tanner, we'll shoot you first with Barclay and then you can get out of the costume. After that, we'll follow with the other guys one at a time, is that good?"

For the first time all morning he let out a wide grin. "Hell, yeah."

"Great, d'you want to get into position? The plan is to have Barclay follow the ball around the bases with you running too. We throw from one base to the next and he sprints to each, but you might need to give him a bit of encouragement. We'll get a few shots of Ace pitching the ball, which we can cut and edit together so it looks like you're all racing."

"Cool," he replied, holding his hands out so we could all help him up. "Let's get this over with before anyone finds out it's happening. I don't need a bigger audience."

"Don't jinx it." I groaned, just as I noticed a couple of figures in the entrance to the tunnel.

He spoke too soon, however, and by the time Tanner had waddled up to home plate to stand with Murray and Barclay, the audience had increased to several of the senior team, including Beulah Holmes, head of legal, Lowe Slater, and the good doctor, Marnie Matthews.

My sixth sense was working overtime because where Marnie went, Jupiter wasn't far behind.

Thirty seconds later and there he was, along with Boomer Jones, Saint Velasquez, Stone Fields, and just to really round this morning out, Coach, followed by several of his assistant coaches. Everyone was in early today, it seemed.

At least Scout was now across the diamond, where I prayed she'd stay.

I kept my eyes trained on Tanner swinging his bat surprisingly well, considering, and moved to stand on the other side of Lux. He was giant enough to keep me out of Coach's eyeline.

"This is quite the audience," he muttered as Ace got into position on the mound.

"Ready?" called Scout. "On my count. Three, two, one."

Ace pitched, but even from where I was standing against the boards, I could see he'd barely put any force behind it.

Tanner hadn't had enough time to acclimate to the size of the costume, not to mention that now he was wearing the head, it was virtually impossible to see what he was doing. He swung and missed it, but the force of his swing had him spinning in the wrong direction, so instead of running to first base, he ran straight toward the mound, tripped, and fell over, only narrowly avoiding Ace.

While everyone else was doubled over laughing as they cheered Tanner, Barclay, the consummate canine professional in his specially made doggie baseball uniform, chased his ball perfectly around each base and, after passing third, sat by Murray's feet and waited for his biscuit.

The guys manning the tripods ran forward and helped Tanner to his feet when it was clear Ace was laughing too hard to be able to help.

"That is the best thing I've ever seen," wheezed Lux, clearing the tears from his eyes.

"I hope Scout didn't think she was going to get this in one take."

The second take didn't go much better, nor did the third. Tanner had tripped over his feet each time. The only one who'd managed to totally nail their performance time and again was Barclay, no doubt everything to do with the biscuits he was getting at the end of each run.

Lux was still trying to contain himself, along with nearly everyone else. Jupiter was making Boomerangs of Tanner falling over. Penn Shepherd was standing with his senior executive team, not one of whom was making any effort to disguise their amusement.

But it was Scout I couldn't take my eyes off.

Her mouth wide open, head back as she belted her laughs to the heavens, her chest heaving with each jagged inhale. I was too far away to properly see her face, but I knew her nose had crinkled up and the line of freckles that had grown over the last few weeks would look almost like a smudge.

It was frightening how long I'd stared at her face while she'd slept next to me.

In the end, Tanner got to second base before Scout called time on the whole fiasco. Removing his lion head, he waddled back to the dugout, his bottom lip protruding in a sulk.

"Buddy, that was awesome," Lux said, still wiping his eyes dry. "I haven't laughed like that in ages."

Tanner grunted in response. "I think I've broken a rib."

"Parker, you're up."

Twisting around to the sound of my name, I found Scout gesturing me over to home plate. I'd been having so much fun watching Tanner that I jogged over with a wide smile trained directly on her, before I remembered where I was and who was watching. But it was too late, I couldn't turn it down.

"Hey there." I grinned, stepping in as close as I reasonably could. Close enough that I could catch her fresh cottony scent. Close enough to breathe her in until my chest flickered. But not being able to kiss her when I knew I could was a new kind of torture. Just an hour of barely acknowledging her while Tanner attempted to get around the bases was hard enough. "You look very pretty today."

"Thank you," she replied, her face almost blank.

She was certainly winning at this secret relationship acting thing. I, on the other hand, may as well have taken a Sharpie to my forehead.

"I like seeing you in a Lions shirt, but you know what would be even better?"

"Let me guess...*your* Lions shirt?"

"Got it in one." I held her gaze, watching her pupils flare as she tried to hold in her smile.

There was something about Scout that made all the usual noise around me quieten, and I could have stayed here all day as she tried to hold in her smile.

"Ace will pitch, try to avoid the cameras when you're running."

"Shouldn't they be trying to avoid me?" I winked.

"Barclay will outrun you, so don't worry about him," she continued, her tone full of tease. "But please try and get it in one take. Tanner took so long that we're running out of time."

"Anything for you, Davison."

"Thank you."

"I missed you this morning," I whispered, taking the helmet she was holding out to me. A zap of static shocked between us as our fingers brushed. "But Monday's a free day, I vote we make it our first date day. And also make up for lost time. Whaddya say?"

She popped a hip, crossing her arms over her chest, and her face filled with sass. "What time have we lost?"

"Well, you know...we could be making out in the closet right now, or I could have stayed over at yours last night." I dropped my voice. "Any time I don't get to spend naked with you is lost time. So...Monday, date?"

There was something about the way she looked up at me, bright blue eyes widening under the almond curve of her thick black lashes, that hit the dead center of my groin.

She took a step back, followed by another, before giving

one single tiny nod, and then the smile she'd been holding in beamed out.

Fucking yes.

We filmed my segment in one take and finished the morning on schedule.

By the time we wrapped, even Tanner was enjoying himself, and with everyone else buzzing hard off all the chatter and laughing, there had been too much going on for me to notice Coach had spent most of the time scowling in my direction.

25

Scout

"Do you wanna slow down on that before you choke?"

I stuffed another handful of popcorn into my mouth. "Huh?"

Alice removed the box from my hands.

The hot dog guy was walking down the steps between the seats, and I was tempted to call him over. Instead, I picked up the giant Slurpee and we watched Boomer Jones walk over to home plate.

The old-school baseball organ—original to Lions Stadium, and one of my favorite things about home games—blared out something sounding a lot like Beyoncé.

For a second, it brought a smile to my lips, though it died again when Boomer missed his first swing.

I shoved my fist back into the popcorn box. "Dammit."

Today we were playing the Cubs at home, the final game of the series and the first time this season I was watching a home game from the comfort of the stands. We'd recorded content before the first pitch, and everything else we'd take from the usual filming around the stadium.

This was my game to enjoy.

Try to enjoy.

Except right now we were bottom of the sixth, trailing the Cubs by four runs. Parker was currently grounded at second. His face filled the screen on the Jumbotron, and from the tension in his jaw, anyone could see how annoyed he was.

I'd missed the 101 on coping with the game-day pressure of dating a baseball player. Combine the dating-in-secret and you had the perfect recipe for stress eating. I'd already been through a packet of Twizzlers. At this rate I'd be downing a bottle of Pepto-Bismol before the day was out.

I shoved another handful of popcorn in my mouth as Boomer's bat finally made contact with the ball hard enough for it to soar high into left field. My answer was drowned out by the deafening roar of the home crowds. Parker passed third and jogged safely to the dugout followed by Boomer, closing the gap on the score.

It was as he ducked down his eyes flicked left and right, and I knew he was searching for me.

So far I was six for six each inning he'd run into the dugout, and my heart had done a little skippity-skip every time. I was undecided whether that was a good thing or not.

Alice moved the popcorn out of my reach. "I take it you've still not heard about the job?"

Oh, that was another reason I was eating my body weight in sugar. This goddamn job.

I shook my head, pulled out my phone, and passed it to her.

FROM: NEW YORK LIONS HR

SUBJECT: SOCIAL MEDIA MANAGER ROLE

Dear Scout,

We'd like to inform you that you are through to the final round of interviews. Please send us your availability over the next two weeks.

Sincerely,

HR

"Another round of interviews?"

"Yup."

"I thought they were done."

"Me too."

"What did Parker say?"

I shook my head. "It just came through this morning. I haven't told him."

It had been a week since I'd promised Parker we'd sign the form once I'd heard about the job. I'd been told I'd hear about it by today, and technically I did. I just didn't hear what I thought I'd hear.

And since then my nerves had been very slowly fraying.

"So is this your second interview?"

I shook my head. "My *first* interview was my second interview. Because I work here, they didn't need a chemistry session, which is what everyone else had. They already know they like me. This will be a third, I guess."

Alice took my Slurpee and brought the straw to her lips. "Of course they like you…but three interviews…feels like a long process just to offer you the job."

I tore my eyes away from the screen showing Boomer and Parker making their way down the gauntlet of boys in the dugout, and turned to her, puffing out a long exhale.

"I guess, but maybe they can't decide. Maybe they like these other people better."

"What about you? Have you decided if you even want it?"

"Nope." I took a giant glug of Slurpee and shrugged. "It's just the way they talk makes it sound like they're going to give it to me, so why drag me through the wait and bring other people in? Either give it to me or don't. It's stressing me out, but maybe that's the point. Maybe it's good experience."

"I hadn't noticed," Alice drawled sarcastically. "What are you going to do about the form?"

My belly did that thing again where it felt like it was turning inside out, which had me reaching for the popcorn again. Right now it was the only thing helping settle my stomach.

The *form.* The goddamn form.

It was all I'd been thinking about because it was literally all anyone had been *talking* about, thanks to the betting pool that someone on the comms team started. Ten dollar entry to pick which of the players would be the first to sign the HR form. The winning pot was already up to four hundred dollars, and Parker was in the lead by a 70 percent margin.

My eyes stayed trained on Lux getting into position.

"I don't know. Wait, I guess."

"Are you still signing it?"

"Of course I am, I didn't know this was going to happen." I waved my phone at her.

Alice was silent, though her brows disappeared under her bangs from the way I snapped my response. While it was a perfectly reasonable question, it only exacerbated the guilt I'd been stewing in since the email had arrived at 9:02 a.m. this morning.

This stupid job was causing me nothing but a headache so far, which didn't bode well for its future. I'd promised

Parker we'd sign the form, and I didn't think he'd want to wait another week, or however long this interview process was going to take.

I'd even come out here early for a little thinking time, and the opportunity to watch Parker warm up before the stadium filled and things got crazy, but that hadn't happened either.

An increasingly annoying group of girls sitting a few rows in front of us also decided to come out early.

Every time a new player stepped up to the plate, they jumped to their feet screaming and waving their Lions banner in the air, only for the screaming to turn to screeching when they'd scored. Alice and I had been here when they'd arrived, each wearing a homemade tee with a player's face on it, including Parker's.

The girl with Parker's face had sat down directly in front of me, and instead of concentrating on the game, had spent all her time talking about how she was going to wait at the gates for Parker and give him her number.

There was a strange combination of emotions coursing through my veins right now—jealousy, annoyance, frustration. I'd never been a jealous person. Even when Mark had spent New Year with his ex, jealousy wasn't the overriding emotion I'd felt.

But now, listening to these girls talk about hooking up with the guys—including Parker—like it was nothing more than a game, had ignited a thick green flame burning in my gut.

"And that's all it is?" Alice asked, after the latest ruckus died down.

"What do you mean?"

"Your hesitation to sign the form isn't about anything else? It's just the job?"

"I'm not hesitating!" I reached for more popcorn but thought better of it when my stomach clenched in protest. "Why else wouldn't I be signing it?"

"I dunno." She shrugged, her eyes flicking to the girls in front. "You wanted to be single this year after what happened with Mark…"

She left the end of her sentence hanging for me to grab onto.

"Parker's not Mark," I muttered eventually.

"I know he's not. I just wanted to make sure *you* know he's not."

"I know he's not."

"Good, because look at how cute he is." She pointed up to the screen where Parker's face was zoomed in as he chatted with Ace in the dugout, laughing along at whatever he was saying. Big smile on full beam. "Shithead wasn't cute."

"Parker *is* cute, isn't he?" I grinned, spinning my entire body around in my seat to face Alice. "Sorry I snapped at you, I didn't mean it."

"I know."

"I'm stressed about the job, that's all, because I didn't think the process would go on for this long. I don't want to get Parker into trouble…" I let out a deep sigh. "I dunno, maybe I should just sign it, especially since I still can't decide if I even want the job. It took me a whole season to get to grips with everything that needed to be done around here, and I'd have to do it all again…" I chewed the corner of my cheek as Boomer Jones's face appeared on the screen.

"But?"

"But…" I took a deep breath as the uneasiness I'd tried to bury for the past few weeks made itself known again. "Okay, hear me out. I know Parker isn't Mark, it's not that at all, and I'm not hesitating. I'm happy to sign it. *But* what if we sign this thing then it all ends? Like twisted karma or something. I just *know* if I sign this form it'll reflect on me in some way. HR will not stay impartial, and then not only will I *not* be dating Parker, I'll also *not* have a job I spent two months of my life working on. And Parker's a star here, he'll take priority. They won't care about me."

"Wow." Alice blinked widely and pulled out her phone. "You need me to call you an Uber from your spiral?"

I rolled my eyes in response.

"Babe, you really need to chill."

"I *can't* chill. Since I got the email from HR I have *lost all chill.*"

"It definitely won't be as bad as you're making it out to be."

"You have nothing to base that off. People are still talking about Boomer and Leanne. There's a goddamn bet running in the office. It's up to four hundred bucks."

Alice glanced away, but I could tell she was trying her hardest not to laugh. "I hope you noticed I didn't enter. Even though I'd have split that money with you."

"Alice," I whined. "I'm serious."

"So am I. Okay, maybe not split. Sixty-forty." She grinned wider as my scowl deepened. "Have you told Parker about the bet?"

I shook my head. "No, he'd only think it was funny."

"It is funny."

"Not to me."

Sensing I might *actually* be about to spiral, Alice picked up the popcorn and passed it over. "The way I see it, that boy is totally gaga for you. Anyone else can see it too. It's why so many have put their money against him."

"It means everyone already suspects. That doesn't make it better."

"It kind of does." She shot back. "All I'm saying is you don't have to worry about it ending before it starts. I don't think that boy is going anywhere, and he's willing to sneak around for you. So that should tell you everything."

I nodded slowly. "You think?"

"Yes. But I do think you should sign that form, if only to stop you stressing out more. They can't hold it against you for signing it, it's like the rules of HR or something."

I pressed into my temples in an attempt to rub away the

tension building there. "Yeah, maybe you're right. I'll go and speak to them on Monday. Or do you think I should speak to Ava?"

"HR"

I nodded. "Okay."

When are you seeing him next?"

"After the game. Tomorrow's a free day, so we're hanging out."

Alice leaned in, lowering her voice to a whisper and nodding to the row in front of us. "You should ask if you can have her T-shirt."

"No thanks. She's probably been sleeping in it," I replied as Ace got ready to pitch.

Even from where we were sitting you could hear the crack of the bat, a split second later the Cubs fans erupted as we all watched the ball fly through the air, heading for the guys in the dinghies out on the Hudson.

The camera followed the trajectory until the screen filled with the dozens of little boats and guys sitting in them with their hands in the air, waiting. A couple of them were brave enough to stand, managing to hold themselves steady on the waves.

"Shit. We're not doing so well," grumbled Alice as the two Cubs players, plus the guy who'd hit the home run, reached their dugout.

"No."

"You'll need to perform your girlfriend duties tonight."

My eyes flicked to Alice from where they were focused on Parker and Ace, both looking serious as they held a quick powwow on the mound. "What?"

She waggled her brows. "You'll need to take his mind off losing."

I smothered a laugh as the girl wearing the Parker's face tee stood up and moved down her row. I didn't want that shirt, but I could cheer Parker up with something even better. Cheer myself up too.

I leaned into Alice. "Will you come to the store with me during the stretch?"

26

Parker

"Is that Scout?" asked Tanner when the buzzer for the elevator sounded, indicating someone was on the way up.

I nodded. "Yup."

"Why didn't she just get a ride home with us?"

Grabbing two bottles of water from the fridge, I kicked the door closed, just as another strike of lightning lit up the living room. The heavens had opened twenty minutes after we left the field, and it didn't look like they were going to close anytime soon.

"Because we're trying not to be seen together. We have to stay a secret until she hears about the job."

"Dude—"

"Not now, Tan," I snapped, interrupting him before he could say any more.

I was already in a bad mood because we'd lost to the Cubs, I didn't want it to get worse by Tanner warning me, *again,* that I needed to get the form signed before Coach found out.

"And don't bring it up this weekend either," I added as an afterthought.

The last thing I wanted was for Scout to get more stressed out about her job, or get annoyed with Tanner. *Or* me. The few sleepovers we'd had so far had been at hers, and this would be the first time she'd ever stayed over at my place.

Therefore, I kind of wanted it to go well, and I *really* wanted her to come back again.

He held his hands up in surrender but thankfully stayed silent as he continued his nightly search through the cabinets for a bedtime snack, which inevitably ended when he found either the Froot Loops or the Cocoa Pebbles.

"Thanks, man," I called out, while sprinting across the living room to where the elevator doors opened directly into our apartment. "Appreciate it."

I made it with a second to spare, and the moment I saw Scout standing in front of me, all the annoyance about losing the game and all the thoughts about the unsigned form vanished.

Yeah, she was totally worth dodging Coach for another

few days.

"Hey." She smiled, tucking a loose blonde strand behind her ear.

Holding my hand out, I tugged her from the elevator and pulled her into me. "You're here."

Taking her face in my hands, I pressed my lips to hers and breathed her in. Immediately my entire body relaxed and calm washed over me, taking with it all the tension I'd been carrying since the game finished. Scout was in my apartment where we'd stay for the next thirty-six hours, and I wanted to savor every single second.

"C'mon, let me show you around."

Easing her bag off her shoulder, I took hold of her hand and guided her into the main room. Just as everyone did when they first stepped around the wide column separating the living room from the elevator, she stopped dead in her stride.

The floor-to-ceiling, wraparound windows provided one of the most incredible views in all of Manhattan, and it was always a lively discussion over which time of day showed the city at its best.

Ace liked sunrise, not that he was ever up that early, so I wasn't entirely sure how he'd discovered it. Tanner and Lux always went with late afternoon when the sun hit the Hudson just enough to make it look like it was golden.

But me? I loved right now when the city that never sleeps was lit up by a million twinkling offices and the lights of the cabs and cars far below.

Right now was when New York really came to life. You couldn't see it from this angle, but in my room, the Empire State Building was so huge stretching out in front of me, that I'd lie in bed at night staring at it while I waited for the adrenaline from that evening's game to subside.

"Wow," was all Scout managed, which was the standard response.

"Awesome, right?" I laughed, pulling her toward the kitchen where Tanner was pouring out a bowl of Cocoa Pebbles.

"Yeah, it's really something. I didn't expect it to be so big," she replied, tearing her eyes away from the windows as we stopped in front of the kitchen counter. "Oh hey, Tanner. Sorry, I didn't see you there."

"It happens," he mumbled, shoveling an overflowing spoon of cereal into his mouth.

"Four of you live here?"

I nodded. "Yep, Tanner and me, plus Ace and Lux. This floor has two apartments on it. We each take half of the building."

"Is everyone here?"

"No, Ace is at his girlfriend's. Lux and Radley went to bed already."

Scout's eyes widened again, I couldn't tell if it was because she was still genuinely impressed with the apartment or if she was nervous at the thought of so many people being here.

In truth, I was kind of nervous too.

We'd never spent time together *with people*—with friends. I'd been to hers a couple of times when her roommate was away, but this would be the first time we'd be in a group, and I sent out a silent prayer I wouldn't blow it.

Although given Tanner was now drinking down the remains of his cereal while spilling milk everywhere, including down his chin, I'd say the likelihood of Scout leaving before sunrise would be down to our caveman ways of living.

When he was done, he swiped an arm across his face, pushed out of his stool, and deposited his empty bowl into the sink. "I'm going to bed. I'm not going to stick around so I can be reminded I'm the only one without a girlfriend."

"Night, Tan," I called, only to get a grunt in response as he disappeared down the corridor leading to his room.

Scout turned to me. "What did that mean?"

"Nothing, just ignore him." I shook my head, picking up the two bottles of water I'd taken from the fridge, and draped my spare arm around her shoulder. "Come on, it's bedtime."

"Do you mind if I shower?"

"Nope, because I'm joining you." I grinned and silently led her down the corridor all the way to the end, where my bedroom door was wide open.

Because Scout hadn't come back with us, I'd taken the opportunity to rush home from the game, steal some of the candles Ace was always burning, and light them around my room. The blinds were open, so between the city lights and the flickering flames, the place looked like it was glowing, and even if I did say so myself, it looked pretty fucking cool. Especially with the rain.

It was the most effort I'd ever gone to, and if I was a girl, I'd definitely sleep with me.

"Wow." She walked straight to the windows at the end, stopping in front of where the Empire State Building stood tall fifteen blocks away, with its top floors glowing green. "This view is seriously amazing."

"Sure is."

I guess she expected me to be looking out the window, too, except when she turned around, my eyes were on her, and her only. Where they'd been since she'd walked in. Where they always were when she was around.

Her head crooked as she peered at me. "What're you doing?"

"Nothing, just watching you."

"Yeah?"

"Yup."

"Why?"

My mind swirled with a million thoughts, a million reasons why I would be watching her. But that's not what she meant.

"Because…because I've thought about this for so long, and now you're finally here in my bedroom…well…" I grinned wide, a poor attempt to lighten the moment and stem the near-overwhelming flow of emotions rising in my chest. "I just hope you're prepared."

"I'm prepared."

Scout stepped back. She was doing that thing she did when she was nervous, where she kind of chewed her lip, *except* she didn't look nervous. Her pupils had flared way too much for that.

I stayed where I was as she slowly removed her sneakers, followed by her jacket, letting it fall to the floor.

My mouth dropped.

I hadn't noticed much about what she was wearing when she arrived, beyond the shorts and a tee she'd had on at the game today. I was too focused on kissing her and dragging her into my lair. If I had seen, there's no way I'd have stopped to chat to Tanner.

We'd have been in my bedroom in under ten seconds, her feet barely touching the floor.

Scout's eyelashes flickered against her cheekbones, and she looked up at me. "I'm sorry you lost today."

Given my current view, I honestly couldn't remember what had happened up to the second we stepped over the threshold to my bedroom and I'd closed the door. Yeah, we lost. It sucked. But if this was my consolation prize, I'd lose every damn day of the week.

Right now, standing before me, looking more glorious than I'd ever seen a human look, was Scout wearing *my* shirt, and if I was correct—which I was—she had nothing underneath. I'd had a couple of girlfriends throughout high school who'd worn my number and the thousands of fans who wore it to every game, but I'd never been *that* bothered about it.

Yet Scout in it...my dick was thickening to the point of painful.

She was the best view of all views.

Holding her gaze, I walked toward her until I was almost touching the tip of her toes with mine.

"My shirt has never looked better."

The hem stopped just below the line of her shorts, and I ran my finger along it just to check that it was *really* real. Her breath caught as a knuckle brushed the soft skin at the top of her thigh. I couldn't tell what I was more turned on by, that sound or Scout in my shirt.

"You like it?"

"No, I fucking *love* it."

"Really?"

"Really. And you're going to be wearing it the entire time you're here."

She rolled her eyes with a smirk. "Okay, hotshot. I packed a bag, but whatever. We're not leaving the bedroom, right?"

"Nope. Not leaving," I repeated, though I wasn't really listening. My focus was trained entirely on my shirt wrapped around her, and what was underneath.

Except in her next breath, she began unbuttoning it.

I stopped her hands from moving further down. "No, Davison, you're not taking that off."

"But aren't we having a shower? It'll get wet."

"And I have a hundred more for you to dry yourself with."

I could tell she thought I was crazy, and there was a large possibility I was, but it was too late. I would never get enough of seeing Scout in my shirt, and if that meant she was wearing it every second of this weekend, then *sobeit*.

"Point me in the right direction then."

I'd never stripped off quicker, and dragged her through my dressing room to the bathroom, at the end of which was a double shower the width of the room. When we'd first moved in, I'd won the master suite with the bath, but Lux traded me for a year's worth of movie-watching privileges because he'd loved baths.

I definitely got the better end of the deal. This shower was awesome.

"Your shower is bigger than my apartment."

I reached in and turned on the water, waiting until it was hot enough for steam to rise and hit the glass walls. "Not quite."

Stepping out of her shorts and panties to move around me, Scout stood just out of reach of the torrents raining down from the two enormous showerheads, one perfectly arched eyebrow raised and directed at me.

"Sure you want me to keep this on?"

"I'm sure."

"Okay," she replied, and moved under the shower, tipping her head back.

I knew she'd look sexy, I didn't know she'd look *this* sexy.

This was my own personal wet T-shirt contest, a *Sports Illustrated* swimsuit edition cover come to life.

The fabric immediately clung to her, emphasizing each perfect, delicious curve of her body.

The swell of her tits, the dip of her waist, the hips I loved to dig my fingers into when I fucked her from behind.

Even through the black cotton, I could see the hard peak of her nipple as beads of water ran down her chest and dripped off the end.

I knew for a fact she had absolutely no idea how perfect she looked, or how gone I was for her already. I wanted to wrap myself around her and never come up for air.

She glanced over at me, wiping the water from her face. "Are you just going to stand there?"

"Uh-uh."

Closing the shower door behind me, I found her staring at me, big blue eyes filled with amusement, and one fist propped on her hip. "Is this what you had in mind?"

My hand slipped across her wet ass and down to her thigh. "Oh, you're way better than what I had in mind, Davison. You're so fucking hot, sometimes I think my head's going to explode."

Just like she always did when I paid her a compliment, her cheeks flushed and she couldn't hold my eye, but I was having none of that today. Gripping her chin, I brought her back to facing me. I needed to see that every word out of my mouth was the god's honest truth.

"You blow my mind, Scout. The reality of you is better than any fantasy I ever had, I like you so fucking much, and I'm never going to stop telling you. So stop shying away when I pay you a compliment."

She paused for a second, I could almost hear the whirring of her brain, and then she sank to her knees. "Was this one of your fantasies?"

Before I had time to answer, her full, pink lips wrapped around my dick.

"Ohhh…fuuck. Yeahhh…"

Her tongue flattened out and ran along the underside of my shaft, catching the sensitive patch of skin near the tip that almost had my knees buckling. My eyes opened enough to catch a glimpse of hers flashing up at me, before her mouth sank back onto my cock.

The sensation of her tongue, the image of Scout on her knees while my dick swelled in her mouth, was almost too much for my brain to compute. It was midnight, I'd played a long, hard-fought game that we'd lost, and I should have been exhausted, but my body was firing on all cylinders, and I didn't want to miss a second of it.

Brushing her damp hair to one side, away from her face, I

watched her cheeks hollow out as she sucked me in.

Pressure shot down my spine, gathering in my balls. I was seconds away from detonating. If she didn't want me coming in her mouth, she needed to move.

"Ahhh, Davison…" I managed to garble. "I'm…so…close."

Instead of kneeling back like I expected her to, her nails dug into my ass until she was almost pushing me into her. Fisting her hair, my hips drove forward of their own accord, fucking her mouth until I couldn't hold it any longer and I exploded down her throat.

Even when I fell back onto the bench running the length of the shower, her tongue worked to stretch out my orgasm until I had to pull her away and onto my lap. Before she even realized what had happened, I'd gripped the back of her head and pulled her lips to mine.

Over and over my tongue swiped against hers, tasting myself in her mouth. It was addicting, she was addicting. I doubted I would ever get enough of her. My fingers ran through her hair, scraping it away from her face, and I slowly moved back so I could look at her.

A lone drop of water ran down from her brow. The steam had turned her cheeks pink, which in turn made her blue eyes appear even bluer, reminding me of a trip to the Bahamas we'd taken last winter. It was becoming harder to ignore the way my heartbeat quickened the longer I stared at her.

"You become more perfect every day." I smacked another kiss to her lips. "Now it's your turn."

Slowly, I slipped each button from its hole until the shirt opened to reveal Scout's beautiful body and perfect smooth, golden skin.

My dick was already getting hard at the sight of her splayed out before me, thighs wide enough that I could see the tiny nub of her clit peeking out. Slipping my hands between her thighs, I eased two fingers inside her.

"Look at you, Davison. So fucking perfect. So fucking wet. All for me."

She let out a garbled moan.

"Do you like that? I know you do, I can feel your pussy tightening. Tell me, I want to hear you say it."

"Yes," she breathed out, "it feels so good."

She arched back, pushing her tits into my face as she gripped my neck and rocked on my palm. I wanted to make this good for her, as good for her as she'd done for me.

Catching sight of it from the corner of my eye, I suddenly found a purpose for the stupid, pointless handheld shower I had never, ever used. Careful not to drop Scout, I leaned forward, switched it on, and held onto it. Her eyes tracked the movement as I hovered it directly above the apex of her thigh, right where she spread over me.

The first powerful hit of spray on her clit had her crying out, her head once more lolling back, and her walls clenching hard around my fingers, still twisting inside her.

"Oh god, Parker..."

From her groan, I could tell she was trying to stay quiet, and that wasn't going to work for me. I wanted her loud.

Dipping my head, I ran my tongue around her taut nipple. "No one can hear you. Not with the shower running, too, you can scream my name all you want, Davison."

"*Ahh*…Parker…yes."

"Better."

It was becoming too much not to join in; she was too close and I was too selfish to let her have this all to herself. I wanted her to squeeze my cock. Her pussy was so slippery I only needed to line her up and ease her down, before I was nestled right up to my balls. Her head was already lolling back as I worked her clit.

Her cries bounced off the tiles as the spray circled over her sensitive skin. Each swipe of the water powering across her skin had her pussy gripping me like a clamp as the pressure inside her built until she needed more.

Tossing the showerhead to the side, I gripped her hips and lifted her, over and over, driving up into her as her thighs shook violently. It only took another few seconds before her convulsions began for real, pushing us both over the edge.

She collapsed onto me, her body heaving as she tried to level her breathing, until all I could hear was the water still pummeling the tiles while the showerhead snaked across the floor, spraying everywhere, but I had no energy left to turn either off.

I reasonably wondered if we could stay here all night.

27

Scout

There's something to be said about starting a day with morning sex.

The hottest guy on earth worshipping you, whispering enough dirty words that you shatter into a million little pieces as he cries your name out like it's the answer to all his questions.

It's exhilarating. Addicting. Ego boosting.

And entirely nerve wracking. Because then you have to come to terms with the fact you could quite easily be falling for this guy. You're beginning to forget what life was like before he bulldozed into your life, taking over every spare second of every day, and pushing out any other thought in your brain until there's no space for anything else.

Now, you're getting dressed in his apartment-sized bathroom while he makes you coffee. It was the reason I was currently running on a high, while also being extra careful not to become overwhelmed, because that was a better word to describe how I was feeling.

Or trying *not* to feel.

Dropping the toothbrush back into my toiletry bag, I gave up attempting to flatten my hair out and pushed it back with a headband, reminding myself I should never go to bed with it wet. It was still kind of sticking up at all angles, but it would have to do.

Tugging on the sweater Parker had been wearing last night and taking one last look in the mirror, I followed the smell of coffee, but not before allowing myself a small smile at the soaking wet Lions shirt still on the floor of Parker's shower.

I wasn't sure what I'd expected turning up to Parker's in his shirt, but I hadn't expected *that.*

Opening his bedroom door, the sound of several voices provided the sober reminder we weren't alone. I might have briefly seen Tanner last night, but after he'd disappeared to bed, and Parker and I had spent the next hour steaming up the shower, I'd all but forgotten that Parker lived with three other guys.

Which came to the second reason my belly had started somersaulting.

These were guys I saw on a daily basis, *at my work.* I mean, I knew they knew about mine and Parker's secret, but it's one thing having knowledge and quite another having it paraded in front of your face. Not to mention between the all-night sex marathon, and again this morning, I'd yet to find a good moment to tell Parker about us needing to stay on the DL for one more week…or however long this job was going to take.

I stepped out in the corridor and stopped.

Unless Tanner had become a ventriloquist overnight, there were at least two other people standing in the kitchen, having a high-stakes discussion over what sounded like breakfast.

"Bacon and maple syrup."

"Bacon isn't a topping."

"It is if I put it on top."

"No, bacon goes on the side."

"But I have it on top."

"That doesn't make it a topping."

"You can have fruit, yogurt, syrup, chocolate chips."

The mention of bacon plus the smell of coffee was too much for my stomach to hold in the rumble. I really wanted breakfast, but I also really *didn't* want to be surrounded by a bunch of people who might question me about work and things I didn't want to answer. Standing in the corridor while everyone ate wasn't an option either, and Parker would only come out to get me.

My stomach rumbled again, kind of making my decision

for me.

Peering around the corner, I immediately caught the eye of the girl standing next to Lux.

Though I'd never met her, she was instantly recognizable, given she was the president's daughter, and therefore a regular feature in gossip magazines, especially since she started dating Lux. But, mostly, from the amount of home games she'd attended, where she'd inevitably appear on the Jumbotron any time Lux scored.

"Hey, Scout's here."

Parker spun so quickly he only narrowly missed Lux and the spatula he was holding. He hurried over, skidding to stop right in front of me with a broad grin curving his lips. I don't know what it was about Parker's smile, but immediately all worry and thoughts about my job quietened.

"Good morning." He breathed in, pressing his lips to mine. "I was just about to come and get you. I'm making you coffee. Happy first date day."

"First date day?"

"Yeah, I said we were going to have a first date this weekend, and here we are." His grin turned sheepish. "Sorry we're not alone and I'm kind of throwing you to the wolves, too, but it'll be fun, I promise."

He looked so pleased with himself, I could do nothing but smile back. "Can't wait. And coffee sounds great. What else is that I smell?"

He slung one of his thick biceps around my shoulder. "*That* is breakfast Casa Grayskull style. C'mon, it's waiting for you."

"What?"

"Casa Grayskull." He shrugged, guiding me toward the kitchen. "It's what we named this place when we moved in. It's from *He-Man*, we're Masters of the Baseball Universe."

I don't know what expression I was wearing because I didn't get any more of an explanation from Parker, only a loud laugh as he pulled out a stool for me to sit on. Immediately a plate was placed in front of me—a stack of pancakes with little smiley faces of chocolate chips.

"There's bacon, fruit, and yogurt too. Plus maple syrup," Parker added, placing the largest bottle I'd ever seen in front of me, next to a glass of orange juice.

My mouth still hadn't closed when Tanner turned around from the stove to watch me, Lux flipped another pancake onto another stack big enough to feed the entire starting nine and waited, eyes on me. Both of them. Guess breakfast also came with an audience.

"Eat, Davison. Don't let them go cold."

I didn't need to be told twice, even though it felt like I was putting on a show, and forked in a mouthful. My entire body melted as I chewed down on the fluffiest pancakes I'd ever tasted.

"OMGawd."

"Good, right?" said Radley, pulling out the stool next to

me and piling up her own plate. "Lux is great at cooking anything, but breakfast is his specialty."

I nodded and forked in another mouthful. I never wanted to stop eating these pancakes.

"Sorry, I shouldn't speak to you while you're eating. I'm Radley, by the way, and I've been very excited to meet you finally. Parker's told us lots about you."

Her smile was so warm and genuine, it took a second for the last part of her sentence to register. The bit about being excited to meet me.

"Radley…" Parker groaned, making her laugh.

"What?" She shrugged, her face a mask of innocence. "You have."

"Yeah, but I'm still trying to play it cool." He turned and winked at me.

I swallowed my mouthful and washed it down with a sip of juice. "I think that ship sailed a long time ago."

"No way," Parker replied, his long fingers digging into my side, making me squeal with a little laughter, but mostly embarrassment. "I know you still think I'm cool."

"You're all right." I shrugged.

Radley picked up her coffee cup, trying and failing to hide a wide smirk. "I think you'll fit in here just fine, Scout. And I'm glad you're here, we need more girls."

"Thank you." My eyes flicked over to Parker, who was watching me with an expression that I felt deep in my chest.

Without saying another word, he turned around to join in with whatever conversation Lux and Tanner were having—from the sounds of it, still bacon as a viable topping.

I glanced at Radley. "Does Lux do all the cooking here?"

She picked up the orange juice and poured herself a glass. "Yup. He enjoys it—plus, the boys would probably live on cereal if he didn't."

"I'm impressed," I replied, staring at the growing pancake stack, even though it seemed the boys were eating as fast as he was making them.

"Yeah, he's great. I don't know if Parker told you, but he also gives the boys cooking lessons."

"That's awesome. Is that why there's so much food? They've been helping?"

"Oh, no, that's normally how much they make when everyone's here. It'll all get eaten." Radley giggled, leaning across the counter to fork up a fat strawberry from a bowl of fruit and swipe it through the maple syrup. "So, what exactly do you do at the Lions? Parker's not gone into that much detail."

Sitting back, I eased a hand over my stomach, congratulating myself for pulling on sweatpants and forgoing jeans, because there's no way I wouldn't be unbuttoning right now. "I'm part of the social media team, I mostly run TikTok, but we all work together on the overall strategy for how the social channels present."

"That's cool. I try not to go on social media because…

you know, there's always someone saying something nasty about my mom, or I'll see some video someone's taken of me walking down the street, or coming out of class, or eating. It creeps me out."

"I can't imagine what that's like." I nodded, because it was bad enough just having Pablo and Alice gossiping at work. The thought of having every move monitored and uploaded to socials gave me hives.

But Radley shrugged it off. "You get used to it, Lux has been so amazing at building my confidence enough to ignore it."

"Your coffee, Davison."

I glanced down at the steaming mug placed in front of me. The one with the whip and sprinkles. It looked exactly like the coffee I ordered from the shop. I sniffed it. It *smelled* exactly like the coffee I ordered from the shop. And it was making my mouth water exactly like the one from the shop.

My gaze darted to Parker, wearing an incredibly smug expression. "You made my coffee?"

"I did."

"My *exact* coffee?"

He nodded, his smile widening with each bob of his head. "I don't know if it tastes the same, but I followed your instructions."

I picked it up and took a sip. It was exactly *my* coffee, but even if it hadn't been I'd have told him it was the best I'd ever tasted, because seriously, *this guy.*

"It's perfect. Thank you."

He leaned over and dropped a kiss on my head. "You're welcome. We're a full-service breakfast apartment here."

"I'll have to remember that."

"But you only get smiley face pancakes on date days."

"I'll remember that too," I replied, hiding my grin behind my coffee. "And do you plan to fill me in on what else is happening on our date today and what I need to wear for it?"

He moved closer, close enough for his lips to brush my cheek. "Lots of things, all of which involve staying in and wearing exactly what you're wearing right now." His head dropped; to anyone else it would look like he was resting on my shoulder, but in reality, he was bringing his lips closer to my ear. "Except for regularly scheduled breaks where I'll be getting you naked."

My core clenched. After last night, I should be waving the white flag of surrender, at least for twenty-four hours, but it appeared that I was far from having enough of Parker's dick.

"We're all going to have a cozy day today," added Radley, totally oblivious of the somersaults my belly was doing. "Lux is baking, and we have movies and popcorn. Perfect for a day of crappy weather."

I was just about to reply when a movement caught the corner of my eye and I turned to find another girl walking down the opposite corridor into the living room.

Even if she wasn't wearing sweats with her blonde hair tied back in a pony and no makeup, and even if I hadn't seen her on billboards plastered all over the city for the latest Gucci campaign, you'd still know she was the type of girl who turned heads wherever she went.

The all-American girl next door, as she was very often referred to.

I just couldn't figure out what she was doing *here.*

Maybe I was hallucinating her from all the sugar I just consumed. That would explain why no one seemed to notice that a Hollywood A-list actress was now standing in the middle of the living room wearing headphones, holding her phone out as she finished a call.

Parker was still close enough to me that I could whisper without drawing attention.

"Is that Holiday Simpson?"

Parker's eyes flicked up, and he nodded. "Oh yeah. She must have stayed over. She does sometimes," he added with a shrug.

"Stayed over? As in…"

"…as in Hol is Tanner's twin sister."

My eyes widened so much they watered. "Holiday Simpson is Tanner's *sister*? They're twins?"

Even as I said it, I knew it was a stupid question.

Or *sounded* stupid.

But I never thought of Tanner as Tanner *Simpson,* as in

Holiday. I never really thought of Tanner at all. Simpson was a fairly common last name. And I swear I'd never heard anyone mention it at work. This was the sort of shit people thrived on gossiping about.

"Yup. Didn't you know?"

"No," I replied. "No, I did *not.* Is it common knowledge? How did I not know this?"

Parker shrugged again but didn't offer any useful response. "She's cool. I'll introduce you."

Oh *god.* No.

I wasn't a die-hard fan of hers or anything, but I'd seen the last couple of movies she'd done and really enjoyed them. Maybe even watched them more than once when Mark cheated—they were *those* types of movies.

And I loved her style, she always looked so chic and cute, and effortless. Even now, in her sweats.

Never in a million years had I ever envisaged meeting her—if I had, it wouldn't have been while *I* was wearing sweats four sizes too big, with last night's wet hair sticking out every which way, and maple syrup likely around my mouth.

I was making a poor attempt to smooth my hair, wipe my face, and simultaneously straighten Parker's sweater I'd thrown on, when Holiday removed her headphones and walked toward the kitchen. Or rather toward *me.*

I found myself enveloped in a hug, and I breathed in the scent of spices and vanilla, and the goodness that came with knowing what scent to buy. It was probably Gucci.

"Hi, I'm Holiday. You must be Scout. I've heard so much about you, I'm kinda relieved you actually exist, to be honest. I was beginning to doubt that you did."

Ohmygod.

Holiday Simpson knew who I was. This was more confusing than when Radley said she was excited to meet me, though it did beg the question how much Parker had been talking about me.

Radley snorted, Parker groaned, Tanner and Lux laughed loudly.

"Holiday, *jeez*. Ease her in, will you? I'm trying to make sure she comes back."

"Sorry." Her big blue eyes rolled dramatically, before pinning them straight on me. "The boys are all a little sensitive before they've had their coffee."

"I've *had* coffee, it's not about that."

"Parker's always a little sensitive when it comes to Scout." Tanner grinned as Holiday opened the fridge, removed a bottle of dark green juice, and shook it.

"Well, we're all friends here." Holiday smiled, genuinely smiled, *at me*. "Nothing to be sensitive about. And I take it everyone knows about you two now?"

"Nope, they're still keeping it secret," Tanner answered before either Parker or I could. I wasn't certain, but I swore I could detect a slight tension in his voice.

"It was only for a week, Tan. I told you," Parker snapped, turning to me. "You hear about the job tomorrow, right, Davison? Then we can tell HR."

I'd left my phone in the bedroom, but even from the distance, and a couple of thick walls between us, I could feel that email burning me. Parker was looking at me so hopefully, I couldn't do anything more than smile and nod, replying, "That's what they said."

Holiday took such a big swig of her green juice, even *I* winced. "Why'd you need to tell HR?"

"They have to sign a relationship form. Coach has been riding Parker's ass about it since the beginning of the season, otherwise he'll get benched or something."

"Tanner! What the *fuck?*"

"What? You will." He shrugged. "That's not a secret. It was in the letter. And we kind of need to make sure you don't get benched."

"Benched?" I blurted.

"Yeah, or suspended," replied Tanner with more seriousness than I'd thought he was capable of.

"What?" My head snapped around to Parker. "You never told me you'd get benched."

"I'm not getting benched, because no one officially knows about us. And it doesn't matter anyway, we're signing it this week and we can all go back to minding our own business," Parker added, with a pointed glare directed at Tanner.

"God, if they ever asked actors to sign a relationship form before a movie, the industry would collapse," went on Holiday, turning back to me. "You work on the social team, is that right? I think I remember Parker saying that…assuming we're not still pretending he doesn't talk about you *all the time*."

I tried to laugh at Parker huffing, and focus on what Holiday was saying, clearly oblivious to the fact that most of the blood had drained from my face. If I looked down, my stomach would be on the floor.

Why had I never asked Parker what would happen if management found out we hadn't signed the form?

For some reason I assumed it would be nothing more than a slap on the wrist, that Coach was giving him a hard time just because he was Coach, and it was a big year for the team. Never in a million years did I think Parker would get into *serious* trouble.

I couldn't be the reason Parker got benched. With any luck I'd get to work tomorrow and Ava would have made a decision. Either that or I'd have to suck it up and confess. But there was no way I'd be responsible for damaging his career.

I focused back on Holiday, trying to channel as much of her acting ability as I could so that no one noticed my internal meltdown, and nodded. "Yes, TikTok mostly."

She let out a loud sigh. "God, I need someone to help me with TikTok. I had a team, but they weren't very good, and I'm too nervous to manage it on my own. It would take up all my time, and I don't have much as it is."

"It's not that hard, Hol. Just set your phone up and do something, then post it."

Tanner was succinct, I'd give him that. Holiday turned to her brother, shooting him a withering glare. "Well done, Tanny, you've just managed to insult both me and Scout."

"What? No I didn't, you know what I mean."

"No, please explain how easy it is to be a content creator. Can't be any harder than catching a ball, right?" she shot back at him, throwing me a wink.

"Ugh. You're so annoying," he griped, and turned to me. "Sorry, Scout, I didn't mean to insult you."

"You didn't, it's okay." I smiled, and Tanner went back to finishing his pancakes, much to the dismay of his twin.

"Um, excuse me. What about my apology?"

Tanner turned to his sister. Identical pairs of eyes narrowed at each other; I could see it now—same mouth, same high cheekbones and smooth brow. Only Tanner's hair was dark, where Holiday's was light. And he had to be nearly a foot taller.

His lip curved up in a smirk. "I don't care if I insult *you*."

Quick as a flash, Holiday kicked her leg out. It would have made contact with Tanner's thigh, but instead he caught it and twisted her around, until she let out a loud yelp. "Tanner!"

The roll of Parker's eyes, and the fact that Lux and Radley were just watching them fight while they finished their breakfast, told me this bickering was a regular occurrence.

"God, you're annoying." Holiday rubbed her ankle as she took a seat at the countertop, next to me. "Anyway, where were we? Scout, maybe this afternoon you can give me a crash course in social media."

"Sure, I'd be happy to," I replied with a smile, trying as hard as I could to push away the niggling anxiety, at least until I got to work tomorrow, and glanced out of the window where it was still raining heavily. "What are the plans for today?"

"Lux is teaching me how to make cinnamon buns, and then we're watching a movie," answered Radley. "You want to learn too?"

"Oh…sure, why not. I've never made them before."

Tanner clapped his hands together. "Okay, if you guys are baking before movie time, I'm setting up the PlayStation. Parker, you in?"

Parker's eyes flicked from Tanner to me, like he was about to say yes, then thought better of it. "Um…"

"Hey, I'm good here, I'm learning to bake."

"Thank you." He rounded the counter and wrapped his arms around my waist, pulling me in. "I'm so happy you're here, Davison. Promise you'll shout over to me if you need anything."

"She'll be fine, Parker."

He ignored Radley and held my gaze. "Promise?"

"I promise."

"Good." He smacked his lips against mine, before going back in for a softer kiss, lingering an extra few seconds. "And I've already shotgunned my lap for you to sit in when we watch the movie."

"I appreciate that." I grinned at him. "Now go and play video games."

He didn't need to be told twice, running off and vaulting over the back of the couch.

Turning back to the kitchen, Lux had almost finished cleaning breakfast away, Holiday was still drinking her juice while scrolling on her phone, and Radley was in the pantry loading her arms up with flour, sugar, and everything you needed for baking.

A buzzing started up on the counter, I glanced down to find Radley's phone ringing. I assumed it was hers anyway, given the cover was pink and the screen saver was of Lux.

"Um…Radley, I think someone's calling you."

She hurried out of the pantry, dumped everything on the counter, and swiped the Answer key. The sound of traffic, rain, and people shouting blared through the speaker.

"Millie?"

"Rad? Radley?"

"Where are you? I thought you were coming this morning, Lux saved you pancakes."

"I'm at Grand Central, can you come and get me? It's so wet, and impossible to get a cab."

"What're you doing at Grand Central?"

"It's a long story. But I have a huge case, and a box and I can't carry it."

"Yeah, sure, I'll be there as soon as I can."

"Thanks, you're a lifesaver. I'll wait by 42nd Street."

"Cool."

The phone cut out just as Tanner walked back into the living room holding a remote control. "Was that Millie? Is she here? Did I hear her voice?"

"No." Radley shook her head. "She was calling."

"She's still coming over, right? She was supposed to be here for breakfast."

"Yes, she's still coming. I'm going to go get her in a second."

Tanner's eyes widened. "Get her, where from?"

Tanner had launched the remote onto the couch next to Parker and was tugging on a pair of sneakers before Radley had time to say, "Grand Central."

"I'll do it, you look busy…and you also come with Secret Service. Don't worry, I got it. I'll save everyone the trip." He snatched up his keys and hit the elevator button as fast as he could, crying, "Be back soon," as the doors closed.

It felt like we'd all just been stuck inside a tornado, or the drum of a dryer, the calm returning only now that Tanner had disappeared.

Parker got up and walked back over to the kitchen. "What

just happened? Where'd Tanner go?"

"Um...he went to get Millie."

"Millie?"

Radley nodded.

"Where from?"

"Grand Central."

Given his PlayStation buddy had just sprinted for the door, Parker pulled out a stool and sat down. "Oh man."

I'd heard Tanner mention Millie in passing once or twice, but based on how quickly he'd sprinted out, and the look Parker and Lux were currently sharing, plus Holiday shaking her head, I'd say whatever happened was much bigger than a passing mention. I just wasn't sure what.

"Is Millie going to be happy about Tanner picking her up?"

Lux shrugged, scooping out a cup of sugar and passed it to Radley. "I guess we'll find out."

We didn't find out.

Even through baking two batches of cinnamon buns—one of which went to Radley's security—a movie, a game of Twister, then another movie, this time with pizza, Tanner and Millie never came back.

According to Radley, Millie had decided to go back to her dorm to deposit whatever she'd been carrying, and the boys figured that was a good enough explanation to not bother asking where Tanner was too. Holiday left before we'd started the movies, and everyone kind of forgot about it.

As Parker and I crawled into bed, and his arms wrapped around me, I couldn't remember when I'd last had a day as fun and as unexpected as this one.

"Today was the perfect first date, Davison," Parker whispered, turning me in his arms until I was facing him enough that I could make out his features in the dim light. His lips were so close to mine that I could smell the mint of his toothpaste. "I can't even explain to you how happy it makes me that you're here. For so long I thought being with you was going to have to live in my fantasies, but now you're really here and I have to pinch myself every morning to remind myself I'm not living a dream. But I am…you're my dream. And I know that we're only just beginning."

I didn't say anything. I couldn't. For the first time ever, the feeling of dread was beginning to set in at the thought of going to work in the morning.

The very stark reminder of Parker getting benched catapulted back into my brain. Benched because of me. I managed to stem the prickle of tears inching up from my belly, scratching at my throat, my chest, my nose, until he drifted into sleep.

28

Scout

"Did you tell Parker?"

I shook my head, pulling my hair from the tie and refastening it. It was totally pointless, just as much hair fell in my face. I should have never cut it so short.

"No. I couldn't. It was such a perfect day together, I didn't want to ruin it." I groaned, blinking from my trance of staring down at the boys in practice. "I can't do this. I can't wait another two weeks of sneaking around. If it was just hiding it from work colleagues, that's one thing. But hiding from management is another. It sucks, you think it's going to be fun, and it isn't. It is *not* fun. It's stressful. And now I've found out Parker could get into real, serious trouble. It's not worth it—"

My rant was stopped mid-flow by Alice cracking open her Diet Coke and taking a big sip, only to pound at her chest when the carbonation got stuck.

"What're you gonna do?" she croaked.

I sighed, leaning so far back, the chair almost tipped. "I'm going to tell HR Parker should be done at practice soon, then we can go. I think he has to get the form, I don't even know. This whole thing is so dumb."

"What about the job?"

"I don't want it." There. It was the first time I'd said it aloud.

I'd been thinking about it all weekend—since the email had come through, since I found out about the possible benching, *or worse.* The way I saw it, if they wanted to give me the job, it would have been mine already. As much as I loved being here, I didn't want to work somewhere that had me jumping through hoops for each promotion.

"I like my job now, I'm just going to stay doing it."

For the first time in Alice Tan's life, she stayed silent, except for the occasional slurp through her Diet Coke. But even though I was staring out of the window down at the field, I could tell she was looking at me, assessing me, probably judging. I didn't blame her, I'd judge me, too, if I was the reason Parker got in trouble.

"Alice…if you have something to say, say it," I snapped

eventually.

"I don't know what I have to say. I'm trying to figure out both sides in my head."

"And?"

"*And*...I think you're right. Even if you take Parker out of the equation, you've never been excited about this role and it's not only causing you to hold yourself back from working, it's stopping you from living your life too. But you feel obliged. I don't think you would have been set up for success and you'd have resented all the traveling."

Obliged. Yes, the perfect word for it.

I'd been put forward for an incredible sounding job, and it hadn't ever occurred to me to ever say no. It hadn't occurred to me that it wasn't the right time. That I should be concentrating on making my current job the best it could be. That a new job and a new challenge wasn't necessarily a good thing.

I nodded slowly. That was it. *Even without Parker* it wasn't the right time for me to take a new role. The weight lifting off me at making the decision was almost tangible. The anxiety vanished, I could breathe a little easier, my shoulders lightened.

I stood up, no point putting off the inevitable. "I guess I should go and find Ava."

"The management meeting just started, she'll be in it."

I sat back down again. "Okay, I'll go in an hour."

"Good idea." Alice drained the rest of the Diet Coke and

tossed the empty can in the trash. The pair of us resumed our watching of the field. The bullpen was empty, which meant the boys were done with practice. "Remind me who this next series is against."

"The Mets."

"Ugh, I hate the Mets. I hope we win, and I hope Shithead is watching."

I chuckled. I hadn't thought about Mark in so long, but I hadn't forgotten about how pissed he'd get when the Mets lost. Or the Lions won. "Yeah, it adds a little sweetness to the win, don't you think?"

"Yup. Sure does. If you and Parker become official, and we nail a win, it could turn out to be a real banner day."

She sat forward again, resting her head on the glass like she always did, and I turned back to my screen where this week's content calendar was up.

Joey and Cyrus would be down on the boardwalk, setting up the time lapse we had for all the fans coming through the Lions arch today. We were almost coming to the end of their internship, before they moved onto the PR team, and I would get another couple of interns to teach.

I was deciding whether I'd actually kind of miss the guys when my phone buzzed, my heart juddering when I saw the name pop up, and a broad smile spread across my face.

Parker: Come meet me

downstairs for a kiss, and I'll give you a coffee for free

Scout: I'll do anything for free coffee.

Parker: Get your ass downstairs, Davison, and I'll show you what I do for a free coffee

Luckily, Alice had gone back to her desk, there was no one else around to notice when I snorted with laughter. Swiping up my key card, I glanced over to the meeting room where senior management was, and hurried downstairs to find out what free coffee would get me. I'd be back up before they were done, then I could find Ava.

I expected Parker to be in the supply closet where he usually was, but as I rounded the corner downstairs, I found that he *wasn't.* Nor was he alone. Unfortunately, I didn't notice exactly who he was talking to until it was too late, nor that Parker's face was filled with tension as he stared at me.

"…And I suppose *this* is a goddamn coincidence," barked Coach, turning to see what Parker had been looking at.

Crap. Crap crap craaapp.

Blinking hard, I tried my best to keep my face as blank as possible, but I'd been horrible at lying as a kid and it I hadn't gotten any better at it. I didn't dare look at Parker or his two cups of coffee, instead pulled out my phone, ignored the pair of them, and kept on walking.

I couldn't quite make out what Coach was saying as I passed by, but his tone was just as growly and no less quiet. It wasn't good, I knew that much.

What I didn't know was where this corridor was leading to, except the fire door now right in front of me. Didn't really think this plan through, not that I *had* a plan beyond getting as far away from Parker and Coach as I could. Now I was stuck. If I pushed through the doors, I would definitely set off the fire alarm.

Turning around, Coach was still talking to Parker. Or maybe he was simply glaring at Parker. I literally had nowhere to hide, except behind the large Ficus plants flanking the corridor.

I was still debating whether to duck behind one when Coach stormed off, leaving Parker standing there, his head down. Even when Coach disappeared around the corner, his head remained dropped.

I ran back toward him. "Parker?"

When he turned around, the expression on his face hit me right in the chest. A combination of anger, hurt, and frustration all teetering on the edge of defeat. This was all my fault.

"What happened?"

"Coach saw me going into the closet and pulled me out. He saw these," he held up the coffees, "and then you arrived."

"Oh, no. Parker…I'm so sor—"

"I'm going to be in deep shit if I don't sign that form, Scout. Did you hear yet?"

I nodded. "Yeah, but…"

"What?"

"They're still interviewing, it'll be a couple more weeks. But I'm—"

His eyes widened, his eyebrows almost disappearing into his hairline. "*Weeks.* Fuck. I can't wait that long, I'm going to get suspended. Coach will be glued to my ass."

"It's okay, I'm going—"

"It's *not* okay, I'm in deep shit," Parker snapped, once more interrupting me. "Nothing's okay about it. This is my job, Scout. My fucking *job*."

I stepped back and stared at Parker, or whoever this guy was in front of me. It wasn't the one who'd wrapped his arms around me last night and whispered into the dark that his dreams had come true. Not the one who'd pursued me since the beginning of the season. Not the one who was always laughing and joking.

This one's face was a mask of fury and frustration, mirrored by the hard tone of his snapping.

And while I understood exactly why he was so pissed, and that it was a position I'd put him in without realizing the gravity of the situation, I was beginning to get kind of annoyed at the constant interruptions.

Because if he'd let me speak, I'd have told him exactly what I planned to do—go to HR and pull out of the interview. But from the way he was glaring at me, nostrils flaring, this guy didn't seem to care about hearing what I had to say.

"Are you done?"

His jaw ground hard. From the tension running through him, I was amazed he hadn't squeezed the coffee from the cups. "I need the form signed today, Scout. I have a job to do, and I can't do it with this distraction. Coach was right."

Distraction. I took a deep breath. I didn't need an interpreter to translate what he was really saying. That my job didn't matter.

"I have a job, too, Parker."

"Yeah, but—"

"But what?"

He broke the stern gaze he'd been holding me with, his eyes flicked down to his sneakers. "Nothing."

"But what?' I repeated, my voice barely disguising my anger. "Mine's not as important?"

"No, I wasn't going to say that."

"Then what were you going to say?"

"Nothing," he snapped, though he still couldn't look me in the eye.

I had no illusions about the pecking order of this company. Parker *was* more important than me. Fans lined the gates to see him. They barely moved out of my way to let me enter the grounds.

But hearing *Parker* say those words, or hold back from saying those words, was different.

"Okay, I'll go then. If you'd let me speak for one second, I was going to tell you I was going to HR today to sign your dumb form. I'd already planned on doing it, but I thought you'd want to come with me. Even though you failed to tell me about the benching or suspension, I should never have asked you not to sign it, and for that I'm very sorry." I paused before my hurt got the better of me. "But after that gross display of condescension and egotism, maybe we don't need to sign it."

His eyes flared as they found mine again. "What? What does that mean?"

I threw my hands in the air. "You're the big shot around here. You figure it out."

"Scout—"

My finger prodded into his chest. "Let's not forget that *you* were the one who pursued *me*. I told you I wanted to stay single, but you decided we were going to be together. And of course, *you* get what you want."

"All I've wanted for the past year is you. But I'm keeping us a secret because of you, I'm doing this *for you*." I couldn't tell if Parker's voice was on the verge of breaking or if he really was that angry at me. "That's what you asked."

"Well, I'll make this easy for *you*. I'm not asking you to do it any longer."

My sneakers squeaked as I spun on my heel and stormed back to the elevator, leaving him standing there with the two rapidly cooling cups of coffee. He was still calling for me to come back as I tried to swallow down the thick lump lodged in my throat.

Today definitely wasn't going to be a banner day.

Parker and I just had our first fight. I had a horrible feeling that not only had I lost it, I'd lost Parker too.

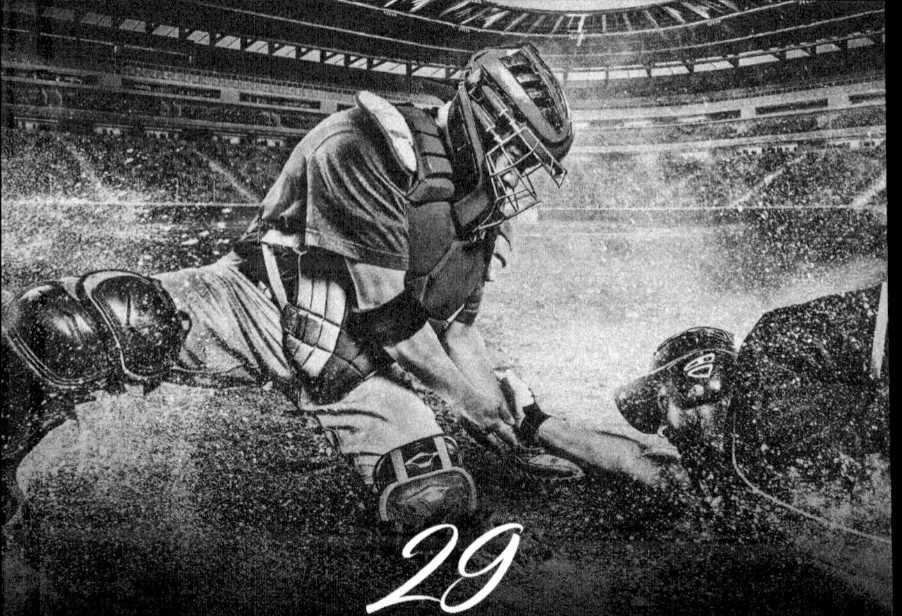

29

Parker

"KING, YOU SUCK. YOU *SUUUCCK.* KING, YOU SUCK."

Fucking Mets fans.

We'd been out at pregame warm-ups for five minutes now, and they hadn't let up once. I could hear them loud and clear, even over the deafening levels of music playing out of the speakers. Whoever was shouting meant business, and was about to get a baseball launched into his face if he wasn't careful.

I might not have a power arm like some of the guys, but I could hit a target at fifty yards without breaking a sweat. It was irrelevant that I kind of agreed with him.

"KING, YOU SUCK."

Ace walked over from where he'd been throwing the balls I'd been catching.

"Hey, bud, switch places with me."

I shook my head. "No way, I'm not giving them the satisfaction."

He glanced over my shoulder to where the chants were still going strong and looked back at me as confused as I felt. I wasn't normally one who received the hate from rival fans, that honor usually went to Jupiter, or even Ace, but I guess someone woke up this morning and decided to make my shitty day even shittier.

"Let's go in then, or move to the other side of the field where Lux and Tan are. They can switch places with us. Even if those dicks aren't getting to you, they're getting to me. Fucking douches. How have they not been shut down yet?"

I shrugged. "Dunno. But fuck 'em. Get back to position, we're not going in. And we're not moving."

Ace turned and trudged back to where he'd been standing, but I could tell from the force of his throw how pissed he was. That made two of us, and at least being pissed at the guys behind was distracting me from who I was really pissed at.

Myself.

Everything about this entire day from start to finish had been a shit show and I only had myself to blame.

I should never have been so cocky this morning. I should have checked like I always did when I walked down the corridor, making sure no one else was around before I ducked into the supply closet. But I was riding on the high from my sleepover with Scout, it was like she'd burrowed deep into my chest and was radiating out like a beam of sunshine.

I was deep in thought about the last time I'd felt this happy, when the door had been yanked open and instead of the girl I was desperate to kiss, Coach had been standing there, nostrils flaring.

What the fuck are you doing? Out. Now. He'd snarled, taking in the two cups of coffee I was holding. *You have got to be fucking kidding me.*

What d'you mean? I'm just looking for cleaning spray. Ace spilled... I'd started, confident I could bullshit my way out of the situation, but then Scout decided that was the moment to walk around the corner, and the shit really hit the fan.

Do you have any concept of how badly Shepherd wants to win the World Series, King?

Yeah, I'd answered, before I realized the question had been rhetorical. Although the empty plinth in the entrance atrium said enough.

No, I don't think you do. He stepped forward, he was close enough that his glasses could probably steam up from my breath. *The trade deadline is in less than two months. Every week we have a discussion on who's playing the best in the league and who we can swap out. Penn Shepherd will not let anyone stand in his way of winning the trophy this year. Not me, not you, and not your girlfriend standing behind the giant plant over there.*

Coach—

Does it look like I'm done talking? You will get traded if he thinks you're not up to the task, if it looks like your head's not in the game. His eyes flicked to the closet door, still open, and down to the coffee cups. *Do you think it looks like your head's in the game?*

I had said nothing. I'd been with the Lions my entire career. A punch in the nuts was an easier blow to take than the thought of being traded because of something I'd done off the field.

This is your final warning, Parker. You have until the end of the day to decide whether you want to stay as starting catcher, or if you want to watch the Lions win the World Series while you're over in Colorado, or holding your umbrella in fucking Seattle. And I don't know if you're aware, but long-distance relationships don't work.

I'd been so preoccupied with getting Scout's attention that I never stopped to think about what would actually happen if we were caught. Coach was right, I *had* been distracted. I'd been too arrogant in our position teetering at the top of our league to care.

Coach's words were still ringing in my ears when Scout ran over, and it took one look at her face for utter panic to kick in. Panic about being traded, about leaving the Lions, and more importantly *her*, and I lost it.

The Mets fans had nailed it, I did fucking suck.

And to top the entire situation off, from the way she stormed off, I think I might have lost Scout too.

"Parker, heads up..."

I swiveled in time for Ace's bullet throw to miss me by an inch, bounce on the ground, and roll all the way to the boards under the crowd, still trying to drill into me how much I sucked.

"CAN'T EVEN CATCH A COLD, YOU LOSER."

Running after the ball, I glanced around for security but couldn't spot them anywhere. We needed to have stricter rules about who we let in early to watch the warm-ups, especially when beer was being served. Or where the rival fans sat. I didn't fail to notice that none of the social team were out here, either, particularly the one member I wanted to see.

The guilt of shouting at Scout flared up again. As I bent to pick up the ball, my eye caught one of the guys in the group. I thought my blood had already reached boiling point today, but I'd been wrong.

From the way I was storming back to him, Ace could tell something was up, and he jogged toward me, his frown deepening with each step.

"Are we going in now?"

"Yeah, I need to find Pablo."

"Pabs? Why?"

"Because that guy telling me how much I suck is Scout's ex. And I want him removed."

Ace was still glancing over his shoulder as he caught up with me, jogging toward the dugout. "Rangers Douche?"

"Yup," I replied as another heckle was sent my way.

"CATCH YOU LATER, KING. SHAME YOU WON'T BE CATCHING ANYTHING."

I was still holding the ball, and spun around, throwing it as hard as I could against the board, right below where he was leaning over.

I shouldn't have done it, I should be mature enough and experienced enough to rise above it. But he was more than an opposing fan, and he'd made it personal.

There was no denying I enjoyed how quickly he flinched back at the sound of the ball making contact.

"Next time it'll be your head," I added with a smile that didn't reach my eyes, and ducked into the dugout. Snatching up the phone on the wall, I hit Speed Dial for reception. "Pabs, it's Parker."

"My favorite catcher." He chuckled. "Why aren't you warming up?"

"I am. I was. But there are some hecklers in the bleachers, can you have them escorted out? I can't find security."

He tutted loudly. "Parker, you know as well as I do we can't kick out the fans we don't like, no matter how much we might want to."

"It's Scout's ex. The one who came to see her."

I thought he'd hung up, the line was so quiet. But then, "Give me five minutes."

"Thanks, Pabs, appreciate it."

"No problem, now concentrate on winning."

The line went dead before I could tell him I'd do my best, and I turned to Ace, who was trying to keep his pitching arm as loose and warm as possible.

"Is he doing it?"

"Yep." I nodded, dropping down onto the bench with a heavy sigh.

He thumbed over to the tunnel. "And are we going in now?"

I nodded again, though stayed where I was. Instead, glanced out to the field where everyone was still warming up; Lux and Tanner were over in the outfield, tossing and catching, Jupiter was standing at the side talking to his third base coach and Marnie, Boomer Jones and a couple of the other guys were sprinting over in the corner.

On the other side of the field were the Mets players, all doing much of the same.

"Where's Scout watching from today?"

"I dunno," I replied, kicking at a discarded peanut shell on the floor, one left over by Saint Velasquez, no doubt.

"Dude, are you okay? Ignore those guys, they're dicks."

I rubbed at my chest; the heaviness which had been dragging through it all day now felt impossible to move. Like an elephant was sitting on my rib cage doing its best to slowly crush me. Crush my heart. Stop my breathing.

"It's not the guys." I curled my hand around the rim of my cap. "I think Scout and I might have broken up."

"What?"

"I fucked up. Coach caught us and threatened me with getting traded, and I took it out on her. I shouted. I made her think her job wasn't important to me. Or she wasn't important to me. And that's so far from the truth," I added, my voice cracking as I failed to swallow down the lump in my throat. "And now I have two fuckups to fix. Scout and Coach. Three, if you count Scout's job."

"Oh, bud." Ace joined me on the bench, threw his arm around my shoulder, and pulled me in for a hug. "You won't have broken up. It's just a stupid fight. Everyone has them, then you move past it and it makes you better."

"I dunno, she seemed mad." I dropped my head into my hands. "Rangers Douche was such a dick to her and I've proved I'm no better."

"Parker, come *on.* You aren't anything like him." He rolled his eyes. "Coach really threatened to trade you?"

"He said nothing will get in the way of Shepherd winning the trophy this year."

Ace let out a low whistle. "You're not getting traded and I'm not playing without you. Coach is just mad because he thinks you've been sneaking around with Scout."

"I have been."

"Right, but…" He paused while I assumed he tried to figure out what his point was. "But you've not been together very long, officially, only a couple of weeks. Not as long as he thinks. And it's not like you were being defiant on purpose, Scout had her job thing. Who d'you want to fix things with first? Coach or Scout."

"Scout," I replied without hesitation. "But I think I'll run into Coach first."

"Did you explain anything to him?"

I shook my head. "No, he stormed off too. Right after he was done threatening me with my position."

"You don't want to leave the club, do you?" Ace asked, his voice quieter.

"No. Of course I fucking don't. I've been here my whole career. I just want to be here with Scout too." I pushed my cap up and rubbed along my brow. "Fuck. I've messed this up so badly. I have to make it better, I have to apologize. Beg her to forgive me."

"Hey," he nudged into my ribs, "I'm the only one of us who gets to be this dramatic. You've fucked up nothing. It's this stupid form that's caused all the problems. Just go and sign it, tell Coach you're not leaving, and go get Scout back."

I turned to him, suddenly feeling way more hopeful than I had all day. "You think if I go to HR for the form, I can explain about Scout's job too?"

"Definitely." He grinned at me, slapping my back. "Everything is fixable. It won't be as bad as you think it is. But we have a game to play first."

Looking out to the field, everyone was making their way off except Lux and Tanner, heading over to us.

"Why are you two sitting in here?"

"We're not, we're heading in now." I stood up, catching the ball Lux tossed to me and stepping out. The timing could not have been more perfect, either, for over where Rangers Douche and his friends were drinking beers, a group of security guards was making their way down the steps. "Wait one second, I want to see this."

The four of us stopped to watch as the guards calmly rounded the guys up and escorted them away.

"Damn, I thought we might get a fight," said Ace.

"No way, those guards easily weigh two fifty. I wouldn't take them on."

Lux pushed up his ball cap with a frown. "What's just happened?"

"Rangers Douche was asked to leave." Ace grinned.

Tanner turned to me, his brows knotted and looking as confused as Lux. "Scout's ex? What was he doing here?"

"Trying to be a pain in my ass. And reminding me I need

to be a better boyfriend."

"What?"

"Nothing, let's go. We have a game to win."

"Damn right we do."

Man, I really hoped Rangers Douche was watching the Lions cream the Mets from some shitty dive bar with the volume turned way down. We were currently top of the fourth, leading the Mets by seven runs to three, and a perverse type of pleasure was warming my veins better than the 90-degree heat that had me sweating my ass off in practice this afternoon.

This day was turning itself around.

We'd win the game, I'd find Scout, Coach, and HR, fix all my fuckups, and then we could get on with our lives.

The next Mets batter took his sweet time walking up to the plate. Enough that I could already tell from Ace's stance what his next ball was going to be without me needing to give him a signal. We'd talked about it during the last break—fastball, curveball, or change-up—and this ball was going to be fast.

Behind me, the umpire was hopping about from one foot to another. I dropped into my squat, shifting my weight from side to side as the batter got into position, and rested my right knee.

Ace's leg raised high, his arm pitched back. I dropped lower.

The ball shot through the air.

The batter swung. And missed. The ball spun.

I reached out to catch it. But instead of hitting center of my glove, it found a different target.

In less than a second, my life flashed before my eyes.

I'd never felt pain like this. Searing uncontrollable pain.

My entire body convulsed like it was trying to turn me inside out. Every cell, every nerve ending exploded as I tried my hardest to stay upright.

And then I hurled my guts up, rolled over, and passed out.

This *fucking* day.

30

Scout

The doors slammed back as I charged through them.

I barely slowed to check which direction the hospital reception was, which in hindsight, I should have, seeing as I ran right past it. The nurse behind the desk gave me one of those withering looks only a nurse who has years of dealing with bullshit under her belt can deliver as I skidded to a halt and tried to catch my breath.

"Parker…King…brought…in…" I puffed, squeezing the stitch running down my left-hand side. I *really* needed to exercise more.

Without saying a word, and barely glancing at me, she

typed into her computer and pointed behind her. "Second floor."

"Thanks," I cried, taking off again. At least the elevator forced me to stop running, allowed me to take a full breath, and gave me another chance to rub away the pain in my side.

I glanced down at my phone as it buzzed.

Alice: Where are you? Ava's looking for you.

Yeah, I probably should have told someone I was leaving before I took off. But that would have required common sense and rational thinking, and after seeing Parker go down and get stretchered off the field, I was all out of that.

This wasn't just a simple baseball injury.

I'd been out on the boardwalk watching on the big screen when he went down. I'd heard the ambulance red light him away, and after Pablo had told me he'd been taken to Columbia Pres, I'd flagged down a cab to get me there as quickly as possible.

Unfortunately it got caught in traffic around Madison Square Garden, so I hopped out and ran the rest of the way, forgetting it was nearly fifteen blocks.

But I didn't matter, as long as I got to the hospital and could be with Parker. The only place I wanted to be.

As soon as the doors pinged I was back running again,

only this time the reception was right in front of me, so I didn't get far, and the nurse behind the desk was slightly less judge-y than the one downstairs, but only by a fraction.

"How can I help you?"

"I'm looking for Parker King. I was told he's on this floor."

One thick eyebrow raised at me, and her lips pursed. "Are you family?"

"I'm his…um, his…girlfriend."

God, could I sound any less believable? They must have a dozen people in here every day trying to pull the girlfriend card. Columbia Pres was the number one hospital in New York for sports injuries, and the city's teams certainly kept them busy.

"You're going to need to sit and wait over there, I'm afraid." She nodded to the chairs behind me.

"Can you tell me what's happened?" I blurted, realizing I didn't actually know, because flicking through different social media channels to find the answers hadn't helped. About as helpful as the staff here.

"No, I cannot."

"Can you just tell me if he's going to be okay?"

She nodded. "No, I cannot."

Cool. I thumbed behind me. "I'll just be sitting over here then."

I plodded over to the chairs. I had my pick, they were all empty.

I decided on one near the side, not in direct eyeline of the desk but close enough that I'd be able to tell if there was any news. I thought someone from the Lions might be here, too, at least one of the coaches, but maybe they'd be coming once the game was done.

I slumped down and checked my phone again.

Scout: I'm at the hospital, I came to check on Parker.

Alice: Is he okay?

Scout: They won't let me in.
I don't know what happened. Do you?

Alice: On the slo-mo the commentators said it looks like a groin injury, but from the way he went down I think it's a little further north

Scout: North? What does that mean?

Alice: *eggplant emoji*

Oh *god.* Poor Parker. The thought of how hard the hit must have been had my legs crossing.

Alice: He sure will appreciate having you to kiss his injury better *smirk emoji*

Scout: *eye roll emoji*

Scout: What did Ava want?

Alice: Don't know, I told her you'd had an emergency and had to leave.

Scout: Thank you. I owe you.

I shut off my phone and rested my head back against the wall. The nurse didn't look like she had any news, or knew any more. It was so quiet here it was hard to believe we were in a hospital, the windows were thick enough that I could barely hear the sirens or city traffic.

There weren't even any TVs to muffle out the sound of silence, or the distant beeping of machines. If I listened carefully enough, I'd probably be able to make out the frantic beating in my chest, which sounded a lot like this was my fault.

I swiped a tear away, searching around for a tissue before I gave up and used my sleeve instead. What a mess. Picking up my phone again, I opened the Lion social app. From the last post on TikTok it appeared the Lions had won the first game against the Mets; Robson Barry had taken over as catcher, and the final score came in at 10–5 to the Lions. And a Lions win was always guaranteed to bring out the haters.

One of my favorite things to do when I needed cheering up was respond. Clicking into the last post, there were nearly three thousand comments already, and I scrolled through until I found exactly what I was looking for.

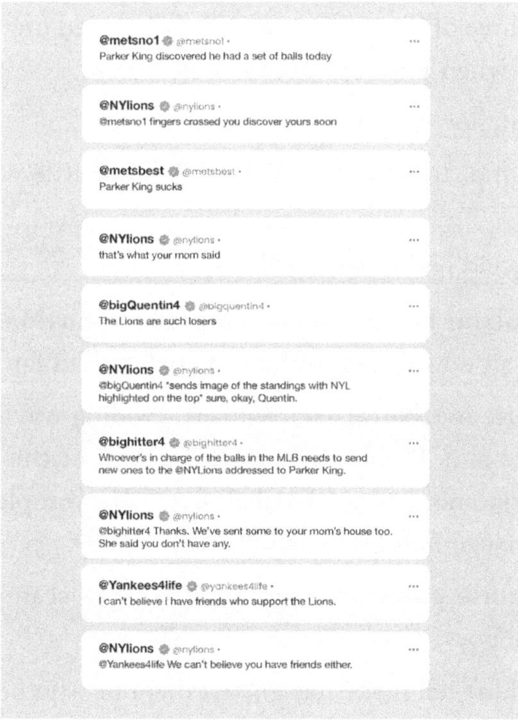

I was quietly giggling to myself, when the elevator pinged and out sprinted Tanner, almost as quickly as I had. He skidded to a stop in front of the desk, followed by Lux and Ace at a much more casual pace. From the grass stains on their pants, it was clear they'd come straight from the game.

"Hello? Nurse?" Tanner slapped the desk, hoping to get her attention, but her back was turned and she didn't appear to be in any hurry to acknowledge new visitors. "Is Parker King here?"

"They won't tell you anything unless you're family," I said, walking over to them.

The three of them spun around, Ace pulled me into a hug, which is when I noticed how pale he was.

"Scout, how long have you been here?"

"I dunno, an hour maybe. It took me a little while to get here."

"Do you know how he is?"

I shook my head. "She wouldn't tell me anything. Just said I had to sit down. I don't think she's a baseball fan."

"Excuse me, Nurse," started Lux, exuding way more calm than Ace and Tanner, who looked aghast at the possibility of someone not being a baseball fan. "Can you please tell us where we can find Parker King?"

The nurse pulled out her chair, her eyes scanning across the three boys.

I couldn't tell if she recognized them or whether her nose was turned up purely because of how dirty they were in her clean hospital. To be fair, given half of Lux's uniform was red from where he'd skidded on the diamond, she had a point.

"No, but the two who came in with Mr. King are in the

private waiting room, down the hall to the right. They'll be able to update you."

My head shot up. "There's another waiting room? Didn't think to tell me that?"

"Hey, honey, you're not the first girl coming in here claiming to be a girlfriend. You ain't gonna be the last."

I hoped the glare I fixed on her as I walked away told her exactly what I thought of her. Tanner burst through the doors of the waiting room the same way he'd exited the elevator, where we found one of the team doctors with an assistant coach.

"How is he? Can we see him? Why are you in here?"

"Easy, Simpson." The doctor poured out some half-and-half into his coffee and stirred it. "He's still in surgery."

"SURGERY?" cried the four of us.

Any remaining blood drained out of Ace's face and he dropped into the nearest chair, his face in his hands. Lux sat next to him and wrapped his arm around Ace's shoulder.

"This isn't your fault, man. Could have happened to anyone."

"Can someone tell us what actually *has* happened?" asked Tanner.

The coach's eyes flicked over to the doctor, clearly waiting for the expert to explain. In hindsight, he didn't really want to speak the words.

"Ruptured testicle."

All three boys winced. Tanner looked like he was about to puke. I have to say I felt pretty nauseous myself.

"Didn't he wear a cup?" I asked in an attempt to break the silence.

"Yep, but the force of the ball had it bouncing off his glove, and he was squatting forward, which caused it to hit at the wrong angle. The cup is cracked, that should tell you all you need to know."

I glanced at Ace, his head now between his knees.

"Does he need his balls amputated?" Tanner whispered, his face the same color as Ace's.

Coach and the doctor shrugged in response. No one wanted to think about Parker and his balls, especially if he lost them.

"How long is he going to be in surgery for?"

"We don't know."

I was just about to ask if anyone wanted me to go and find snacks, if only for something to do, when the door burst open and in ran Radley, who immediately hugged Lux, followed by Holiday, looking as glamorous as ever in a pair of ripped jeans and a vintage Fleetwood Mac T-shirt.

"Hol? What are you doing here?"

"Came along for the ride. Radley and I were watching on TV; Lux messaged to say he was coming here, so we headed over. Any excuse to see that handsome agent of hers."

Tanner's eyes darted back to the door. "Is Millie with you?"

I swear he looked relieved when Holiday shook her head and took a seat next to me. "Are you doing okay?"

I nodded, slowly. It was the first time anyone had asked me, and the first time I'd even considered the notion that maybe I wasn't, especially when my eyes filled with tears.

"I'll be better once we hear about Parker."

She patted my knee. "I'm sure he's going to be okay. These boys are resilient. Tanner got into enough scrapes when we were little that made me believe they're all part cat with nine lives."

I sniffed, drawing my arm under my nose again because I was still missing tissues. "Yeah, I hope so."

"He will, you'll see." She smiled. "And once he's better, maybe you and I could have a coffee, there's something I'd like to talk to you about."

I was wondering what on earth Holiday Simpson would want to talk to me about when the door clattered open again.

"Doesn't anyone walk in like a regular person," someone behind me grumbled.

This time, we were joined by a woman I didn't recognize, who immediately knelt in front of Ace, followed closely by one I did. One who had me sitting up straighter as the knots started twisting in my belly again.

"Scout?" asked Lowe, because obviously I was the first person she spotted. "What are you doing here?"

"Um…I…"

"She was filming with us, we brought her," jumped in Tanner, before I stuttered any more, because there was no reason why I *should* be here, but Lowe seemed happy with his explanation and went over to join the rest of her friends.

The door was closing behind her, only for a set of fingers to grip the frame and push it back open. The knots in my belly became a ball, tangled and twisted. Tanner stiffened next to me. Of course, Coach would come, and *of course* he'd be accompanied by Penn Shepherd. I wasn't the first person Coach spotted when he walked in, but I was a close second, and the glare of his eye told me I was exactly who he held accountable for Parker being in the hospital.

Fuck fuck fuck.

I was saved from my spiral of panic by the door once again opening, this time by the only person we wanted to see more than Parker.

"Doc." Penn Shepherd crossed the room, his hand outstretched to shake. "How is he? What's the verdict?"

"He's out of surgery and in recovery. We need to monitor him for a little longer before he has visitors"—the surgeon peered around the room—"and I'd prefer you not all descend at once, but he's going to be fine."

The relief was as palpable as the sighs from everyone present. Parker was okay.

"Doc, was anything…um…removed?" asked Tanner.

She shook her head, and I swear I saw the tiniest hint of a smile. "No, Mr. King is still in one piece, but he'll be out of *any* kind of action for six to eight weeks."

I stayed as still as possible, praying none of the boys, Radley, or Holiday glanced in my direction.

"I'm going to check him in post-op, but I'll send the nurse in if anyone has more questions." There were murmurs of *thanks, doc*, and she was about to leave but turned back to the room. "Does anyone know if Mr. King volunteers with children, or any type of outdoor clubs?"

The boys all shook their heads.

"Hmm, strange, must have been the morphine. He kept babbling about how much he loves the Scouts," she replied, before walking back out of the door.

There was absolutely zero chance that no one was looking at me; not the boys, not Coach, not my boss's boss's boss, not the owner of the New York Lions, or any of the other people in here I'd never met. I didn't know if it was worse when Tanner tried to cover his laugh with a cough.

Probably, but I couldn't see how.

Either way, getting up and walking out of the room to save face was the only viable option I had. I was barely down the hallway before the tears burst forth.

All the stress of the past few weeks—my job, the waiting, the sneaking around, the argument with Parker, his accident, the guilt, his drugged-up declaration of love—erupted out of me in huge, wrenching sobs. I sat there, crying until I thought I couldn't cry anymore, and that I'd really need a tissue this time because there's no way my sleeve would suffice, when a box of them was thrust under my nose.

Lowe shook it at me. "I think you need these."

"Thank you." I sniffed, pulling a bunch from the top. I was wondering if it was impolite to blow my nose in front of her before I decided I didn't care.

"Are you okay?"

I shrugged. "I don't know."

"Is there anything I can do to help?"

That was it, that one simple question and my tears dried up. Before the day had swiftly gone south, I'd been planning to pull out of the interview process, and Lowe sitting presented a unique opportunity I was unlikely to get again.

"Yes." I sniffed, wiping my nose again. "I appreciate this isn't the time or the place, but I've decided to pull out of the social media role. It's not the right time for me. I love my current job and I want to keep working at it until I've outgrown it. I've still got so much to learn. I'm really grateful for the opportunity you gave me, but I'd be even more grateful if you'd allow me to continue in my current position. Also, if you haven't guessed from my being here and all, you should know I'm dating Parker King. I haven't signed the HR form yet, but it was on my list of things to do today, but things got in the way, and then this happened…"

There. That should cover everything.

Lowe sat back, rolled her mouth together, and nodded. "I can't say I'm not disappointed, but if you feel you're not ready for the role, then I appreciate your honesty in telling me. I've said it before, but we're lucky to have you here, and I stand by that. You might not feel you're ready now, but when you feel like taking on a new challenge, you let me know, and we'll talk."

"Thank you."

"And in regard to Parker…hey, I'm dating my boss." She laughed, before her smile softened. "It's not easy to have a work relationship, but that doesn't mean it's impossible. If he makes you happy, that's all that matters."

"He does make me happy." I smiled, genuinely for what was probably the first time all day.

Lowe nodded, pausing like she was about to say something then changed her mind. "C'mon, let's go back, I'm sure you'll want to see him."

Tanner was laughing at something on his phone when we walked into the waiting room. "That's what your mom said… never not funny."

Instead of taking my seat, I walked to where Coach was sitting and stopped in front of him. I'd been honest with Lowe, may as well rip the whole Band-Aid off.

Here goes nothing.

"Sir, you should know that it was me who asked Parker to wait until we told people about our relationship. He did it for me because I was scared it would jeopardize a job role I was interviewing for. If anyone should be punished for not following the rules, it should be me. All Parker wants to do is play well for you and this team. Please don't take that away from him."

Coach removed his reading glasses, which made his eyes seem even more piercing. I was tempted to ask him to put them back on.

"I think Parker's saved me the job of punishing him, don't you?"

I nodded.

"He's going to be on the injured list for sixty days, perhaps you two could use the time to get your story straight."

"Yes, sir." I nodded again as Lowe walked over with Penn.

"We can talk more about this tomorrow," Lowe announced, resting her hand on my shoulder. "It's late, we should be going home. There's another game against the Mets to win tomorrow, and you all need your rest. Parker will be out until the morning, and we can't do any more tonight. He's in good hands here."

There were murmurs of agreement as everyone stood up and made their way to the elevators. Penn, Lowe, Coach, and the team doc all took the first elevator, while the rest of us waited back. I could tell they were all reluctant to leave Parker on his own, especially Ace, but I had no plans to go anywhere, and I didn't need to be in top shape to play a game of baseball.

"Guys, you heard Lowe, you all need your sleep. Don't worry about Parker, I'm staying. I'll message you if there's anything urgent, but I'm sure he's going to be fine."

"She's right," said Lux, his arm around Radley, who looked like she was about to fall asleep. "We'll come back first thing."

After a few quick goodbyes and the promise to meet Holiday for breakfast, I followed the nurse to Parker's room and crept in.

The glow of the machine lights lit my way as I leaned over to kiss his cheek, taking extra care not to disturb the morphine drip in his arm, then pulled a blanket over me and hunkered down on the couch.

31

Parker

I must have dreamed it.

The couch under the window was empty, but I swear I'd woken up in the night and Scout had been asleep on it. It was the only thing from this entire twenty-four hours that would have made me feel better. That and the morphine I was hooked up to.

Because this stuff was fucking incredible.

I also had a brief recollection of the surgeon coming in this morning to tell me how lucky I was I still had two balls, along with the ability to have children. Assuming I was ever allowed to have sex again, which would only happen once the intense throbbing in my groin stopped underneath the enormous diaper I appeared to be wearing.

My head dropped back against the pillow, and I tried my hardest to remember what had happened after Ace pitched, but maybe it was best that I couldn't. It was bad enough that I'd woken up with a surgeon peering over me telling me she'd fixed my junk. I could kind of do with her returning, however, so she could fill me in on the more salient points, like what to do when I needed to take a piss.

Or walk.

And it was probably out of her area of responsibility, but maybe she could also help me fix things with Scout. Because after using the bathroom, and figuring out how to put one foot in front of the other without causing myself excruciating pain, Scout was the priority. I had to fix everything I'd fucked up yesterday, before I'd fucked myself up.

Scout was the number one thing on my list once I was out of here. *When* I got out of here.

A bubble of panic rose in my chest and popped.

Oh *shit,* what if I never got out of here?

Coach had said being traded was a likelihood if I couldn't make a decision about my career by the end of the day. End of the day, *yesterday.* I'd missed my deadline to fix everything. What if this was my punishment and I had to stay here for weeks? Until I fully recovered.

Was this how Coach would trade me? Would he use this injury as an excuse to bolster the team, and the next time I crouched at the plate would be in Seattle? I didn't want to go to Seattle. I wasn't built for rain. Scout wouldn't like the rain. What was I saying? Scout wouldn't come to Seattle. The long distance wouldn't work. We'd break up.

This was bad. Really bad.

The machine monitoring my heartbeat had begun beeping in double time. But I needed to get out of here. I could withstand a little throbbing in my groin, because I needed to find Scout. I needed to find Coach. I needed…

Arrrrggghhhh.

"Mr. King. Get back into bed. *What* are you doing?" The nurse rushed over to me, gripping my arm as I attempted to move my left leg back into bed, but honestly the pain shooting through me was crippling to the point where it pierced my brain, and I could do nothing but fall back. "You need to stay in bed and stay still. Tsssk. What were you trying to do? Tsssk."

I caught sight of her name tag—Deirdre—while she continued scolding me under her breath. I thought it probably wasn't wise to tell her I'd planned to find the girl who may or may not be my girlfriend and beg her to forgive my stupid ass until she definitely *was* my girlfriend. Oh, and also beg for my job.

Deirdre shut off the heart rate monitor and took my blood pressure. From the soft huff she let out, I assumed that meant it was okay. At least the beeping had stopped.

"Okay," Deirdre said. "You stay here now. Don't be trying

anything stupid again. You heard the doctor this morning, you can get out of bed this afternoon once your bandages have been changed and we hook you up to a portable IV."

I don't remember him saying any such thing, but for the first time, I noticed the small tubes I was attached to, not just the one in the back of my hand.

"Could I get some more pain meds, please?" I croaked, wincing from the expectation that even talking might hurt.

"I'll see what I can do," she grumbled, plumping up my pillow and tucking the sheet around me like she thought it would keep me in. "But only if you stay in bed this time. You'll pull out all your drips if you're not careful."

I'd hand over my firstborn if she could stop this throbbing in my balls. That's if I ever worked up the courage to have sex again. From the way I felt, just taking a piss would be akin to climbing Everest.

"I promise."

She huffed loudly, giving me the distinct impression she didn't believe me. She didn't need to worry about me moving. I wouldn't move again even if I wanted to, the pain was incapacitating. I was almost too scared to breathe.

I wouldn't dare tell her I was kind of uncomfortable with the way she'd pushed the pillow behind me, and I didn't think she'd appreciate me calling after her.

"There he is."

My eyes flew open to find Lux, Tanner, and Ace walking

in. Ace pushed past the other two, marching over to the bed, and pulled me into a hug before I knew what was happening.

"I'm so sorry, Park." His voice cracked. "I'm so sorry."

"Hey, you're all good." I wrapped my arms around him as best I could without tugging on the tubes, or moving my body *in any way*. "It wasn't your fault. It was an accident."

He stepped back, wiping a hand over his eyes. "I'm still sorry."

"Don't be, it would have been an awesome ball if I'd caught it." I grinned. "But while you're feeling like you owe me something, could you move my pillow, please?"

Tanner fell onto the couch and rearranged the cushion under his head. "You kind of did catch the ball."

His chest shook as he tried to hold in his laugh. Lux didn't bother holding it in, even Ace looked a little happier than he had been two minutes ago.

"How long am I going to have to put up with jokes about my balls?" I asked, my mouth twitching with a smile.

Lux scratched along his jaw, his head tilted. "I'd say at least until you're back on the field, and then maybe for another couple of weeks."

"Cool cool, just so I know what to prepare for."

"How are you feeling?" he asked, opening his backpack and pulling out a container, which he handed me along with a fork. "Thought you might like some pancakes."

I glanced down at the stack, covered in maple syrup and

raspberries. My favorite.

For a second I couldn't speak, my throat was too thick. These drugs were messing with my brain. I was either going crazy or on the verge of tears. Or feeling deliriously happy and grateful that I had the best friends in the world, like right this second.

"You gave me a smiley face."

"Special occasion." He grinned.

I forked a mouthful of pancakes in, immediately deciding they were the best thing I'd ever tasted. "Deesarewelygoob."

Ace poured out a glass of water and passed it to me. "How are you feeling?"

I took a large gulp, I could get used to being waited on like this. "I'm feeling okay, except I tried to get out of bed earlier and won't be doing that again in a hurry."

"Painful?"

"Never experienced anything like it," I replied as a thought occurred to me. "Oh, hey, did we win?"

Ace grinned. "We sure did. And we're gonna win again today."

"That's good news at least. Don't want to have almost lost my balls for nothing." My eyes sliced over to the TV. "I guess I'll be watching here."

"Have you seen the doctor? When are you getting out?"

I shrugged, taking another bite. "Don't know. She came by this morning, but only to tell me the surgery went well.

I'll ask when I see her later, but it's going to be a few days, I think."

"Coach said you're gonna be on the injured list for sixty days."

I turned to Tanner, brows furrowed. "You saw him?"

He nodded. "Yeah, he was here last night."

"Coach was?"

"Yep. Him, Shepherd, Lowe Slater, Payton, Hol, Radley…"

He paused. I waited to see if he was going to say Scout, but there was only silence. Maybe I *had* imagined her on the couch. Even before I felt the panic rising in my chest, the beeping on the monitor quickened. I shoved another mouthful of pancakes in, hoping to focus my brain on eating instead of how I would get Scout back.

"Oh, and Scout, plus one of the team docs and your assistant coach."

"Scout?" Pancake sprayed everywhere as I blurted her name. Ace got up and passed me a paper towel. "Thanks."

"Yeah, she was the first here. She was waiting when we got here, and she stayed."

"She stayed?" I blurted again, this time without the pancake. I hadn't imagined it, she really had been here. But that begged another question. "Then where is she now?"

No one had the answer to that, however, and I slumped back.

"She told Coach, by the way," said Tanner from behind the

copy of *GQ* he'd found on the table.

I perked up again. "She told Coach what?"

"That it was her who'd asked you to keep them a secret and you shouldn't be punished for it. If anyone should be punished, it should be her. She did it in front of Shepherd too."

"What? What did they say?"

"Coach said he thinks this was enough punishment. I guess you got benched without being officially benched."

"Huh." I glanced around, half expecting to see her sitting there. But no. The same thing happened when I went to find my phone, because I couldn't find it, I didn't have it here, so I couldn't even check to find out where she was. "Do you guys have my stuff?"

They all shook their heads.

"It'll still be in your locker, I'll ask Pablo to pack it up and bike it over here this morning," added Ace.

"Thanks, man." I smiled at him. "And if you see Scout, will you ask her to come back?"

"Sure." He nodded, just as a soft knock sounded on the door.

"You can ask me yourself if you'd like."

And there she was, standing in the doorway, holding a large backpack. She looked so perfect I could almost be convinced I'd dreamed her up. My heart thudded again, and I couldn't hold back the smile that threatened to split my face.

"Hey."

"Hey," she replied, her eyelashes batting as she took in the guys. "Hey, guys."

Ace jumped up from the end of the bed. "Hey, Scout, we were just leaving."

Tanner peered over the top of *GQ*. "We were?"

"Yep," replied Lux, knocking Tanner's feet to the floor. "Let's go, Tan."

Tanner put down the magazine and stood up, all with very little grumbling. "Okay, guess we'll see you later, big guy. I'll dedicate my first home run to you."

"You better. I'll be watching." I laughed. "Thanks for stopping by."

"Bye, dude, Bye, Scout."

"See you later." Her eyes followed the three of them. My eyes followed her until the door closed and it was just the two of us. She turned around to find me looking at her. "Was it something I said?"

"Maybe." I chuckled before my smile dropped a little. "I thought I dreamed you sleeping on my couch."

"You didn't." She pushed up the sleeves of her pale blue sweater and sat at the end of the bed. Too far away, in my opinion.

"Why did you leave?"

"I went to meet Holiday. And then I went to the club to pick up your things. I thought you'd want your phone." She bit down on her smile, and from the angle she was sitting, her entire body was backlit by the sun pouring through the windows. The ever-escaping strands of blonde highlighted her face like she was wearing a halo.

She was my angel.

We both turned as the monitor started beeping faster. Goddamn machine giving away all my feelings. Lacing my fingers with hers, I pulled her in closer. From a night sleeping in here, she should be tired, but she'd never looked prettier.

"Thank you."

I don't know if we were waiting for the machine to slow down, but as we stayed there, our gazes locked, it was clear that wasn't going to happen.

"I'm so sorry about yesterday." Our voices chorused. "No, I'm sorry. No, me—"

I paused, holding my hands up. "Let me go, please. It's the only time I'll ever ask to go first."

Her lips pursed, holding back her smile. "Okay."

Holding onto her gaze, I took a breath. "I'm sorry I was such an asshole to you yesterday. I never should have shouted, and I never should have made you feel like your job wasn't as important as mine, or as important to me. It is. *You* are important to me. Your job, your happiness, your future. All those things are important to me, and I'm so sorry I ever made you think or feel otherwise."

Blue eyes bored into mine; the longer they held there, the

quicker I could feel mine misting over.

"I'm sorry *I* was such an asshole." She grinned, holding her hand up before I could object, which I was about to do. "It was an asshole move asking you to lie for me. The interview process was stressing me out and I didn't realize what I was asking of you. I didn't know how serious the implications were. But I've fixed it, you're not going to get into trouble."

"I heard you spoke to Coach. You didn't have to do that."

Her thumb moved against the top of my hand, taking care not to touch the drip tube. "I did. I also spoke to Lowe Slater, I told her I didn't want the job."

My brow furrowed hard. "You did what?"

"It's okay, I did it for me as much as you. I want to stay in my current position, I'm not ready to move on from it."

"Did they even offer it to you?"

She shook her head. "No, I pulled out before. I don't think it would have been mine, they wouldn't prolong the process if they wanted me to have it."

"Are you sure?"

"One hundred percent. I don't want the added pressure, I want to stay loving the job I have now. And I want to stay with you, if you'll still have me."

My brows shot up. "If I'll still have *you?* Are you kidding? What about you still having *me*?"

"I'll still have you," she replied, inching a little closer up the bed. "But no more sneaking around. When you get your phone, you'll find an email from HR with the form to sign."

"Does that mean we can go back to our morning coffees?"

"I'll do you one better, sometimes we can drive in together and I won't make you drop me outside the gates."

My hand eased out of hers and found her thigh. "Wow, Davison, I have to say, that's a real turn-on for me."

"Yeah?" She leaned in.

"Yeah," I mumbled against her lips, just as I realized what a huge mistake I was making. "ARRRGH. FUCK."

I doubt Scout had ever moved quicker in her life. If I wasn't writhing in pain, I'd be laughing at her sitting on the floor where she'd landed.

"Oh my god, Parker. Are you okay?" she cried, just as the door burst open again and I was once more the recipient of Deirdre's disapproving glare.

"What are you doing? Why are you on the floor?" Deirdre barked at Scout, marching past her and over to the bed. "Mr. King, you have just had surgery. No hanky-panky. What did you think would happen?"

I was concentrating too hard on wishing away the pain to provide a cohesive answer. Plus, I hadn't been thinking about anything other than Scout, and the feel of her lips on mine.

Nope. No. Do not think about *that.*

"Young lady, I suggest you sit over there." Deirdre pointed to the couch and left the room with a louder *tsssk* than she had last time.

“Are you okay?” Scout whispered, as though speaking at any kind of volume might set me off again.

“Yeah,” I groaned, “but I should probably take this opportunity to warn you I can’t have sex for at least six to eight weeks.”

“I think I can manage that. We’ll play Twister instead.”

I groaned louder, my eyes squeezed shut.

“Okay, maybe not Twister. Monopoly, or we can learn to bake. Or watch movies and eat pizza.”

“Pizza. I can eat pizza, and while I’m being honest, I should also tell you that I think I’m falling in love with you.” I waited a second, then eased one eye open. “You don’t look surprised.”

“I’m not.”

“I’m that obvious?”

“No.” She bit down on her cheek, sucking it in, as she moved to perch on the end of the bed again. “I just know how loveable I am. Plus, the surgeon said you were blabbing about how much you loved me.”

I let out another groan. “Oh man. How am I so uncool with you?”

“It’s okay, I think I’m falling in love with you, too, Parker King.”

My eyes flicked to hers, bright blue and sparkling bright. Her entire face was lit with happiness, reminding me of the first time I’d laid eyes on her waiting outside the stadium with the box of apples. I could still feel how strong I’d jolted, and the memory of it hit me square in the chest and began moving lower.

I pointed to the couch. This was going to be a long eight weeks. "Scout, I love you, but please go and sit over there. And tell me why you met Holiday."

"She offered me a job." She grinned.

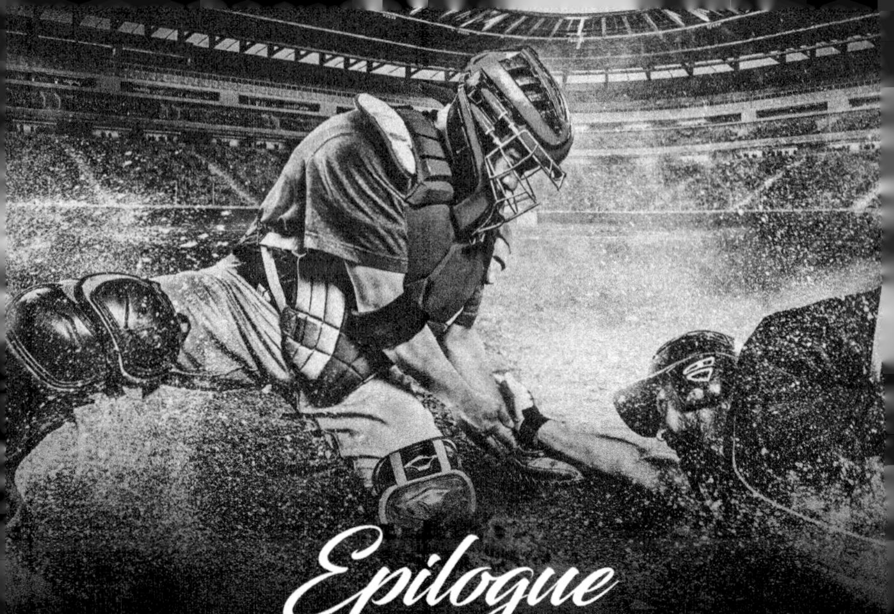

Epilogue

Parker

SEVEN WEEKS LATER

"Babe, hurry up."

My eyes scanned over my closet shelves until I found the sneakers I was looking for, sat down, and pulled them on. Scout walked out of the bathroom, towel wrapped around her with a toothbrush in one hand and a mouth full of paste.

"What?"

"We need to hurry up."

Her brows dropped, and she turned and left without

another word, only to return thirty seconds later, this time holding a hairbrush. "Your appointment isn't for two hours. It's not going to take me two hours to get dressed."

Tugging her hand until she had no choice but to sit on my lap, I wrapped my arms around her, reveling in the heat of her damp body, fresh from the shower.

"I know, but this appointment is a big deal. And you never know, we might get there early and they see us being punctual and bump us up."

Scout twisted herself until we were face to face and I took the moment to soak her in. I'd never get enough of looking at her. We'd entered the height of summer, and in the last few weeks, freckles had erupted all over her forehead, down her nose, and across her cheeks like tiny little sprinkles of happiness.

That's what she was to me, happiness.

Her hair was now almost long enough that she could tie it back without any of it escaping, but I took the opportunity to tuck a lone strand behind her ear.

Her mouth rolled as she tried to hold in the smirk, but I could see it twitching on her lips. "Bump us up?"

"Yes," I replied, nudging her nose with mine. "Bump us up. Which I, for one, am all for. The sooner we get to the docs, the sooner she can give me the all clear and sign me off, and the sooner we can get back here so I can show you exactly how much I've been missing you."

"Oh yeah?"

"Yes. Two months, Davison. It's been two months."

"It's been *seven weeks*," she shot back, with an eye roll. "Barely a month and a half. And we can't come back here, we have to be at work, remember?"

I groaned; work had temporarily slipped my mind.

It was true, we did have to be at work. It was the Lions for Dogs game today, something Scout had been working hard on, and in my temporary position as bench warmer, I'd been given the responsibility of posing with all the rescue puppies looking for homes, and signing autographs. Scout was super excited about it, too, because since she'd made the decision to pull out of the interview, she'd thrown herself into her current job and was once more loving it. Today was her day as much as mine.

Holiday was still begging Scout to come and work for her, but for the moment, Scout was happy, therefore I was.

"Okay, but then after work we're coming back here. Because that seven weeks has felt like a lifetime, and I'm not waiting a second longer." My lips ghosted along her jaw, tasting her skin. "Don't pretend it's not been a lifetime for you too."

Out of habit, her neck tilted, allowing me to breathe her in; the clean scent of the soap she loved, the toothpaste lingering on her breath, the earthy tones of her shampoo—all of it sending me into a tailspin. I wasn't lying, the last seven weeks really had felt like a lifetime. A torturously long lifetime of having Scout next to me, and this, right now with her sitting in my lap, was the closest I'd gotten to being able to touch her without the worry of causing myself some real permanent damage.

I'd learned my lesson the first week home.

I'd been in hospital for three days. After the second, I'd been allowed to walk, allowed to use the bathroom, and two of the five tubes attached to me were removed. I was sent home bandaged up like an Egyptian mummy, with a list of rules, including no sex and no strenuous exercise, but I wasn't complaining.

It felt logical to me that while *I* might not be able to have sex, that didn't mean Scout had to miss out. I was only human, and I wanted to make it up to my girl and there was no harm in getting creative. I could still make her come, right? *Wrong*. It hadn't occurred to me I'd still get hard the moment I laid eyes on Scout's naked body and slipped my fingers inside her silky, dripping pussy, but I had.

And what had started out as a day full of promise, had ended back in the emergency room with a scolding. Thankfully Dierdre wasn't on duty.

After that, we enforced a sex sabbatical for both of us, which turned into the most prolonged case of edging on record. It no longer felt like my balls were on fire every time I caught her scent or brushed my lips to hers. Even when I deepened our kiss to taste her, explore around her mouth, I could cope, but the fire in my balls was now happening for an entirely different reason.

So, yeah, I wanted to get to the doctor as early as possible, and based on the way Scout's breathing had shallowed, I'd say she did too.

"Think about how good it's going to feel, Davison. It's been seven *long* weeks. My dick will be so hard for you, so fucking *hard*..."

The second my fingers inched underneath her towel, she jumped from my lap and ran into the bathroom. "Okay, you win. Let's go. We'll get you bumped up."

"See," I grinned at myself, "that's the enthusiasm I was after."

"Can we get coffee on the way?"

"You bet," I called to her. "In fact, I'll go and make you one right now to take with us."

I wondered if a hop, skip, and jump counted as strenuous exercise as I wandered out into the living room to find Ace and Lux in the kitchen.

"Big day today, bud." Ace grinned, peering up from his cereal as I flicked on the coffee machine.

"It sure is."

"Do we need to warn the downstairs neighbors that all the banging they'll hear tonight isn't a construction project?" Lux chuckled.

Ace held his fist out to pump. "Nice."

I showed the pair of them exactly what I thought of their joking by flipping them off. Seven long weeks of jokes hadn't just worn thin. It was see-through. "Where's Tanner."

Lux shrugged. "In his room, maybe. Haven't seen him yet."

"He's not come in for breakfast?"

The pair of them shook their heads.

"Weird." I pulled the milk from the fridge. "I figured he'd be up, he's been so excited for today."

"Your sign-off?"

"No, idiot, the dogs thing." I frowned. "He's not stopped talking about it."

"Only because he's front page of the charity calendar," replied Ace, pouring another bowl of Cap'n Crunch out and focusing back on reading the magazine laid out in front of him. "He's probably doing his hair, making sure he looks his best for all the puppies. It's your turn to wake him up anyway."

I glanced at the clock. He really should be out by now. We had a rule on game days—if he wasn't with us, last one out of the door had to check Tanner was awake. He had a bad habit of oversleeping, and the last time it happened, Coach reamed us *all* out.

"Okay, I'm going to check."

Tanner's door was closed when I reached his room. "Tan, you up, buddy? I'm making coffee?"

No answer. Knocking didn't result in anything different either. I pressed my ear to the door, *carefully*. I'd been caught out before listening at Tanner's door when we thought he'd overslept, and was subjected to hearing things I could never unhear, but this time it was silent.

It was no use walking away either. Like the wellness checks they implemented in Vegas, we needed proof Tanner wasn't in his room. He could sleep through an earthquake.

Bright sunshine sliced through the gap in the door as I opened it. Pushing it wide, I found his bed unmade, which meant he was either in his bathroom or he'd already left the apartment—something he'd never do.

"Tanner?" I called out again. "Tan?"

"Find him?" Lux asked when I walked back to the kitchen.

"No." I shook my head. "Can you call him? Maybe he went in already?"

"No one's that excited about dogs," he replied, hitting Speed Dial on Tanner's number.

The three of us waited for him to pick up, only it rang out.

"This isn't right. There's no way he would have left without us, he's slept in his bed. Can you two go and get ready, we need to find him."

Ace drained his cereal, placed the bowl in the sink, and jogged down to his room, the opposite direction Lux had gone. I'd finished the coffees for Scout and me, and was grabbing an apple when the elevator pinged, and out walked Tanner.

"Hey! Guys, he's back…" I called out loud enough for them all to hear me. "Bud, where've you been? We called you."

He could have been mistaken for a robot for how still he was. I watched as he walked to the couch, his face a mask devoid of expression, and sat down. When the bright morning light caught him, it only highlighted how pale he was.

I perched on the coffee table opposite him. "Tanner, what's going on? Are you okay?"

For the first time since he'd walked in, he focused on me instead of looking into the distance. While I waited for him to speak, he removed his cap, slowly pushed his fingers through his hair, and sat forward. "Millie's pregnant."

My inhale was so sharp, the bite of apple I'd just taken was sucked into my throat, where it lodged. Panic ensued. Not that Tanner noticed, he was back to staring into space while I tried to cough out the apple—it didn't work. I tried to scratch it out, I tried anything I could to loosen it because *I couldn't breathe*.

This is how I would die, by Tanner telling me the girl he liked was pregnant with another man's baby.

Somehow, I managed to stand up and throw myself against the edge of the couch. Where the fuck was everyone else? Why had no one else rushed out to see where Tanner had been? I'll tell you why, because they were all selfishly going about the same business, whatever the fuck that was, as I fell onto the back of the couch over and over.

I was about to give up hope when the apple projected through the air, landing by Tanner's feet, and I collapsed to the floor, coughing and gasping for oxygen.

"Tan…fuck…" I crawled to where he was still sitting. It was only when I arrived back in front of him that he seemed to notice that I hadn't been there for the past minute.

He blinked at me. "Are you okay?"

"No," I croaked, picking up the apple and launching it as far as I could into the kitchen and out of my sight. "Are you?"

"I'm not sure."

"What happened?" I turned back to the kitchen, where the fuck were Lux and Ace? "Guys? Can you come here? It's urgent."

Lux appeared first, typing away on his phone, while Ace sauntered down from his bedroom holding a coffee cup. Both of them frowned when they saw me on the floor.

"What's up? Are you okay?

"No,"Tanner and I answered in unison.

Ace stopped by the couch. "What are you doing?"

"Tanner has something to tell you, but can you put the coffee down first?" I wasn't about to get sprayed with it, and our housekeeper was already annoyed with the amount of spillages she'd had to get out of the rugs.

Ace frowned but placed the coffee on the table. I turned to Lux, who looked equally confused.

"Okay, Tan. Go."

He paused and took a deep breath. "Millie's pregnant."

Ace's mouth dropped, and my eyes flicked to Lux. "Did you know about this?"

He shook his head, again mirroring Ace's expression. "No.

No, I didn't. Does Radley know?"

"No idea." Tanner shrugged, and a smile spread across his face. He was clearly in denial.

Ace dropped down and swept him into a hug. "Man, I'm so sorry."

I started to mentally plot out how we could ride through this storm together, how we could support Tanner, because fuck me…if this had been me, and Scout had gotten pregnant with Rangers Douche, I don't know what I would have done.

There was still a smile on his face when I turned to him, but Lux got there first. "Tan, why are you looking so happy?"

Slowly Tanner eased himself from Ace's grip and peered at each of us in turn as his smile stretched from ear to ear.

"Because it's mine. Millie's pregnant with *my* baby. I'm going to be a dad."

Want to know what happens with Tanner and Millie? Their book is out in June, and you can preorder now.

Read on for the first chapter.

MILLIE:

I don't know it yet, but today is the day I get pregnant.

It stands to reason, seeing as the last twenty-four hours had absolutely sucked, that I was standing outside Grand Central Station in the pouring rain holding a suitcase, a duffel bag, and a rapidly disintegrating box filled with some of my most precious memories, while I figured out what to do.

In true New York style, the second the heavens opened, the cabs disappeared.

To top it all off, the most annoying human being I know had just pulled up to the curb, popped his trunk, and jumped out, totally oblivious that he was blocking the road with his giant Escalade.

But that's Tanner Simpson for you.

The cacophony of honking increased tenfold.

"There's the most beautiful girl in the world." Tanner grabbed my suitcase, flashed me one of his signature smiles, and opened the passenger door. "Mills, get in the car, it's raining."

"Where's Radley?" I asked, not moving from the spot where I'd transformed into a wet, bedraggled mess.

I'd been expecting my best friend to pick me up. I'd called her twenty minutes ago, and she said she would hurry. I *needed* her to come and get me. I needed to download the last twenty-four hours of my life to her because only she would understand.

Tanner wrestled the duffel bag off my shoulder and tossed

it in the back of the car with the suitcase.

"She was in the middle of baking with Lux, so I volunteered. And she comes with Secret Service, so I saved everyone a ride. Plus, I *wanted* to come." He grinned. "Seriously, why aren't you getting in the car?"

I yanked my box out of his reach before he tried to take that from me too. There's no way I was giving the box up, he'd have to pry it out of my cold, dead hands.

Tanner's brows shot up. He placed one hand on the door frame, and stared at me with those blue, *blue* eyes of his. You could get lost in them if you weren't careful, therefore I was *always* careful.

A droplet of rain fell off his baseball cap and hit one of those sculpted cheekbones, before disappearing into the short stubble hiding a dangerous pair of dimples.

He might be the most annoying person I'd ever met, but he was easily the most handsome too.

Top three most handsome, without a doubt, which only made it worse.

"Are you okay?"

I nodded, because if I opened my mouth to say yes, I knew I'd start crying. Maybe he wouldn't notice, though; it was raining enough.

"Jeez, why's everyone being so loud this morning?" He turned around, uncharacteristically snapping, but it worked to raise a little smile on me. And release some of the tension jammed in my throat.

"Because you're blocking the road."

Tanner frowned, like he'd only just realized he was stopped at an angle and cars were having to go around him. *He* was the cause of the noise.

"Oh. It was only two minutes, people need to calm down," he replied, his head quirking. "Now, you wanna make it three, or are you getting in?"

I had a choice.

I either stayed here, getting soaked through while he drove off with most of my stuff, or I sucked it up.

What's the worst that could happen? He'd talk my ear off for twenty minutes. I could cope with that if it meant I could get out of the rain. *Just.*

Ducking under his arm, I stepped up into the warm, dry car and Tanner slammed the door behind me.

ACKNOWLEDGMENTS

If I could live in the New York Lions world forever, I would. I love it here, and I hope you find the same joy in Parker and Scout that I do whenever I return to these boys.

As always, I could never do it alone. I have a team helping me bring my books to life, supporting me, listening to me and I am eternally grateful to each and everyone of you.

To Georgana, I truly don't know what I would do without you. I'm so lucky to have you in my corner, and I'm so excited for what we have to come this year and next.

To Valentine and everyone at Valentine PR, Taylor, Glav and Sydney. Forever grateful for all the help and advice you give me in building the Luluverse. I bow to your creativity because it's so much more than anything I could come up with. And without you it would take me five times as long to do everything.

To Stephanie, what a year! I can't wait until we can have more adventures together.

To the Jupiter Reeves Fan Club, OG members and newbies, and everyone joining the Luluverse, I'm so grateful to you all for giving me the chance. And I'll keep bringing the stories to you for as long as you'll let me. Your support this past 12 months has been so incredible and truly made me feel less alone during long bouts of imposter syndrome.

And finally I can't write a book without thanking the one who is by my side 24 hours a day. My puppy.

xo

ABOUT THE AUTHOR

Lulu started writing by accident, and somehow found herself stuck in a fictional world of ice hockey, baseball and billionaires. A world she has no plans to leave.

More recently she's ventured across the Atlantic to where her latest novel is set - the beautiful cities of Oxford and Cambridge, and the annual rowing showdown on the River Thames.

She's a big fan of strong heroines, because those fierce alphas need someone to keep them in check. You'll find her navigating her way through Romance Land one HEA at a time, and trying to figure out the latest social media platform she needs to post to.

She'd love to hear from you, loves hearing your opinions and thoughts, so please message her on any of the social platforms @lulumoorebooks and she'd love you to come and join her reader group on Facebook - aptly named The Jupiter Reeves Fan Club.

But if you don't want to do any of that, there's always her website - lulumoorebooks.com

The New York Players

Jasper

Cooper

Drew: The Vegas Edition (extended prologue)

Drew

Felix

Huck

The Tuesday Club

The Secret

The Suit

The Show

The New York Lions

The Third Baseman

The Shake Off

The Baller

The Strike Zone

Home Run (coming June 2025)

The Oxbridge Series

Oar With Friends

You Float My Boat

The Valentine Nook Chronicles - coming September 2025

Once Upon A Christmas Tree

Valentine Nook

Wylder Ranch

Honeysuckle Lane

Foxleigh Park

Burlington Hall

Printed in Dunstable, United Kingdom

63841692R00251